THE MAN In the *Leather* JACKET

Devils & Dames

P.E. BOROCH

20 Twenty Literary Group

ISBN
978-1-962868-79-2 (Paperback)
978-1-962868-80-8 (eBook)
978-1-962868-78-5 (Hardcover)

To Uncle Steve

You said you would love to read one of my books
one day, so get comfy wherever you're at, crack open
a cold one, and enjoy! This one's for you!

Steve Allen Boroch

1961-2023

Table of Contents

Nearly at the exit, the approaching squad cars were so close Porter could see each driver clearly behind the wheel. Half were angry, and the other half was scared as hell. There was one person whose facial expression differed from the rest. In the unmarked silver SUV sat a passenger with a sadistic grin, and it was Captain Easley.

As Porter reached the highway off-ramp, he engaged the emergency brake and spun the wheel for the drift, but he couldn't help but stare back at Easley.

"What the fuck are you smiling about?" Porter murmured.

Porter heard tires squealing first and saw the black unmarked Ford Crown Victoria second. Third, he saw the driver, Gunther. His vehicle, modified with a steel push bumper, broke from the group of pulled-over cars and, accelerating, smashed into the passenger side of Porter's truck.

The force sent Porter's truck spinning uncontrollably across the road. Within moments, the Ram crashed through the shoulder barrier and toppled over the highway's edge.

Plunging towards the reservoir, Porter gripped the steering wheel and held his breath, bracing for the inevitable impact. The drastic change in scenery from road to water to the free-fall floating sensation to the sudden hood first impact shook Porter to the bones.

The truck immediately sank and took on water from the open driver's side window. Porter tried for the door, but it wouldn't budge due to the water's pressure against it.

As the vehicle continued to plunge and the water reached his chin, Porter took a final deep breath just as water completely engulfed the cabin.

1

A pale '87 Bronco crept across an uneven snow trail. A rotting wooden sign read, "Last bar before the border. Drink up!" The Bronco veered off the path and into the lot of Payne's Bar.

Hector Guvera took a sip from his travel mug, putting the vehicle in park. He listened to Johnny Cash's 'The Man Comes Around' through his garbled speakers and looked out his cracked front windshield.

The Bronco's headlights illuminated the faded tin exterior of the bar. The siding was peeling, and the metal roof was dented and patched from years of neglect. A handful of advertising signs hung in the window, partially illuminated, partially flickering. Across the door, green cursive read, 'Greetings From El Paso.'

Loud country music assaulted Hector as he entered the bar. On the back wall, a large, flat-panel TV played a music video of Reba singing "Fancy."

The roper heels of Hector's black and white rattlesnake boots drove loudly into the scratched wooden floor. He passed a rowdy group and made his way to an empty table. Hanging his dark red suede jacket on the back of the chair and placing his black felt pinch front cowboy hat on the table, he sat and rolled up his flannel sleeves.

The loud smack of a cue ball performing a break on a billiards table drew his attention.

With his gaze fixed on the table, a trio of blond-haired men slithered to his table.

One of the men pushed his knuckles into the wood top. The second crossed his arms and pressed his groin into the table's edge. The third pulled up a chair and got comfortable.

Hector knew Trevor, Simon, and Drew. They were local boys who worked at the automotive store– brothers. They had been popular in high school and still thought they were twenty years later.

"Gentlemen," Hector said.

Drew slapped Hector on the back. "Well, would ya look at that? It's ole' Heck. What's it been, sixteen years since you last were here?" There was alcohol on his breath, and he spoke with a thick Texas drawl.

"Seventeen," Hector corrected him.

"Seventeen? I'll be damned. Has it been that long? What you been up to?"

Hector searched the eyes of each man.

They were thirsty for action.

"Guys, I don't want any trouble."

"Trouble? Heck, me and my brothers want to buy you a drink."

"That's not necessary."

"Becky!" Drew yelled, waving to the bar where a woman served a drink. She was short and cute, sporting thin glasses and a bow clipped into her wavy auburn hair. "Becky! Goddammit, woman, I'm talking to you!"

"You shouldn't talk to her like that," Hector said.

"What?"

"I said, you shouldn't talk to her like that. She doesn't deserve that."

"Don't be so serious. Heck, we're just having fun!" Drew laughed.

With a notepad, Becky approached and glanced over the faces before stopping at Hector's. "You're back." She beamed.

Drew snapped his fingers, "Focus, woman. I'd like to buy this man a drink." He slapped Hector on the back. "Ain't that right?"

"Okay," she said, putting her pin to the pad. "Hector, what can I get ya?"

"He'll take a water," Drew said. Once more, he slapped Hector across the back. "Ain't that, right? Water, that's all a dirty Spic like you deserves. Only American citizens deserve a beer."

"Drew, he joined the Army out of High School," Becky said. Hector waved her off.

"Of course, he was in the Army," Drew continued, "that's all that illiterate Spic's like him are good for. Bullet sponges, ain't that right, Heck? Damn, I'm surprised the government hasn't deported your ass yet. Does the U.S. government know you're in this country?"

"Got your green card?" Trevor asked.

"I hear he likes dirt in his water. It reminds him of his homeland," Simon added.

Their laughs echoed that of hyenas.

Trevor reached back and grabbed a near-empty glass of water from the table behind him. "Look what I found, just for you, buddy." He placed it on the table.

"Wait," Drew leaned back and, hacking, spit a long loogie into the cup.

"C'mon, cut it out," Becky said.

"There we go, now it's ready," Drew pushed the cup towards Hector.

"That's enough."

"It's fine," Hector said.

Standing, Drew pointed to the drink. "That's all you, buddy, courtesy of me and everyone in 'Merica. You're welcome."

"Drink up," Simon laughed.

"Welcome back," Trevor said, slapping Hector hard on the back.

Hector watched as they walked back to their table.

Becky grabbed the cup. "I'm sorry about that."

"It's not your fault."

"Well, it's my family's bar, so I take responsibility."

"It's not your fault," Hector repeated.

Her eyes searched his.

What was she looking for?

"You still like Budweiser, right?" Becky asked.

"I used to."

"Used to?"

"I've been sober for a while now. I'll take a glass of warm milk."

"Of course," she began to write on her pad but shook her head, "I'm throwing in some nachos too. Don't worry about the bill. It's on the house. Drew and his brothers can be real dicks."

"Rebecca, it's okay."

She brushed a strand of hair behind her ear.

"You alright?"

"Yeah, I mean, it's just no one calls me Rebecca."

"I can call you Becky if you want."

"No, I like you calling me Rebecca."

"Good," Hector said. "Let me ask you something."

"Uh, okay."

"Did you ever get your doctorate? I remember it was all you used to talk about."

"No, I mean, not yet –" she twirled a finger in a strand of her curly hair, "you think I'd still be working here if I did? I got my Associate's last year, and I will start going for my Bachelor's next year when I finish paying off my student loans. Money's just a little tight right now."

Hector nodded, "I understand."

"So," she pushed up her glasses, "I heard about your parents. I'm sorry. They were nice people."

"Thank you."

"Are you just here for the memorial service?"

Hector nodded.

"That's a shame. It'd be nice to catch up."

"Yes, it would be."

He watched her walk away and wondered what else had happened in her life since they had spoken last. She was still kind and beautiful– that hadn't changed.

Minutes later, Becky approached his table, nachos in one hand and a glass of milk in the other.

From across the bar, the cackle of hyenas stopped. Hector watched Drew tap one of his brothers before getting up from his table. He made a beeline to Becky and violently shoulder-checked her on his way to the bathroom.

Hector rushed forward and caught her before she fell over, but the tray she held crashed into the nearest table. The nachos splattered them with hot cheese and chili. The milk splashed into their faces.

Drew laughed, and his brothers followed his lead. The hyenas left through the emergency exit with cigarettes dangling off their lips and beers in their hands.

⚜

Hector had watched them for over an hour. It was nearing one in the morning, and the remaining customers had cleared. Drew and his brothers were huddled outside the bar's entrance, smoking and drinking, exchanging stories of their sexual conquests.

"After five minutes of plugging her, she finally woke up and mumbled, 'Stan?'" Drew said. "I just said, yeah baby, it's me, Stan." He laughed and downed his beer, "Dumb bitch fell back asleep, so I just finished up."

All his brothers laughed and belched like teenagers in a beer-drinking contest.

"You still got the video?" Simon asked.

Drew chucked his empty bottle into the exterior of the building and pulled out his phone. After thumbing away, he handed the phone to his brother and stole his beer. Simon leaned over Trevor as they both watched the video.

"What a dumb bitch," Trevor said.

"Look at you, flexing your arm for the camera," Simon said to Drew, "That's my boy."

"You need to upload this shit," Trevor told him.

"Already did. Dumb bitch doesn't even know she's famous."

They laughed and continued their stories for a few more minutes. Drew tugged on the front door, needing another beer, but it was locked.

The 'Payne's Bar' sign flickered before turning off.

"Fuck," Drew said.

The brothers watched as a blue Jeep with a torn open black canopy pulled to the front of the bar and exited the lot. An El Paso Community College Alumni license plate frame was affixed to the dented rear bumper.

After complaining about 'that bitch' Becky, the brothers said their goodbyes and parted ways.

Trevor's car was a yellow Chevrolet Camaro with black pinstripes running down the hood. Beat-up leather seats filled the inside.

The driver's side door was cracked open. Trevor shrugged, too drunk to remember if he locked the door. Getting behind the wheel, he fumbled in his pocket for the keys. Finding them, Trevor turned over the engine. Rubbing his hands in front of the vents, he put a cigarette to his lips and lit up.

A chord slipped over his head and tightened around his neck.

The cigarette dropped from his lips.

Trevor gurgled as he tried to pull at the chord pressed against his throat– it didn't budge.

He looked into the rearview mirror, and his bulging eyes screamed so many things his voice couldn't.

Trevor kicked out violently, and the Camaro rocked side-to-side as he fought against the inevitable.

A final gasp escaped his pursed lips before his head slumped and his body went limp.

Hector let loose the chord and retracted it into the wrist of his glove.

Pulling Trevor's body to the passenger seat and crawling into the driver's seat, Hector shifted the car into second gear.

Across the lot, Hector watched Simon open the door to his silver Pontiac Firebird.

Reaching into his jacket, Hector pulled out a mouthguard and fitted it to the underside of his mouth. Fastening his seatbelt, he turned on the headlights and pressed the accelerator.

Before Simon could get into his car, Hector shifted into third and traveled across the lot. His headlights blinded Simon, who defensively put up his hands before Hector slammed into him and the Firebird.

With the engine still growling, Hector stepped out and pocketed his mouthguard.

Simon squirmed between the crushed hood of the Camaro and the warped driver's side of the Firebird. Pinned and coughing blood, Simon cried, "Help me. Please, help me."

"Of course," Hector said, condensation making his breath visible in the frigid blackness.

He unclipped his Strider SMF knife from his belt and unfolded it.

Pressing his forearm against Simon's face, he forced the head to turn, exposing the left jugular vein.

"What are you –"

"Relax," Hector said.

With a quick jab, four inches of steel pierced the man's neck.

Hector took a calculated step back as blood squirted like a draining hose. The color faded from the man's face before the final drop painted the snow in a cherry splatter.

Wiping his knife blade across the yellow jacket of Simon's slumped shoulder, a pair of headlights from a Chevrolet Corvette illuminated the carnage.

As the car slowly passed, the driver looked at them through his open window. Illuminated by the blue glow of the Corvette's dash, Hector could see Drew's shocked face.

The shock turned to disbelief.

Drew slammed on his brakes and gawked at his dead brother, "Simon, oh my god. Simon!"

Walking across the lot to his Bronco, Hector popped open the rear window and pulled out his Mossberg 590 shotgun fitted with a Salvo 12 suppressor.

A horn blared. "Hey! Fucking Spic, get back here!" Drew yelled.

The Vette's V-8 engine roared as Drew performed a slushy U-turn across the lot.

Holding the shotgun at his side, Hector walked into the open.

The Vette accelerated towards him.

Hector fished a 12-gauge out of his front flannel pocket and cycled the action back on the weapon. Dropping the shell into the loading gate, he pushed the pump forward. Hector leveled the shotgun and took aim through his rear sights.

The Vette was moments away from hitting him.

With a trigger pull, the shell spat out the eighteen-inch barrel.

Drew slumped, and the Vette swerved, barely missing its target.

Seventeen-inch wheels jumped the front entrance parking blocks, and the car crashed through the front of Payne's Bar.

Hector slung his rifle behind his back and listened to the night. He could make out the jagged silhouette of the Franklin Mountains painted against the blackened sky.

A moment passed.

The churning V-8 and the spin of Goodyear tires were the only sound.

Hector walked across the lot and, getting into his Bronco, repositioned the vehicle parallel to the bar's new opening.

With the vehicle running, Hector grabbed the winch hook attached to the rear bumper.

The cable unspooled from the drum as he walked it into the bar.

Billiards tables were overturned, and wooden chunks of chairs and tables exploded across the floor. The bar top was caved in with the smoking Corvette, now a fixture centerpiece.

Navigating the wreckage, Hector investigated the Vette's shattered driver's side window.

Drew sat slouched, wearing a dripping crimson mask. His chest was a pool of red where the buckshot from the 12-gauge had peppered him.

The driver's side door was smashed inwards and wouldn't budge.

With the wench hook, Hector cleared out the remaining glass in the driver's side window. He extended a finger under Drew's nose.

There was faint breathing.

Hector yanked the body out the smashed window and onto the floor. After securing the cable around Drew's ankles, he returned to his vehicle and started the winch.

A trail of blood smeared across the floor as the cable retracted Drew's body.

Hector stopped the winch when the body reached his truck. With a nudge of a boot, Drew awoke and coughed blood.

"You should have stayed asleep. We've got a long way to go," Hector told him.

Sitting behind the wheel, Hector turned up his speakers listening to the end of Cash's 'The Man Comes Around.'

Hector took another sip from his travel mug, put the Bronco in drive, and pulled away.

Nearly 600 miles away, Detective Ryan Porter sat in his parked '95 Ram 2500 truck, looking up at a billboard. With his driver's side window open, he blew a plume of smoke into the Walgreens blacktop as electric guitar chords reverberated throughout the cab.

The billboard was a charismatic businesswoman in her early forties with mid-length dyed red hair. She stood with her arms crossed over her chest in front of a waving American flag. In bold white letters, it read, "Bobbi Johnson for U.S. Senate, show them WE WON'T BACK DOWN!"

At the song's conclusion, the DJ came onto the air. "Enter Sandman by Metallica was released on the classic Black Album in 1991. Personally, my favorite album. Now for some uncheerful news: another teenage girl has gone missing. Authorities say Claire Walters was last seen leaving her High School last Monday. This marks the fifth missing teenage girl in Colorado Springs in three months. Any information regarding these disappearances should–"

Porter turned down the radio and glanced at the image of Claire Walters on his phone. She had short brown hair, peace sign earrings, and a terrific smile. The news article said she was sixteen.

Flipping his phone closed, Porter took a drag on his cigarette and looked out his window.

He watched the girl with blonde pigtails and frosted blue and rep tips for half an hour. She was standing across the street doing her best Harley Quinn impersonation.

Porter thought the girl looked damn cute in her white crop top, shiny red and blue jacket, matching shorts, and fishnet stockings. There was only one problem. The girl was young, much too young. Her face was naturally pretty, but it was hard to see under the heavy layer of dark mascara and loud bubblegum lipstick.

Few cars had slowed at the sight of her. The hookers on the adjacent corner by the Comic bookstore weren't having much luck either.

Cherry wore a skin-tight grey and black catsuit complimented with the Catwoman mask and claws. Porter didn't remember Selina Kyle having an Adam's apple, but life was full of surprises.

Velvet sported a revealing, green-leafed outfit resembling Poison Ivy. The short Latina was deceptively cute, but if any guys got too close, they'd undoubtedly be poisoned by more diseases than they bargained for.

Taking off his sunglasses, Porter closed his eyes and massaged his temples. A headache was in full swing.

He popped open his glove box, reached past his Beretta, and took out the bottle of Excedrin. He chugged down a trio of pills with a swig of coffee.

Loud thrumming sounded from a car's stereo as it cruised across the road. The source was a blue Cadillac intentionally modified to be a low rider with shiny spinners.

Porter remembered being a kid living in Fort Bliss. He would walk to his middle school, and daily, those same low riders would drive down the road, playing that same beat– He hated that beat. The locals would blare it like it was their national anthem.

Distracted by memories, Porter almost overlooked a black Escalade with tinted windows pulling alongside the young girl.

Porter reached into his leather jacket and pulled out his pocket scope. Putting the monocular to his right eye and adjusting the focus, he watched the girl approach the vehicle and lean into the passenger window.

Half a minute passed.

The girl got inside.

The vehicle rolled off.

Porter picked up the handset of his CB radio and said, "We're on."

He turned over the engine, crept out of the lot, and onto Academy Blvd. Traveling Northbound, he gained on the Escalade and let a few cars pass before him. He changed lanes to avoid a massive pothole and got caught behind a light after a quarter of a mile. So did the Escalade in the center lane, four car lengths ahead.

Looking in his rearview mirror, Porter noticed a trailing yellow Jeep Wrangler. An attractive blonde was behind the wheel.

A horn blared from somewhere– traffic was moving.

Accelerating, Porter nearly caught up with the Escalade that had merged into the left turn lane when a semi crossed over and pulled in front of him.

He looked over his shoulder, and the lane was blocked.

The traffic light transitioned to yellow.

The Escalade made the light and turned onto the intersecting road.

"Shit," Porter murmured.

Just as the vehicle was nearly out of sight, it turned into the parking lot of a hotel.

❧

The Escalade pulled into a spot.

The passenger introduced himself as Joshua in a slow tenor voice. He had a long hook nose and thick brows. Joshua turned to the girl in the backseat, "Gumad, what'd you say your name was again?"

"Roxy," she said.

"What's that like, a stage name or something?"

"Or something," she told him.

"Right, Roxy, gotcha." He gestured a gunshot and winked.

Roxy's door opened from the outside, courtesy of the thick man who had been driving. He wore an expensive dark suit and sunglasses. His baldhead and stocky build reminded Roxy of a stereotypical movie villain.

"Thanks," she said.

There was no response.

"Lorenzo doesn't talk much, but he's loyal," Joshua said.

Roxy stepped out and looked at the hotel's yellow and white facade. She read the large glowing yellow text above the main doors, "Every Seasons Inn, classy."

Joshua skipped over to her and put a long arm around her shoulders. His overpowering vanilla and lavender cologne traveled down his red windbreaker sleeve and into her nostrils. "Nothing but the finest for you, Gumad."

"Gumad, what is that? Italian?"

"Highest marks," Joshua said.

"What part of Italy are you from?"

"A little city called Scandicci. Have you heard of it?"

"No," she said.

"Few have, but you know of places like Rome, Venice, or Florence, right?"

"Yeah, Venice is a place I've always wanted to visit. Well, Italy in general, but specifically Venice."

"Yes, Venice, beautiful place, beautiful people. A pretty girl like you would fit right in."

"How sweet. I bet you say that to all the girls."

Joshua shrugged playfully.

"So, what brings you all the way to Colorado?"

"Let's just say I oversee a joint venture with my American partners. I'm checking in on the operational side of the house. This is what you would call a business trip."

Lorenzo led the way into the lobby.

As the sliding glass doors opened, there was an immediate scent of pine sol and lemonade. They walked across the white-tiled floor to the check-in desk, where a young man with freckles and a goatee stood. The name tag affixed to the red jacket of his suit read 'David.'

"Mister Joshua, welcome back," the receptionist greeted.

The name, Mr. Joshua, reminded Roxy of Lethal Weapon when Gary Busey, playing Mr. Joshua, showed his loyalty by extending his forearm. The General scored it with an open flame from a lighter.

The scene always made her cringe.

Joshua extended his fist over the counter, and the receptionist fist-bumped him in return.

With a grin, Joshua put an arm around Roxy's shoulders. "David, meet my new friend –" Joshua looked down at her and gritted his teeth. "Her name is escaping me at the moment."

"Roxy," Lorenzo said in his growling bass voice.

"Right, Roxy," Joshua repeated as he snaked his thumb under her bra strap and, lifting, snapped it back onto her shoulder.

David smiled as he eyed her.

Roxy knew the look all too well. Many young and older men had undressed her with their eyes. It came with the job.

David licked his lips and averted his eyes. He dialed the phone, "Mr. Joshua's on his way up and bringing a guest. Yes, one." He reached into his pocket, produced a key card, and handed it to Joshua. "Number 615, sir."

"As always, you are my number one guy," Joshua said, handing over a cash fold.

Roxy was guided forward.

At the hallway intersection, they took a turn, and halfway down the hall was an elevator. A large 'out of order' sign was magnetized to the door.

Lorenzo pushed the call button, and they waited.

Roxy was nervous but tried not to show it.

Joshua squeezed her shoulder. "Don't be nervous, Gumad. We're just going to take a little ride." He buried his nose in her hair and kissed her neck. "Then we'll get to know each other better. Capiche?"

The elevator rang, and the metallic doors spread open.

Two thick men in suits with heavy walrus mustaches stood inside. On their belts sat Berettas.

Turning into the Hotel lot and finding a space, Porter killed the engine and stood on the step bar smoking a cigarette. He watched the yellow Jeep roll into the lot and park beside him.

The driver stepped out.

Robust features defined her face hidden behind a pair of reflective aviators. Her body was athletically built, with just the right curves in just the right places. Even at a distance, Porter could smell the Rainforest Fresh Suave shampoo in the long blonde hair she wore in a ponytail.

She sported a dark turtle neck and a black leather jacket. A thin necklace with a silver cross hung off her neck. She appeared more like a casual coffee drinker at a Starbucks after Sunday Mass than a veteran cop.

"Ready?" Porter asked.

"Whatever happened to formalities?" she replied in her husky voice. "Hello? Good afternoon? Something like that?"

Porter smirked and, taking a final drag on his cigarette, flicked it into the blacktop. "Good afternoon, Detective Evans. Want to fuck or something like that?"

"There's something seriously wrong with you."

"That's not a no."

Evans sighed and took the lead as they entered the lobby.

A young couple stood before the receptionist's desk and debated whether they needed one or two beds. The man was saying one, the woman, two. There had obviously been a cheating scandal from their banter, and he was over it. She wasn't.

The young buck behind the counter, whose nametag read 'David,' waited patiently. As the two continued to argue, he motioned to Porter and Evans. "Hello, can I help you?"

"Let's cut the bullshit, David," Porter said, pushing up his shades. "You know the drill." Porter pulled back his bomber jacket and flashed the badge clipped to his belt.

David stiffened, and his face flushed. "Uh, Officers, I have no idea what you're talking about."

"It's time for our monthly allowance," Porter said.

"Allowance?"

"He's screwing with us," Evans said. As she lowered her gaze to meet his, Porter saw David's anxiety reflected in the aviators she had yet to take off.

Porter motioned to his hands. "David, you like how your fingers work?"

David retracted them. "What do you want?" he whispered.

Porter exchanged a glance with Evans before answering, "Preferably a blonde,"

"Nope, make it a redhead," Evans said dryly.

"Why can't we have both?" Porter said.

"We're not that type of a hotel," David said.

"We're not that type of hotel," Evans mocked.

"Right," Porter said, "and I'm not the type who would plant drugs on you and then call it in." Porter tapped his fingers impatiently across the counter. "Listen, we all know what my partner and I will find if we start opening some doors, so stop playing the dumbass card."

Evans leaned across the counter, "I came here last month, and the other guy didn't give me this much crap."

"What other guy?" David asked.

Evans looked at Porter and nodded.

Porter grabbed him by the tie and yanked David's body across the counter.

"The one with all his fingers intact," Evans said.

"Okay," David said.

They had drawn the attention of the arguing couple.

"Don't mind us," Porter told them, presenting his badge. "David here is under investigation for storing child pornography on his company computer."

The couple walked out of the lobby.

David took a big gulp as a new group walked in.

"You want me to introduce you to them?" Porter asked.

David reached over awkwardly and picked up the phone.

Porter released him.

"Yes, I have some VIPs here," David said into the phone. "They say they want their salary payment. Uh, yeah, they want a number two and a four."

"Sounds like he's ordering us fast food," Evans whispered to Porter.

"Well, they may be greasy and –" Porter whispered back.

Evans put a finger to his lips and gave him a familiar look Porter could recognize even behind her aviators.

"Okay, I'll let him know," David placed the handset back on the receptacle and handed Porter a keycard reading 612. "They'll meet you at the elevator."

"The elevator?" Porter said.

"Yessir."

David's nodded to the intersecting hallway.

Porter and Evans stepped off and walked the hallway. Each was going in a different direction. There were a few elevators in either direction, but only one with an 'Out of Order' sign.

Spotting the elevator first, Evans notified Porter with a quick whistle.

Standing together at the elevator, Evans pressed the call button.

After a few seconds, the button illuminated. A chime sounded, and the doors opened.

Two thick men wearing suits stood inside the enclosure. They had walrus mustaches, bulging guts, and hairy skin smelling like the inside of a Pizza Hut box. Beretta APX pistols sat nestled in leather holsters on each man's belt.

"Who are you guys supposed to be, Beavis and Butthead?" Porter asked.

The two looked at one another. The joke didn't register.

"Be nice," Evans told him.

"Let's see it," the monkey on the right said. His English was broken but understandable.

Evans flashed the keycard, and they both flashed their badges.

The two men spoke Italian to one another, and then the left monkey looked at the beretta holstered on Porter's side, "Gun." He then looked at Evan's Glock, "You too."

"Really?" Porter said.

"You want a girl, yes? We want to make sure you two won't cause any trouble, yes?"

Evans nodded to him, and they reluctantly took their pieces out. They ejected their clips, and Porter pulled the round from his gun's pipe before handing it over.

Evans went through the motions of clearing the pipe, but Porter noticed she didn't pull the round out.

Interesting.

The monkey on the left took Evans Glock, and the right took Porter's beretta. Righty examined the piece, "92FS, good gun." He pocketed it and motioned them inside, "Come, Amico."

"Right, Amico," Porter repeated as they walked inside the shaft.

Righty pushed the button for the sixth floor.

The warm hallway smelled of sweat and urine. Roxy could hear moans and bed frames knocking against the back of the walls. The bay window at the end of the hall was covered in newspaper pages.

Two gutty men with pit sweats paced the hallway. They had their coats off and their white sleeves rolled up. In one hand was a silver travel mug, and a cell phone resided in the other. Holstered pistols sat on their belts.

"Over here," Joshua told her, stopping at room 615.

Inserting the keycard, the light indicator on the reader winked to green, and a 'click' sounded. Joshua turned the hand lever and pushed her forward. "Here we are." He handed the keycard to one of the men in the hallway, who stuffed it in the front pocket of his dress shirt.

The room was like any other hotel bedroom she'd been in. The same off-white carpet. The same bathroom entrance to the right, just as you walked in. The same mini-fridge, oak furnishing, and soft blue linens on the bed.

The similarities stopped there.

Steel bars lined the windows. One cuff of a chain link set was affixed to each bedpost. The nightstand beside the bed had various syringes and small bottles filled with a milky substance. Instead of a mint, a roll of duct tape sat on the center pillow. A bottle filled with something green sat on the nightstand.

Lorenzo produced a pair of latex gloves from his coat pocket and put them on.

"What the hell is this?" Roxy turned for the door, and Lorenzo caught her in a bear hug. He lifted her off her feet and turned her around. Roxy struggled against his grasp but couldn't break it. "Let go of me, please! Help!"

"Scream all you want. We own this floor," Joshua said.

The hallway man who had taken their key card smiled at her and closed the door.

Lorenzo walked her across the room and threw her forcefully onto the bed.

Roxy tried to get away, but Lorenzo straddled her. Holding onto her forearms, he pinned her down. He attempted to cuff her left wrist, but she squirmed too much.

In anger, Lorenzo smashed her wrist into the bedpost.

Roxy screamed as he overpowered her and cuffed her left wrist. She spat into his face, and Lorenzo responded by smacking her and then beginning to choke her.

Walking to the end table, Joshua penetrated the syringe's tip into the bottle filled with the milky green substance. "Lorenzo, be nice."

Lorenzo eased up.

"Please, stop! Let me go. Please!" Roxy pleaded in between coughs.

Joshua pumped the needle, and green droplets bled out of the syringe tip. "Gumad, I'm sorry, I lied. You won't be seeing Italy anytime soon."

Roxy leaned over and bit Joshua's hand as the needle pricked her arm.

Joshua screamed in pain and let go of the needle. He stepped back and, coddling his hand, yelled, "Control her!"

Lorenzo wrapped his hands around her neck again.

Roxy kneed him in the groin. She plucked the needle from her arm and jabbed it into Lorenzo's neck. She pushed the plunger, and he screamed, rolling off the bed.

Roxy then brought her right knee to her chest and grasped the bottom of her boot. Pushing down on the release button, she disconnected her stun gun.

She activated the weapon, rolled to her side, and sent 25 million volts of electricity into Joshua's chest.

❦

As the elevator ascended, there was back-and-forth chatter in Italian. Porter exchanged a glance with Evans and then looked at each man as they pointed at his jacket and continued their conversation.

"Is there something I can help clarify, Amico?" Porter said.

The right monkey motioned to a cluster of patches on Porter's A2 Aviator bomber jacket. "My brother, Sergio, he says your jacket reminds him of the one in Top Gun. The one Tom Cruise wears."

"Is that right?"

"Good movie," Evans said.

"But I told him the one Tom Cruise wears is different." There was more chatter, and the brother asked, "He wants to know how you get a jacket like that? He wants one."

"You gotta save the world a couple times," Porter said.

Evans rolled her eyes.

The brother on the right translated for Sergio.

There was a crackle in Porter's ear before a voice came through his earpiece. "Boss, I'm compromised. Room 615, I'm —" A loud bang ensued.

Sergio brought his hand to his earpiece. He exchanged a worried look with his brother and mouthed out something inaudible.

Porter didn't need to know Italian to know what would happen next.

Some things are universal: the shift in the eyes, the deep breath, the stillness of everything.

Porter exchanged a glance with Evans, and with the years of history between them, that's all they needed.

Before the brothers could grab their pieces, Porter reached into his jacket and grasped the K-Frame of his Smith & Wesson Model 15 revolver in his shoulder holster. Turning his back to Sergio, he jerked the trigger, sending a .38 through his jacket and into the man's chest.

Evans' back was to the other brother on the opposite side of the elevator. She held back the man's firing arm with one hand and pulled at the meaty arm wrapped around her neck with her other.

Sergio's corpse pressed down on Porter's back, nearly toppling him and hindering his movements. Porter struggled to free his revolver out of its holster.

"If you're not too busy," Evans strained to say, still fighting off the second brother.

Porter kicked out, pinning the remaining man's firing arm against the elevator panel.

A stray 9mm round fired off into the floor from the Italian's Beretta.

Evans wrestled her Glock from the man's inner jacket pocket and, shoving the four-inch barrel under the man's chin, yanked the trigger.

❧

Sitting at the base of the door, Roxy reached up and fasted the securing chain. Taking a deep breath, she put a finger to her earpiece. "Boss, what's your location?"

There was no response.

She rubbed her left wrist and glanced at Joshua and Lorenzo. Both were still lying unconscious on the carpet.

From the opposite side of the door, she heard a gentle knock.

"Mr. Joshua, are you done?" A man called out.

A click sounded as a card slipped into the reader.

The handle moved, and the door crept open – it stopped at the width of the chain.

Roxy touched the active prongs of her stun gun to the door lever.

A scream sounded from the other side, immediately followed by a loud *thump*.

Unfastening the door chain, Roxy peered out. A man was lying on the opposite side of the hallway – spasming.

Down the opposite side of the hallway, she saw the other man. His gun was drawn, and his phone was pressed to his face. He turned towards Roxy's' door.

A loud ding sounded.

The man turned to the elevator. A fire extinguisher rolled out and down the hallway to greet him.

The man looked down as the extinguisher stopped at his feet.

A revolver peeked out of the elevator. A .38 round shot out, impacting the fire extinguisher and exploding it into the man's chest, sending him flying across the hallway.

Porter and Evans stepped through the elevator.

The door to their right opened, and a man with a bath towel secured across his waist hung onto the door frame and leaned out– curious about the commotion.

Porter sent the man to his back with a kick to the chest. "Check the other rooms!" he barked to Evans.

"Secure them, Porter. We're taking them in!" Evan yelled as she rushed across the hall to a door creeping open. "CSPD, come out with your hands up!"

"I ain't going back to jail, I ain't!" the man in Porter's room pleaded.

Porter looked past him, past the stained blue carpet littered with used condoms and blood, and saw a naked girl chained to the bed – her body was severely bruised, and her wrists bloodied. She had long, unkempt red hair and a freckled face peppered with dimples. She couldn't have been older than sixteen.

Porter sent two to his chest. Walking over the body, he unloaded his last round into the man, "No shit."

Scurrying footsteps sounded as a group of half-dressed, panicked men ran out their doors and made a beeline for the elevator.

Porter began to pursue them when he saw Roxy peering out her door.

"Back in your room!" Porter barked.

Evans yelled as she entered a room further down the hall, "Police Officer, get down on your knees, hands behind your head!"

Across the hall, a door opened. A shirtless man with orange spike hair peaked out and slurred, "Ah, shit." Catching sight of Porter, he slammed the door.

Porter ran and sent his shoulder into the door, forcing his way inside. Holstering his empty revolver, he pulled out his Beretta.

The shirtless man stood between Porter and a bed with a young girl cuffed. His thin face and bare chest were covered in tattoos of various animals. He held an iron in one hand and pointed angrily with the other. "Get the fuck back, bro!"

He threw the iron.

Porter deflected the iron with a forearm, but a bull rush caught him off-guard, and his back slammed into the wall.

Shirtless held Porter's firing arm back, and with a key ring in his hand and a key between each finger, he repeatedly jabbed at Porter's side.

Porter smacked the butt of the Beretta into the man's head, but the man kept jabbing ferociously. Porter's body armor absorbed the initial blows, but one jab got through, and a key tore into his side.

Yelling, Porter dropped his gun.

Sending a knee to Shirtless' chest, the man rose, and Porter cracked the top of his head into the man's nose.

The man stumbled back, blood rushing down his face.

Porter stepped forward and cracked his fist into the man's face.

The man stumbled back and swiped wide with his keys. "You're dead, motherfucker."

Porter stepped back and, reaching in his jacket, pulled out and slipped on brass knuckles, "Waiting on you."

Shirtless jabbed out wildly, and Porter dodged and tossed his jacket over the man's face. As the man struggled to get it off, Porter struck him with a powerful haymaker to the side of the head, dropping him.

The girl on the bed coughed and wearily cried out for help.

Porter walked to her.

She was young and barely developed. Her eyes were lucid, and her body was patterned with bruises and cuts like the other girl's. She had short brown hair and wore small peace sign earrings. The girl was Claire Walters.

Porter focused on Shirtless. Pulling his jacket off him and grabbing the man by his orange hair, Porter dragged him into the bathroom and, standing him to the sink, smashed the man's face into the faucet.

Falling back and writhing on the floor, Shirtless moaned in pain and tried to stand after a few moments. Failing to return to a vertical base, he sank to the carpet and sat with his back to the wall. Blood dripped from his mouth, and he spat out teeth.

Shirtless turned to Claire as she pleaded for help. He coughed and, forcing a blood-riddled smile, looked at Porter, "She liked it."

Porter grabbed the iron from the carpet and bashed Shirtless in the skull with all his might – crushing it.

Holstering his Beretta, Porter knelt at the girl

"Please, help," she pleaded in a low whimper.

"You're safe now," Porter said before yelling out for Evans.

Evans swept the room as she entered, but upon seeing the girl, she holstered her weapon and knelt beside her. Running a thumb over the girl's face, she nodded, "You're alright. Help is on the way." She turned to Porter, "I cleared the other rooms. Go on."

Donning his jacket, Porter made his way to Roxy's door. Two men were down. One was in a business suit and drooling something green, the other in a windbreaker, passed out at the foot of the bed. He was cuffed at each wrist, with the link passed through the front bed frame.

The girl sat on the floor. Her clothing was torn and lipstick smeared. There was a shiner under one of her grey eyes.

"You can't catch bad guys sitting on your ass," Porter said, offering a hand.

"I'm fine, thanks for asking." She stood on her own and took off her wig, revealing her shoulder-length green and black hair.

"Damn, Mindy, I was getting there."

Mindy thumbed back to where the two bodies lay. "The guy in the windbreaker is Mr. Joshua. He's the ringleader."

Porter took a knee next to him, "Mr. Joshua, like Gary Busey from– "

"Lethal Weapon," she finished the sentence.

Porter felt a pulse on Joshua, then walked to the man in the business suit. "What's his deal?"

Mindy picked up the bottle of green liquid, "They were going to drug me with this shit."

Porter inspected the bottle, "What is this?"

"I don't know."

Feeling eyes on him, Porter turned to her, "What?"

"You're bleeding," she pointed to the blood running down Porter's side and dribbling onto the carpet.

"Did you get his phone?"

Mindy retrieved the iPhone from her pocket. "Here you go."

Porter turned it on and saw that it needed a pin. "Biometrics won't work on it?"

"Yeah, even when he used it around me, he'd always put in a pin."

"Did you catch what it was?"

"Nope, he always turned away." Mindy shook her head, "Who the hell doesn't use biometrics on their phone?"

Porter stared at Joshua, "People with something to hide." Porter put the phone in his jacket. "There's another girl in the first room at the end of the hall." Slapping a new clip into the Beretta and chambering a round, he handed it to Mindy, "Check on her."

"Right," Mindy said. She looked at Joshua, "How will you get the pin out of him?"

Grabbing a tuft of greasy black hair, Porter inspected him. "You really want to know?"

Mindy hesitated before answering, "Yeah, I do."

"Check on the girl," Porter said, motioning her out.

As Mindy exited, Porter closed the door and, leaning his back on it, reached into his jacket and pulled out his pack of Lucky Strikes. Freeing a cigarette, he lit up and took a deep drag, sending a jet of smoke through his nostrils.

With his gaze fixed on Joshua, he took the cigarette out of his mouth and squashed the tip into Joshua's face.

The flesh sizzled.

3

Porter leaned against the door frame, watching Mindy as she spun a Daisy 1903 bolt action Springfield rifle.

Holding the rifle handguard and the butt, Mindy flicked it into the air, and the weapon spun a revolution before she caught it. "That's called a single," she said.

Porter swigged some coffee and put a cigarette to his lips, "Yep."

"Now, let me show you a double." She crouched before tossing the rifle higher into the air. It turned two revolutions, and as Mindy tried to catch it, the rifle fell onto the snowy ground. "Dammit."

"Smooth."

"Hey, this isn't as easy as it looks."

Porter blew out a plume of smoke, "You're trying to force a catch. Let it fall naturally into your hands."

"Right, naturally," Mindy said, picking the rifle up and wiping the snow off. She tossed the Springfield once more. The rifle spun two revolutions, and as Mindy tried to catch it, the barrel smacked her right hand across the knuckles and fell into the snow.

Mindy shook her right hand, "Son of a bitch!"

"Rub some snow on it," Porter said. Setting his coffee on the entryway steps, he plucked the rifle from the snow and wiped it off.

"I don't know how the other guys do it," Mindy said, patting snow across her knuckles. "They make it look so easy."

"What other guys?"

"The armed drill team. Chief Casper said I have to show him a double before he'll let me join."

"Take a step back," Porter told her.

"Are you kidding me? This I gotta see."

With the cigarette hanging out of his mouth, Porter smirked at her. He positioned his hands on the rifle and spun it in a single tight revolution before catching it. "The trick with the single is not to throw it but to let it roll over your hand and then catch it. Here's a double," he put a hard spin on the rifle and tossed it into the air. He caught it after the second revolution.

"You need to toss it high enough and put a hard spin on it to go faster." He performed the double again and caught it. "You see how I didn't reach up for the rifle? I just let it fall back to me." He handed the rifle back.

"Did you learn that in the Marines?"

"Marines taught me to kill people. I learned how to spin a rifle in NJROTC."

"You never told me you were in NJROTC."

"Never asked," Porter said, returning to his coffee and taking a sip.

A black SUV turned into the trailer park as Mindy was about to spin the rifle again. The vehicle rolled slowly down the road towards them.

"Expecting company?" Mindy asked.

"Not that I know of."

They watched as the SUV slid to a stop alongside the foot of the gravel path leading to the carport. A thick, seasoned bald man with a medium-length, curly white and brown beard, sunglasses, and a dark business suit with an American flag pin on his lapel stepped out from the driver's side. He stared at Porter for a long moment before walking around the vehicle and opening the rear passenger door.

"Smells like government," Porter said.

Out walked a lean man with slick blond hair and a thin face from the rear door. He wore dark sunglasses, partially covering the scar on his left brow. He wore a business suit, but with disdain, like he was uncomfortable in his own clothes. No American flag was pinned to his lapel.

Last was an attractive woman with fiery red hair that Porter instantly recognized from the billboards and TV ads. Former Governor Bobbi Johnson wore a neutral trench coat over her dark pencil skirt.

"Wait, is that?" Mindy whispered.

"Yep," Porter said.

The former Governor smiled with soft pink lips as she approached them, "Hello, you must be Detective Porter." She extended an expensive leather-gloved hand. She smelled of flowers after a Spring rain.

Porter looked at the hand, paused, and exchanged glances with the two men accompanying her.

"Hello," she said more firmly, stabbing her hand in his direction.

Porter hesitantly exchanged the shake, "Mrs. Johnson."

"It's Ms."

"Okay, Ms. Johnson, Porter corrected himself." She had the softest beige face that over-the-counter product could manipulate to hide her thin wrinkles. Her contacts changed her iris from auburn to emerald.

"Please, call me Bobbi," she said with a polished politician's smile.

"Okay, Bobbi," Porter thumbed behind himself, "this is my partner, Mindy Miller."

Bobbi began to extend her hand towards Mindy and stopped. She crossed her arms, mimicking her posture on the many billboards lining the city roads. "Aren't you a little young to be playing with guns?"

"It's a Daisy 1903 bolt action rifle with a cemented barrel. It can't fire. On the other hand," Mindy pulled up her jacket and tapped on the Beretta 92 FS holstered onto her belt, "I'm a deadeye with this."

Bobbi wagged a finger at her and grinned at Porter, "I like her."

"Fantastic. Why are you here?" Porter said.

Bobbi kept her grin, "You know I'm the reason you two were released from the Police Station a few hours ago, right?" Without anyone answering, she continued, "Let's just say Captain Easley was convinced that it's in her best interest to build a good rapport with me."

"Since you're running for Senator?" Mindy asked.

"The U.S. Senate seat for Colorado, young lady," Bobbi corrected.

"Right," Porter said. With deliberate slowness, he drank his coffee and blew out a plume of smoke, "Thanks for the assist. Your medals are in the mail."

Bobbi nodded, "Aren't you a callous one? I heard that about you, but it's not a problem. I'll be needing that. I want to employ your services, Detective."

Porter puffed on his cigarette and stared at the two suits accompanying her. The driver with the bald head and tattoo on his neck looked like nothing more than a muscle for hire. He wasn't the issue. The other one, though, was. "What type of job?"

"If you would be so kind as to give me a few minutes, I'll review the details."

Porter rolled his wrist and looked at his watch, "You have ten."

"That should be enough," as Johnson walked up the steps, the two suits followed.

"They stay," Porter said.

"Excuse me?" Bobbi asked.

"You've got ten minutes, well, less now, but I don't want them stepping inside my house."

"I assure you they're —"

"Not American," Porter interrupted. "Mr. Clean, who looks like a fatter and balder version of Ivan Drago from Rocky, has a dagger tattoo stamped on his neck. In Russia, that means he's murdered people and has no problem doing it again if the job demands it. There are also quite a few drops of blood stemming from the dagger's tip. That's the number of people he's killed, and the drops go past the neckline."

Porter pointed to the other suit and flicked his cigarette at the man's expensive dress shoes.

The blond looked down at the cigarette and then at Porter — his thin face was lifeless.

Porter returned the stare. The man was hard to gauge. "And Simon Gruber here isn't wearing an American flag on his lapel. I'd peg him as German with his blond hair, blue eyes, and black, red, and yellow tie. Habe ich recht?"

The blond's thin upper lip curled ever so slightly in amusement.

"They told me you were good, but you're terrific," Bobbi said.

Porter walked up the stairs to his screen door, "Let's go." He nodded to Mindy, "Keep an eye on them."

"You got it, Boss," she said. Setting the rifle against the outside of the trailer, Mindy pulled out her phone. "You guys into TikTok? They have a new conversation starter for first dates, fuck, marry, kill – Superhero actor edition. Robert Pattison, Henry Cavill, Ryan Reynolds, who wants to go first?"

The two men exchanged a glance.

Bobbi followed Porter inside the trailer. She looked around the home, and her disapproval of the makeshift office setting was obvious.

Porter topped off his coffee in the kitchen, "Can I get you a cup?"

"Uh, no, thank you."

Porter shrugged and, adding sugar and cream, swirled the inside of the cup with his finger. He gestured to the futon littered with blankets and Mindy's assortment of hoodies, "Have a seat."

Bobbi squinted at the coffee-stained red futon, "I think I'll stand."

"Suit yourself," Porter sat on the futon and sipped his coffee. He lit another cigarette and flicked his wrist to look at his watch. "We're at eight minutes and ticking."

"Okay, you're aware of the crime wave in the city, yes?"

Porter blew out a plume of smoke, "Crimewave? How dramatic."

"Excuse me?"

"Crimewave, hell, it's what keeps me employed."

"Well, Mr. Porter."

"Just, Porter, Mr. Porter was my dad."

"Okay, Porter, getting rid of the crime wave will ensure my selection as the next Colorado Senator."

"Aren't there two seats for the U.S. Senate?"

"Yes, but Tate's term limit is up, which means his seat is free for the first time in decades. Bernard is in the other seat. He's not going to lose. So that only leaves the one seat."

"Right, by the way, cute billboards."

"Uhh…thanks. Did you know that Colorado Springs has the worst crime rate in the state? It has spiked 300% in the last six months."

"Are you telling me or asking me?"

Bobbi began to answer, "All I'm saying is –"

"Make it quick. You're down to seven minutes."

"Dammit, would you stop counting me down? Do you talk to all your clients like this?"

"Which one do you want answered first?"

Bobbi groaned in frustration.

"Get to the point," Porter said.

"I need you to take down American Iron."

"The home security company?"

"Yes, certain people in the CSPD tell me –"

"Certain people?"

"Yes, they say they're the culprit behind the increased crime in this city, and they need to go. I'm told their home security company is just a front. They offer their business to homes and companies, and if they reject, things get interesting. Most of those places get vandalized or broken into that same week."

"Forcing them to buy into the company?" Porter asked.

"That's right."

"Sounds like the old mob protection service in New York. Give us 20% of your monthly income to protect you, or we bust up your shop and your kneecaps."

"Exactly. Everyone knows it's going on."

"What do you know about their hired muscle?"

"That's where you come in. I want you to find out who they have contracted to commit these crimes and stop them. Their company won't last long without their hired muscle. There's a name that's come across my desk recently. He may be the one you're looking for, Frank Marion. Heard of him?"

Porter put his mug down and kicked his boots onto the table, "Can't someone with your connections just get the cops to round up Frank and the rest of them?"

"You know all too well it doesn't work like that. The police need to follow the law. American Iron operates smart enough not to do anything illegal, at least on paper. Not to mention, it takes time to build a case. I don't have that type of time. So, I need someone who isn't afraid to…let's say, bend the law to get results and get them fast. And after what you did to solve the Sandman case, the things you did that weren't reported in the papers, you're just the person I want for this job."

"Things that I did that weren't reported in the papers?"

"I have connections everywhere in this city. Even with certain Safeway managers."

Porter shook his head, "I'm stuffing that asshole into another locker."

"So, I need you to do whatever you do to end this. I don't care how you do it or what it costs. I'll cover the overhead if that's a concern. I'll cut through any red tape along the way if you need me to. I want the muscle behind American Iron out of my city, and I want them out before the polls open in three weeks."

Porter sipped his coffee, keeping eye contact, "So you can tell the voters it was you who got them out?"

"If I can't even bring order to this city with a worse crime rate than Denver or Pueblo, people won't have confidence I can do it for the state. It's simple. Win this city, win the state. So, what do you say?"

"Win the city, win the state," Porter said. "I'm sure it would make one hell of a campaign poster. Where would I start? You want me to bust into the American Iron corporate office and waterboard the head boss for answers?"

"Waterboarding? No. That's some Jack Bauer stuff."

"Actually, I'm pretty sure Jack Bauer would do something far more interesting than waterboarding," Porter said.

Bobbi rolled her eyes, "I have an old friend, Audrey Peterson. Her family just moved into town. She believes American Iron was behind an attack on her family business earlier this week. I'll have the Petersons come here tomorrow morning and give you the details. Work their case and go from there. It should be a good starting point and lead you to Frank Marion."

"So, work your friend's case and shut down Frank Marion, American Iron's muscle? Which will then lead to the crime rate dropping?"

Bobbi nodded. "Do what you need to do."

"Do what I need to do?" Porter squashed his cigarette into the ashtray on the table, "Sounds illegal."

Bobbi put up her hands defensively, "In no official capacity did I say to do anything illegal."

"Yeah, okay, still sounds illegal."

Bobbi shrugged, "Your words, not mine. Is that a problem?"

"Of course not, but it's gonna cost you something extra. My standard rate is fifty dollars an hour–"

Bobbi held up a finger. Plucking a Leathernecks Detective Agency business card from the holder on the table, she pulled out her phone. She thumbed away on the screen and then entered the email address from the card, "There you go." She presented her phone screen, "I've paid you for two weeks. Double the normal rate deposited to your PayPal account. And this is just the first installment. You'll get the second deposit when you finish the job."

Porter's phone buzzed, and pulling it out of his jacket, he saw a notification from PayPal on the front display screen.

Bobbi nodded, "It goes without saying, but – "

"You were never here? And we've never met? Right?"

"Right, so we have a deal?"

"Sure," Porter said.

On the table sat a black mug with a picture of Britney Spears and the caption, 'If Britney survived 2007, you can survive today!' The cup was filled with a collection of various pens. Bobbi grabbed a red pen and scribbled on the back of the business card. "This is my personal number and the number and address of the Petersons. I expect daily updates."

Porter took the card and asked, "What if I find out American Iron's not behind the crime wave? Maybe you've got the wrong people."

Bobbi shook her head, "I'm never wrong."

"Right," Porter said.

"Well, I'll leave you to it then," she held out her hand, and Porter stood and shook it. She reeled him in, "One last thing, Porter. Don't abuse my trust, don't waste my money, and most importantly, don't cross me. I'm not someone you want as an enemy."

Porter pulled her in closer, "Good thing you got a cute ass, or I might have taken that as a threat."

Bobbi's eyes dangled in his for a moment. After the disbelief subsided, a subtle pink grin escaped. "You're just full of surprises, aren't you?"

"If you really want to know, I've got time," he motioned to his rear bedroom.

Bobbi rolled his wrist and, looking at his watch, shrugged. "Would you look at that? Our ten minutes are up."

"You sure about that? Watches can be wrong," Porter said.

Bobbi laughed, shook her head, and reached for the door. "Call me when you have an update." About to leave, she lingered in the doorway and tapped her fingers on the faded white wooden frame. She parted her lips with her tongue, "Who knows, play your cards right, and we might arrange a meeting at my office next time and schedule a few extra minutes."

Porter followed her out.

As the car rolled away, Porter turned to Mindy. "Thoughts?"

"Not sure. The two guys were quiet. I took pictures of all of them and the car license plate. I'll start running a background check."

"Right."

Mindy stared at him for a long moment, "What's wrong?"

Porter shook his head, "I'm not sure yet."

4

At 5:37 in the morning, Mindy poured freshly made coffee into a dented steel thermos cap. She brought it to her nostrils and breathed in the aroma of French Vanilla. She took a sip and drew back the window's curtains next to the door.

The warm glow of exterior lights was the only sign of life in the snow-blanketed trailer park. Yawning, she sipped her drink again and sat behind the computer.

Launching YouTube, she clicked on a video featuring a compilation of the ten best skateboarding tricks performed at the X Games.

Before the clip played, a commercial showed Bobbi Johnson wearing a red polo shirt and blue denim jeans, walking up a lane at an indoor firing range. She wore clear-lensed eye protection and American flag-themed shooting earmuffs.

A caption of 'Bobbi Johnson for U.S. Senate' scrolled across the bottom of the screen.

Mindy had the option to skip the advertisement but decided to watch.

The concrete floor Bobbi stood on was littered with 9mm casings. The camera zoomed on her dark face as she squinted and fired off a round from a Glock.

She hit a man's silhouette on a paper target with a bullseye to the head.

"I'm a straight shooter when it comes to taking care of Coloradans. I took care of this state as your Governor, and I'll do it again as your Senator," Bobbi said, holstering her gun. "People like current Governor Tim Styles want to give long-drawn-out answers when asked about their stance on lowering the crime rate in Colorado. Answers filled with political nonsense that don't answer the question."

A clip played of an overweight fifty-something, shaggy blond-haired man with a walrus mustache nervously pulling at his tie while standing behind a podium.

"When I was Governor of Colorado, crime was down 30%. Since I stepped down two years ago, crime has risen sharply," she said. A graphic showed the percentage change. "I vow to protect your places of business from looting, your streets from violent protests, your homes from invasion." A clip depicted citizens brawling in the street, a masked man throwing a brick into a store window, and a hate group marching down the road with racist picket signs.

"As Governor, I raised $100s of $1000s of dollars for our police forces. This money went towards increased police personnel, upgrading body armor, and ensuring our POST academies had the best technology and equipment for incoming recruits." A clip played of Bobbi giving a speech at a Police Academy graduation ceremony.

"Everyone knows my stance on handling crime in this state. Let me get back into the fight, not only in Colorado but in Washington. This is our state and our country. Let's show them we won't back down." She fired off her Glock once more.

Wearing a sharp business suit and standing before a waving American flag, she said, "I'm Bobbi Johnson, a true Colorado Native, running for U.S. Senate, and I approve this message."

Mindy yawned and sipped her coffee as the skateboarding video began to play.

At the video's conclusion, she closed the browser and, navigating to her desktop, opened the 'Cases' folder.

Mindy was in the middle of adding an entry when she heard a car pulling up. The sound brought her to the window.

She watched a snow-dusted Honda Accord slide to a stop in front of her trailer. After a moment, a couple walked out. They wore gloves and matching puffy yellow jackets with hoods pulled over their heads.

After a few steps, the man fell on his back. He waved his arms like a turtle on its shell. The woman helped him to a vertical stance, and locking arms, they shuffled to the door.

Mindy put a hand on the hilt of the Beretta holstered on her side.

Just as they were about to knock, she opened the door the length of the securing chain. "Can I help you?"

"This is Leatherneck's Detective Agency, right?" the woman said with panic. "Are you guys open? Your website says to drop by and see if you get lucky. Are we lucky?"

Mindy sized them up and unhooked the securing chain. "You must be the Petersons. Bobbi said you'd come by." She gestured them inside.

As they walked in, they saw the holstered pistol. The woman stopped in place and put a hand on her chest.

"Have a seat." Mindy gestured them to the futon she had cleared for them.

"It's okay," the male counterpart said, pushing the woman to the seat. The two stripped off their gloves and pulled back their hoods upon sitting. They rubbed their hands, absorbing the heat extruding from the noisy furnace.

They each shook Mindy's hand and introduced themselves as husband, Mike, and wife, Audrey. Mike had a firm grip and a certain hardness to his eyes. From his stocky build and short hair, Mindy assumed he was military or had been from the stubble on his chin. On the other hand, the woman had long legs and a face covered in makeup. Mindy knew she was a military spouse, always having to look nice whenever she went to those family readiness group meetings.

"Coffee?" Mindy asked.

Both shook their heads.

"Is Detective Porter around? Bobbi said to talk to him," Audrey said.

"Porter's working another case right now."

"Are there any other detectives around? I mean, other people in the agency we can talk to?"

"Other people in the agency?" Mindy repeated. "Just me."

"What my wife meant to say," Mike interrupted, "are there any adults we can talk to?"

"Boo, don't be rude," Audrey said as she squeezed his leg.

"I am more than capable of helping you. I'm Porter's partner," Mindy told them sternly.

"Sorry, we meant no disrespect. It's just you look…." Audrey looked over Mindy, taking in her ripped jeans and Metallica halter top, "Young."

"So, how do you know Bobbi?" Mindy asked to advance the conversation.

"We went to college together, CU Boulder," Audrey said. "We both majored in Political Science. I ended up in the Public Relations field, working for News Stations. She's Bobbi Johnson, former Governor of Colorado and now running for the U.S. Senate. One of us obviously did a little better than the other."

"Don't say that," Mike said, "you've got two beautiful boys and me."

"More like I got two puberty monsters who won't pick their dirty-ass drawers off the floor and a husband who doesn't know how to cook dinner or run a vacuum to save his life. Lucky me."

"Oh, so that's how it is? Good, love you, too," Mike said.

Mindy smiled and sipped her coffee. They seemed like a fun couple. "Why don't you tell me what happened."

The couple looked at each other, and Mike reluctantly took the lead. "Where to start?"

"At the beginning," Mindy told him, producing her phone and opening her recorder application. She took a seat in the computer swivel chair, facing them.

"Go ahead," Audrey said, slapping Mike's leg,

"Woman, I can speak for myself," Mike told her.

"Then you had better start talking, Boo. You're sitting there all quiet and nervous, white-people-like." She batted a hand to Mindy, "No offense, honey."

Mindy shrugged and continued sipping her coffee.

After a long stare, Mike submitted to his wife. "Go ahead. You gonna hijack the conversation anyway."

"No, I won't," Audrey retorted.

"Okay," Mike began. "So we just –"

"Last month," Audrey said, "We moved here from El Paso. You see, my husband's a fiber optics guy, a contractor. There was an opening here at Cheyenne Mountain Space Force Station. That's why we came. He worked at Fort Bliss, but the El Paso area is bad, especially for raising little ones."

"Hold on," Mindy said, "the media always says El Paso is one of the safest cities in America."

"Yeah, spend a week there watching the local news," Audrey said. "Trust me, I had to put a positive spin on every murder, illegal crossing, and human trafficking incident for El Paso Channel 2 Action News."

"I think they only take metrics from U.S. citizens," Mike added.

"Yeah, but what happened has nothing to do with work," Audrey said. "It's the new neighborhood we live in now. The neighborhood looked nice on paper. It has a nice view of the mountains, a low crime rate, affordable houses, and is even close to the base. It all seemed great."

"But it's not?" Mindy speculated.

Both shook their head.

"The first day we're there, unloading packages–" Audrey began to say.

"I was unloading boxes. You were just standing there," Mike corrected.

"Boo, we're a team. We've talked about this." Audrey continued, "I was supervising when those people walked right up my driveway, smiling like we were old friends."

"What people?" Mindy asked.

"Ya know, the people asking if you're interested in purchasing their home security system," Audrey said.

"They're worse than roofers after a hailstorm," Mike added. "Vultures."

"The security guys were pushy," Audrey continued.

"So there was more than one?"

"Two. One said he was training the other, but both were real pushy," Mike confirmed. "I told them we weren't interested."

"You see, my husband was in the Army. Did three tours."

"Four," Mike corrected, "woman, you call yourself my wife?"

"He's delirious. It was three," Audrey insisted. "Damn sand dementia. Anyway, we can take care of ourselves. That night around…what would you say, two?"

Mike held up three fingers.

"Yeah, two," Audrey confirmed to herself. "We woke up to a loud noise, our bay window downstairs breaking. Mike got up to grab the gun out of the safe and…."

The two exchanged a worrisome glance.

"What?" Mindy said.

"Boo, might as well tell her," Audrey told Mike.

Mindy inched forward in her chair.

"I almost had the safe open when I heard them come up the stairs, and then I smelled something. There was smoke, and then I couldn't breathe."

"You couldn't breathe?" Mindy asked.

"They threw a CS grenade into the room," Mike said.

"My eyes burned, and I couldn't stop coughing," Audrey said. "I thought I was gonna die."

"That's a CS grenade for you," Mike said.

"At some point, I fell over, and when I looked up, I saw them – they weren't human," Audrey added. "They had glowing blue eyes."

"What?" Mindy said.

"They were wearing NVGs," Mike said. "Night Vision Goggles, combine that with the gas, and it explains what she thought she saw."

"Thought I saw?" Audrey asked. "I know what I saw. They were some sorta ghosts or demons."

Mike shook his head.

"Phantoms," Audrey said. "Like something out of a damn horror movie. Four of them."

"Needless to say, she started babbling her nonsense to the cops and instantly discredited our situation. I'm telling you, it was just off-duty military wearing NVGs."

"Right," Mindy said. "Why do you think they were military?"

"Their maneuvering, the way they held their rifles, hell, their boots."

"Okay, did they say anything to you?"

"Well, they had guns pointed at us," Audrey said.

"Rifles, M16s with laser sights," Mike clarified.

"I know how it sounds," Audrey told her, "but they didn't say anything."

"Nothing?"

"Not a word," Audrey repeated.

"They just wanted to scare us," Mike said.

"Wanted to? Well, they did. Thank God they didn't go to the boy's rooms," Audrey said, putting a dramatic hand on her chest.

Mike looked blankly at the floor, "I got a powerful impression they wanted us to move out of the house. To be honest, I've never been so scared in my entire life, and I've been to many places and seen a lot of stuff. But it was all in different countries. I never thought I'd see this type of stuff back in the States."

"Are you going to move?" Mindy asked.

"No, how can we?" Mike said, "All of our money is tied up in the house."

"You said you talked to the police?"

"We talked to Detective Evans," Audrey explained. "She said break-ins were happening to a few other houses in the neighborhood over the year. None of them reported people with glowing eyes."

"NVGs," Mike corrected.

"Glowing eyes," Audrey said again. "She doesn't think this was a race crime because each house had different ethnicities."

Mike continued. "Evans told us none have ever been resolved out of the half dozen similar cases. She's had the cops sitting outside our house for the last three nights, but nothing's happened."

"Did your neighbors see or hear anything?" Mindy said.

"No," Mike told her, "Supposedly, none of them even heard the window break."

"Or the loud-ass music they were playing," Audrey said.

"What music?" Mindy said.

"I don't know, rock and roll. It started blaring in the house when we heard the window break."

"It's called Heavy Metal," Mike corrected.

"Whatever, all our neighbors are lying sons-of-bitches," Audrey grumbled.

"So, you think they're lying?" Mindy said.

"Honey, have you ever heard a glass break that wasn't loud?"

"Be nice," Mike told her.

"Boo, tell her about all those signs in the neighbor's yard," Audrey said.

"I'm telling the story, woman," Mike told her. He continued, "Get this–"

"All our neighbors have the signs for the home security system those people were pedaling at the door," Audrey interrupted.

"The neighbors say once they got the security system, they ain't had any problems."

"When you say all of your neighbors, how many are you talking about?" Mindy said.

"Basically, the entire neighborhood," Mike told her.

"You think this is a scheme by the security group to get you to buy their system?" Mindy asked.

"Absolutely," Mike said. "But my wife thinks I'm crazy."

"You are crazy," Audrey told her.

"Why, because ghosts don't have motives?"

"Well, there's that, but If something like that was happening, the po-lice would have caught them by now."

"You would think." Mindy said, "What's the name of this security group?"

Audrey reached into her purse, "This is what they gave me." She handed over a business card. The texturized ivory card had a Bald Eagle grasping onto an Iron bar and branding the words 'American Iron' across its spread wings. The text beneath said, 'Security, Safety, Reliability – trust us with all your home security needs.' Contact information followed.

"After we talked to the po-lice and realized they weren't going to help, I reached out to Bobbi," Audrey explained. "She said you could help us."

"Yeah, uh, we'll see what we can do," Mindy said.

With a squeak, the rear bedroom door opened. A mature, well-maintained woman with wavy, long, dyed blonde hair walked out. She went to the kitchen and poured herself a cup of coffee.

"Oh, my Lord," Audrey whispered. "That woman ain't got no clothes on."

"Well, she's wearing panties," Mindy said.

"And nothing else," Mike said, his eyes traveling from the pair of butterfly tattoos above her panty line to her ample breasts.

The blonde smiled, eyeing him with her sexy raccoon eyes hiding behind faded dark eyeshadow.

Mike waved, and Audrey smacked him on the back of the head.

"Uh," Mindy said, gesturing to the woman, "Alice, here is a battered woman we rescued on one of our cases."

Alice gave Mindy an amused look.

"She's, uh…French," Mindy said.

Alice met Mike's gaze. "Voulez-vous coucher avec moi?"

Mike remained speechless.

"Okay, time to go," Audrey said. "You have my number and contact information, right?"

"Bobbi provided it," Mindy said. "We'll be in touch."

Audrey guided her husband out the door and smacked him again as he snuck a final glance at Alice.

Mindy downed her coffee and refilled her thermos cap in the kitchen.

Walking to the hallway coat closet, Alice reached into the inner pocket of Porter's jacket and fished out his pack of cigarettes and a lighter. Shaking out a cigarette, she lit up.

Alice advanced to the window and watched the Honda pull away. With arms crossed over her chest, she puffed on the cigarette. "Damn, I didn't think those two would ever leave."

"Yeah," Mindy agreed.

Blowing out a plume of smoke, Alice noticed a shiner under Mindy's eye, "Where'd you get that?".

"It's nothing," Mindy said. "Just the case we worked on yesterday."

"Umm, hmm. Take a seat," Alice said.

Mindy rolled her eyes and sat on the futon, "I told you, it's nothing."

Alice grabbed her clutch purse from the kitchen counter and sat beside her. After some digging, she pulled out a makeup case and, pressing her finger into the foundation, smeared it across Mindy's bruise. "Don't want people asking questions."

"Thanks."

Alice gently worked it in, and Mindy held back a smile as she did so. Alice was like an older sister. She was always looking out for her and offering advice. Even if it was more stripper knowledge than anything else. Last week, Alice told Mindy to always wear shoes with straps so you don't propel high heels at a customer's face.

Alice had been a sex object in earlier years, but she had been in the game for too long. Though, she was still pretty.

"After all the assholes I've been with," Alice said, "this is second nature." She finished and inspected the bruise, "Good as new."

"How's Porter doing? He seemed a little on edge after Bobbi left yesterday."

"He's having nightmares again."

"Nightmares?"

"Yeah," Alice said. "They're getting worse." Alice took another puff on her cigarette.

"How so?"

"Shouldn't you be getting to school?"

Mindy checked the time on her phone and cursed. Walking to the hallway closet, she threw on her bomber jacket. Then, she grabbed her backpack and skateboard beside the desk and opened the door.

"Mindy?" Alice called out as Mindy had one foot out the door.

"Yeah?" She said, putting in her earbuds and thumbing away at her phone playing 'Complicated' by Avril Lavigne.

"Gun."

Mindy stared at her in protest.

"Gun," Alice repeated. "I'm asking nicely."

Sighing, Mindy unclipped her holster and slapped it on the kitchen counter. "Happy?"

Alice puffed on her cigarette. "Have a good day at school, dear."

Walking out the door, Mindy flicked her off, put her board on the icy asphalt, and stepped off.

After dropping Alice off at Fantasies and driving through the double-wide entry gates of Scraps Disposal Transfer Station, Porter turned his truck up the snow-dusted trail leading to the vehicle weigh-in station. He kept to the right of the cones separating inbound and outbound traffic and followed the bend to the top of the hill.

Stopping short of the weigh-in station and the adjoining building, he pulled off and stepped out.

A pungent odor emanated from the massive indoor dumpsite 100 feet past him. He could almost taste the stale food, rotted cardboard, and molded drywall.

Walking to the weigh-in building, Porter watched a Toyota truck with a bed of toilets and sinks pull forward, stop at the ramp, and get weighed.

"Okay, you're good," a woman's voice blared through the speaker affixed to the railing on the ramp.

The Toyota went down the opposite side of the ramp and advanced to the dump site.

At the payment counter, Porter rapped his knuckles on the security window.

A young woman in a burgundy puffer jacket rolled her wheelchair into view. She had a soft face and dyed pink hair, sported in a bob. Her short, freckled nose held up pink sparkle-framed glasses.

"Porter," she greeted with a beaming smile.

"Molly, how you doin' beautiful?"

She brushed a strand of hair behind her ear peppered with various earrings, "Good."

Porter leaned on the counter, "So, what do I gotta do to get you to have a drink with me?"

She rolled her eyes, "You know I'm not old enough."

"You let me worry about that."

"If I didn't know any better, that almost sounded like a date."

Porter lit a cigarette and shrugged, "You tell me."

She beamed, "What can I do for you?"

"Is the Love Doctor working today?"

"Lemme check," Molly wheeled to her computer and, with fingerless knitted green gloves, typed away on her keyboard. "Yep, the Doc's in today, bay four."

"Thanks, beautiful." Blowing out a plume of smoke, he smirked, "Catch you later."

Making his way to the bay, Porter watched a skid loader roll back and forth. The loader beeped as it collected trash material from the various bays and piled them into a vast mountain at the center of the dump site.

As the loader collected another heap of trash, a man wearing a hard hat and reflective vest jogged out and waved his arms. The loader stopped, and the man picked through the pile and pulled out a wooden candlestick holder. Examining it, the man stepped aside and waved the loader to continue.

"Anything good?" Porter asked.

Doc was known as 'that funny-looking guy' with his scraggly appearance, bulgy eyes, and pointy nose. His Ph.D. and reputation for being horny gave him the alias of 'Love Doctor.'

"Oh yeah, I got a perfect one here," Doc said in his scratchy voice, examining the candle holder. "The wife will love this, the kids too. They can use this to build a rocket ship or something."

"You don't have any kids," Porter said.

"I might. You never know."

"And you're not married. Five times divorced."

"Good point. Though that fifth one didn't count," Doc tossed the holder behind his back. "Vic, I'm taking my fifteen!" he yelled to his supervisor at the opposite end of the bay. Walking outside, Doc extended a hand, "Porter, how the hell are you?"

"I need some information," Porter reached into his jacket.

"Jesus Christ, don't shoot me," Doc said, putting up his hands defensively. "I don't know what Mindy told you, but I swear to God, she never told me her age. I saw her at the club that night and assumed she was legal and –"

"You talk too much," Porter handed him the iPhone he had taken from the hotel, "I need you to break into this."

"What do we have here?" Doc withdrew his glasses from his vest pocket and put them to his face. "No biometrics, huh?"

"Nope."

"Porter, I have a Ph.D. in Mathematics. This is a little beneath me."

"You also have that program you use to crack into ATMs. What was it, a Bank of America ATM last time?"

In the distance, Doc saw a customer unloading a toilet from his truck. Laughing, he waved him off, "We're just joking, man, just a joke." Turning back to Porter, he whispered, "Want to say that a little louder? C'mon, man."

"I need into this phone, at the soonest."

Doc pocketed his glasses, "You know this shit is illegal, right?"

Porter stared at him with a neutral look.

"You're not going to deck me, are you?"

"You really think I would tell you before I did?"

"Point taken," Doc pocketed the phone. "Okay, but this can take me hours or days, maybe even a week."

"Doc, don't bullshit me."

"Fine, give me a day or two, but listen, my work isn't free. It's gonna cost you."

Porter sighed, "What this time?"

"Introduce me to the redhead at your club, you know, the one I'm after."

"She's not a real redhead."

"Like I care if the curtains match the drapes."

"Jessica?"

"Yeah, Jessica Rabbit."

"You know that's not her real name, and she has kids."

"No problem, kids are great. I was looking for someone to wash my car."

"She's sworn off, guys. A hundred percent die-hard lesbian now."

"Hot. Maybe her girlfriend will get jealous."

"And I hear she has crabs."

"Sounds crunchy. Seriously, Porter, you'll have to try harder than that."

"Fine."

"One more thing, maybe get her to give me a lap dance or two on the house."

"Sure, but no guarantees she won't just kick you in the nuts and take your money."

Doc shrugged, "Wouldn't be the first time."

⁂

Alice spun around the center pole before lowering to her hands and knees. Locking eyes with a young guy upfront with a military cut sporting large oval glass, she crawled across the dollar bill-littered hardwood stage to him. As she began nibbling on his earlobe, the men surrounding him yelled and slapped his back.

The song, 'Monster Mash,' ended.

"Find me later if you want more," Alice whispered into the young man's ear.

Collecting the bills, Alice tucked them under an orange thong strap, picked up her matching bra, and stepped off stage.

Putting her bra on, she went to Porter's table and sat on his lap. Wrapping a sweaty arm around his neck, she plucked the cigarette from his lips and took a puff.

"How'd you do?" Porter asked.

Alice plucked the bills from her panties and counted, "Cheap fucks."

"What do you expect?" Porter said. "They're all Army. Payday's not until the end of the month."

"Fucks shouldn't even bother coming in."

A brute wearing shades crossed their view and hunched over a distant table– passing out business cards.

Alice flicked cigarette ash toward him. "Your buddy has been making rounds for the last hour."

"Is that so?" Porter said, stealing the cigarette back.

Sweat was dripping from Alice's forehead to her brow. In her early forties, she wasn't the age of most girls here and a few years older than himself, nor was she in perfect slender condition, but he'd be damned if she didn't belong. Ever since Maggie left, she'd been the only girl *seriously* worth his time.

Maybe it was because Porter felt he wasn't as young nor in the top physical condition he had once been, and she was the best he would get. Maybe it was because, no matter what, she didn't judge him as everyone else did. Perhaps it was because he knew that she knew it wasn't real – *they weren't real.*

"He's recruiting for some sort of security firm," Alice said.

A loud 'Hooah!' broke out from the center stage table.

Porter shook his head.

"What, don't Marines say that too?" Alice asked.

"Yeah, if we had dicks in our mouths."

They looked to the stage where a slim redhead with freckles wearing a bunny-eared headband took the stage and danced to the surrounding customers' hoots, whistles, and hollers.

As they watched, the young guy Alice had been flirting with earlier stood from his seat and faced them. He looked embarrassed and scratched the back of his stubble head. As he approached their table, he looked back at his buddies, who egged him on.

"Looks like you got a secret admirer," Porter told Alice.

"Gotta make the rent somehow." Alice craned to Porter's ear, "We need to talk about something."

Porter squinted in suspicion, "What's going on?"

"Later." She kissed him on the cheek before meeting the young man.

Wrapping an arm around his torso, Alice led him away.

Porter watched them momentarily and wondered what she needed to tell him. He shook the thought and, scanning the room, found the brute wearing shades was now at another table.

The brute wore a skintight black shirt, like all the cool guys in the movies – and with his high and tight haircut and chiseled jaw, he looked like Uncle Sam's poster boy for the war effort.

Porter smelled the scent of Suave shampoo before Evans sat in the vacant seat next to him. She crossed her legs and stared interestedly at the stage, cradling her hands on her lap. "She's flexible. Must be new. Let me guess, red hair, bunny ears, Jessica Rabbit?"

"You guessed it." Porter turned to Evans, and a flash of red light from the stage reflected off her silver cross necklace, drawing his gaze. He followed the cross as far as he could, the tip of which sat between her breasts.

"Focus," she said, nodding to the stage.

"I am," Porter told her.

She pointed to her eyes and then to the stage.

They watched Jessica perform a series of spins on the pole and sway her body to the 'Ghostbusters' song.

"She's not your type," Evans said.

"Is that right?"

"Ryan Porter, I've known you since the 7th grade."

"Indulge me."

Evans motioned to Alice, giving a lap dance to the young buck in one of the club's dark, sticky corners. "You're more into the middle-aged, used-up, blonde types."

Porter studied Evans, "Damn right."

"Asshole."

"Is that an invitation?"

Evans sighed, "In your dreams."

They watched Jessica for a bit longer. She took off her top and, securing the undergarment behind a man's head, pulled him into her breasts.

"So, I assume you didn't come here with the intention of me making an honest woman out of you?" Porter asked.

"You assumed correctly, for once."

"Let me guess, Captain Easley."

"Yep."

A slender waitress with a soft face wearing an orange Halloween-themed bustier, black leggings, and a giant bat bow in her ponytail wine-red hair walked over with a limp. She wore black lipstick and orange eyeshadow. Twisting off the beer cap, she handed Porter a Coors Light, "You were looking thirsty, Boss." She spoke loud and slow.

Porter pulled a five from his wallet and slipped it under her shiny black belt, "Thanks, Erica."

She winked at him and turned to Evans.

Evans waved her off, and Erica limped back to the bar illuminated by a string of purple lights.

"Erica, huh? She seems cute," Evans said. "So, no spiffy fantasy name for her?"

"She's the barmaid, not a dancer."

"And special?"

"Erica was in a bad car accident as a teenager. The accident left her hearing impaired and messed up her legs."

Evans grinned, "Wow, you know quite a bit about her."

Taking a swig, Porter nodded, "Listen, just because I know a girl's history doesn't mean I've slept with her."

"So, you're saying you haven't slept with her?"

"I never said that."

"She's a cripple."

"Cripples need love too."

Evans sighed, "Alright, you have to answer something for me."

Porter sighed, "Yes, I'll support the local police and screw you too."

Evans ignored him and continued, "How the hell do you know Bobbi Johnson? Not every day a U.S. Senate candidate vouches for your release from police custody."

"Only met her yesterday," Porter took a swig of his beer. "We've been hired for a job, starting with the Peterson case. It seems Bobbi Johnson and Audrey Peterson are old friends."

"Wait, Bobbi Johnson hired you?"

"Appreciate the vote of confidence. So, what happened on your end?"

"After you and Mindy gave your statements, I had to have a little chat with my Lieutenant."

"Go on."

"To put it nicely, she's pretty upset we went into that hotel before the backup arrived. She's labeled you a vigilante, and me–"

"What?"

"Soon to be unemployed."

"Well, two places are always hiring, McDonald's and the Army. I'm sure you'll figure it out."

"Army, hell no, and if I ever have to make you a burger, I'm spitting in it."

"I always knew you were a spitter."

Evans rolled her eyes, "She also wasn't too thrilled you used your teenage partner as bait."

Porter took a swig of beer. "Easley told me as much. Though, if it's any consolation, it was Mindy's idea to be the bait, not mine."

"Doesn't change the facts–"

"We found Claire Walters and the other girls," Porter said. "Not to mention I put that Spaghetti eating fuck Mr. Joshua on the shelf so you could bleed him for information. And once he gets out of the hospital, I'll rip out his God damn throat. As far as I can tell, that's a win-win for everyone."

"Ryan, I'm on your side."

"I feel there's a conjunction coming."

"But she doesn't want me to help you with the Peterson break-in case."

"There it is."

"In fact, she ordered me not to talk to you about the case or solicit you and Mindy in any future sting operations."

"If you're not pissing people off, you're not doing your job," Porter said.

"Regarding the Peterson case –"

"Atta' girl."

"You know they reported seeing ghosts?"

"Audrey reported seeing ghosts. Mike's pretty sure it was just some clowns wearing NVGs," Porter corrected. "I'm going to go with Mike on this one."

"We've got two units patrolling the neighborhood, but it's been quiet since the break-in. We can swing by after this if you want."

"Any leads?" Porter asked.

"Nope, we've tried to get a hold of the Scooby gang to see if they knew anything, but they're not answering," Evans said.

"Next time, give Buffy a call."

"I know Buffy's a blonde, but not Willow, Faith, Dawn, or Cordelia?"

"Well, it would be a package deal, obviously."

"Obviously," Evans said, rolling her eyes.

Porter nodded, "Bobbi believes this is the work of American Iron who has hired someone called Frank Marion to operate the muscle of their business. What do you know about Frank or American Iron?"

"Never heard of a Frank Marion. As for American Iron, well, they're a fairly new home security company and have only had a footprint in the city for about a year now, but –"

"What?"

"In the last year, their profits have boomed. As they've risen, other security companies in the city have left. Companies like ADT, Vivint, and America Burglary, to name a few."

"Are they running these other companies out?" Porter asked, sipping on his beer.

"Don't know, but they'd need some serious backing if they are." Evans watched as dollar bills showered the stage following the redhead's performance. "Bribing profitable companies to leave town takes a lot of money."

"Any leads?"

"I didn't get that far. I sent what I had to Mindy since I'm officially not on this case. Also, speaking of which, how is she doing? What she did for those girls was brave."

"She can handle herself," Porter said.

Evans sat forward and, interlocking her fingers, raced her thumbs around each other. "Be careful you don't treat her tougher than she is. At the end of the day, she's just a teenager without her parents. She needs guidance."

"Noted."

"Ryan, I'm serious."

"I'm not a guidance counselor."

"If you aren't willing to be a father figure, why bother adopting her?"

"Tax write-off."

Evans chuckled, "Sure."

"That there is a salty-looking jacket," a man said.

Evans and Porter turned to the brute who stood to Porter's side, eyeing a cluster of patches on his bomber jacket. "Military, right?"

"Bought it on eBay," Porter told him.

The brute laughed, "Good one. But you can't fool me, man. Look at you. You got the look. I can tell." He read some of the patches, "Marine Corps, huh? I was Army, Special Ops."

"Spectacular. Should I send you a friend request?" Porter asked.

"Don't mind him. He's always an asshole," Evans said.

"It's all good," the brute said, "I can be too. Hope you don't mind me intruding, but one of the girls said you were the owner."

"What's it to you?" Porter said.

"Hey man, I'm not looking for a fight. I just wanted to introduce myself." He extended a beefy hand and forced Porter into a handshake, "Names, Scott."

"Porter," he told him.

"Sarah," Evans' said, shaking his hand next.

"Military, too?" Scott asked her.

"No, not me," Evans said.

"Maybe she's the smart one," Scott said, trying to force a laugh. It didn't work. "Okay, let's cut the bullshit." He reached into his pocket.

Both Porter and Evans reached for their pieces.

"Whoa, settle down, guys," Scott said. He pulled out a stack of business cards bound together with a rubber band.

Porter and Evans retracted their hands.

"The Second Amendment is hard at work here. I like that," Scott said. He handed a business card to each of them. "I represent American Iron. Have you heard of my company?" Scott asked.

Porter and Evans exchanged a glance, and both shook their heads.

"We're a home security company based here in the local area. Veteran-owned and operated. I hope you don't mind me passing around some of my cards."

"Man's gotta make a buck," Porter said. "Just make sure my girls see some of those bucks too."

"Yeah, absolutely."

"Home security?" Evans said, examining the card.

"Yeah, my company specializes in smart home technology. What sets us apart is we do it all. We install, monitor, provide technical support, and respond to alarms. We also –"

"What do you mean you respond to all alarms?" Evans asked. "Don't the monitoring services just reach out to the police?"

"Most do," Scott agreed. "But we have our own private security. Hell, we can deploy a QRF," he snapped his fingers, "just like that."

"Quick reaction force," Porter told Evans.

"Yeah, I know," she said.

"We'll get there in half the time it would take for our local tin Gods to put down their doughnuts and actually do their job," Scott said.

"How Convenient," Porter said, smirking at Evans.

Evans wasn't amused.

"That's where you come into play," Scott told him, pointing to the business card. "We're always looking for a little muscle for our private security. My company only hires vets, so call us if you need extra holiday cash. I mean, not that you need extra cash with a place like this. But maybe tell your Marine buddies about us, whether they need work, part-time, full-time, whatever, we can make it work."

Porter looked over the business card and pocketed it. "I might know a few guys."

"Sweet, man." He looked around the club. "Hey, mind if I ask who you got for security on this place? I noticed some areas where a couple more door locks and security cameras would be useful. Those big bouncers I saw can only do so much, know what I mean, man?"

Porter was about to tell him to "fuck off" when Evans put her hand on his thigh. "Let's meet in a few days to discuss what you have to offer," she said.

"Alright, sounds good," Scott said. "Here," he took out another business card and wrote his number on its back. He handed it to Evans, "You guys give me a call on my personal line whenever you're ready, and I'll bring some brochures, play you guys a demo on my laptop, all sorts of shit."

"Sounds great," Evans said. She turned to Porter and squeezed his thigh, "Right?"

Porter nodded, "Thrilled."

"Alright," Scott said, shaking their hands and lingering on Evans. "I gotta say, Miss, you would look much better up there." He pointed to the stage, "Just saying." Grinning, he walked off to another table and began chatting.

"Charming," Evans said.

"You ever meet someone for the first time and feel like breaking their fucking neck?" Porter asked, taking a final puff off his cigarette before snuffing it in the ashtray on the table.

"You always were the jealous type."

"Were? Hell, your boy Finley's still dead to me."

Evans rolled her eyes, "Listen, we'll get closer to American Iron's products and, with any luck, see some of Scott's books when we discuss profits. Win-win, right?"

Porter looked down at her hand on his thigh, "Only if you move your hand slightly higher."

"Yeah," Evans said, slapping his leg, "but why give you the satisfaction?"

"Well, Scott's right about one thing," Porter said, downing his beer.

"What's that?"

Porter walked towards the stage, "Hell, I'd pay." He pulled out a wad of cash from his wallet. "Think of it this way, Captain Easley might fire you soon, and if your Army and McDonald's jobs fall through, then there's option three."

"I'm confused," Evans said, following Porter. "Are you trying to bribe a cop to get naked on stage or solicit one for sex?"

"Do I get a discount for both?" At the stage, Porter tossed the cash onto it.

Jessica blew him a kiss.

"You could wear your old flat-foot uniform," Porter said, heading for the exit. "Hat, baton, the works. Just like Senior Prom. Remember Senior Prom?"

"You and I remember Senior Prom quite differently."

6

Parking behind Evans Jeep, Porter stepped out of his truck, took a drag on his cigarette, and looked around.

The middle-class HOA neighborhood was odd, for nothing was out of place, which was the point of an HOA neighborhood. Identical two-story houses, well-maintained lawns, similar paint color schemes, white picket fences, and quiet streets. Everything seemed almost perfect.

Thick white signs with the American Iron logo were in front of each house. Every door had identical keypads, camera doorbells, and motion floodlights over the garage.

"Is this place freaky or what?" Evans said, walking to him.

"This is like the beginning of every horror movie I've ever seen," Porter said.

"I'm thinking House of Wax. Remember when we watched that?"

"The remake?"

"Yeah, the remake."

"That was a horrible movie."

"Yes, it was," Evans led the way up a driveway to a house with a blue tarp duct taped over a busted front window.

Porter rapped his knuckles across the door.

There was no answer.

Evans looked back, scanning the roads, "That's weird."

"What?"

"There should be a squad car patrolling this area."

"Tax dollars hard at work." Porter knocked a second time, and the door creaked open.

"Yes," a woman said. Upon seeing Evans, she opened the door fully, "Detective Evans." She turned to Porter, "You must be, Detective Porter? I'm Audrey."

"Can we come inside?" Porter said.

She motioned to them, "Sorry, do you mind if I ask you to put out your cigarette?"

Porter shook his head, "No, I don't mind if you ask." Taking a puff on the cigarette, he continued, "My partner has filled me in on the case, and Detective Evans offered to show me your home."

"I hope you don't mind us stopping by," Evans said.

"Not at all. Thank you for coming," Audrey told them, staring at the cigarette and shaking her head. "My husband's at work, and the kids are at school, but I can answer your questions. Where are my manners? Can I get you two something to drink?"

"I'll take a Coors Light," Porter told her.

"Uh, we actually don't drink alcohol. I can get you juice, milk, coffee, or water."

"Your husband is a vet and doesn't drink?"

"He got gout in his foot the other year and needs to avoid alcohol now."

Porter waved her off. "Your husband, Mike, works at Cheyenne Mountain Space Force Station, right?" Porter walked through the living room littered with an assortment of cardboard and stackable plastic storage boxes and stared at a black scorch mark on the carpet.

"That's right," she said.

Burn marks spanned across the living room.

Dropping to a knee, he sniffed the carpet and smelt the faint scent of sulfur. He turned to the tarp-covered window and envisioned the window being busted and the CS grenade tossed inside the house. "They hit you when again? The home invaders?"

Porter walked to the front door. The deadbolt had been kicked in.

"Around three in the morning," Audrey said.

"Ballsy," Porter looked down at the baseboards. Boot scuffs were apparent at the entry corner of the front door. The exact place someone trained to clear a room would check after the initial weapons sweep. "Most home invasions happen in the daytime."

"I didn't know that," Audrey said, following his movements.

"They usually want to avoid encounters." Porter pointed to the kitchen, "You mind?"

Audrey shook her head.

He searched the linoleum floor until he found another scuff mark by the rear patio door.

Porter mentally saw an armed man running across the kitchen, abruptly stopping and standing guard.

"Is this your only other exit out of the house?" Porter asked.

"Yes, the garage outside is detached."

Nodding, Porter walked back into the living room and saw a picture frame canted on the wall.

"You told Mindy there was loud music playing?"

"Loud music?" Evans said, confused.

"Yeah, my husband says it was heavy metal. It shook the entire house," Audrey said.

"Music torture," Porter said.

"Music torture?" Audrey asked.

"It's a form of physiological warfare. In 1989, Bush Senior sent troops into Panama to get General Noriega. Surrounded by U.S. troops, Noriega holed himself in the Vatican embassy. Troops played heavy metal on full blast from speakers mounted on Humvees for three days and nights to get him out. Noriega eventually surrendered."

"Really?" Audrey asked.

"Yeah, they still do it on occasion." As Porter said this, he imagined heavy metal riffs blasting through the house as men charged up the stairs on the surprised family.

"Do you need to look upstairs?" Audrey said. "It's where we were threatened."

"Threatened?"

"Well, where we felt threatened," Audrey clarified. "I think they set off another grenade up there."

Standing at the base of the stairs, Porter looked up and shook his head. "No, I've seen all I need."

"Are you sure?"

"Yeah," Porter said, snuffing his cigarette out.

"So what now?" Audrey asked.

"Well," Porter said, "I'll look into it."

Taking out his pack of cigarettes, Porter began packing it into his palm. Walking to the front door, he looked at the damaged door frame where the deadbolt had been kicked in. The deadbolt lock was in working condition, but the strike plate was missing, where the structure was damaged.

In the center of the door and on either side were screw holes. A 2x4 was propped upright in the corner of the room with six screws penetrating through its back. A cordless drill and a battery charging station sat beside it.

"That's how you're securing the door?" Porter asked.

Audrey nodded, "Yeah until our good-for-nothin' home insurance shows up and assesses the damage. And, even then, that doesn't mean they will fix it immediately."

"You guys going to be home tonight?"

"Why?"

"Leave the coffee running. I'll be around later, around six-ish."

"Alright."

They all shook hands, and Evans and Porter exited the house.

Porter put his shades on and lit up. He stared at the blue sky streaked by the exhaust of F-16s practicing.

"What are your thoughts?" Evans asked, adjusting her Aviators.

"For starters, this sucks."

"Well yeah, their house was broken into."

"Everything in that house leads me to agree with Mike. That invasion was conducted by vets. They broke in using a grenade, kicked in the door, performed their sweeps, placed guards, and the disorienting music."

"So, what does that mean?"

"Training only gets you so far. You need the right gear to pull off something like this. The grenades, rifles, NVGs, that stuff doesn't come cheap. If they are military vets or off-duty military, you would think they are being supplied by a military armory. From what I saw, though, nothing actually ties this to American Iron."

"Alright, a theory could be that American Iron hires these guys, possibly vets, to terrorize houses that refuse their services," Evans said. "American Iron contracts these guys to get homeowners to invest in their services and put out the competitors,

"So American Iron is the only game in town."

"Exactly," Evans said.

"It makes sense on paper," Porter said.

"The flaw in the theory is that something like this would require the entire neighborhood to play along. You can't tell me the Petersons are the only ones to experience these Phantoms."

"Phantoms?"

"Sounds better than your NVG-wearing vets," Evans said.

"True. Fear is a powerful tool. Make an example of one house, and no one talks about the next."

"In a world of social media, someone would've talked."

"Let's test that theory." Porter focused on a house across the street that was for sale. "Follow me."

A black plastic brochure box was staked in the house's front yard by the curb. Porter took out a flyer and read over it. Since June, the house had been on the market, meaning it was completely vacant.

Porter plucked a palm-sized rock from the road and walked up the yard to the green metal edging separating the landscaped lava rocks from the grass.

"What are you doing?" Evans asked.

Tossing the rock to himself, Porter went to the nearest window. "Your report said none of the neighbors heard the break-in. They all slept through it, right?"

"Right," Evans agreed cautiously.

"Okay," winding up, Porter tossed the rock into the window, and it made a crack but failed to break. "Hmm."

"Just what are you…"

Porter pulled out his revolver and let loose a .38 into the window. It burst open in an explosion of glass.

Upon doing this, occupants from three surrounding houses poked out their doors to investigate the noise.

Porter turned to a few houses and waved, "Looks like they can hear just fine. Why don't you monitor their social media feeds and tell me who talks about this."

Those who looked out quickly ducked out of view.

"You made your point." Walking across the street, Evans unlocked her car. "You know you'll have to pay for that window, right?"

"Put it on my tab."

"Right, your vigilante tab?" Evans checked her phone, "I'm late."

Porter motioned to the cross hanging off her neck. "Afternoon Mass?"

"You know, there's always plenty of room if you ever wanted to tag along. Clear that consciousness of yours."

Porter leaned on his truck. "Interesting date proposal. Hell, if you want to fuck, Sarah, just say so. No need to get God involved."

"In your dreams."

"Yeah, 11th-grade dreams. I remember it like it was yesterday. You, me, your parent's basement, a little Britney Spears playing."

"You just had to bring that up, didn't you?"

"Of course."

"We all make mistakes in life."

"Yeah, but not every mistake is bad."

"C'mon, you seriously got anything better to do tonight?"

"Probably Alice or someone just as willing."

"Seriously, Porter."

"I am being serious."

"C'mon, when's the last time you went to church?"

"Man, aren't you persistent?"

"What can I say? I like to help the less fortunate."

"Sarah, you know me better than anyone. Your God and I don't have a cordial relationship."

"It's alright," Evans said, grabbing onto his hand.

Her touch surprised him.

"I know you've been through a lot and have lost faith. But remember, even if you don't believe in him anymore, he still believes in you."

Porter caressed his thumb over hers, feeling her skin. It had been too long. "Sarah, I –"

"You're not a lost cause."

"That's not the consensus."

"Well, I'm not the consensus." She took off her glasses, and her powder blue eyes shone. She cocked her head that little way she does when she is full of concern.

Porter stared into her eyes, "You haven't looked at me like this in a long time."

Porter remembered their Senior year of High School. Porter stood in his NJROTC uniform, and Sarah in a shiny blue dress with a slit up the side. She held his hand outside the ballroom at the NJROTC military ball as they anxiously awaited to hear who had won the title of King and Queen. Next to them stood Finley in his uniform and his date, Heather Johnson. She was pretty in her white satin dress, but she wasn't Sarah.

The announcement was made inside the ballroom: Finley had won King, and Sarah had won Queen.

The two couples exchanged dates, and Finley whispered to Porter, "I always win."

Sarah gave Porter that concerned look before Finley walked her into the ballroom.

Returning to the present, Porter realized her eyes lingered on him.

Porter advanced his lips onto hers.

Evans returned the kiss, which lasted a long moment before she pushed him away and smacked him.

"Okay, I deserved that," Porter said, massaging his jaw.

"No," she said, pushing him further back. "I am not one of your two-dollar whores!" Getting in her car, she slammed the door.

"Sarah," Porter protested, palming the driver's window. He wanted to apologize. Needed to tell her more. Maybe get in another kiss. Anything, but leave the situation like this.

Turning over the engine and rolling her window down, she snapped, "Porter, I am engaged to Finley, you know that?"

"You asking me or telling me?"

"You're such an asshole. You had no right."

"I call bullshit," Porter said. The more he thought about Evans and Finley's relationship, the more it pissed him off. Evans was excellent in every way, and Finley, Finley was a walking cluster fuck in every way.

Finley was a former Army Ranger and was now in the not-so-secret Secret Service. He cared more about making the next promotion than trying to know anything relevant about Evans.

"I am engaged, dammit," she said.

"To who? A fucking guy who doesn't know shit about you?"

"He knows enough."

"Does he know your favorite season is Fall because you're pumpkin crazy about fucking everything? Does he know you liked Jim Carrey movies as a kid because they were the only thing to make you laugh when your dad came home drunk? Or how about that you love the smell outside just before it rains? Does he know any of that stuff? Tell me. How much longer are you going to be engaged to that prick? Another year?"

Evans stayed quiet for a moment, taking in everything Porter had said. Her knuckles turned white on the wheel, and it was evident that she was straining to say something. Evans was usually reserved, always the better person. *Not this time.*

"At least Finley's committed to someone. You wouldn't know anything about that, would you?"

"You forget I was married?"

"Yeah, and Maggie left you, didn't she?"

The words stung, and it wasn't something Porter was ready to hear.

From the apologetic look on Evan's face, it wasn't something she was expecting to say.

They both looked away from one another and as Porter shook his head and walked off, Evans drove off in a hurry.

"I deserved that," Porter said for the second time today.

Sitting in his truck, Porter thought of all his time with Evans over the long years they had known one another. Friends and part-time lovers like her were rare. Friends as you got older, real friends were even rarer. Porter didn't have more than two or three left in his life.

He was okay with that.

7

Taking off the final halter, Hector opened the stall gate for each horse.

"Go on, get," he told them.

One of the horses neighed and turned to the side. The other stared at Hector, ears forward, alert to what he was telling them but not comprehending. The third horse's head was lowered, and its ears hung to the side.

Hector withdrew his Sig Sauer P226 from his trouser waistband and fired a 9mm into the stable roof. The horses bolted. They raced across the snow-covered dirt road and into the hills beyond.

Hector had grown up with Sparky, Buddy, and Dusty. He had fed them, rode them, and played with them for so long that, at one time, they felt more like his friends than actual human beings did. He hadn't found much solace with people in school, so his only company was the horses for many afternoons and nights.

Hector walked across the property's snowy front yard and up the rickety old wooden stairs to his parent's house. Leaning on the front door, with its chipped brown paint, he pulled an egg from his pocket and peeled it. He took a salt packet out of another pocket and, sprinkling a dash, took a bite.

A cold bite was in the air, but the radiating sun made it a beautiful day. The country spanned as far as it could before reaching the base of the Franklin Mountains. It was a beautiful sight he didn't appreciate as a child.

There was a rare peace here.

Pulling out the funeral program that he had stuffed in his jacket from this morning, Hector looked over it.

To think someone's life accomplishments could be summed up in a brochure.

Crumpling the form, he let it fall to the ground.

Entering the house, he stood in the doorway.

His dad had left the radio on, and Johnny Cash was singing the song, 'Hurt.'

There was a mix of smells emanating from the kitchen. Folgers from the stained metal pot sitting atop the counter. Peppermint from the Avalon lotion his mother had always put on at least five times daily. Sugar cookies from the open jar on the counter.

Hector stared at the beige walls populated with various wooden frames of jigsaw puzzles. A puzzle box stood upright on the table. It displayed the finished picture and read, "9,000-piece Underwater Paradise." Wax paper and puzzle glue sat beside it.

Hector shook his head.

Hector's old man was the hardest, meanest, most ruthless son-of-a-bitch he had ever known. His father had been a Vietnam vet, served under Hal Moore, and fought in Ia Drang Valley. To think in his wonder years reduced to working on puzzles.

A blue cushioned rocking chair sat idle across from the television in the living room. A Longaberger basket was on the floor beside it. A pair of silver crochet needles stood erect in a red yarn bundle. Knitted socks, a sweater, and a scarf were folded neatly on the side table. A Samsung remote sat atop them – everything Hector's mother needed.

Hector finished his egg and poured milk into a cup. He nuked the mug in the microwave for forty-five seconds. Sitting on his mother's chair, he sipped the drink while rocking back and forth.

Had it really been seventeen years since the last visit?

Hearing a series of loud caws, Hector looked out the window.

Murders of crows enveloped a tree.

Hector could see what was left of Drew through the chaotic fluttering of their black wings.

His legs and body were saran-wrapped around the trunk, and his arms spread out and secured across a pair of extended branches. His eyes had long since been removed – the crows were now pulling at things inside his neck.

Hector turned on the news and continued sipping his milk.

Just as the weatherman in his annoying blue tie made a ridiculous pun about the unrelenting snow throughout the week, Hector let his eyes rest and slipped into darkness.

❧

On a freezing October midnight, an MH-60 Black Hawk helicopter passed alongside the towering dark Hindu Kush Afghanistan mountains. Inside, a tall twenty-eight-year-old with a square jaw and beady eyes recited, "Been around the world twice.

Talked to everyone once. Seen two whales fuck, been to three world fairs…do I really got to say it all?"

"Say it, Hamel!" Murphy egged him on while smearing the last of his MRE cheese on a cracker. Bringing it to his mouth, he got a bit on his thick red mustache.

"Recite the ballad of the Frogman!" Patel sang in his best Shakespearean voice. For a dramatic flair, he vigorously grasped a handful of air.

"That is the worst impression I've ever heard," Murphy told him.

"Sue me, you peesa Irish shit. I'm from fuckin' Jersey," Patel said, flicking him off.

"Keep going," Hector said to Hamel.

"And I met an old man in Thailand with a wooden cock. I've pushed more peeter, more sweeter, and more completer than any other peter-pusher around," Hamel continued.

"Louder!" Murphy yelled over the whir of the chopper blades. "Say it like a man!"

Hamel laughed, "I'm a hard-bodied, hairy-chested, rootin'-tootin' shooting, parachuting demolition double cap crimping Frogman. There ain't nothin' I can't do. No sky too high, no sea too rough, no muff too tough. Learned a lot of lessons in my life."

"Boots on the ground in sixty seconds!" the pilot yelled.

Hamel clammed up at these words.

"Corpsman, don't be nervous," Hector told him. "You've had the best training in the world. You're ready for this."

"I know, Gunny. But it's my first mission. What if I fuck up?"

"Finish it!" Murphy and Patel hollered in unison.

"Fine," Hamel continued. "Okay, never shoot a large caliber man with a small caliber bullet. Drove all kinds of trucks. Two-by's, four-by's, six-by's, and those big mother fuckers that bend and go 'Shhh Shhh' when you step on the brakes."

"We got company." Patel hollered as he looked out the open side. Putting binoculars to his face, he said, "Looks like two, no, make that three unknown vics, rolling up over the hillside."

"Let me see," Murphy said, stealing the binoculars.

Patel pointed at the vehicles, "I swear on my sweet mother's grave if these grimy cocksuckers start any shit with us –"

"Pilot, we got company!" Hector yelled.

"Oh shit, one of them's packing," Murphy said.

"Gimme those," Patel said, stealing the binoculars back.

"What's he packing?" Hamel asked.

"Keep going," Hector told him.

"Anything in life worth doing is worth overdoing. Moderation is for cowards. I'm a lover, I'm a fighter, I'm a UDT Navy SEAL Diver. I'll wine, dine, intertwine and then sneak out the back door when the refueling is done. If you're feeling froggy, then you better jump, because this Frogman has been there, done that, and is going back for more. Cheers, boys."

"Contact left!" Patel yelled.

The buzz of the doorbell awoke Hector.

He looked at the television, and the "Price is Right" was on. Drew Carrey explained the rules of a game involving a giant Tic-Tac-Toe board to a sizable woman wearing a loud yellow shirt that read I LOVE DREW.

The doorbell buzzed again.

Looking past the kitchen, Hector saw a man in a black polo and matching hat looking through the window next to the door.

The man eyed Hector and held up a medium box. "Hello there. I have a package for you."

"Right," Hector said, sitting up from the recliner. After taking a few steps, he stopped.

The deck's floorboards behind the house creaked.

He turned to the window again. The man was still looking through the glass, grinning ear-to-ear. Hector stared at him for several seconds, and the longer he did, the more the grin widened.

Hector slowly opened the kitchen door.

The man was clean-cut, thin-faced, and slender. He wore a lanyard over the collar of an orange polo with a placard that listed the company as 'Global Delivery Service.' A dented white van was parked in the drive. The two cloth front seats were empty.

"Mr. Guvera, please sign," the man said as he pushed a clipboard with a pen tied to it at Hector.

Hector looked over the acceptance form and paused, applying the pen to the board. "What time is it?" Hector read the nametag of the deliverer, "Jeremiah?"

"Excuse me?"

"What time is it?"

"Uh," the man shrugged, "I'm not sure, around four, I guess."

"That's interesting," Hector said, scribbling on the form.

"What's that, sir?"

"I've never met a deliverer who didn't know the time." Extending the clipboard to Jeremiah, the worker grabbed it, but Hector didn't release it. He focused on the 'Molon Labe' tattoo running down the man's forearm.

Perspiration ran down Jeremiah's forehead. Hector traced the bead of sweat as it traveled down the man's face and onto the small earpiece inside the man's right ear.

Hector withdrew his Sig Sauer from his waistband and planted two in Jeremiah's chest and one in his head.

Hector emptied another three into the back door and heard a thud as a body hit the deck behind the house.

Making his way to the back door, Hector inspected the bullet-riddled corpse. The body was hefty and dressed like Jeremiah. A Glock 19 was gripped in his hand.

Hector pocketed the gun and, hugging the exterior, performed a perimeter check.

Hector didn't spot anyone else, only the *seemingly* empty van parked idle in the drive.

At the front doorstep, Hector crouched, inspecting the medium, brown, bulky package that fell at Jeremiah's body. Too much tape was adhered to the box, and oily stains were soaked through the wrapper.

Hector picked up the package and lobbed it onto the van's hood.

Leveling his gun, Hector shot the package.

The box exploded, turning the van into fiery wreckage suspended on melting wheels.

The van's back doors burst as smoke billowed from the open windows.

Something that resembled a human ran out – engulfed in flames and screaming.

Hector watched *it* run frantically for several seconds. When it came within ten feet, he emptied his clip into it.

As the corpse smoldered in the snowy front yard, Hector returned to the kitchen, where he noticed blood splattered on his flannel shirt. He tossed the shirt in the trash. Finding tongs inside a drawer, Hector returned to Jeremiah's body and knelt beside it.

Hector dug through the man's pockets using the tongs to bypass the blood that had trickled from the man's chest and head. One front pocket held a loaded Glock. The other was empty. He rolled the body on its side with his foot and, inspecting the back pocket, pulled out a leather wallet.

Flipping open the wallet, he inspected the ID card within. The Nevada driver's license read Andrew Daniel Reeves.

Hector found Andrew's phone in the side pocket and used the dead man's index finger to unlock the device. Using the phone, he looked up Andrew's name on the web, which came up with an obituary from a year ago. Army veteran killed in a training exercise. The picture from the obituary matched the fresh corpse in front of him.

Looking at the bodies, Hector suspected the others would have similar obituaries.

Quickly looking through the phone, Hector saw nothing of value. Pulling out the SIM card, he snapped the chip.

⁂

Hector handed over a check and deposit form to the large teller with curly black hair and wearing too much perfume at the Wells Fargo bank. "I'll need $10 thousand from this and deposit the rest."

She looked over the check. "That's quite a bit. Let me call over my manager."

As Hector waited, a low buzzing caught his attention. Between two red couches, a long table with a massive fish tank was off to the side. The tank was populated with pebbles and decor with a sunken pirate ship theme. An assortment of blue and yellow fish swam around. There was a Keurig coffee station, a cylinder of sugar, and a half carton of milk to the side of the tank.

Grabbing a foam cup from the silver dispenser attached to the wall, Hector poured himself a cup of milk.

Catching the eyes of the young financial advisor sitting behind a cluttered desk, Hector nodded to him. As the man returned the nod and focused on his computer monitor, Hector wondered how people got so far in life wearing a suit and tie. At the young man's age, Hector was shipping off to Iraq. Hector wondered how fast the kid would fall if subjected to the glass jaw experiment.

An older woman with curly white hair and a blue crochet sweater stepped to the counter and waved him over. "Sir, can I see your ID, please?"

Hector met her at the counter, "My ID?"

"Yessir, it's bank policy."

"Of course," reaching into his suede jacket, Hector pulled out his wallet and handed over his military retiree card.

"Thank you," she read it, "Mr. Hector Guvera." She handed it back and smiled, "I thought so. You're taller than the last time I saw you."

"Taller?"

"Yes, you don't remember me, do you?" Her eyes remained glued to her computer as she typed.

Hector studied her, "Should I?"

"When you were twelve, I opened up your savings account." She laughed, "I remember how proud you were with your twenty-one dollars and twenty-five cents. Oh, yes, I remember. Your mother told me how hard you had worked to earn that. She said the Bennett's had worked the tar out of you."

"Twenty-one dollars and twenty-five cents?"

"Yessir, I remember." She finished typing and met his gaze, "I was so happy when someone told me you had left this place."

Hector sipped his milk. "Happy. Why?"

"A hard-working young man like you – I knew you would go places if you left. Not many people here leave. They say they'll leave, yet year after year, I see them. Like the Swanson brothers, they grow older and crankier, always talking about their goals. But not you. You left."

Hector recalled her name. "Mrs. Hartigan, right?"

"Please, call me Nancy."

"Nancy."

"But now you're back?"

"Just to take care of things."

Nancy stared at the check he had given her. "So, you sold the ranch?"

"Yes, ma'am."

"To the Bennett's of all people, how ironic. Well, your parents would have wanted you to sell." She counted out the $10 thousand, all in $100 bills. Placing the bills in a manilla envelope, she reached over the counter, handed it to him, and grabbed his hands.

Hector froze – physical contact was foreign to him.

She smiled sympathetically. "I'm really sorry about your folks. Getting in a car wreck is no way to die."

He stared down at her veiny, weathered hands. Freeing one of his own, he put it reassuringly atop hers. "My father always told me that life and death are God's will. We can't change what we can't change."

"I know, but they were good people, terrific people." She brushed his right hand with her thumb before letting go. "Just like you."

Hector shook his head. "I'm not one of your good people."

"Excuse me?"

Hector didn't answer. He placed the envelope in his jacket and walked out.

❧

"Hector, so good to see you. Come in, please," Mrs. Chambers said, opening the screen door for him. With her wavy Farrah Fawcett auburn hair and high cheekbones, she had once been the MILF every high school guy had talked about. Now, though, age and chocolate had gotten the better of her.

"There's no need for that," Hector told her. "I'm just here to say goodbye to Rebecca."

"Nonsense, come in."

Hector nodded and, taking off his cowboy hat, entered the kitchen. There was a strong smell of peppermint. She used the same hand lotion his mother had.

"It was a beautiful service," Mrs. Chambers said. "I think your speech was perfect. Your old man would have gotten a good laugh, and your mother, well, she was just a beautiful human being. She knew how much you loved her."

Hector nodded.

Standing at the base of the stairs, Mrs. Chambers yelled, "Rebecca, there's a handsome man here to see you." She turned to him, "I never lie."

"Mom!" Rebecca yelled at the top of the stairs.

"What? I was young once." At Rebecca's gesturing, Mrs. Chambers walked off.

Rebecca came down the stairs and met him in the kitchen. "I'm sorry about that."

Reaching in his jacket, Hector handed over the envelope. "Here."

"What's this?" She looked inside, "Oh my, God."

"I heard about what happened to your bar last night. And that college of yours isn't going to pay itself."

"I can't accept this."

"Yes, you can. Life isn't always fair."

"But Hector, this is so much money. What about you? I can't —"

"I sold the ranch." He pointed to the envelope. "You can thank the Bennetts for that."

"But, the ranch? That's been in your family since your great-grandfather."

"It's just property and land. Ranching has never been in my blood. I couldn't wait to get out of here when I was a kid."

"And now that you're back, you can't wait to get out of here?" Rebecca placed the envelope on the table. "Why do you hate this place so much?"

"I don't hate it. It's just never felt like home."

"But, if you stayed this time, you could make it home."

"This was a peaceful dream for my parents, but I'm not them. I've been all around the world. I've lived in so many places, and even now, I don't have a home."

"But, you could make this your home. People here care about you."

Hector shook his head.

"I'm sorry you feel that way."

He reached for the door, "I belong to the wild."

Opening the door, she rushed to him and hugged him. They held onto one another for a time before she leaned up and kissed his lips.

Hector looked into her eyes, and there was a moment of weakness – but only a moment. Walking away, Hector put on his cowboy hat, started his Bronco, and turned around in the dirt lot. He drove off the property and, making it to a stop sign, looked out at the country.

Hector's phone rang. Few people had his number. The Caller ID said 'CSPD.'

He put the phone on speaker, "Yes?"

"Hello, is this Mr. Guvera?" A gruff-sounding man on the other end asked.

"Go on," Hector said.

"This is Detective Amberson with the Colorado Springs Metro Police Department. I'm sorry to inform you that your brother, Joshua, is in critical condition. We ran his file, and you are his only surviving relative."

"What happened?"

"Sorry, Sir, I can't discuss the specifics. Your brother is involved in an active case."

Hector sipped his travel mug and spotted a skinny grey coyote running across the road. It stopped before fully crossing and looked back at him. Hector could see its sharp golden-brown eyes staring him down even from this distance. Its survival instincts were apparent, clear as day.

The coyote crossed the road and vanished on the other side of the hill.

"Sir? Mr. Guvera, are you still there?" Amberson asked.

"What hospital is he in?"

"Let me check," Amberson paused before continuing, "St. Barbara Hospital."

"In Colorado Springs?" Hector asked.

"Yessir."

"Is Josh going to die?"

"Uh, Mr. Guvera, I'm not a doctor, but it doesn't look good. Unfortunately, that's all I can say. I assume you'll be coming?"

Hector's eyes drifted down each road. One road led South, which would bring him to the El Paso International Airport, and from there, he could catch a connecting flight to Maine and then to Europe. The other road, parallel, would eventually merge onto I-25 Northbound to Las Cruces, New Mexico. The Highway would subsequently lead to Colorado.

"Okay," Hector said, hanging up the phone. He cut the wheel and headed Northbound – into the wild.

8

Porter paid five dollars for his ticket, declined concessions, and entered the Raptors High School football stadium gate. Walking up the home-side bleachers, he found an open seat and got as comfortable as possible on the icy steel bench.

His boots were sticky on the concrete walkway. He looked down at the spilled coke and flattened popcorn. The smell of dried syrup and candy was repulsive.

A decent number of people were sitting in the bleachers, more so on *this* side than the visitors. He recognized a few kids he knew through Mindy.

A stout woman sat next to her rowdy kids and pasty husband a few rows down. She had shoulder-length auburn hair and puffy cheeks. Porter remembered Heather Johnson when she was a cheerleader in High School and a NJROTC cadet for one year. She had been runner-up for NJROTC Queen his Senior year. She was eighty pounds lighter and sexy as hell then. Her nickname had been "Deep Throat Heather."

On the sidelines facing them stood the Raptor cheerleaders. Holding red pompoms in their gloved hands, they made a series of chants and kicks. They wore long-sleeved red and black shirts and skirts. 'Raptors' was embroidered in white letters across their chests. Dinosaur stickers adhered to their cheeks.

Porter checked his watch and saw that he still had time before kickoff.

Pulling out his phone, he opened a recent text from Mindy. The attached link brought him to the website for 'American Iron.' The red, white, and blue banner said, 'Smart home security for smart Americans.' A blinking text box read '24x7 home security' and listed the technology and monitoring offered. Scrolling, he read positive reviews, most written by veterans and gun-toting Republicans. There was a number listed to call for pricing.

The stadium erupted as the JV football team hit the field.

Suited in thick shoulder pads and red and black jerseys, the three dozen kids waved arms, screamed, and jumped around like energized idiots.

Damn, to be young again.

Wearing green and silver, the opposing team hit the field with mild applause.

Sitting in a high box on the opposite side of the field, a thin-necked goatee man wearing a faded tie-dye shirt spoke into a microphone. "Ladies and gentlemen, please stand for the arrival of the colors and the playing of the National anthem."

Porter stood, as did everyone in the bleachers.

The four-person NJROTC Color Guard marched diagonally across the field from the rear pylon.

The right-side rifleman was Mindy. She wore a white cover, matching gloves, and a crisp black uniform. A blue aiguillette wrapped around her left shoulder. On her chest were two rows of ribbons. Her eyes looked straight ahead as she marched in step with the rest of the detail.

The National flag bearer commanded the detail to "Halt" and "Present Arms."

Mindy and the opposite rifleman lowered their Springfield rifles to a vertical presentation in military sequence.

The state colors dipped.

From the Visitor's bleachers walked a woman carrying a glossy blue and white lightning-streaked electric guitar. The petite woman wore a faded black denim jacket full of patches, a white tank underneath, and baggy black cargo pants. Her long black hair blew in the frosty wind, and her orange sports glasses reflected the dying afternoon light.

At midfield, the guitarist stood against the loud electric humming of the 60 Hz AC power system picked up by the amplifier.

She struck the first note.

With his hand over his heart, Porter couldn't help but stare at her. She was beautiful.

The guitarist had sexy, sharp, angular features. With how she carried herself, Porter gauged she landed somewhere between her early and mid-thirties.

And she wasn't wearing a wedding ring.

The guitarist injected some creative liberty into the 'Star-Spangled Banner,' but it was better for it.

Halfway through, his eyes wandered to the trio of football players kneeling. He noticed another player on the opposite side of the field standing with his fist raised defiantly.

The protests left a bad taste in his mouth.

Every American, from football players to Olympians to everyday citizens, had the right to protest during the National Anthem. Still, it didn't mean Porter had to like it.

As the Anthem neared its conclusion, the woman in denim began shredding on her guitar. The crowd hollered encouragement, beat their fists, and clapped as the last notes played out.

Mindy and the opposite rifleman shouldered their weapons at the Anthem's conclusion. The state colors raised. The color guard performed a countermarch, and they stepped off the field.

"Special thanks to the Raptor's very own NJROTC color guard, and let's hear it for Ms. Valentine!" the announcer said.

Valentine raised her pick to the roaring crowd like something from a movie.

Sitting, Porter watched Valentine walk to the opposite bleachers. She sat next to a black guitar case and stowed her instrument.

As the teams lined the field for kickoff, Porter's pocket buzzed. Digging his phone out, he saw a text from the Love Doc.

"Done. Text me."

A screaming kid from the row above spilled popcorn on him.

Porter turned to the kid and was met with a look resembling the fear of God.

"Sorry, man," the kid squeaked.

Porter wiped off his jacket and went down the bleachers to the parking lot, where it was quieter. He lowered his tailgate at his truck, sat, and lit a cigarette. Pulling out his phone, he called the Love Doc.

Porter looked at his surroundings as the phone rang on the other end. A few car lengths down, a trio of kids in letterman jackets were sitting on the hoods of their vehicles. Their music was cranked loudly, and they were vaping and passing around a flask. One of them caught sight of Porter, concealed the flask in his jacket, and laughed.

Taking a deep drag, Porter blew out a string of smoke.

"Yeah," Doc said, picking up.

"It's Porter."

"Yeah, I know it's you, Porter. It's called caller ID. I told you to text me, man. This isn't the '90s. No one calls anymore."

"Uh, huh," Porter said, taking another nicotine hit. "Whaddya got?"

"Okay, I got into that phone you gave me. Porter, I gotta tell you, man, you're dealing with some serious shit. Where'd you get this?"

"You took a peek, huh?"

"No shit, I took a peek. It's like a porn site. Even if you stumble onto it accidentally, you gotta look."

"You telling me you *accidentally* look at porn sites?"

"Okay, you got me."

"So, Doc, what's on the phone?"

"Nope, we had a deal. I get some alone time with Jessica. You promised me, man."

"I never said you get alone time. I don't run a brothel."

"Fine, semi-discreet time, better?"

Porter sighed, "Be there at eight."

"Alright, so she's working tonight?"

"Just be there at eight."

"That's my future wife, ya know?"

Porter hung up.

Taking a final drag, Porter flicked his cigarette into the blacktop and returned to the stadium. He walked past the bleachers and behind the football field and surrounding track. Just outside the opposite bleachers, Porter saw the NJROTC detail as they packed their rifles and rolled up their flags. They were deep into a conversation about gun control while stuffing everything into the back of a late-model hail-dented Subaru.

Porter didn't see Mindy and figured she was in the bathroom underneath the bleachers that led to the visiting teams' locker room.

Standing at the base of the bleachers, he looked up to where he had last seen Valentine.

She wasn't there.

❧

With her garment bag slung behind her back, Mindy maneuvered her skateboard around the pair of second-string cheerleaders gossiping on the track. Rolling out of the stadium and performing an Ollie on the flattop, she landed and, kicking off neared Porter's truck. She swerved around a cluster of cars where three boys in varsity jackets sat atop their hoods.

She didn't know the boys personally but had seen them at school. Bobby, Dolph, and Kevin were all members of the wrestling team. Their rock music was cranked so loud, their voices so obnoxious, it overtook 'The Bitter Truth" Evanescence album Mindy was listening to.

"Hey, ROTC girl!" Dolph yelled.

"Come back, skater girl!" Bobby added.

"How much do you charge?" Kevin yelled.

Mindy couldn't ignore them any longer. Turning, she put her foot on the flattop and, stomping on the tail of her board, caught it. Taking out her earbuds and dropping her bag, she approached them. "You got something to say?"

The three boys looked shocked that she had acknowledged them.

Bobby tapped the shoulder of Kevin and laughed. "Oh, snap."

"What?" Mindy asked.

"Don't be like that, girl," Kevin said. "We just want to know how much you charge?"

"Yeah," Bobby added, thumbing to himself and the other two, "can you hook us up with a group rate discount?"

The three of them laughed as Mindy flushed hot. "You guys think you're pretty funny, huh?"

The three continued to laugh.

"Have fun mounting dudes tonight, butt fuckers." She turned before they could respond and, picking up her bag, stepped on her board again.

Kevin grabbed her arm. "I heard you like older men. I'm a Junior, so..." Kevin rubbed her arm, and his voice softened, "Whadda ya say, Freshman?" He took a twenty-dollar bill from his wallet. "How much does this get me?"

He motioned to his new Ford Fusion. "C'mon, skater girl. You say I'm a butt fucker? Want to find out if you're right?"

Enough of this bullshit!

Mindy dropped her bag and put her dukes up. She twisted her ankle and sent a rabbit jab into Kevin's throat using the whole momentum of her body. As he stumbled back, Mindy sent a front kick to his groin – dropping him.

"Bitch," Bobby said, jumping off his car and taking a swing.

Ducking, Mindy picked up her board and, with an uppercut, cracked its' nose into his.

The boy fell back, blood spewing from his face.

She turned to Dolph. Holding her board like a baseball bat, he shook his head and snaked into his car.

Mindy watched as he drove off, then looked down at the two boys writhing in pain and crying.

She plucked the crumpled twenty-dollar bill from the pavement and waved it in front of Kevin. "This gets you an ass-whooping."

"Mindy," Porter called behind her.

She turned and, breathing hard, nodded. "Sup, Boss?"

Porter looked at the boys, then back at her, "You good?"

"Never better," she said with a heavy breath, holding up the twenty-dollar bill. "Let's get some food. I'm buying." She tossed her garment bag into the bed of Porter's truck and hopped into the cab.

Walking up to the boys, Porter knelt, "Walk it off, drink some water. Trust me, it could have been worse."

Holding onto his bleeding nose, Bobby groaned, "How the hell do you figure?"

"She could have killed you."

They looked at him in disbelief.

Porter shrugged and walked to his truck.

9

Porter sat in his truck, listening to the radio, smoking a cigarette, and sipping his coffee. He watched Mindy through the glass door of the American Iron sales building across the street. She had been talking to the sales representative for almost half an hour.

Clicking away on his phone, Porter continued reading the Wikipedia article on Bobbi Johnson—high marks at CU Boulder, former Mayor of Denver and Governor of Colorado. Johnson won the Republican nomination to run on the ballot for the Colorado United States Senate vacant seat. She has close ties with high-ranking Republicans and is endorsed by the President as "The ideal Law and Order American."

Porter skimmed through the sections on her early life, education, career, political positions, and campaigns. Everything seemed pretty consistent with the gun-toting Republican image her ads made her out to be.

The last part of her write-up caught his interest.

Under the section on 'personal life,' a paragraph summarized that Bobbi invested heavily in a start-up oil and gas field company a few years back. The company went under, and it's rumored she lost up to $500 thousand. Johnson never confirmed the figure. Still, upon being questioned in an interview, she says she lost "A significant amount of money."

After "A Little Bit Off" by Five Finger Death Punch was played, the radio cut to a commercial.

A man with a soft voice spoke. "We all know how to share and compromise in the best interest of everyone. We know that sometimes everyone doesn't agree. That's okay, but what's not okay is Bobbi Johnson running for U.S. Senate."

Porter turned his attention to the radio.

"When Bobbi Johnson was Governor of Colorado, it was her way or the highway. During her term as Governor, she had the highest staff turnover of any sitting Governor in Colorado's history. Those fired from her office cited they felt intimidated and belittled. As reported in the Denver Times, the ethics commission concluded Johnson violated Colorado's workplace safety policies on four separate incidents.

The bottom line is that if she was a bully as a governor, how do you think she'd act in the U.S. Senate? It's a fact. No one likes a bully. Tim Styles, the current Governor of Colorado, has an impeccable ethics record. Vote for Tim Styles for U.S.

Senate, a family man and a trusted leader. He'll continue to stand for what's right."

A deep voice concluded the advertisement, "I'm Tim Styles, and I approve this message."

Porter sighed. Blowing out a plume of smoke, he looked at the surrounding buildings. He saw a towering Tim Styles billboard erected off the highway entry ramp.

Styles stood in front of a green field with a blue sky. He was grinning and fitted into a tailored blue suit with an American flag tie. He was a stocky man in his late fifties. He reminded Porter of an '80s cop from an Action movie with his shaggy blond hair and walrus mustache. Not a good Action movie, but one of those VHS tapes buried in the corner of the lowest shelf of a Blockbuster.

In bold letters, the billboard read, "Tim Styles for U.S. Senate, a COLORADO FAMILY MAN, and TRUSTED LEADER!"

Porter broke his gaze as Mindy crossed the street.

Hopping into the cab, Mindy put her bookbag at her feet and sighed, "Well, that's half an hour of my life that I'm never getting back."

"That good?"

"I swear, that creeper wanted to get in my pants."

"You told him it was a research paper for your High School, right?"

"Yeah. I told Predator 9000 I was writing a paper on successful local businesses in Colorado. He seemed not to listen much; instead, he kept offering me a cookie. Who does that? I swear he's going to be on a future episode of 'How to Catch a Predator.'"

"Or a future character in a Thomas Harris novel."

"Who?"

"Harris wrote The Silence of the Lambs. You know, Jame Gumb, it puts the lotion on the skin."

Mindy shrugged, rubbing her hands at the heater vents, "Never heard of it."

"Shocking." With a flick, Porter sent his spent cigarette out the window. "So, besides Predator 9000, whaddya think about the company?"

Mindy took her dented thermos from her bookbag and, unscrewing the cap, poured coffee into it. "I hate to say it, but they seem legit."

"Really?" Porter said, putting the truck in drive.

"Yeah, they hire employees who already have certifications to cut costs. Like, Security Plus for networks and…" she read her notebook, "CFOT for fiber optics technicians, ONSSI for surveillance cameras, Crestron for programming, Vindicator for entry badging, and a whole bunch of other stuff."

Porter turned onto the main road, "What about their security equipment?"

"They buy stuff in bulk from sites like Amazon and Home Depot to get cheaper rates," Mindy said. Sipping her coffee, Porter hit a pothole, and Hazelnut coffee splashed onto the bottom of her chin. "Dammit."

"You gonna be okay?" Porter joked.

"Screw you," Mindy said, wiping off her chin with the back of her hand.

"I prefer blondes."

Mindy rolled her eyes.

Stopping at a light, Porter caught sight of a blue and white van parked alongside a T-Mobile store. White lettering on the vehicle's side read, "American Iron Security Services."

Porter nodded to the van, and Mindy met his gaze.

Beside the entrance glass door atop a ladder was a man wearing a hard hat, blue polo, and neutral khakis. He was installing a round security camera. His co-worker, tapping away on a tablet, stood at the ladder's base.

"They certainly do look legit," Mindy said.

"What did he say about their security detail?"

"Let's see," Mindy read off her notebook, "they maintain multiple Quick Reaction Forces around the city to strategically and rapidly deploy…yada, yada, yada. Nothing about Frank Marion or outsourcing to gangs or biker clubs or anything."

"Guys full of shit."

"Most likely."

As the light transitioned to green, Porter accelerated and eyed a Starbucks. "You up for a coffee?"

Mindy tipped her thermos cap to him, "I'm good."

"Can I try some of that?"

"Okay," Mindy said hesitantly, handing the cap over.

Porter lowered his window and dumped the coffee out.

"What the hell? Not cool."

Porter returned the thermos cap, "You up for some coffee?"

"You're a dick."

"That's the rumor."

As they pulled into the Starbucks drive-thru lane, Mindy shook her head, "Don't tell me we're only here so you can hit on Alice? Ever since she got this second job, you've made it a point to get a coffee from her every day. I know you're worried about her kid, but you're already screwing her. Why don't you just leave her a tip next time."

"I never do just the tip. Go big or go home."

Mindy stared in confusion for a moment and then palmed her forehead.

Wearing a long white sleeve and a green apron, Alice leaned out the drive-thru window and grinned as they pulled up. "Hey, good looking."

"That's my line," Porter said.

"Hello dear," she said to Mindy.

"Eat shit," Mindy told her.

"The usual?" Alice asked.

"Sure," Mindy said.

"Porter?"

Porter leaned out his window with a twenty-dollar bill, "I want something hot and steamy with whipped cream."

"Cherry on top?" Alice said, licking her lips.

Mindy sunk in her seat and buried her head in her hands, "Kill me now."

❦

"Just don't throw any camera into the basket," Mindy said, removing the box from the Lowes shopping cart.

"You said a cheap camera, under fifteen dollars," Porter said, finishing his caramel macchiato.

"Newsflash, that's not a real camera," Mindy ran her finger across the text on the box, "interior/exterior simulated security camera, a.k.a., not real. It looks and moves like one, but it's not one. This won't do the Peterson's any good." She returned it to the shelf and replaced the basket with a Ring doorbell camera.

"Well, how was I supposed to know that?"

"Try reading."

"And people say I'm a dick," Porter said.

"I heard that."

"Good."

"I also said it had to be Wink compatible," Mindy said.

"What the hell is a Wink?"

"We've been over this. It's the name of the Hub we're going with. All the security products have to be Z-Wave and Wink Compatible to integrate."

Porter buzzed a hand over his head.

Mindy plucked items off the shelf left and right, continuing down the aisle. The cart was filled with security signs, external cameras, a siren and strobe, glass breaker sensors, door and window sensors, smart lights, motion lights, and a hub.

"This isn't going to be cheap," Mindy said, leading the way to the door keypads. Spying out a Z-Wave Schlage lock, Mindy threw a pair of them into the cart.

Porter's eyes went wide as he read the price tag. "No shit, that's why you're paying for dinner, remember?"

❧

Porter and Mindy sat atop the truck toolbox mounted on Porter's bed, eating hot dogs and staring out across the Lowe's parking lot.

The air was crisp. Ice clung to the thin tree branches barely visible within the Lawn and Garden department. The few sprinkled flakes glinted in the faint moonlight that had just begun to rise over the horizon. Traffic on the main street behind the Lowes died down, and besides the distant chug of a train, the evening was quieter than most.

Porter and Mindy could quickly tell the serious contractors from the everyday mom and dad looking for a fun winter project. The serious contractors who pulled up in their beat-up trucks were bundled adequately in paint-splattered and heavily worn attire and took their time entering the store. The everyday person wearing their tee shirts and jeans pulled up in their Dodge minivans and Honda Civics and ran into the store to avoid the cold.

"I used to do this with my dad," Porter said.

Mindy turned to him, "Yeah?"

"When I was a kid, we didn't go to the mall or movies on the weekends. We'd go to the hardware store. Well, more like he'd go to the hardware store for what seemed like hours and drag us along."

"Fun childhood."

"Yeah, we'd play with the display tools when Dad wasn't looking. The only thing to look forward to was the hot dogs afterward."

"These are good," Mindy said, chewing on her own.

"Well, it certainly gets the taste of sawdust out of your mouth."

Taking another bite, Mindy put a hand over her mouth, "You don't talk much about your family."

"Not much to talk about," Porter said, finishing his hot dog and chugging his can of coke.

"What do you mean?"

"I don't know, I guess it's just..." Porter struggled to describe the situation, "I haven't really talked to them in a while."

"You mean your parents?"

"Well, my mom, brother, sister," he clarified, "it's been a while."

"What about your dad? You didn't mention your dad."

"He died when I was about your age. He was in the Army and went to Iraq. He never came back."

Mindy stared at him hard, "You never told me that."

Silence ensued for several moments.

Eventually, Porter shrugged, "It's not something I like to talk about."

"Sorry, I didn't know." Mindy changed topics, "Your mom, what does she do?"

"Teacher, North Carolina. And before you ask, my sister's in the Air Force, and my brother's working in Europe doing some business thing."

"Wait, your sister's in the Air Force?"

"Yep, Olive, well Olivia, is a Colonel. In a few years, she'll be eligible for retirement."

"What's her job?"

"Fighter pilot."

"Sweet, like Captain Marvel?"

"Tell me you didn't just make that comparison?"

"You guys close?"

"Not really. Olive enlisted when Chris and I were in Junior High. Needless to say, she is a mean, cold-hearted bitch and would find any reason she could to kick our asses," Porter said with a smirk.

Mindy chuckled, "A girl kicking your ass? I don't believe it."

"Well, believe it."

They both laughed.

"Can I ask you a question?" Porter asked.

"Sure," Mindy was curious about what he would ask. Porter usually didn't ask her many questions. On the one hand, she liked that he didn't get into her personal business. On the other hand, sometimes she wished he would.

"What was going on at the football game?"

"You talking about those assholes I beat up?"

"Yeah."

"It was, uh, nothing. Just stupid stuff," Mindy finished off her hot dog.

"What type of stupid stuff?"

"I don't know. Those guys –"

"What?"

Mindy looked at her phone, "It's getting late. Shouldn't we get going? I thought you said you wanted me to install all this stuff tonight."

"Mindy," Porter said sternly.

Mindy huffed, "Fine, they were calling me a slut and trying to get me to have sex with them. Happy?"

After finishing his drink, Porter nodded and scanned the parking lot. "Why would they think you're a slut?"

"Well, people know about my sister working at the club a few summers back, and word got out that I worked at the club this summer, and well –"

"You took food and drink orders, that's all."

"They don't know that, and well –"

"Well, what?"

"There's you."

"What about me?" He said, forcing eye contact.

"It's stupid, don't worry about it."

"The longer you keep shit bottled inside, the worse it will get. You might want to take my advice. I got the high score on this one."

Mindy shrugged, "People see me with you, and they think we're having sex."

"Why would people think that?"

"They don't see my mom or sister anymore. They only see you, giving me rides and stuff. They think I left my family to live with you, and we sleep together. It's the talk of my school."

Porter stifled a laugh, "Jesus, as your legal guardian, I'm pretty sure that's not allowed. It's gotta be in the fine print somewhere."

"Yeah, but –"

"They're fucking idiots."

"That's not much comfort."

"I know," Porter said. "Alright, keep this story to yourself."

"What?"

"Back in the day, Sarah and I hooked up."

"You mean like slept together?"

"Slept together?" he repeated. "Have I ever told you how cute I find that 7th-grade vocabulary of yours?"

"Fuck off, Porter."

"I'd recommend you fuck on. You get better results."

"Fine, you two *fucked*. Is that better?"

"It's such a privilege to see your mind at work."

"Shut up. What happened?"

"Well, word got out. I'm not sure how, Sarah's not sure how, but somehow it leaked. For a good year, while I was getting high-fives and guys were buying me drinks, everyone called her a slut and a whore behind her back. It made me sick because she didn't deserve that, and neither do you."

"Yeah?"

"Yeah, and you know what? After a while, no one gave a shit. Believe it or not, all of High School will be a fleeting memory one day. Don't get so choked up over what people call you. It's just not worth your time. Plus, unlike those fuckers, you're alright."

"Uh, thanks?"

"I'm telling you, four years from now, none of this shit will matter, okay? So, there you go, there's my pep talk," he said, crumpling his coke can and chucking it into the truck bed.

"You love her, don't you?"

"Who?"

"You know who, Sarah."

Porter shrugged, "Hell, I don't know."

"What do you mean you don't know? You obviously do."

"It's not that simple."

"Sure it is, do you, or don't you?"

"Here's the thing. After Maggie left, I realized I didn't know the first thing about love. The whole idea is a foreign concept."

"Did you and Maggie ever get a divorce?"

"Jesus, you're nosey."

"Sorry, you don't have to answer —"

"Good," Porter jumped over the edge of his truck and made his way to the driver's seat. As he turned over the engine, Mindy joined him on the passenger side.

"Porter," Mindy said, "you don't get to ask me serious questions if you won't answer mine."

Putting the truck in drive, Porter put a cigarette to his lips, "Technically, no. One morning, I woke up, and she had left her ring and a note on the table. I haven't seen her since."

"You never tried looking for her?"

"What's the point? She wanted out of my life, and she's out." Porter pulled out of the lot, and they made their way to the Peterson house.

10

As Mindy climbed the ladder to install the glass breaker alarm to the ceiling in the Peterson's living room, Roger Peterson held the ladder. He eyed the holster attached to her belt and, in his best, manly voice, asked, "Is that a real gun?"

"Yep," Mindy told him. She held out a hand, "Drill."

Roger handed up the cordless drill. His eyes drifted from the holster to the silver and black belt overpopulated with double grommets. His eyes then wandered to her rear, fitted in tight denim.

Nick Peterson stood on the other side of the ladder and asked, "What type of gun is that?"

"Beretta 92 FS," Mindy said, securing the final screw.

"Have you killed anyone?"

"Boys!" Audrey said from the kitchen table where she, Mike, and Porter were drinking coffee. "Nicholas, Roger, stop pestering her. The girl's workin', something you two knuckleheads don't know nothin' about!"

"How old are your kids?" Porter asked.

Nick wore a Dallas Cowboys tee. Roger sported a University of Texas-El Paso basketball jersey. Both boys had matching flattops and their father's chiseled faces.

"Roger is sixteen, Nick is twelve," Mike said with a yawn. "They're good boys."

"They're lazy, Boo," Audrey said, "don't deny it."

Mike shrugged and, with groggy eyes, downed more coffee.

"How's the new job treating you?" Porter asked.

"Busy," Mike said, "I was up in the bellows all day pulling out copper wiring and replacing it with fiber. It's a confined space, so it's really cramped."

"That sucks."

"You're telling me, but the pay's not bad." He poured himself another cup and stared at the patches adorning Porter's jacket that hung on the back of the chair. "So, how long were you in the Marines?"

"Six years."

"Only six?"

Porter knocked on his right prosthetic knee, which *clinked*, "Didn't have many choices."

"Sorry," Audrey said.

Porter shrugged, "Shit happens."

"I see some Iraq and Afghanistan patches," Mike said. "I did four tours in Iraq with the Army. It takes a toll, doesn't it?"

"Yeah, it does."

Mindy finished mounting the glass breaker to the ceiling. She handed the drill to Nick and thumbed away on her phone, integrating the glass breaker with the hub.

Stepping down the ladder, she unpackaged a door sensor and inserted the lithium-ion battery.

Roger repositioned the ladder for her and grinned.

Mindy returned the grin and asked, "Level?"

"Uh, yeah," Roger said. "Of course, I'm on the level. For sho'."

Mindy laughed, "Good to know, but I really need the level."

Roger flushed red as Nick laughed. Roger shot him an evil glare and hissed, "Shut up."

Nick searched through the brown toolbag and handed over the level.

"Thanks," Mindy said. She positioned and marked the top of the front door and the frame above it using a Sharpie.

Roger pulled out his phone as she began securing each sensor's backplates to their markings. "Hey, uh, Mindy, you on Insta or TikTok?"

"Both," she casually said. "Why?"

"Oh Lord, if that ain't obvious enough," Audrey whispered from the table, "that boy is embarrassing himself."

"I heard that," Roger said. "I just think she has some serious drip."

"Drip?" Nick said. "Oh, man, you're so lame."

"Shut up," Roger hissed again.

"Next, you gonna ask her to do a drip check."

"I said, shut up."

Mike, Audry, and Porter looked at each other and shrugged in visible confusion.

"So, Detective Porter –" Mike began to say.

"Call me Porter," he said.

"Porter, is installing our own security system really cheaper? Wouldn't it be better to just hire a different company?"

"They all a bunch of scam artists," Audrey said.

"I'll let Mindy explain this," Porter said. "She knows the business a lot better than I do."

Mindy continued working as she said, "Okay, say you hire a security company." She paused and wiped the sweat off her brow, "Sure, they would probably provide and install the basic equipment for free. That's always one of the perks."

"Right…" Mike hesitantly said.

"But here's where they screw you."

"From the beginning," Audrey said.

"Let the girl finish," Mike told her.

"Most companies lock you into a $40 dollar a month, five-year monitoring plan that's nearly impossible to cancel without a huge cancellation fee. You're paying nearly $2,500 over the life of the plan."

Mindy opened and closed the front door, ensuring the sensors were communicating. Satisfied, she thumbed away on her phone, integrating the sensor into the hub. "But, American Iron charges $60 a month. Now we're talking $3,500."

Mindy began unpackaging a Schlage keypad and stripping unneeded parts from the box.

"$3,500? That could buy me a new washer and dryer," Audrey said.

"I could buy a car with that," Roger added.

"Yeah, a cheap one," Nick said.

"You're getting on my nerves," Roger told him.

"Beer money," Mike muttered.

Mindy directed Roger and Nick to remove the old deadbolt and doorknob from the front door.

"Just removes those screws," she said, pointing to them.

"It's a business," Mike continued, "no different than paying for internet or Cable? Is that so bad?"

"Not if the service justifies the cost," Mindy said. "Anyone who uses local boys to enforce their security, not the cops, spells shady-as-hell to me. And if that's shady, I can only imagine their call centers are operated by local bubbas trying to make a quick buck. No one really qualified."

Porter added, "Plus if those guys are breaking into businesses and residents who don't buy into their services, they're freakin' assholes on a whole different level."

"Good point," Mike conceded.

"Amen," Audrey added.

"You have any drill bits?" Mindy asked the boys, taking a breather and drinking her coffee on the living room table.

"Yeah, hold on," Roger said, running off.

"No, I'll get it," Nick said, chasing after him.

Mindy set down her coffee and returned to the door, inspecting her work.

"How old is Mindy?" Mike whispered to Porter.

"Sixteen," Porter told him.

"Look who decided to play matchmaker?" Audrey said. She walked around the living room, inspecting Mindy's work. "Dang girl, you've done this sort of thing before?"

"Once or twice," she said.

Porter motioned his cup towards her, "Mindy has forgotten more about security systems than I'll ever know. She's good. I'll give her that."

"Hmm, almost sounded like a compliment there, Boss," she said.

"Almost."

The boys returned, each carrying a drill bit case.

"Mindy, you about done?" Porter asked.

"Just need to install the doorbell camera and the siren."

"You and your partner sure have an interesting relationship," Mike told Porter.

"You have no idea," Mindy said as Porter nodded.

"So, does it work?" Mike said as everyone stood in the living room, looking at the finished work.

"Let's see," Mindy opened the door and closed it.

Nothing happened.

"Okay…" Audrey said.

"Roger, open the app and alarm the house," Mindy told him.

Roger thumbed away on his phone, "Okay, go ahead."

Mindy opened the door once again. The white and red siren on the living room back wall screeched a high-pitched whine as the strobe light within pulsated.

Everyone put their fingers in their ears, and Mindy made a cutting motion across her neck.

Roger de-alarmed the house with the app, "Wow, that's loud."

"What'd you say?" Nick asked, laughing.

Mike gave a thumbs up.

"Girl, you know your stuff," Audrey told Mindy.

"Well, that's not all. Check your phones," Mindy told them.

The Petersons pulled out their phones.

"All your phones are linked to the app," Mindy said, "so whenever one of your home security devices goes off, everyone will get a notification. You can also view outside your house with the doorbell cam and talk to people through the microphone. Plus, you can program the app so that when an alarm goes off, the police are notified, whether you're home or not."

"This is great," Mike said.

"I ain't good with these app things," Audrey said, thumbing her phone.

"We'll teach you, Mom," Roger said.

"Yeah," Nick said, "Mindy taught us. It's easy. We can even lock and unlock the doors from our phones. How cool is that?"

Mike extended a hand to Porter, and they shook, "I don't know what to say. You guys went above and beyond."

Audrey nodded and hugged Mindy, "Good job, girl."

"Glad we could help," Porter said.

"Here's the million-dollar question," Mike said, looking at the various devices Mindy installed, "how much do we owe you guys for –"

"Bobbi already paid us for the job," Porter told him, "consider this included."

"Bless your souls," Audrey said, wrapping her arms around Porter. "You two have restored our faith in people."

"Sure," Porter said, gingerly patting her on the back.

Mindy held back a laugh.

Walking to Porter's truck parked on their curb, Porter bit down a cigarette. Lighting up, he saw that Mindy was staring off at something. "What's up?"

"What does that look like to you?"

Porter looked to where she did.

Porter could make out a silhouette of a man standing in the second-story window a few houses down. He was holding something to his face, something elongated and pointed at them.

For a moment, *just a moment,* Porter thought the man was holding a rifle. He could feel phantom pain in his missing leg, and a cold shiver ran down his spine.

The cigarette dropped from his lips as he remembered the snap of the sniper rifle shot that took out his leg all those years ago.

"Looks like a camera with a hell of a lens on it," Mindy said. "We're popular."

Porter breathed a sigh of relief, "Right, a camera."

Mindy looked down at the cigarette, "You alright, Boss?"

"Get in the truck, now," Porter said. He stomped towards the house. He was pissed off that this man had made him feel fear and pissed off that he could still feel fear, royally pissed off. "Hey! You want an autograph with that?"

As he neared the house, the man ran from the window.

"C'mon out, you pussy!"

A few seconds later, the same man ran out the front door.

The guy was skinny and sporting an aggressive military cut that looked like he had escaped from the chow hall in boot camp. He wore a tan shirt, military-issued ACU pants, and combat boots, but what really stood out were his large, oval BCG glasses.

Porter was sure he was the same punk from the club. He was the one who had bought a lap dance with Alice.

The boot camp escapee entered a silver SUV parked alongside the curb in front.

The vehicle came to life, and high beams shot out, blinding Porter.

The brightness intensified as the vehicle headed toward him.

"Fuck me." Porter turned and ran for his truck.

"Run!" Mindy said out the truck's passenger window.

"No, shit!" Porter said.

The roar got louder and was nearly on top of him when Porter reached his truck and, stepping onto the rear bumper, flung himself into the bed.

The SUV skimmed the side of his truck, shaking Porter violently and taking out his driver's side mirror.

Bones aching, Porter regained his orientation and uprighted himself onto a knee. Reaching into his shoulder holster, he pulled out his piece and let fly two rounds.

One .38 kissed the trunk, and the other shattered the rear windshield.

The SUV swerved before heading out of the neighborhood.

Porter jumped out of the bed and ran to the driver's seat.

"You okay?" Mindy asked.

"Nothing a steamy dose of coffee and sex won't cure." Turning over the engine, he cut the wheels and pressed the accelerator.

The tires groaned as he spun the truck around.

Mindy produced her thermos and poured coffee into the cap, "Here, you're on your own for the sex."

Porter grabbed the cap and downed its contents, "Fair enough." He sped the truck out of the neighborhood and onto the intersecting main road. The SUV was five cars ahead.

He swerved around a van, bullied through a red light, and veered onto a long stretch of road.

Porter passed several vehicles and was close enough to read the SUV's Kansas license plate. Just as Porter began reading the numbers aloud and Mindy scratched them into her notebook, a car cut in front.

"Oh, c'mon," Mindy protested.

"Out of the way!" Porter said, waving a hand to no avail.

The car in front pulled back, allowing an 18-wheeler to get in front.

"You gotta be kidding me?"

Getting ready to pass and accelerate, another 18-wheeler pulled alongside him. "C'mon, do I have 'shit magnet' tattooed on my forehead?"

"Just face it, the world's conspiring against you," Mindy said.

"Story of my life." Porter followed the traffic to the exiting lane leading to the interstate.

Porter bided his time at the red light, and the SUV turned onto the road when the light turned green. Porter did the same and passed by the pair of 18-wheelers in the merge lane. Nearly on him again, the car exited for Cheyenne Mountain Space Force Station.

Porter saw the driver's eyes flash in his rearview mirror before flooring it.

"That's right, get a good look, asshole," Porter said.

"Catch him before he gets to the gate," Mindy said.

"Mindy! You want to drive?"

"Yeah, I'd love to."

"Well…you can't."

"Then why'd you ask?"

"To make you feel better," Porter said, gaining on him.

As the SUV neared the guard shack leading onto the base, the entry bar lifted, and the armed contractor in the black jacket, matching beanie, and yellow security vest waved him in.

As Porter approached the gate, the contractor lowered the entry bar, and Porter slammed on his brakes, nearly hitting the guard who stood in front.

"Move!" Porter said.

"Sir, I need you to turn around," the guard said. He was beefy, with prominent bushy brows, thin spectacles, and a deep voice.

Reaching inside his jacket, Porter produced his wallet and pulled out his retired military ID. "Let's go. I'm following that guy." He pointed to the SUV that had finished maneuvering around the staggered concrete barriers and was heading up the road.

The guard glanced at the ID and waved away, "The base is on Lockdown. You need to back up and turn around, sir."

"Lockdown? You just let that car through. Hell, you didn't even check his ID."

"This is bullshit," Mindy said.

"Listen!" the guard said firmly. He put one hand on the M-4 strapped to his chest courtesy of a three-point sling and placed his other on top of the truck's cab. Leaning into the driverside window, he said, "You make me tell you again, we're going to have trouble and trust me, you don't want trouble."

Porter stared at the man's beady dark eyes for a long minute and shifted the truck into reverse. "I can't wait until you guys lose your contract."

"What was that?"

"You heard me, rent-a-cop. Soon, you'll be a security guard at Sears. They have a big empty parking lot I can kick your ass in."

"Yeah, Jarhead, you and what fucking army?!" the guard barked, patting his chest and extending his arms in a show of strength.

Porter knew he couldn't win a fair fight with this guy, but then again, Porter knew nothing of fair fights.

"What, no comeback?" the guard asked.

"You want my comeback? Go scrape it off your wife's teeth," Porter said as he backed the truck in defeat and drove away from the base.

Walking into Fantasies, Porter and Mindy saw Doc. He wore a loud yellow Hawaiian shirt with big red flowers and dancing naked tiki girls. With a green margarita, Doc conversed deeply with Erica, who was working the bar.

"So, this Martinez guy saw a Slurpee Machine at a 7/11 and thought, hey, how about a frozen margarita? And that's how they were created," Doc said, sipping his drink.

"Wow, that's really interesting," Erica said with a fake smile as she wiped down a glass. Seeing Porter, Erica motioned to Doc, "Says he's here to see you?"

Doc spun his chair to Porter and shook his head, "You said Jessica would be here, but Erica said she was off tonight. What the hell, man?"

Porter nodded to Erica, "The usual." He then turned to Mindy.

"You know, I could really go for some chips and salsa," Mindy said.

"Look through the camera feeds first, chips and salsa later," Porter said.

"You're killing me, Boss," Mindy said, walking through the bar and into the backroom.

"I'll get you that beer," Erica said. "Want me to tell Alice you're here? She's in the back, getting ready."

"Sure," Porter said.

"You said she would be here. I wore my best shirt and everything," Doc said, tugging at it.

"That's your best shirt?" Porter said.

"So, sue me, and hey, just for the record, it's pretty classy for a place like this."

"A place like this?" Porter asked, raising a brow.

Seeing the error of his ways, Doc said, "Yes, a fine gentlemen's club you've got going here. Impressive, man. Cool lights and décor and the scenery, you can't beat this scenery." He slapped Porter on the shoulder, "Am I right?"

Porter looked at Doc's hand, which was still on his shoulder.

Doc retracted his hand, "My bad."

"She'll be here. A deal is a deal."

"She better."

Porter sat beside Doc and lit a cigarette, "So, what did you find out?"

"Lady Luck."

"Uh…I'm going to need a little more than that."

"There are a ton of texts about meeting up at Lady Luck."

"Who is meeting up at Lady Luck?"

"Gunner."

"What?"

"That's what it says, man, here, read this." Doc handed over the phone.

Porter read the screen aloud, "Gunner will be at Lady Luck at sunset."

"Keep reading," Doc told him.

"Lady Luck is nice. Even Renegade and Mogul would approve."

"Yeah, it's all a bunch of nonsense," Doc said. "The more you read, the more confusing it all gets. I don't know what the hell any of this means, do you?"

Porter shook his head.

Erica returned, handed Porter an open Coors Light, and grinned, "So, I know something you guys don't?" Erica said, "Oh, this is great."

"Here we go," Porter said, taking a swig of his beer.

"Okay, am I missing something here?" Doc asked.

Erica held up a finger, "Give me a minute. I'm going to soak this in."

"Is she serious?" Doc asked.

"Dead serious," Porter answered.

"I mean, I might just have my Associate, not a Ph.D.," she said to Doc, "or traveled the world in the Marines, like some," she said to Porter, "but even I know what those texts mean."

"As usual, I am honored by your presence," Porter told her. "Now spit it out, genius."

Erica smiled and, leaning across the bar, planted a kiss on Porter's cheek, "As long as you know where you stand."

"Hey, I think you're a genius, too," Doc said, tapping his cheek.

Erica shook her head, "Nice try."

Doc shrugged in defeat.

"Those are Secret Service Code Names," Erica told them. She plucked the phone from Porter and read the screen, "Even Renegade and Mogul would approve. Renegade was Obama's name, and Mogul was Trump's." She continued reading, "Lady Luck is a meeting spot, probably a bar or a club, and Gunner, not sure about that one."

"Another code name?" Porter asked.

"Yep, that only makes sense," Erica said, returning the phone.

"So, if Renegade and Mogul are code names for Presidents, wouldn't Gunner be a President too?" Porter asked.

"Not necessarily," Erica said, "the Secret Service has code names for Presidents, their families, important persons, and locations. Some Senators running for Office have even gotten them."

"How the hell do you know all this?" Doc asked.

"Bartender by night, college student by day. My Major is in Political Science and Government."

"Well, better change majors then. You're much too truthful and pretty to be in politics," Porter said.

"Ahh, thanks, Boss."

"School, huh? You need a private tutor?" Doc asked as he raised and lowered his brows. "You and I could cram in some late-night sessions."

"You wish."

"Erica, do me a favor, call in Anna," Porter told her.

"Wait, who the hell is Anna?" Doc said. He thought for a moment, "Never mind, I get it. That's Jessica Rabbit's real name. Well, continue."

Porter took a swig of beer, "Tell her she needs to come in for half an hour and service my friend here with the Gold package on the house. She does it. She gets a full day of PTO."

"That's right," Doc said with a grin and danced in his seat. "The Gold package, yeah, baby, yeah, baby. Wait, what's the Gold package?"

"Something good," Porter said.

Erica put down the glass she had wiped down a dozen times. "Did you clear this with Ursula?"

"You let me worry about Ursula."

"Okay," Erica said, producing her cell phone from her back pocket. Before dialing the number, she mumbled, "Why don't I ever get PTO?"

❧

"I'm back," Mindy said, sitting dramatically beside Porter on the leather couch in the Fantasies showroom. With her shoes propped on the couch arm, she plucked a tortilla chip from the basket atop the circular table between them. She dunked the chip into the container of salsa. "Looking through the camera footage, I found the guy, and I've got good news."

Porter was only partially paying attention to the conversation. His focus was centerstage, on Alice. She sported a pumpkin on her lacy black panties, working the pole to "The Devil Went Down to Georgia."

"Ya know, the one Alice gave a lap dance to earlier today. He almost ran you over?"

The older guys sitting around the stage were grinning ear-to-ear, hopelessly in love.

Mindy nudged Porter's leg with her shoe, "Did you hear what I said? I've got good news."

Porter downed his Coors and held a finger to Erica at the bar, "I'm listening."

Mindy yawned, "Damn, don't sound too excited. Our guy is Jason Beasley."

"So, I take it you tracked him by the credit card he paid for drinks?"

"Nope, didn't have to. Jason dated my sister last year. He started out as one of her dealers, then they started dating. Things didn't last long." She showed Porter a phone picture of Jen and Jason standing side-by-side at a Mexican restaurant. They both wore sombreros and grinned like idiots.

"Yep, I never forget an asshole. That's him, alright."

"Yup."

"How well do you know this guy?" Porter asked.

"I know Jason's in the Air Force, stationed at Cheyenne Mountain if you couldn't have guessed. Jen would sometimes pick me up after school, and we would go to his place afterward so she could pick up drugs or screw him or whatever. He lives off base."

"Right," Porter said, unimpressed.

"Anyway, I'd wait in the car because I sure as hell wasn't going into his house, and most times, she wouldn't come back for hours, nights even. Sometimes, I'd have to take the bus home."

Erica walked over, "You let me know when you want a real drink, Marine," she said, cracking the top off a Coors and handing it to Porter.

"Keep them coming," Porter said, handing over a five.

She winked at him, "Of course, sugar." She turned to Mindy, "Anything for you, hon?"

"No thanks," Mindy continued, munching on chips. Thumbing her phone, she said, "His Facebook profile says he's stationed at Cheyenne Mountain Space Force Station. Jason is a Satellite Communications Systems Operator-Maintainer, whatever that means."

"It means he has a bright future with T-Mobile making minimum wage," Porter said, sipping his beer. "Do you know if he's part of an American Iron? Maybe a side gig or something?"

"He rode a bike, but I don't recall him being part of any biker gang when Jen was with him."

"People change."

"True," Mindy agreed. "He has a recent post that says…" she read off her phone, "I don't really care about my day job. It's my night job that pays the bills. Call me The Nightrider, bitches."

"Someone's a Mad Max fan," Porter said.

"Who's that?" Mindy asked.

Porter shook his head in disappointment.

"Excuse me for not being versed in old '90s movies."

"Came out in '79."

"You're showing your age, Boss."

"Keep it up, and I might just find your receipt and return you."

"Speaking of receipts, have you checked the bank account today?"

Porter chugged more of his beer, "That's your job, not mine."

"Well, how much did Bobbi Johnson pay you for this job? There's quite a bit in there."

"She said she'd pay us double the normal rate for two weeks. Half now and the other half when it's done."

"So that should be $4000 now and $4000 later, so $8,000, right?"

"If you say so. I didn't major in math."

"Well, this is pretty simple math. Look, $50 an hour normal charge, double is $100 an hour, times that by 80 –"

"What's your point?"

"My point is, she's made multiple payments into the PayPal account and already paid too much. She's literally put like thirteen grand in there."

"Her loss."

"It doesn't bother you at all?"

"Nope, not in the least."

"Well, it does me," Mindy put up a finger as she yawned. "This entire case is supposed to stay 'off the books,' right?" Mindy asked, using air quotations. "What if we're being used as, I don't know, money launders or something."

"For a U.S. Senate candidate?" Porter turned to her, "That's pretty thin, Rookie."

"Look, all I'm saying is –"

"Fine, if it means that much to you," Porter cut her off, "I'll bring it up to her the next time I check in, alright?"

He expected Mindy to comment, but he noticed she had dozed off.

Reaching into his jacket, Porter pulled out a cigarette and lit up. Inhaling the nicotine, he stared at Mindy.

"Ahh, is it past someone's bedtime?" Alice said, sitting beside him on the couch and stealing the cigarette from his lips. She took a puff, "She's a cute kid?"

"She's alright," Porter said.

Alice put the cigarette to Porter's lips, and he took a drag. She wrapped an arm around his shoulders and forced him into a deep kiss. The smoke in his mouth traveled into hers. "You're cute, too," she said. She breathed out his smoke and ran a hand up his leg to his groin.

"Nothing down there is cute," Porter said.

"Trust me, I know," she said, straddling him.

This lasted until Porter gently pushed her aside and stole the cigarette, "Listen, I need to ask you something."

"Ooh, are you finally popping the big question? I'm flattered."

"Well, I'm popping something, but it ain't that."

She squeezed his crotch, "Go on."

He blew out a plume of smoke, "That guy you gave a lap dance to this morning, Jason. Do you know if he works for American Iron?"

"Why, you jealous?"

"I'm not the jealous type. Just ask any of my girlfriends."

"Right," she kissed his neck, "I don't know a Jason."

"He had on BCGs."

"BCGs?"

"You know, birth control glasses? The Democrats call them boot camp glasses. He was kind of young and had one of those high and unnecessary haircuts. A real target indicator."

"Right, I remember. The only tip Jason had was the one in his pants, which was small."

"Does he work for American Iron?"

"Not one for conversation tonight, huh?"

"The little shit tried to run me over earlier tonight."

She shrugged, "Maybe he's the jealous type." She moved her head towards the cigarette, and he transferred it to her lips.

"I'll ask him about it when I beat the shit out of him."

"Ladies and gentlemen!" Erica spoke into a megaphone from behind the bar counter.

She was so loud she woke Doc, who had fallen asleep at the bar waiting for Jessica. Looking around and not seeing her, Doc left his seat and stumbled to the bathroom.

"It is now midnight," Erica said, "and officially George's twenty-first birthday!" A trio of men around the center stage cheered as the fourth man with black curly hair and a plaid shirt stood, blushing. "As a special treat, his buddies have all chipped in to buy our premium package, fifteen minutes of fame! George and his buddies will be treated to more hot girls than they know what to do with. Girls set up the table!"

A pair of girls walked over, pulling chairs away from a table and ushering over George and his buddies.

"Ah shit, here we go," Alice mumbled.

"So, I need all the ladies in the club to head over to George's table to give him his birthday present," Erica said. "Fifteen minutes of fame."

Lady Gaga's "Paparazzi" blared over the speakers.

As the girls walked to his table, Erica said, "You'll be treated to Belle and Jasmine." She pointed to the back of the room, "Aurora, get over here." She directed her megaphone to another corner, "Ariel, c'mon now, George is waiting on you." Lastly, she pointed to Porter's table, "Alice, I see you over there, and you're tonight's Jell-O Shot! C'mon, girls. Everyone out of the backroom, hustle, hustle, hustle! A man only turns twenty-one once!"

"Lucky me," Alice sighed. She kissed Porter and planted the cigarette between his lips. "Jason didn't tell me he was with American Iron, but I'm pretty sure he is. Hell, he was bullshitting with that American Iron recruiter guy like they were buddies."

Porter grabbed her hand as she tried to leave, "Earlier, you said we needed to talk about something. What's up?"

Alice stared at him for a long moment, and her expression changed from amused to grief. "Not tonight, Porter."

"Alice?"

"Really, it can wait."

"You wanted to tell me something, so tell me."

"Alice, waiting for you!" Erica blared over the megaphone.

"Yeah, I know!" she yelled to Erica. Turning to Porter, she shrugged, "I gotta go."

Porter held her back, "Tell me."

Alice nodded, "Jeff got out of prison today. He wants to see Amber and try again with me. Porter, I owe it to Amber to try and make this work. Jeff says he's a different person now. I'm going to give him one more chance."

Porter shook his head, "You can't be fucking serious."

"Porter, Jeff is her father and –"

"He shot up and hit her. How old was Amber at the time?"

"I know, but it was five years ago."

"Then with you –"

"I know."

"This is a fucking stupid idea." Porter sighed and shook his head, "If that fucker so much as raises his voice towards you or Amber, call me, and I'll break every bone in his body."

Alice kissed him, "You're so damn cute when you care."

"Hey, I mean it, alright?"

Alice threw him a wink before walking to George's table and lying down with her back across it.

At George's table, Erica stood with an assortment of Jell-O Shots on a silver tray and poured one into Alice's naval. She then ushered George forward with a curl of the finger. He laughed before diving in and slurping the shot from Alice's belly. All the girls laughed, and the guys hollered, "Next," as Erica poured the next round.

Porter chugged his Coors dry and tossed his spent cigarette into it. He watched as the guys took turns drinking from Alice's naval as the girls cheered them on. Alice's fingers and toes curled with every shot.

As the guys began getting their lap dances, Porter knew he had to get some fresh air before he found a reason to do something stupid to George or one of his buddies.

He turned to Mindy, but she was still out. Taking his cigarettes and lighter out, he placed his jacket on her.

Walking across the club and nearing the exit, he stopped at the beads that led out, for a rosy scent was in the air.

12

Porter would be the first to admit that he knew the scent of every girl in the club, and this scent didn't belong to any of them. It was the perfume his ex-wife used to wear – some Bath and Body thing. When he came from the field, deployments, hell, the aroma greeted him.

He followed the scent to a familiar woman sitting alone at the bar wearing a denim jacket assorted with patches and a guitar case at her feet. Her right hand shook as she brought a cocktail to her pink lips.

Porter recognized her from the football game, Valentine. Even with all her clothes on, she was beautiful in the club, full of naked women.

When did she slip in?

Porter sat next to her and knocked on the counter. Getting the attention of Erica, who had stepped behind the counter, Porter nodded to Valentine. "I'll have what she's having and her drinks on me."

"No, thanks," Valentine said as she watched the mounted television playing ESPN.

"Careful with this one, Boss," Erica cautioned.

ESPN was doing a countdown of the top ten football comeback plays. At number two was John Elway's 'The Drive' against the Cleveland Browns in the '86 AFC Championship game.

"Don't you even want to know my name?" Porter asked Valentine.

Valentine continued watching the show and sipping her cocktail.

Porter looked to Erica for relief.

Erica shrugged and slid a similar cocktail to him.

Porter lit his cigarette and, downing his cocktail in one gulp, remembered how much he hated Strawberry Daiquiris. Turning his attention to Valentine, he asked, "So, I guess a blowjob in the parking lot is out of the question?"

Erica facepalmed and walked off.

Valentine sighed and turned to him. "Listen, asshole, I don't know who the hell you think you are, but…" she stopped mid-sentence, staring at him with emerald and orange eyes. She took in his eyes, lips, build, shoulder holster, revolver, and badge. "Okay, if you're a cop, then I'm John Elway."

"Detective Ryan Porter," he told her, extending a hand.

She cautiously shook his hand. Her hand trembled in his, "You're a Private Investigator?"

"That's right, and you're Valentine?"

She eyed him suspiciously.

"I was at the game. You played a kick-ass rendition of the National Anthem."

"Okay," she said, "that explains that. For a second, I thought you were stalking me."

"That hasn't been ruled out."

She smiled and pointed to his holster, "Nice Smith & Wesson. My dad used to carry one too. You're not issuing me a summons, are you?"

Porter nodded to her guitar case, "You're one to talk. You're not going to go all Desperado, Antonio Banderas on my ass, are you?"

"Lugging around a guitar case full of guns sounds like a lot of work. Plus, I'm not sure I fit Steve Buscemi's description of the biggest Mexican he's ever seen."

"Big as shit," Porter said as they exchanged a grin.

"This guitar was given to me by James Hetfield."

"From Metallica?"

"You know another James Hetfield?" Valentine asked, "So yeah, this stays with me wherever I go."

"Makes sense."

She sipped her drink, "So, blowjob in the parking lot? Helluva pickup line, Detective."

"Well, you were playing hardball."

"Still am." She squinted at him, "Veteran?"

"Yeah, Marines." He squinted back at her, "You're a Vet too."

"You think so?"

"That American flag patch on your right denim sleeve gives it away. Most people would make it face the other way, with the stars to the left and the stripes to the right. Yours is the reverse. Like it's flying in the breeze because you're running into battle."

Valentine nodded, "I was in the Army."

"No one's perfect."

"Oh, it's gonna be like that?"

"Yeah."

There was silence as the two sized one another up. Lady Gaga's song 'Paparazzi,' was blaring in the background:

Valentine's stare was predator-like, hungry.

"Can I buy you that drink now?" Porter asked.

She studied him a bit longer and then said, "Sure."

Porter ordered her another cocktail and a beer for himself.

"So, what do I owe the pleasure, Detective?"

"Would you believe me if I told you I just wanted to buy a pretty girl a drink?"

"Not a chance in hell," she finished off her drink.

"Fair enough." Porter extended his pack of cigarettes, and with a flick of the wrist, a cig extruded, "I haven't seen you around here before."

She plucked the cigarette from the pack and tugged on the lapel of her jacket. "Does my excess attire give it away?" She nodded in George's direction, where the girls were still performing lap dances. "This usually isn't my scene, but I was looking for a gig, and this was the first club I saw."

"Yeah, this place isn't big on live music."

"Yeah, Erica told me. But I figured, hey, I'm already here, might as well get a drink." She extended her cigarette, and Porter lit it.

"So, do you just drive around looking for work?"

"No, nothing like that. I'm visiting my uncle, who lives in the area. He's in the middle of work, so I figured I'd make a few bucks."

"And the football performance?"

"Damn, you're just full of questions, aren't ya?"

Erica slid their drinks to them.

Porter's fixated on her shaking hand holding the cigarette.

"IED blast, Afghanistan," she said, taking a puff. "I got so many metal plates holding me together, under an x-ray, I look like Wolverine."

"I would have never guessed with how you play the guitar."

She nudged the case with her boot. "When I play, the shaking stops. It's hard to explain." Sipping her drink, she shrugged, "So yeah, full disclosure, I'm a cripple."

"You're not the only one." Porter knocked on his prosthetic right knee.

"So, did you go down with the ship?"

"Ship?"

"Yeah, Captain Ahab."

"Ah, well, substitute a whale for an RPG and the open waters for Iraq."

"Would you look at that," she said, "we're just a couple of broke dicks now, aren't we?"

"It would seem so, though full disclosure, I'm *still* fully functional."

"Okay, I'll drink to that."

They raised their glasses, clinked, and downed them. Their eyes remained locked on one another.

"Married?" she asked.

Porter held up his left hand.

She pulled his hand close and wiggled his ring finger, "No ring, but you've got a wedding band indentation."

"Wife has been out of the picture for quite some time."

"You didn't kill her, did you?"

"No, unfortunately, I missed the opportunity."

"Okay," she smirked. "Plus, how awkward would it be if two serial killers were sitting at this bar?"

"Extremely awkward."

Porter liked her. She was tough but had humor buried in there.

"Not married, huh? Well, Detective, that's a shame."

"A shame?"

"Yeah," she said, "married men are much easier to seduce."

"Is that right?" He snuffed his cigarette into a silver ashtray on the bartop and lit a new one.

She held up two fingers, "Single men come in two stocks, depressed," she lowered a finger so that she was flicking him off, "and overconfident. The depressed ones are the ones who never get laid. They let themselves go to shit and probably become serial killers one day or simply blow their brains out. The overconfident ones are the assholes who still look *halfway* decent," she eyed him up and down, "and screw the dumb young chicks and the used-up whores. Women like me, who are neither, aren't their clientele."

She took a deep drag and pointed her cigarette tip to George's table where the action was happening.

"I wouldn't be so sure," Porter told her.

"Umm, hmm," she said, unconvinced. "Then you got the married ones who have that natural urge to cheat. It's in their biology. They can't fight it. They always have that fantasy lingering in the back of their mind. That 'what if' scenario is constantly playing out. They don't care who they screw. They just want something different."

"Makes sense."

Valentine studied him, "Interesting."

"What?"

"You never asked if I was married. I could have just removed my wedding band. You never know."

"You're not married," Porter said.

"So sure?"

"A married girl would have reacted in one of two ways by now."

"Go on," Valentine said.

"One," Porter extended his middle finger, "you would have immediately rejected me and walked away."

"And two?" Valentine asked.

Porter added a second finger, "We'd be in bed already. A lot of married women just have that natural urge to cheat. It's in their biology."

Valentine leaned forward, puffing on her cigarette and smirking that cute, uneven smirk, "You're pretty sure of yourself, aren't you, Detective?"

"Damn right." He stared at her thin pink lips as she put her dying cigarette to them.

Porter gently pulled the cigarette from her lips and placed a fresh one in its place. Leaning forward, he touched the cigarette's tip in his mouth to hers, lighting it.

They shared a fleeting moment before Valentine looked past him and said, "What the hell?"

Porter followed her gaze and saw two men in flannel standing over Mindy. They were staggering and laughing.

The one closest to Mindy wore a tractor hat, had a shaggy beard, and was plump. Shaggy put down his beer, leaned over Mindy's resting head, and pulled down his pants.

The other had a long, hooked nose and was as tall as he was thin. Hook Nose crouched and pulled out his phone.

Porter sprang from his chair. He maneuvered around tables, chairs, customers, and girls across the club. Reaching Mindy, he sent a steel-toed boot between the legs of Shaggy, who wore no pants.

Shaggy howled in pain.

Porter grabbed Shaggy by the back of the flannel collar and tossed him over a table.

Mindy awoke and yelled, "Look out!"

Porter turned to Hook Nose. He had a switchblade, and a knife sprung from it.

Hook Nose slashed out.

Porter jumped back and caught the beer bottle Mindy tossed to him. With a swing, Porter shattered the glass across Hook Nose's face, dropping him.

A punch kissed Porter's jaw, and he stumbled back.

He looked at Shaggy, who had put his pants on and regained a vertical base. Even though Shaggy was taller than Porter and had a good 100 pounds on him, the man looked scared.

Porter put two fingers in his mouth and, swabbing the inside of his cheek, pulled them out, revealing blood. He spat on the floor.

"C'mon," Shaggy said, putting his fists up in an Irish fighting stance.

Porter cut the distance between them with a leap and grabbed Shaggy by the flannel collar with one hand. With the other, he repeatedly punched Shaggy in the face, backing the man into the couch and knocking off his tractor hat.

When there was more blood than face, Porter kicked him in the chest and sent Shaggy toppling over the couch and onto the floor.

On his back, Shaggy groaned in pain, holding his face as blood flowed from between his fingers.

Porter pinned him down with a boot to the chest and took aim with his revolver.

"No! Don't fucking kill me, man, please. I have a family!" Shaggy pleaded.

Hook Nose stood, holding his bleeding face.

Mindy pointed her Beretta at him, and Hook Nose dropped his switchblade and put his hands up.

The music stopped, and Porter looked around. All the customers and girls were standing at their tables and watching.

Two club bouncers ran over and kept their distance from Porter and Mindy. Valentine remained at the bar, staring at him.

Doc returned from the bathroom and, walking to the bar, stopped and nodded to Porter, "Hey, man, you good over there?"

"Uh, we better step back from this one, sugar," Erica told him, handing him another margarita.

Doc sipped the drink and smiled, "I like this club. It's exciting."

"Mr. Porter," a thick-necked bouncer said, "just put down the gun, Boss. We'll kick them out."

"Back off, Beast," Porter said. "You don't want none of this."

The other beefy bouncer began to sneak up from the side.

"Don't try it, Herc. You're not quick enough," Porter said, keeping his gaze locked on Shaggy.

Hercules stopped in place, and the two bouncers took a step back.

Only Alice dared to approach. She touched Porter's shoulder, "Babe, he's not worth it."

"Yeah, man, listen to her," Shaggy pleaded.

"Two things I got tonight: beer and your opinion. Last I checked, I only fucking asked for one of them," Porter said, cocking back the hammer of his revolver.

A series of jingles rang out from a phone.

On command, everyone checked their phones.

The ring continued.

One by one, everyone realized it wasn't their phone.

"Boss, I think that's you," Mindy said.

Porter glanced at his jeans pocket and saw a light flickering within. He focused again on Shaggy and said, "Alice, you mind?"

She grabbed the phone from his pocket and awkwardly flipped it open, "Uh, hello? Porter's phone."

All around the club, there were whispers of, "Flip phone?" and, "They still make those?" one person said, "What is that?"

"Uh, hold on," Alice said. She handed the phone to Mindy, "This chick is losing her shit. I think it's one of your clients."

Mindy put the phone to her ear, "This is Mindy." She listened and nodded, "Calm down, nope, you're good. Okay, listen to me, turn on all the lights, make lots of noise, we'll be there in like, I dunno, like ten minutes, K?"

Mindy twirled her gun as she listened to the speaker on the other end, inadvertently waving her barrel at the customers and girls who scrambled underneath tables for cover. "Yeah, Porter's right here. He's just, uh…"

Porter had the four-inch barrel of the Smith & Wesson leveled between Shaggy's crying eyes.

"You know what?" Mindy continued, "He's, uh, super busy." She shook her head, "What sound? No, don't be silly. No one's crying. Everything's fine. Yeah, we're totally chill. Listen, take a deep breath. We'll be right over." She lowered the phone and tapped on the screen, "What the hell? How do you end a call with this thing?"

Alice grabbed the phone, flipped it closed, and slid it back into Porter's pocket.

"Boss, we gotta go," Mindy said. "The Peterson's house is about to be broken into."

"Please, man, please," Shaggy pleaded.

Porter reset the hammer and lowered his piece, "Get the hell out of my club." He turned to Hook Nose, "If I ever see either of you in here again, I'll kill you."

Holstering his gun, he watched as Hercules and Beast escorted them out.

After they left, he looked at the mess he had caused and the faces of the astonished customers. The girls looked annoyed more than anything. He pulled out his wallet, took out a bundle of fives, and tossed them like a game of 52-card pickup.

"Drinks are on me."

The customers cheered.

Porter looked to the bar, but Valentine was gone.

As Porter followed Mindy out of the club, Anna walked in. Porter pointed her to Doc.

Doc pumped his hand victoriously.

T ake a right," Mindy said as Porter's Ram growled through the night.

Approaching an intersection, Porter blared his horn and bullied through a red light. They barely missed a collision with an oncoming SUV. As they continued, horns sounded behind them, followed by middle fingers hanging out car windows.

Mindy thumbed away on the GPS app on her phone, "Follow this road for another mile, and then we're going to get off on exit 152."

"Got it," Porter said.

"Were you really going to kill that guy at the club?"

"Shaggy?"

"Yeah, Shaggy."

"Yeah."

"Jesus, Porter, we've talked about this. You can't just go around shooting people because they're dumbasses."

"Sure, you can."

"But –"

"Mindy, those two guys were going to do some nasty shit involving their nuts and your face. I'll let you do the math. No one fucks with you while I'm around, got it?"

Mindy couldn't stay mad at him. She laughed instead.

"What?" Porter asked.

"Nothing," she said, "exit here and get in your right lane. You'll turn right at the stop sign and follow the road until you see the entrance to their neighborhood. The Peterson's house is 5114 Bloomington Street."

Nearing the neighborhood, Porter pointed to the glovebox, "There's a remote in there."

Mindy sifted through an old CD storage case and a spare Beretta. She pulled out the remote key – there were two buttons.

"Click the LIGHT ON" button twice."

Mindy clicked away, and the IR light on the remote blinked twice. "What did that do?"

"Look."

Mindy saw alternating flashing lights atop the truck, illuminating the snow-dusted road ahead of them, "Sweet, strobe lights."

Sliding across the ice and nearly spinning out of control, Porter cut the wheel into the slide, gained traction, and said, "Reach in the back and grab the megaphone."

Mindy found the white and red bullhorn and looked it over. "There's a siren button on that thing. When we get close –"

"Blast it."

"Get ready," Porter said as the Peterson's house became visible at the end of the culdesac. There was a trio of bikers on Choppers, revving their bikes and making a wasteland of the front yard with continuous doughnuts.

As they approached, Porter saw the riders wearing vests covered in patches and bandannas concealing their mouths. It was too dark to see all the details.

"Hit it," Porter said.

Mindy rolled down her window. The megaphone blared an obnoxious police siren.

Porter drove into the Peterson's front yard and slammed his truck into the nearest Chopper before stopping.

The biker fell off, and the others yelled out in disbelief.

Porter stepped onto his step bar and fired at the narrow snow patch between the toppled biker's legs.

The biker looked at the sizzling snow, "Holy shit!"

"Next time, I won't miss," Porter pointed his gun toward the two other bikers. "Want to call my bluff?"

One of the bikers was about to grab the gun holstered at his side, and his eyes locked onto Porter.

Porter nodded to him, "Go ahead, try me."

The downed biker got up and waved off the other two. Wiping snow and blood off his face, he hobbled across the yard to the closest Chopper and straddled the back seat.

They sped off, chanting "Fuck you" and "you're dead."

Mindy heckled them over the megaphone, "That's right, run away, you pussies! Leave and don't come back!" She exited the truck and turned to Porter, "Nice work, Boss."

Porter shielded an ear, "You trying to kill me? Turn that thing off."

"My bad."

Audrey and Mike opened the front door, both armed with guns.

"Oh, thank the Lord, you two are here," Audrey said with a hand on her chest. She turned to Mike, "See, I told you they'd come."

"Woman, I never said–" Mike began to say.

"But you were thinking it, weren't ya?"

"Really, woman?"

Making his way to the wrecked Chopper in the front yard, Porter knelt and opened the saddlebag secured to the bike's rear. Inside the bag were a pair of NVGs and a gas mask.

Mike and Audrey corralled them inside the home.

Walking inside, Porter placed the NVGs and gas mask on the kitchen table. "I took these off your visitors."

"So it was the bikers," Mike said. "Not damn ghosts, after all."

"Okay, I have an active imagination, so sue me," Audrey said.

"Apparently," Porter said.

"Did you call the cops?" Mindy asked.

"Yeah, that's the first thing we did after calling you guys," Mike said.

"And as you can see, their lazy asses ain't here," Audrey said.

"Are they gone?" Roger said from the staircase, armed with a baseball bat. His brother Nick was standing behind him.

"Yes, now go back upstairs," Audrey told them.

"I would have taken their heads off," Roger said, swinging at an imaginary biker.

"Next time," Porter said.

"Did you kill any of them?" Roger asked.

"Not for lack of trying," Mindy mumbled.

Porter shrugged.

"If they come here again, then I'll kill them myself or die fighting," Roger said. "I know where my dad keeps his gun, and I'm not afraid to use it."

"Don't say stuff like that," Audrey said.

"Roger!" Mike said, "Shut your mouth about things you know nothing about."

"Dad, I'll do it. I swear!" Roger shouted.

"Die fighting," Porter said. "Let me ask you something, Roger. Have you ever watched a man die?"

Roger looked at Porter with a blank stare, "What?"

"Have you ever killed a man? Have you pulled the trigger of a gun?" Porter asked.

Roger shook his head.

"Your dad and I, we've watched men die and heard men die," Porter stepped up the stairs to meet Roger. "We've killed men, and let me tell you, there's nothing heroic about it. There is nothing heroic about killing or dying fighting. You don't get to say that type of stuff until you know something about it, you understand?"

Roger gulped uneasily and said, "Yes, sir, I understand." Roger hung his head low, "Detective Porter, I'm sorry, I didn't mean to –"

Porter grabbed his shoulder, "It's okay, I know."

Breaking the tension, Mike showed them his phone and tried to open the Ring app, "Okay, so the doorbell camera was recording the whole time. I think I figured out how they pulled this scam off." He thumbed away and grunted in frustration.

"Dad, let me do it," Nick said, pulling out his phone and walking past Roger and Porter, cozying up next to Mindy. Everyone gathered and watched as Nick scrolled through the last ten minutes, which showed the three bikers rolling up to the house, huddling together in discussion, and then causing mayhem.

They wore different bandannas over their faces and matching black vests. The word 'Wolfpack' was embroidered above a large howling wolf patch.

"I thought I recognized their vests. Fuck, this doesn't make sense," Porter said, lighting up.

"Detective, language?" Audrey said. She then nodded to the cigarette, "You mind?"

Porter puffed, "What, did I not offer to share?"

Audrey shook her head.

"Do you know their gang?" Mindy asked.

"Yeah," Porter said. "I know the club President. They're known for doing a lot of good around the community. I'm surprised they're mixed up in this."

"Maybe it's not a club involvement, just a few bad actors," Mike said.

"That would be my guess," Porter said.

"Here's what I wanted to show you." Mike scrolled to a video of a red, white, and blue Chopper pulling alongside the curb. There was a familiar man behind the chrome handlebars.

"Is that Scott?" Porter asked.

A woman was in the rear seat. She stepped off and, pulling down the mouth bandanna of the rider, kissed him.

"Yeah, Scott," Porter said.

"The woman on the bike came by and said she worked for the U.S. Census Bureau," Mike said. "She wanted to verify our name, how long we lived here, how many kids we had, and all sorts of stuff. Something didn't seem right. After a few questions, I asked for her identification, and she just clammed up and walked away."

"White girls always be doing creepy shit like that," Audrey said.

As the woman in the video approached the door, they saw her wearing a blue hoodie. As she got closer, Porter immediately saw a resemblance to Mindy. They both had identical soft faces, broad shoulders, and slender builds.

"Jen?" Mindy asked.

"Wait, do you know her?" Audrey said.

"Yeah, that's my sister."

"Well, shit," Porter said, blowing out a plume of smoke and heading for the door. "This just got a Helluva lot more complicated. We'll be in touch." He motioned Mindy to follow.

"Wait, where are you two going?" Audrey said.

"To work," Porter said.

"Wait," Mike said as Porter walked out.

Porter turned to meet him.

"What you said to Roger back there, uh, thanks. Sometimes, a father's words aren't enough and need to come from someone else to sink in. You seem good for Mindy." He forced Porter into a handshake. "Just remember, Mindy hasn't seen or done the things we have yet."

Porter shook his hand, "I know, and you're right. I'll keep it in mind.'

Porter waited by the truck and watched Mike walk inside, and Mindy walk out. As Mindy got in the truck, Porter did the same and pulled out his phone.

Dialing a number, he put the phone to his ear, and when the other end failed to pick up, he said, "It's Porter, call me back. It's about your biker club."

Pocketing the phone, he murmured, "If that old bastard dies from a heart attack before calling me back, I'm going to dig up his grave and beat the shit out of him." Turning his attention to Mindy, he said, "Start talking.'

"I had no idea Jen was involved," Mindy said.

"Yet you text her every day?"

"Well, we used to, then about a month ago, she stopped texting me regularly. I only get updates occasionally, and they are usually one-word answers. I ask how she's doing, and she'll send something back like FINE."

"Call her."

"Then what?"

"Call her."

"You think if she talks, we can find Frank Marion and expose American Iron?"

"Here's the thing, I recognize that G.I. Joe she rode in with. He was passing out business cards at the club." Porter dug his wallet out of his jacket and pulled out a business card. He handed it to Mindy. "Don't bother with the personal number scribbled on the back, it dials their call center."

"Scott Winters, American Iron," Mindy read.

"I think he's the leader of American Iron. We're having no luck with Frank, but we can put a face to this guy."

"Wouldn't his business card say President or something?"

"If I was part of a sketchy organization, I wouldn't post my title on a business card."

"What makes you think he's the leader?"

"When Sarah and I talked to him, he kept saying things like, 'my company.' That and he has massive swagger and an ego. You usually get that in an organization if you're in an upper management position. Add all those up. He's gotta be the leader."

"So, you're thinking, we find, Jen –"

"We find him and get him to tell us Frank's whereabouts." Porter smirked, "Hell, there's a chance this just might work. Slim as hell, but a chance." He blew out a plume of smoke, "Like you getting laid before Senior year."

"Or you not getting an STD by the end of the year."

"Too late."

"Ewe."

"It was a joke."

"Right."

Porter shrugged, "Call her."

Mindy dialed and put the phone on speaker.

There was no answer.

Prompted to leave a message, she said, "Hey, Jen, it's me, again, listen, call me back as soon as you can, it's important, bye."

Porter blew out another plume of smoke, "She's not going to call you back, is she?"

"Probably not."

Porter shook his head.

"So, I've got a question. Why didn't you take out Scott when you had the chance?"

"Well, I didn't put two and two together at the time."

"You couldn't just look up American Iron info on your phone? I'm sure they have their company hierarchy posted on their website." Pulling out her phone, Mindy thumbed away. "Yep, Scott Winters, President."

"I was distracted by a club full of naked women."

"Poor you," Mindy scoffed.

As he lit a cigarette, Porter nodded, "The struggle was real."

"Okay, this might be a long shot," Mindy said, "but let's go after Jason."

"Who?"

"C'mon, I thought you said you never forget an asshole."

"Depends on the angle."

"Of course it does," Mindy said, shaking her head. "Jason Beasley, Jen's ex and Alice's new boyfriend, remember?"

"That asshole."

"Right, so I'm thinking we go to Jason's house and politely ask where Jen's at. You know, the Porter version of polite."

Porter massaged his temples, "You said yourself they haven't dated in a while."

"Yeah, but it's our only lead. Maybe Jason will lead us to Jen. Jen will be with Scott, leading us to Frank, and we shut them down."

"Yeah, and maybe Britney Spears will show up naked at my front door tomorrow morning."

Mindy grinned and shrugged, "Maybe. You never know."

"A lot of maybe's flying around in this conversation." Porter opened his center console, pulled out a bottle of Excedrin, and popped a handful of pills into his palm. Downing coffee, he turned over the engine, "Fuck it, who knows, maybe we'll get lucky."

14

At midnight, a mist enveloped the blackened sky of Raton Pass. Tall LED lamp lights and alternating illuminated billboards of U.S. Senate candidates Bobbi Johnson and Tim Styles reflected off the slick, icy highway, casting a ghastly glow. The only other visible lights on Raton's Colorado-New Mexico border town were a diner and hotel off the I-25 exit.

Inside the Motel 5 lobby, Gary Suthers popped the tab on his Coke and reclined in his seat. With his boots propped on the desk, he took a swig and belched as he watched the late Broncos and New England game, which had extended into overtime.

The channel dropped during the middle of a Broncos field goal attempt, and a 'low signal' message flashed across the screen.

"Oh, C'mon," Gary yelled. He flipped to another channel. The message repeated.

A low guttural growl sounded from the parking lot, and headlights flooded the lobby.

Gary watched a white Ford Bronco slide to a stop in a vacated space.

A thin man wearing a cowboy hat and red suede jacket and holding a travel mug stepped out. With his rough skin, he looked like a hired hand you would pick up on the side of the road for day labor.

A cold chill sifted into the lobby as the man entered,

Gary sat up, "Hello, sir, sir, sir. What can I, I, do for you?"

Taking off his cowboy hat, the man walked to the side counter with a Keurig coffee maker and rummaged through the basket of creamers, "No milk?"

"Sir, would you, you, like a, a, room?" Gary asked.

"People think creamers are the same as milk."

"It's, it's not?"

"No, most creamers are dairy-free, just water, sugar, and vegetable oil."

"I, I, didn't know that."

"That's quite the stutter," the man said.

"Yes, I've had had, had it my whole life."

"Why would they put someone who stutters behind the front counter of a hotel?"

"I only work p- part-time, during the gr-graveyard shift."

"I see," he said, sipping on his mug.

The way this man spoke and stared at Gary was methodical. It would have creeped Gary out most times, but the man didn't seem to be mean, just calculated.

"Forgive me for asking," the man said, "but do you have mental disabilities?"

Gary shrugged, "That's one way to s-say it."

"There's another way?"

"In school, they would always call me re-retard."

The man took a deep breath and stared at him. "People used to call me names too. All sorts of names."

"W-What did did you do about it?"

The man looked out the window at the barren stretch of highway, "I killed them."

"Right," Gary said, stifling a laugh. The laugh wasn't returned, "You're j-j-joking, right?"

"I need a room."

Gary forced himself to look away from the man and wiggled the mouse on his desk, "One night?"

"Yes, do you have a room without a Bible?"

"What?"

The man turned to him, "I don't want a Bible in my room. There's always one on the end table or inside the dresser. I'm not paying for a Christian-themed room."

Gary nodded, "Okay, I'll make sure to take it out." Gary typed away, "One bed?"

"Yes."

"Name?"

"Hector," he told him, "Hector Guvera."

After a few more taps on the keyboard and a mouse click, Gary said, "It'll be sixty-five dollars."

Hector produced an envelope from his suede jacket and counted out sixty-five dollars. He slid the money across the desk.

Gary looked at the bills. "Uh, we-we only t-take credit cards."

"Credit card?"

"Yeah, credit card. You know, for uh, uh, inci-incidental purp purp – "

"Incidental purposes," Hector said.

"Yeah, that."

Hector slapped down a twenty-dollar bill, "That's for you to keep."

Gary crawled his fingers across the table and took the bills, "F-for what?"

"I don't pay with credit cards and need a room for the night. I'll let you figure out how to book me in the system."

Gary grabbed a key card from his drawer and programmed it. "Room 117. I get off shift soon and will come by for the B-Bible."

"Good," his eyes wandered to the highway again and then to the Waffle House and convenience store on the other side of the parking lot. He pointed to the restaurant, "You know if that place has good milk?"

"M-m-milk?"

"Milk," Hector reiterated.

"I-I guess. My sis-sister Emily works there. She'll t-take care of y-you."

"Is she a good sister?"

"A g-good sister?"

"Yes, is Emily a good sister?"

Gary nodded, "The best."

✺

"If you're feeling froggy, then you better jump, because this Frogman has been there, done that, and is going back for more. Cheers, boys!" Hamel said with a waver in his voice.

"Contact left!" Patel yelled.

Rounds began impacting the side of the chopper.

"Murphy!" Hector yelled.

"Shoot that hooptie," Patel said.

"Yup, outta the way," Murphy said, pushing Patel aside. The Irishman laid on his belly and, aiming down the scope of his Mk 11 sniper rifle, said, "Slán leat," before pulling the trigger.

The man standing behind the M2 Browning heavy machine gun mounted in the bed of the black truck fell backward. With another trigger pull, a 7.62mm x 51mm NATO round spat out the twenty-inch barrel and impacted the driver. The truck swerved, and the following truck crashed into it, sending both off the road.

"We're clear!" Patel yelled, removing the binoculars from his face.

"No, we're not," Hector said, leaning out and seeing a trail of smoke from the tail rotor.

"Oh, stall the ball," Murphy added.

"Going down!" the pilot yelled.

"Shit! Now that ain't right!" Patel bellowed.

"Gunny!" Hamel yelled.

"Here we go!" Murphy said.

"Brace yourselves!" Hector yelled.

Alarms sounded, and as Hector looked out the opening, the world spun chaotically and –

⁂

Hector stirred from his sleep. He pulled the Sig Sauer from his side holster and trained the sights on the door. The temporary silence was broken by the air conditioning module attached to the wall, humming to life and exhaling hot air.

A trio of knocks sounded on the other side of the door. "I'm, uh, uh, here for your B-B-Bible," a voice said.

Hector glanced at the neon numbers of the clockface on the nightstand. He had only gotten a few hours of sleep.

Getting to his feet, Hector leaned on the door and looked out the peephole at Gary. "One moment." Pulling the Bible from the nightstand drawer, Hector twisted the deadbolt and opened the door.

The frigid night air bit into his flesh.

Hector looked down both sides of the empty outside corridors before handing the Bible to Gary.

"Th-thanks," Gary said. "Have a g-good night."

Hector saw Gary's eyes staring at the dog tags stuck to his bare chest.

"Were you in the the Army?" Gary asked.

"Yes, for a time. I was also in the Marines."

"Hey, I kno-know a M-M-Marine. He saved my life."

"You were in the service?"

"Me? Oh, no-no. I was…" Gary trailed off, deep in thought. "Earlier this year…It was a b-bad time for me and others. We were….we were…" a tear ran down his cheek. Gary chuckled and looked at the wet cement ground, "Whew, just thinking about it is p-painful."

"Thinking about what?"

Gary locked eyes with him, and there was no stutter as he said, "Demons walk this Earth, Mr. Guvera. True demons. I have seen the face of evil, and I'll never forget what he looks like."

"Evil," Hector repeated. "At the end of the day, when the lights go out, and it's just you and your thoughts, everyone has demons they must face. It's how we confront those demons that define the outcome."

"Do y-you ever f-fight demons?"

"Every night."

Gary nodded, "Have a goo-good night."

"Gary," Hector said. "What happened to the evil you speak of?"

Gary smiled, "The Marine killed him."

Hector watched as Gary walked down the side of the building, past the pool, and around the corner.

Securing his door, Hector took a shower and got dressed. He then walked across the frozen lot and into the convenience store. After purchasing a few items, he headed towards the Waffle House.

Before entering, Hector pulled a two-liter bottle of RC Cola from the bag, unscrewed the cap, and poured the contents onto the parking lot – he did the same with a can of Coke.

Walking through the Waffle House's double glass doors, heat from the HVAC hit him, followed by the smell of coffee and bacon. The restaurant was small, with red and white benches hugging the interior walls and red bar stools lining the long front counter. The subway-tiled walls were complemented by a yellow and black diamond banner. A digital jukebox played, 'I Walk the Line' by Johnny Cash.

"Welcome in, sit wherever," the cook behind the counter said to him. The cook was short, with facial features full of stress and bushy brows on a clean face. He wore a faded black Waffle House hat, matching apron, and a blue shirt with a graphic on the back that read 'Rockstar Grill Operator.' The cook opened the back door and yelled, "Emily, you got a customer!"

Walking across the empty restaurant, Hector set his cowboy hat down on the furthest booth and sat with his back to the glass wall. He looked out at the deserted highway before focusing on the laminated menu on the table.

A young freckled waitress in a blue collared shirt and black apron walked over. A flower was pinned to her visor, giving her that cute girl-next-door look. She was a brunette, easy on the eyes, with short hair and her brother's pointed nose. A gold cross hung down her long neck. Her nametag read Emily.

"OJ's car," Emily said, pointing out the window to the hotel parking lot.

"What?" Hector asked.

"I saw you pull up a few hours ago. White Ford Bronco is the model OJ Simpson drove in that '93 car chase. FX did a show on it a few years back. Did you watch it?"

"I don't watch much TV." Hector read her yellow nametag, "Emily, your brother, says you'll take care of me?"

"You betcha. What can I get ya? Coffee? I just made a fresh pot."

"I'll have milk, warm, microwave it for forty-five seconds," Hector placed his travel mug on the table and unscrewed the top.

"Uh, yeah, I guess I can do that."

Hector nodded and emptied the contents of his convenience store bag across the table. The empty two-liter toppled over, and Hector stood it up.

"That's quite an assortment there," Emily said. "Anything to eat?"

Hector nodded, "I'll have an order of hashbrowns with ham, cheese, and chili."

"Right, warm milk at forty-five seconds and an order of hashbrowns."

"With ham, cheese, and chili," Hector reiterated, unclipping the Strider SMF knife from his belt. He unfolded the weapon and stabbed it into the two-liter.

"You got it," Emily said, scratching the order on her pad.

"Thank you."

"Of course."

Walking behind the counter, Emily yelled, "Johnny, drop one scattered, covered, chunked and topped."

Johnny repeated the order and began making the food.

Hector continued to work the knife into the bottle as she passed the order to the gangly cook with a cleft lip. He serrated the bottle lengthwise but kept the neck assembly. Finding the roll of duct tape, he found the opening seam, stretched out a few pieces, and then adhered the strips to the bottle's sharp edges.

Hector paused and looked out to the highway. Headlights were visible at the top of the pass.

Emily returned with a glass of milk, "There you go, nice and warm, forty-five seconds, just like you asked."

Hector took a sip, "Perfect." He poured the glass into his mug.

"So," Emily said, "You working on some sort of Science Fair project?"

"Something like that," Hector said. Grasping the empty Coke can, he pushed his blade into the aluminum and cut it in half.

Emily nodded, "You're not from around here, are you? Well, most people who stop here aren't."

"Not really."

"Just passing through, huh?"

After opening the pack of facial cotton pads, Hector nodded and lined the can's ventilated bottom.

"That's a shame. I think everyone should have at least one friend in Colorado. Gives you an excuse to go skiing, see Cave of the Winds, or see a Broncos game."

Emily watched as he twisted open a bottle labeled 'Activated Charcoal Dietary Supplement.' He poured a handful of black pills into the soda can. Taking out another cotton pad, he sandwiched the drugs.

Hector looked up at her.

Emily grinned, "Don't mind me. I'm just nosey. Your food will be right up." She looked out the window, "Johnny, it looks like we're about to get real busy."

"Alright, alright," Johnny said smoothly. The grill hissed as he worked the hashbrowns with his spatula.

Hector cut a hole into one last cotton pad and laid it atop the can. He pushed the two-liter's open neck through the opening and bonded the two with a strip of duct tape.

Six motorcycles pulled loudly into the lot.

"Emily," Hector called out, applying a final strip of duct tape.

"Yessir," she said from behind the counter where she was tallying up tickets with a calculator.

"Is this place insured?"

"Insured?" She shrugged, "I don't know, I guess?"

"All Wafflehouses are insured by the bank," Johnny said. He finished the hashbrowns and added chili on top. "Order up."

Emily grabbed the plate and walked it to Hector, "Here you go. Let me know if you need anything else."

"Yes, I need you and Johnny to leave," Hector said, sipping milk.

"Excuse me?"

"Now," Hector said, taking off his jacket.

At those words, the six men in the parking lot stepped off their bikes. They were geared in goggles, bandannas over their mouths, and dark leather jackets full of patches. Each was armed with an M4 assault rifle.

The oldest biker had a bald head with a spider web tattoo stretched across his dome. Plucking a 40-MM grenade from the bandolier strapped across his broad chest, he popped open the bottom barrel of his M203 rifle and slid in the explosive.

The grenade broke through the window– landing on the floor between the counter and the grill.

Emily screamed, and Johnny yelled, "Time to go!"

"Go! Now!" Hector said.

The grenade hissed and enveloped the restaurant in a thickening white cloud.

In a panic, Emily and Johnny ran out the restaurant's back door.

"Light it up!" Max growled.

The remaining windows shattered as a hailstorm of 5.56x45mm rounds harassed the restaurant.

The barrage lasted until every man had emptied his 30-round magazine.

One by one, a series of 'clicks' sounded as each man ejected their empty magazine and reloaded.

"Move in!" Max said. "The first one to retrieve Guvera's body gets an extra 500."

They entered the restaurant staggered and crouched, with weapons leveled, butts pressed against their shoulders, and sighting down their ACOG scopes. Green dots danced across the smoke from the mounted laser sights.

Reaching the table where Hector had been sitting, the first two sifted through the smoke. The bullet-riddled table was empty. Only a cowboy hat, suede jacket, travel mug, and plate of hashbrowns remained.

"Max, it's clear," a man said.

"Keep looking," Max said from the rear.

Gunfire sounded from the kitchen.

"Take cover," one yelled as they all slid and ducked behind the remaining furniture.

"Contact front!" another said, firing away into the kitchen.

Others joined in, and a barrage of lead laid waste to everything before them.

"Hold your fire," Max said. Walking into the kitchen, he plucked a piece of the exploded brass casing from the grill. "What the hell? A diversion?"

A single shot sounded behind him, and Max ducked, "I said, hold your fire!"

A thud sounded as a body fell to the floor.

The smoke was too thick to get a clear look, but Max thought he saw a human-sized blur make its way through the smoke toward one of his men.

Two shots from a pistol later, a second man dropped.

With the barrel of his M4, Max followed the blur. He watched it move to another man, shoving silverware into the M4 barrel, watching the barrel implode, and seeing a third man drop with a blast to the head.

A fourth man screamed as the blur riddled him with bullets.

"Max, help!" Another man yelled.

"Get back to the bikes!" Max ordered.

Gunfire followed him as he rushed through the smoke in a panic. He slammed a shoulder into a wall, cursed as he slid on blood, and landed on the corpse of one of the bikers.

He stared into the grotesque insides of a blown-apart head.

Getting up, Max stumbled outside and puked. Rebalancing himself, he watched another flash of gunfire from the blur. His final man inside screamed and fell back as his rifle fired into the ceiling.

Max emptied his magazine into the restaurant, "Die, you son of a bitch!"

Panting, he pulled the remaining magazine from his side pouch. Before he could insert the magazine, he felt hot steel nudging against the back of his skull.

Max gulped a lump of fear and, putting his hands up, slowly turned.

Hector stared at Max through the plastic two-liter bottle of the makeshift gas mask. Beneath his bandolier, Max wore a vest embroidered with a nametag reading 'SGT. AT ARMS.' Beneath the rank was his name, 'MAD MAX.' A circular logo of a green serpent eating its tail adorned the opposite side of his vest.

"Fine, you got me, brother. I'll tell you whatever you want to know," Max said. "You probably wanna know how we tracked you. GPS tracker on your car, brother."

"Who from the CIA hired you?"

"CIA? Listen, brother, I don't know what the hell you're talking –"

Hector circled and aimed at the giant serpent patch on his vest, shooting him in the lower back.

Max held onto his back, screaming, bleeding, and cursing in pain, painting the blacktop red. "My back, you shot my fucking back!"

"I won't ask again."

"Okay, not CIA. He said he was NSA."

"Who?"

"I never got a name."

Hector shot him in the leg, "You'll have to do better than that."

Max screamed out once more and yelled, "You mother fucker!"

"I'll let you choose where the next bullet goes."

"I'm telling you, he never gave me his name," tears of pain streamed down his face. Max rolled onto his side to meet eyes with Hector. "I swear to Christ, he never gave me his name. I swear, I swear –"

Hector took aim at Max's groin.

"Okay, brother, wait, we called him Scarface."

"Scarface?"

"Yeah, real thin Nazi-looking bastard with scars across his face. That's all I know. I swear to Christ, that's all I know."

"I believe you." Hector pulled the trigger, and the side of Max's skull exploded.

Hector crouched at the body and removed the two-way radio clipped to Max's vest. In doing so, he noticed a small blood-splattered rectangular device attached to the other side of the vest.

Unfastening the bandanna off Max's neck, Hector used it to pluck the device off.

Smearing away the blood, Hector saw a video lens and an LED screen displaying information.

Someone was watching.

Hector looked into the device and said, "You're next."

He dropped the GoPro to the ground and smashed it with his boot.

Making his way to his Bronco, Hector turned the two-way radio channel to 17 and the sensitivity and volume to max. He waved the radio around the Bronco until it gave a high-pitched whine.

In the direction of the whine, Hector crouched and reached under and into the rear driver-side wheel well. He yanked out the GPS tracker magnetized to it.

15

Turning off Academy onto Airport Road, Porter and Mindy traveled Eastbound past a Burger King on one side and a mix of low-rent townhomes on the other. The crowning achievement was an intersection with a '90s Shell gas station in front of a run-down Dollar Store and laundromat shopping strip. The glow emanating from the buildings was warm orange compared to the cool white LEDs of the newly installed towering street lights.

"Turn here," Mindy said.

"Alright," Porter said as he puffed on his cigarette.

Turning into the dark neighborhood, Porter slowed, for a shirtless potbellied man rocking a mullet walked across the road drinking a beer. The man shielded his eyes from the truck's headlights and flicked them off.

The neighborhood was an assortment of chain link fences, barking dogs, and, upon closer inspection, what looked to be condemned townhomes. In several front yards, people sat on folding chairs, gathered around burn barrels, and, from the smell sifting into the truck's cab, smoking pot. A group of kids was huddled together in the road, looking at their phones. They didn't move for the truck.

"What the hell is wrong with these kids?" Porter asked.

"Social media never rests," Mindy said.

As Porter swerved around them, the kids looked up from their phones and shouted obscenities.

"Little assholes," Porter said, blowing out a plume of smoke.

"I told you it was a rough area," Mindy said.

"I'm pretty sure I've seen this neighborhood on an episode of Dog the Bounty Hunter."

"Turn in here," Mindy said, pointing at an intersecting road.

The neighborhood transitioned from townhomes to houses. Turning onto Wendy Ct., Porter slowly navigated through a narrow street of parked cars lining both sidewalks.

Mindy lowered her window and scanned each one-story house. Upon crawling towards the worse-looking one on the street, she poked a finger out, "That one."

Red curtains obstructed their view, but they could still make out silhouettes of people inside. Loud rock music escaped through the outer graffiti walls and into the night, and even from out here, they could smell traces of booze and weed. A half dozen Choppers cluttered the poorly shoveled driveway, and frost-sprinkled weeds made up the front yard.

"Jason's got company tonight," Porter said.

"Yeah," Mindy agreed.

Parking at the end of a cul-de-sac, Porter took a final drag on his cigarette before tossing it out, closing the window, and killing the engine.

Mindy began to open her door, and Porter put up a finger. "What?"

"Calm down there, killer."

"C'mon, we can take them."

"We?" Porter asked.

"Well, you can take out the big guys. I'll go for the smaller ones. You know, the weaker ones."

"Or, we try being smart about this," Porter reclined in his seat and, zipping up his jacket, stuck his hands in the pockets. "We wait until either the pack thins out or Jason leaves."

"So, what is this, a stakeout?"

"Stakeouts are half the job. I once did one for thirty hours to catch some husband cheating on his wife. C'mon, get comfy."

"Wait, if you did a lookout that long, what did you do when you had to, you know, use the bathroom?"

Reaching back to the bench seat, Porter picked up an empty plastic Coke bottle and dropped it in her lap.

"You're kidding, right?"

"You're telling me you've never pissed in a bottle?"

Mindy motioned to her lap. "Boss, I don't have the necessary plumbing."

"Excuses, excuses," reaching back again, Porter produced a yellow oil funnel. "That's why God invented this."

"Gross, I'm not taking a piss in that, or in front of you for that matter."

"Ah, you still have dignity. That's cute."

"You don't?"

"You lose a lot of it in Bootcamp."

"Yeah, I'll just hold it in if I have to go," Mindy said. Rubbing her hands together, Mindy looked out the window. It had stopped snowing, but a thin layer of frost was still on the ground. She pulled out her phone and checked the temperature, which read fourteen degrees.

"The car needs to stay off while we do this," Porter said.

"Yeah, I get it. We don't want to give away our position, makes sense."

"There's a blanket under the rear seat," Porter said.

"I'm fine, really," Mindy said, zipping up her leather jacket.

"So, you're shivering because it's cool?" Porter asked. "Alright, suit yourself. Wake me up if you see Jason."

"Wait, why do I have to stay up?"

"Because you're the rookie."

"Well, that's bullshit."

"Yep," Before drifting to sleep, Porter smirked as Mindy reached in the back, pulled out the blanket, and wrapped herself.

⚶

Two hours had passed, and even with earbuds in and Avril Lavigne's 'Love Sux' album blaring, Mindy could hear Porter snoring. Sipping down her coffee, she looked at his sleeping face.

She could see all the pain and scars of his life fade away. All the stress-induced aging disappeared like it was a bad dream.

Sleeping, he looked young.

The front door of the house opened. Jason, wearing a Wolfpack vest, stumbled out.

Mindy smacked Porter's shoulder.

"I'm up," he grumbled.

Jason's balance was off, and he seemed to be plucking at the stars as if they were right in front of his face. Looking at the bikes parked in the driveway, he tapped the top of each and shook his head while he moved down the line. He finally found his bike, mounted it, revved it, and drove off in a zig-zag.

"Mindy, you're up," Porter said, opening his door.

"What?"

Porter pointed to the steering wheel.

"I've never driven before."

"Listen, it's like fucking for the first time. You just dive in and figure it out." Porter squinted, "Are you gonna tell me you've never done that either?"

"You can be a real asshole, you know that?"

"That's the rumor," Porter said, walking around to the passenger side.

Mindy scooted into the driver's seat, turned the engine over, shifted the truck into drive, and pressed hard on the accelerator. The truck coughed forward, and she slammed on the brakes.

"Relax," Porter put a hand on hers, clutching the steering wheel, "take it slow."

She applied less pressure to the accelerator and began crawling the truck out of the neighborhood.

"Go a little faster. Keep it under twenty-five."

Following the road, she reached around the steering wheel, "How do you turn on the lights?"

"Leave them off for now. Wait until we get to a decent stretch of road with a few more cars."

"It's too dark. I can't see anything. What if I hit one of those kids?"

"Evolution in action."

"What if I wreck your truck?"

"I'll take it out of your paycheck."

"Wait, I'm supposed to be getting a paycheck?"

Turning out of the neighborhood, they could see Jason on his bike in the distance, illuminated by dim streetlights lining the road. The motorcycle swerved across lanes and even veered into the shoulder. It nearly collided with a guardrail but regained balance at the last moment.

When a few cars merged onto the road between them, Porter instructed, "Speed up to fifty and turn on the lights. The switch is to the left of the wheel. Two clicks."

"Two clicks," Mindy repeated. As she accelerated, the V8 roared, and a smile crept across her face.

"Feels good, doesn't it?"

"Yeah." Getting a feel for the road and the truck, Mindy used her blinker and passed up a vehicle. "Are we following him to another house?"

"He won't make it that far?"

"No?"

"With all that beer in his system, he's going to stop somewhere to piss. I bet you twenty bucks. It's that gas station." Porter pointed up the road. On the intersection of Airport Road and Powers, a gas station sat next to a McDonald's. Besides the attendant's beat-up '80s blue Pontiac, the lot was empty.

Jason pulled into the lot and walked into the Run 'N Go convenience store.

"Not bad," Mindy said.

"I have my moments."

Mindy crept the truck into the station, and Porter directed her to pull alongside a pump. Parking and killing the engine, they watched Jason stumble out of the convenience store, holding a key chained to a hubcap. He entered the exterior bathroom.

"Now what?" Mindy said.

Porter handed over his wallet, "Fill her up and get me a pack of Lucky Strike."

"Uh, they won't sell to me."

"Figure it out. All else fails, show the attendant a little ankle like a nice Amish girl."

Mindy called out as he walked off, "Where are you going?"

"To check on our friend."

❦

Porter crossed the blacktop and, at the restroom, tugged lightly on the handle. It was locked. Putting his ear to the door, he could hear piss splashing into a toilet.

Taking a knee, Porter reached into his utility belt and pulled out a bronze key with jagged teeth. He shoved the bump key into the lock and twisted it with the doorknob.

Porter got a full-frontal of Jason leaning over the urinal. Holding himself upright by the forearm and thumbing away at his phone, Jason was shaking out the last bit of piss, most of which hadn't reached the urinal.

"What the hell?" Jason slurred.

Porter kicked him in the side, knocking him over. "Remember me?"

Jason dropped his phone, and Porter stomped on it.

Laying on the yellow and blue cracked tile floor, Jason felt around his belt before finding his holster. He struggled to get his gun out.

Porter stepped on his hand, "Having trouble?" Before Jason could answer, Porter punched him in the gut.

As Jason doubled over, Porter yanked the belt out of the loops of the kids' pants, and the holster fell to the ground. Porter picked up the holster and, tossing away the dime bag of weed stuffed in the side pocket, examined the piece, "SIG Sauer M17. Where'd you get this?" Turning the tan pistol in his hand, he saw a bar code etched into the weapon, "Military issue?"

"Fuck you," Jason spat, now wielding a red-handled pocketknife.

"Really?" Porter asked, clipping the holster onto his belt. "With your dick hanging out and covered in piss, you're going to cut me?"

Seething with anger, Jason attempted to stand but slipped in urine. He got to his feet on his second attempt and leveled his knife. Porter now saw that embroidered on the front of his vest was a rank patch of "Member" and a name patch of "Pup."

"You are so fucked, man," Jason said. "I'm a badass mother fucker. You see my colors," he tugged on his vest.

"Okay, badass mother fucker, your move."

Jason flared his nostrils and, taking a deep breath, threw his pocketknife.

Instead of sticking, the knife's handle impacted Porter's chest and bounced off, landing on the floor.

They both looked down.

"That was your big move?" Porter asked.

"Yeah, that was my big move."

Porter stepped forward and clocked Jason in the face, dropping him.

Mindy walked inside and closed the door behind them. She took a noisy slurp from her Big Gulp and tossed the pack of cigarettes to Porter, "Happy Halloween, here's your treat."

Porter eyed the Lucky Strike pack.

"Showed a little ankle," she said.

"Atta' girl."

"Hey, I know you," Jason said from the floor, blood dripping between his fingers, grasping his nose. "You're Jen's sister. You and that bitch are gonna pay."

"Hey, Jason, sup?" Mindy said. Finding the dime bag on the floor, she examined it, "Betcha, I can sell this for ten whole dollars. Porter, I got breakfast."

Porter nodded to Mindy, "You got your Ka-bar?"

"Yeah, what do you have in mind?" Taking another sip, she unzipped her leather jacket and, reaching to her side, pulled the knife from its sheath.

Jason's eyes widened in fear.

"You ever scalped someone?" Porter asked.

"Are you fucking serious?" Jason asked.

"Did I stutter?"

"Seemed pretty clear to me," Mindy said.

Crouching next to Jason, Porter grabbed what little hair he had and yanked. "The first thing you'll want to do is give the hair a quick, strong jerk."

"Hey, that hurts, man," Jason protested.

Porter banged the back of Jason's head into the rear stall, "Shut up, I'm talking." He yanked again, "Then, take your knife," he used his hand to illustrate the movement, "and start at the turf and work it in a saw-like motion." He looked back to Mindy, "Wanna give it a try?"

"Sure, why not?" She approached and set the blade's edge on Jason's head below the front hairline, "Saw-like?"

"Okay, I'm sorry," Jason said.

"For what?' Porter asked.

"I tried to hit you with my car, man. Is that what you want to hear? My bad."

"Oh, that was you. I hadn't noticed, jerkoff," Porter said.

"What do you guys want?" Jason asked frantically. "Just tell me what the fuck you want."

"Porter, you didn't ask him?" Mindy asked.

"I was getting there," Porter told her. "Alright, Jason or Pup, whatever the hell you go by, who do you work for?"

"I'm in the Air Force."

"Uncle Sam ain't your only employer."

Jason's eyes shifted side-to-side, "I don't know what you're talking about."

Porter tugged his hair again, "You're not making a believer out of me, kid."

"Is this because I bought a dance with your Old Lady?"

"My Old Lady?"

"You know that blonde slut at the club. I saw her hanging all over you."

Porter punched him in the face again.

Jason cried out in pain.

Porter tugged Jason's hand away from his face, "C'mon, it's not that bad. Let me have a look."

Jason lowered his hands, revealing a disfigured nose adhered to a bloody face.

Porter punched him again.

"You mother fucker!" Jason yelled. "You broke my fucking nose."

"Oh, did I? Let me see," Porter said.

Jason glued himself to the stall and waved him off, "Get the fuck away from me."

"What'd you call that woman at the club, the blonde one?"

"Fuck…fuck…I don't remember her name."

Porter lit up a cigarette, "Think hard. Starts with an A."

"Alice, yeah, Alice, she's an angel, man. A damn angel."

"That's what I thought," Porter said as he blew a plume of smoke at Jason. "Now, who are you working for? Who ordered you to run me down? Unlikely, I pissed off Uncle Sam that much and I know for a fact your Wolfpack President didn't order the hit."

"American Iron paid me to do it."

"What's your relationship with them?"

"My relationship?"

"We already know the answer," Mindy told him. "Best for you to answer before Porter starts getting impatient."

"You've been patient this whole time? Shit," Jason said.

"Yeah, shit," Mindy agreed.

"Fine, a couple of us Pack boys do odd jobs for them."

"How many of you work for American Iron?"

"I don't know, maybe two dozen. American Iron only hires military or vets from the Pack. They pay us monthly to be on standby and available after hours to do whatever jobs they need."

"Who is your intermediary with American Iron? I doubt you're the brains between the Wolfpack and American Iron."

"Tattoo Tony cuts us the checks." Jason looked at Porter, "What? Were you not expecting that name?"

"Tattoo Tony is the Treasurer for the Pack?" Porter asked.

"Yeah, he says the money comes from American Iron."

"And Tattoo Tony is working behind the Wolfpack President's back?"

Jason shrugged, "I guess."

"Is Tattoo Tony's real name Frank Marion?"

"Frank Marion? No, who the hell is Frank Marion?"

Porter and Mindy exchanged a glance.

"Do these jobs involve breaking into homes and terrorizing people?" Porter asked.

"Whatever they need," Jason answered. "Look, I ain't proud of it, but money is money. Hey, some of the work is honest, too."

"Yeah, I'm sure you fucks are saving kittens outta trees," Porter said, puffing on his cigarette.

"Do you guys disguise yourselves on these jobs?" Mindy asked.

"Disguise ourselves?" Jason asked.

"Like wearing NVGs and gas masks?" Porter clarified.

"That's right," Jason answered.

"You check out the gear and weapons from the armory on base?" Porter asked.

"I know the armorer. I hook her up with the good shit, and she hooks us up. Lends us stuff off the books."

"Yeah, thought so," Porter said.

Mindy made an obnoxious slurp as she finished her drink and tossed it in the can. Crouching before Jason, she asked, "Where's Jen?"

"How the fuck would I know? She ditched me last year," Jason said.

"Say it ain't so, a stand-up piece of shit like you?" Porter said.

Mindy thumbed her phone and showed him a picture, "This is from a doorbell cam today. Do you recognize who she's with?"

"Shit, I don't know," Jason said.

"Wrong answer," Porter said, yanking on the hair once more, "On second thought, let's scalp his nuts first, and then we'll move to his head."

"If you say so," Mindy touched the blade to his groin.

"Wait, wait, let me look again," Jason studied the phone, "Okay, she's with Scott. Wait, you know Scott?"

"Yeah, we're old war buddies. We used the same port-a-shitters in Iraq. Very exciting. Where is he?" Porter asked.

"How the hell would I know? I only met him once when he was recruiting us for his organization."

Porter shrugged at Mindy, "Should we flip a coin for left nut, right nut?"

"One-Eye!" Jason yelled.

"One-Eye?" Porter asked. He looked at Mindy, and she exchanged a look of confusion with him.

"He works for American Iron, too?" Mindy asked.

"Yeah, One-Eye Jake is former Special Forces or something. He's the Sergeant of Arms for the Pack. He and Scott are close. He'll know where he's at."

Mindy nodded to Porter.

"Where is One-Eye now?" Porter asked.

"The bar, he's always at the bar."

"Which bar?" Mindy asked.

"Britney's."

"I know this place," Porter said. "You're not lying, are you?"

"No man, I swear, man, I swear."

"What does he look like?" Porter asked, "Your Sergeant of Arms, One-Eye?"

"I don't know, kinda fat, a bald spot on the top of his head. He has one of them, Mr. Monopoly mustaches."

"Mr. Monopoly mustaches?"

"Yeah, a curly one. You know what I mean, doncha?"

Using her Ka-bar, Mindy drew an imaginary curly mustache on her face.

"Alright," Porter looked at Mindy, "Satisfied?"

"I will be once he puts his junk up," Mindy said, pointing at his groin with her knife. "The damn thing is staring at me."

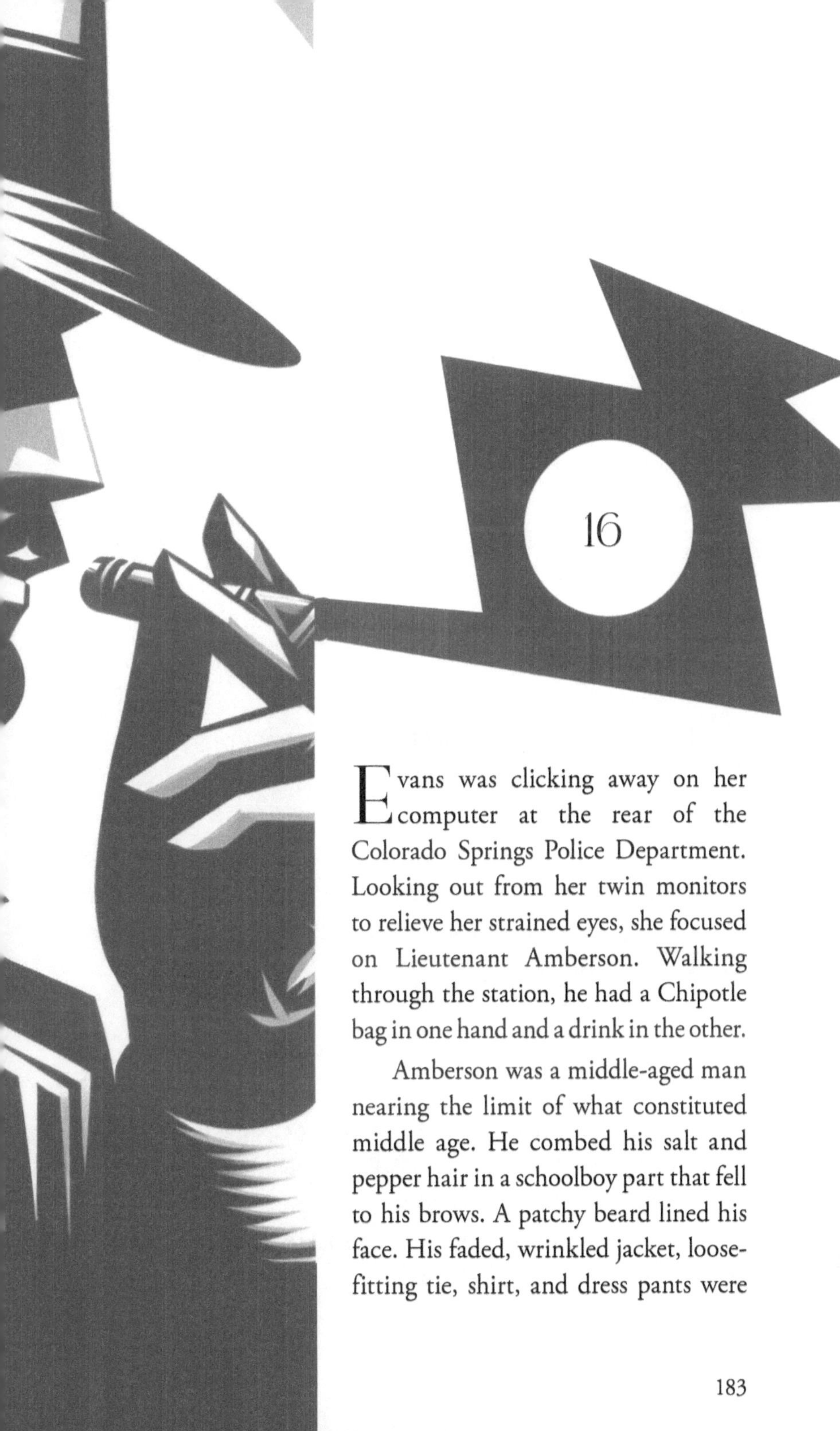

16

Evans was clicking away on her computer at the rear of the Colorado Springs Police Department. Looking out from her twin monitors to relieve her strained eyes, she focused on Lieutenant Amberson. Walking through the station, he had a Chipotle bag in one hand and a drink in the other.

Amberson was a middle-aged man nearing the limit of what constituted middle age. He combed his salt and pepper hair in a schoolboy part that fell to his brows. A patchy beard lined his face. His faded, wrinkled jacket, loose-fitting tie, shirt, and dress pants were shades of grey. Amberson was a sixteen-year veteran and only second to the Police Captain.

Before arriving at his desk, he stopped and joked with the rookie front desk Officer. Amberson was always chit-chatting with the rookies, getting to know them and making them feel welcome. He was a real people person.

Making his way to his desk facing Evans, he sat down his dinner and eyed her suspiciously, "I thought you went home for the day."

"Good evening, Detective Amberson," Evans said, rolling her chair out.

"Sarah, you and I are on a first-name basis. You're not a flat-foot anymore," he said, taking a noisy drink slurp.

"Sorry, Harry, it just –"

"After two months, being Detective status still hasn't sunk in, right?"

"No, I mean yes, but it's not that. Only one other person calls me Sarah."

"Boyfriend?"

"Not exactly."

"Umm, hmm, someone leads an exciting nightlife. But, hey, I'm not judging," Amberson said. "Believe it or not, I was young once, too."

Evans shook her head.

"Chips and salsa?" He said, producing them from his bag.

"No, thanks."

"So, not that I don't like the evening company, but I take it you're not here to chat?" Amberson said, munching away on a chip and getting a few pieces stuck in his beard.

"Well, I had just finished evening Mass and was on my way home when the Captain called me in."

"Yikes, surprise meetings with the Captain are never good."

"Tell me about it," Evans said, returning her concentration to the computer. "Until she calls me in, I'm just working on a few reports."

Amberson dipped a chip in salsa and, leaning back in his chair, looked at the ceiling, "You know, my ex was into the whole church scene. And I must admit, it was always good for the soul when I went. But, I gotta tell you, Sarah, I've never met a religious person without a guilty conscience." He wagged a chip at her, "But I've worked with you long enough to think you might be the exception."

Evans shook her head, "I'm no angel."

"No one is, but you're a good person." Amberson chuckled, "This may be the wrong job for you."

"Or, it might just make me perfect for the job."

"You're a glass-half-full type of person, aren't you?"

"Always."

As Amberson continued munching on his chips, he logged into his computer and began clicking away.

"Lemme ask you something. Were you nervous when you made Detective?" Evans asked.

"Now we're digging deep into the history books," Amberson said, wiping his mouth and beard. He thought momentarily and grinned, "When I was promoted, it took what seemed like a year for it to sink in. I would still report to the desk Officer out of habit – telling him every time I stepped out of the building or took a piss. One day, I accidentally put on my patrol uniform. I nearly got to work before remembering I was supposed to wear a suit and tie. But, trust me, it'll wear off."

"That's good. Hey, changing topics, do you know why the patrols were pulled from the Peterson's house?"

"Yeah," he said slyly.

"Well?"

"Well, last I checked, you've been pulled from that case."

"I know, but —"

"You're going to have to take it up with the Captain," he said, taking a bite out of his burrito. Harry's phone rang, and mouthing 'every time,' he wiped his mouth and, speed chewing and swallowing, answered. "Detective Amberson," he paused and nodded, "okay, I'll let her know." He hung up the phone, "Speak of the Devil. She has summoned you to her fresh new layer of Hell."

"She knows I have a phone, right? Why does she always call you?"

"Let's just say…" he took a bottle of Tabasco out of his drawer and sprinkled the burrito, "if I were you, I'd go in swinging. That *statie* has a hard-on for you."

Grabbing her case files, Evans stood and danced her fingers on her desk. "Go in swinging, huh? You really think that'll work?"

Amberson's phone rang again. He looked at it sorely, reluctantly put down his burrito, and shook his head as he picked up the line.

Walking down a hall of cubicles and past the records office, Evans stopped at the frosted glass door, which read 'Captain Denise Easley.' Evans felt like she was back in High School, standing before the Principal's Office. This had only happened in Sophomore year when she and Porter got caught making out in the janitor's closet.

With a deep breath, she rapped her knuckles across the door.

"Come in," the voice within the office said.

Evans entered and met the long stare of Captain Easley. She was a thin woman in her early fifties who wore her obviously dyed black hair in a bob. Her high cheek-boned face was smoothed over with foundation covering her wrinkles. She wore a pressed suit with a neutral texture, giving her a masculine look.

Easley had been a high-ranking state cop recently transferred to the Captain's seat. Her office looked almost moved in, but a few boxes still needed unpacking. Sitting atop one of them was a framed 8x10 of Easley and the Denver Mayor shaking hands on the green in front of City Hall.

"Close the door," Easley said, adjusting her framed Master's degree, which hung behind her Mahogany desk. The degree was from Stanford, so naturally, she must have thought it meant something extra special.

After closing the door, Easley motioned Evans to the leather chair facing the desk. Evans sat as the Captain continued to stand.

This was all mind games.

"Good, I meant to speak with you," Easley said.

"Yes, ma'am, you did call me in," Evans said.

"You can lose that micro aggressive attitude right now. Last I checked your salary, I can call you whenever I want and make you work as many hours as possible. Got it?"

"Okay," Evans said. She had a bad feeling about this conversation.

"I wanted to ask you a question."

Evans wanted to scream, "Well, no shit," but she remained silent. A Mark Twain quote, etched on a sign hanging in her apartment, rang in her ears: "It's better to remain silent and be thought a fool than to open one's mouth and remove all doubt."

"When did you get promoted to Captain?" Easley asked.

"Excuse me?"

"It's a simple question. I know you were recently promoted to Detective status two months ago, but when did you get promoted to Captain?"

"I didn't." Evans knew where this was going, but unfortunately, she had to play it through. Once upon a time, during her High School years, her father, the policeman, had a similar conversation with Porter.

Word had gotten around town that she and Porter had slept together. When her father found out, he insisted Porter come over for dinner. When Porter entered the house, her father locked the door behind him. He removed his tie, rolled up his sleeves, put up his dukes, and asked, "So, when did you become a real man?"

"Ah, that's right, you didn't make Captain," Easley said, breaking Evans from reminiscing further. "Did you?"

This would be a by-the-book ass-chewing, and like any ass-chewing, you just had to sit there and take it like a champ. Just as Porter did all those years ago, hopefully with fewer punches.

"Well?" Easley asked.

"I'm not the Captain," Evans hissed.

"Good, we're on the same page. So, who the hell do you think you are to dispatch two of my units to the Peterson's house?" As she said this, her pink lips curled into a Disney villain-like smile. "After your O.K. Corral stunt at the hotel, I pulled you from the case, remember?"

Evans had dealt with people like Easley her entire life. People so high on their self-righteous pedestal they thought they could never fall off, like her father.

"Captain, the call was made before you took me off the case. Their house got broken into," Evans said, placing the case file on Easley's desk. "They're boarding up their doors and putting tarps over their windows every night just to stay safe."

"Are they now?" She didn't bother looking at the case file. It was beneath her. "Thanks for that new information, Detective. Let's return to my original question. Who do you think you are to dispatch two of my units?"

The grin of hers was beginning to annoy Evans. On second thought, Evans wished she would have gone in swinging as Amberson suggested, and perhaps that would have wiped the smile off her Stanford-educated face.

"I didn't think I needed the approval to dispatch two units," Evans said. "After an event, should the family feel threatened, it's standard operating –"

"Don't preach the SOPs to me. You ran wild here when Gordon was in charge, but that ends now. Starting with you," she pointed a thin, frail finger at her. "We are doing things by the book. Do you understand me?"

There was an air of silence as Evans absorbed the statement, and Easley waited for a response.

"Okay," Evans said, "do you have those books available for everyone to review?"

Easley's smile dropped, and she sighed, "Alright, let's address this." Leaning on her bookshelf filled with course books on Psychology, Sociology, Forensics, and Criminology, Easley crossed her arms over her chest. "I'm going to be frank with you because of your rank. You and I have a different relationship than most of your patrol pals outside that door, okay?"

"Okay."

"To be perfectly honest, I'm not overly impressed with you."

Evans had known this because, for starters, she had gotten *that* sort of vibe the first day she had met Easley. Second, it was the talk of the station. According to Harry, who gossiped with everyone, the rumor was that either Easley would fire Evans or Evans would get Porter to inflict harm on Easley. Some of the boys even had bets going. Third, this wasn't their first talk.

So, how else did you respond to someone saying they weren't impressed with you, other than, "Okay."

"Okay, is that all you say?" Easley asked.

"What do you want me to say, Captain?"

Easley's grin resurfaced, a perfected eat-shit-and-die grin of a face. "Your file says you went to a community college for your associate degree," she said disappointedly. "Then you went to CSU Pueblo for your bachelor's in criminology. CSU is not a prestigious college like Stanford, but it is accredited. You had a solid career in homicide, was promoted to Sergeant pretty quickly, then promoted to Detective following your actions in the Sandman case."

"That's right," Evans said.

"This entire department, even the Mayor, think of the Sandman case as quite successful. But anyone who reads that case file and really reads between the lines," Easley squinted as she continued, "can easily see how you guys dropped the ball. Talk about embarrassing. I hate to say it, but you were promoted under false pretenses."

"False pretenses? We broke up a massive weapons deal, got the killer, and freed the people who had been held hostage."

"We? This department hardly did anything. All it did was show up in the eleventh hour to take credit. Your little buddy, the vigilante, Private Investigator Ryan Porter, interfered so much that, as dumb luck would have it, he inadvertently solved the case. All while killing people left and right, including the main suspect. Not to mention costing the city over a $100 thousand dollars in damages." She counted on her fingers, "Automotive, structural, road –"

Evans interrupted, "Without Porter, the case –"

Easley interjected, "You would have made Detective years ago. Porter's an unwashable stain on your somewhat respectable career." She picked up the tablet on her desk, "I ran a background check on your buddy. Porter has hero syndrome tattooed across his forehead."

"I'm going to have to disagree, Captain."

She read the tablet, "Ex-Marine with two combat tours –"

"Former Marine," Evans corrected. "The only ex-Marine is Lee Harvey Oswald."

"Stop interrupting me," Easley said. "Let's continue, shall we? Combat tours in Iraq and Afghanistan. He was taken as a POW in Iraq when his unit got ambushed, rescued by a U.S. raid after two months, and returned to the States, highly decorated.

A medical discharge forced him out of the Marines at the rank of Sergeant. He got his Private Investigator License online last year," she sighed. "He was credited with solving a dozen cases, including the Sandman case a few months back."

"Doesn't sound like too bad of a resume."

Easley put down the tablet. "Well, the devil is in the details. Every case he's involved in leaves bodies, shell casings, and mountains of paperwork for this department. He has a kill count on his file. A kill count!" She smacked her hand on the desk so hard she began rubbing it afterward.

"Uhh –" Evans began to say. She was unsure if she was going to defend Porter's actions or not. Before she could say much more, Easley continued.

"Who has that? His count is in the double digits." Easley shook her head, "His tactics and his interrogation techniques are inhumane," she sighed. "Quite frankly, he's worse than half the inmates we lock up. The only notable achievements he has is, let's see," she inspected the tablet again. "A winning lottery ticket a few years back, an Associate of Art, and he owns a strip club."

"I'm not sure I would label him worse than the inmates we lock up."

"At the hotel, he tortured the main suspect, Joshua, excessively, might I add, and you didn't even bother to stop him. You realize he inflicted multiple cigarette burns on the victim and broke nearly every bone in his body?"

"Mindy and I were tending to the two girls until backup arrived."

"Oh yes, Mindy Miller, the underage girl you used in the sting operation. How could I forget?"

"Without her help, we would have never known what they were doing there."

Easley shook her head, "It was only a matter of time before we raided the hotel."

"Only a matter of time? Captain, tell that to the victims."

Easley leaned against her desk and crossed her legs, "Detective, I don't know how you two got a U.S. Senate candidate in your back pocket. But trust me, Bobbi Johnson is the only reason you two aren't facing charges for killing those people."

"Those killings were justified. Internal Investigations proved it."

Easley nodded, "Yes, *excessive use of force was justified,* was their conclusion. You two found those missing girls, didn't you? But you got lucky this time. Had you gone in there and killed those men and not found anyone, not even Bobbi Johnson could save your ass."

"Porter's good," Evans said. "His methods may be unorthodox, but every time I've worked with him, it's been for the best."

"You stick up for him a lot, don't you?"

"Excuse me?" Evans said.

"Yes, I know you two were High School sweethearts. The hallways talk."

She was out of line. "Captain –"

"I get it. You're still close to Porter, but move past High School. He's dead weight. It's only a matter of time before he screws up. I nail him with something, and he finds himself in a holding cell. This is a professional recommendation, and I can't make you stop sleeping with him –"

"I'm not sleeping with him!" Evans snapped.

Easley grinned and asked, "Defensive?"

Evans was gritting her teeth, which she hadn't done since her days at the Academy. A force of habit before getting tasered in the chest or pepper-sprayed in the eyes. Ironically, these were the two specific things she wanted to do to Easley.

"Your personal relationship with Porter is impacting this department. I've already counseled you about this once. This is now the second time. There won't be a third. Now, I don't know how many times you blew Gordon and Amberson to make Detective before I got here, but," she gestured to her groin, "I got nothing to blow on. So, let me make something perfectly clear. If you test me on this, the Peterson case, or your relationship with Porter impacting my department, I will make your career a living hell. You understand me?"

Evans could only stare in controlled anger. At her sides, her knuckles turned white. This belittling reminded her of her father.

"Five words I want to hear," Easley said. "Yes, Captain, I understand you," she paused, awaiting a response. "What's wrong? Do they not teach syntax in Community Colleges?"

Evans stood and, reaching for the door, met her stare. She didn't know whether to bark "fuck you" or beg for her career and say, "Yes, Captain, I understand you." Evans was always good at taking the high ground and being the better person, but today wasn't her day, including her earlier meeting with Porter.

She remained silent, fuming.

Easley shrugged, "Fine, I wouldn't get too comfortable with your fancy new desk." She held up the case file, "Don't forget to give this to Detective Amberson."

Evans snatched it from Easley and left the office.

Storming down the length of the station and with fury pulsing through her veins, she sat and, crossing her arms on the desk, buried her head in them and let out a long groan of annoyance.

"That good, huh," Amberson said.

"That statie hates me," Evans growled, peeking up.

Amberson slurped on his drink, "Look at it this way…in this city, chances are she'll be out of a job in six months. She'll either get shot, kidnapped, or fired."

"That's six months too many."

"Ain't that the truth?" Amberson licked his lips as he often did when coming up with something witty, "Sarah, you can't let that statie see you like this. It'll just add fuel to the fire. We all have days when we want to take our gun and shoot up the place. But listen, you gotta keep trucking."

Evans stared at him in bewilderment, "Shoot up the place?"

Amberson rolled his eyes, "Oh great, now I'm the monster?" Harry's phone rang, and picking up the receiver, he said, "Graham Central Station, Detective Amberson," he nodded, "Right, I'll be right there."

"What's up?"

"Statie wants to chew my ass now." Locking his monitor, he stood and stretched, "Finish up and get out of here. I'll hold Lucifer's daughter at bay as long as I can so you can retreat."

"Thanks, Harry. Sorry if I got you in trouble."

Amberson shrugged, "Pretty girls getting me into trouble? I got over that two ex-wives ago."

17

Walking into Britney's, Mindy stayed close to Porter. There was the smell of alcohol, the old jukebox hard at work, and the clang of a cue ball connecting with the siding of a billiards table. Mindy was familiar with the same atmosphere after working at a strip club. The clientele in biker vests with wolf patches embroidered on their backs was the difference.

Porter seemed right at home, sporting his well-worn leather jacket and packing as if walking into a business meeting.

Eyes followed them as they headed to the bar and took a seat. A mason jar full of crumpled dollars was sitting atop the counter, and a sticky note that said 'JUST PUT THE TIP IN, SEE HOW IT FEELS' adhered to the glass.

Ordering a Coors Light, Porter seemed oblivious to the dozen occupants staring at them. But Mindy knew Porter saw more than he let on. He was constantly surveying, continually strategizing.

"You want a drink?" Porter asked.

"Uh, water."

"Add a water," Porter told the older woman behind the counter. She looked like she had been pretty once, but age and wrong choices had gotten the better of her. She would be perfect in a cigarette commercial, "This was me at twenty." The commercial would show a picture of a cute girl. "Now look at me," flashforward to age sixty, baggy eyes, skeleton cheeks, veiny throat, the works. "You must be, Britney."

"Umm-hmm," Britney said as she fixed the drinks. "You two look lost." She stared at Porter's jacket, "This ain't no air hangar, Maverick." Her eyes rested on Mindy, "And it's a bit late for kids." There was a hint of a North Eastern drawl, maybe Boston.

"Nope," Porter said, "not lost."

"And it's not a school night," Mindy told her matter-of-factly.

Britney slapped the drinks on the counter. Her eyes lingered on Mindy. "Why are you here?"

Porter downed half the Coors and gestured to the window, "Where's the guy who rides that girl's bike out there?"

"What the hell are you talking about?"

"The Harley Davidson Sportster out there. It smells like potpourri and shits glitter from its exhaust."

"Careful, mister," Britney said in a hushed voice. Her eyes surveyed the bikers behind them, and Mindy saw her giving them a 'stay-put' look. It was evident she was in charge.

"I'm looking for One-Eye Jake," Porter said.

Britney picked up a glass and began wiping it with a rag. She worked the glass with authority and years of stress. "What do you want with One-Eye?"

"You know him?"

"I know everyone here."

"I want to talk to him."

"About what?"

"I'm working on a case and was hoping he could help me."

She stared at them hard, "You two don't look like pigs."

"Private investigator," Porter said, flashing his badge.

"Detective, huh?" She didn't look amused. "Should have told me you were a cop. I might have believed that." Britney snickered and turned to Mindy, "You a detective too?"

"Aspiring," Mindy said.

"It's good to have goals," Britney said to her. "I used to be pretty like you. I was going to be a famous actress. In the '90s, I was an extra on an episode of Friends. Then I got knocked up, and here I am." She grinned wide and inspected the glass she was cleaning, "What's this case about?"

"We're looking for someone," Mindy told her, taking the lead in the conversation.

"Umm-hmm."

"Goes by the name of Jen Miller."

"You look like her," Britney said.

"She's my sister."

"Okay, I'll buy that. So, what does One-Eye have to do with Jen?"

"You already know the answer to that," Porter said.

"Sure I do," she said with a sly grin. "But I want to hear it from you."

Before Porter could answer, Mindy retook the lead, "I hired Porter to find Jen, and we're led to believe she's dating some guy named Scott."

"Some guy?" Britney asked with a smirk.

Mindy continued, "We can't find Scott but hear that One-Eye is his buddy. We were going to check if One-Eye knows where Scott is, and hopefully, we'll find Jen."

Britney wasn't sold and exchanged a glance from Mindy to Porter. After a long moment, she said, "You two seem to hear quite a bit."

"Is One-Eye here or not?" Porter asked.

"You're not much of a people person, are you, Detective?"

"You're one to talk," Porter said. "The people who tolerate you daily are the real heroes."

Britney shook her head and turned to Mindy, "You shouldn't let him talk."

"Easier said than done," Mindy said to Porter's annoyance

"I haven't seen Jen in a few days," Britney said. "Yep, she's Scott's girl, but be careful poking around here." The bathroom door opened, and Britney pointed to the man who walked out. "There's One-Eye. Talk to him, and then I suggest you leave. My boys don't like cops or a Detective, for that matter. It gets them jumpy. I hear it's bad for your health."

Porter downed his Coors and slapped a five onto the counter, "I'm livin' on borrowed time."

They walked to the Billiards table where One-Eye was at. A chunky man with a bald spot and a spindled mustache was caressing the tip of his stick with chalk. He wore plastic aviator wings and a name tag that read 'ONE-EYE' on his black leather Wolfpack vest.

"You lookin' for me?" the man growled.

"One-Eye?" Porter asked.

"One-Eye Jake, the one and only."

"You have both eyes."

"That I do," he said.

Mindy chimed in, "Then why are you called One-Eye?"

"Britney didn't tell you?" He unbuckled his belt and grabbed his jeans. "Let me show you, behold the marvel!"

"Not in front of the girl!" Britney yelled from the bar.

"C'mon Mama, they want to know," he argued.

"Put it up, or you're gonna be called No-Eyes."

One-Eye waved her off, buckled his belt, and readjusted his jeans.

"So, I take it you've only got one, uh –" Mindy began to say.

"Nut?" One-Eye looked down at his lap, "Lost it in Iraq."

"Okay, I gotta ask," Porter said.

"You been to the sandbox?"

"Once or twice."

"So, you know those camel spiders out there?"

"Yeah."

"Yeah," One-Eye told him.

Porter cringed. "Didn't know they could do that."

"Neither did I."

"We're looking for Jen Miller," Mindy said, changing subjects.

"Don't I know you?" he said, staring at her. "Something about you looks familiar."

"I'm her sister."

"Yeah, I can see that," he said. He wagged his pool stick at Porter, "And you are?"

"He's a Detective," Britney shouted from behind the counter, "play it cool. Just answer their questions."

"You going to arrest her?" One-Eye asked.

"No," Porter told him, "just need to find her."

"Why?"

Porter looked to Mindy, and she audibled.

"Our mom has terminal cancer," Mindy said. "She's only got a few days left to live. She and Jen are close, and I know she'd want to see her before…." Mindy began tearing up, and her voice cracked as she said, "Well, you know."

"Yeah, I know. Damn, cancer, huh?" One-Eye said, twirling his mustache, "My Uncle had that. Talk about some nasty stuff. Uh, sorry."

"Thanks," Mindy said. She glanced at Porter, who was holding back his famous smirk.

"I just had dinner with Scott and Jen a few hours ago. That's where I got these fancy wings," he said, smirking and poking at his plastic aviator wings.

The bar doors opened, and Jason appeared with a bandage across his nose and sporting a black eye. He took two steps, reared his head to a tall, thick guy who had followed him and pointed to Porter and Mindy. "There they are. Those are the two that tried to scalp me!"

The bar went silent, and all eyes lasered in on the guests of honor.

"You rough up, my boy?" One-Eye asked.

Reaching into his jacket, Porter pulled out his pack of cigarettes and pulled a death stick out. He lit up, took a deep drag, and, running his fingers across the green felt of the Billiards table, grabbed a ball. "Mindy, take a step back."

She did so.

One-Eye swung out with his pool stick.

Porter ducked and shot up, bashing the red-striped 11 under One-Eye's chin. Before One-Eye could hit the floor, Porter pitched the 11 into the throat of the thick biker standing next to Jason.

Pulling the plastic wings off One-Eye's vest, Porter pulled out his revolver and leveled it at Britney, who was reaching for her gun under the counter. "Don't, just don't."

Mindy pulled out her Beretta and pointed it toward the occupant bikers.

"You won't shoot us," one of them told her.

"Let's rush them," another said.

Mindy pointed her gun at a table and blasted away an empty beer can. "Try it."

The bikers stopped in place.

"You two are making the biggest mistake of your lives," Britney said. "No one roughs up my boys and gets away with it."

"Lady, this can end one of two ways," Porter said. "First, we walk out of here, and no one has to die."

"Second?"

"People die, and we still walk out of here."

Britney stared at him hard before announcing to the bar, "Let them leave."

Porter and Mindy backed out of the bar. Their weapons were leveled at any pair of eyes crossing their barrels. Mindy was first to leave, and as Porter was nearly out the door, he passed by Jason.

Jason poked a blood-crusted finger into Porter's chest, "We're going to kill you. You hear?"

Porter grabbed the index finger and bent it until it snapped, "Shut up."

Porter kept his gun trained on Britney as he backed out. When the doors closed, he holstered his piece and rushed to his truck. Along the way, he saw the row of bikes had been kicked over.

"Waiting on you," Mindy said from the truck's passenger seat.

"No shit," Porter said, hopping into the cab, turning over the engine, and peeling out of the lot. Looking in the rearview mirror, he saw the bar patrons standing by their knocked-over bikes, cursing, shoving, and yelling at one another. "They're really pissed off."

"Yeah, about that, I kinda slit their tires too."

Porter chuckled and lit a cigarette, "Not bad, Jailbait. Not bad at all."

"Learn from the best."

"By the way, nice waterworks back there with the cancer mom bit. You were pretty convincing."

"What bit? She actually has cancer."

Porter turned to her, "Damn, Mindy, I didn't know."

Mindy giggled, "Damn, I am good."

"Enjoy the moment. A broken clock is right twice a day."

"Love you, too." Mindy laughed. Looking at the dark road, she asked, "So, where are we going?"

Porter stopped at a light and turned to her, "Oh, this is precious. I'm going to savor this."

"What?"

"You're telling me there's something that Junior Detective of the Year Ms. Mindy Miller doesn't know and needs my expert knowledge to figure out."

"Shut up," she laughed, "just tell me where we're going."

As the light turned green, Porter accelerated and cut into the far lane. "You didn't find anything weird about Mr. Monolopy?"

"You mean besides the story of why he's called One-Eye?"

"Yeah, besides that."

"I dunno, he was wearing aviator wings."

"Plastic aviator wings," Porter said, taking them out of his jacket and handing them to her.

"Okay, plastic, what difference does that make?" she inspected the silver wings.

"Let me ask you something? Where in this city can you get plastic aviator wings?"

"Just tell me."

"Just answer the question."

"I dunno, a Halloween store or toy store."

Porter turned onto an intersecting street, "A toy store? Have I told you lately that seeing your mind at work is a real honor?"

"Screw you."

"I'm not that bored, and you're not that lucky."

"Fine, an airplane. Don't they give them to kids on airplanes?"

"And the lightbulb finally goes off," Porter slowed and merged into the right-turn lane. Sitting at the red light, he pointed out the window to a ninety-seven-foot Lockheed C-130 Hercules military transport aircraft parked parallel to the adjacent road. A sizeable brown and tan building adjoined the port side of the plane.

"The Aircraft Restaurant," Mindy said, reading the long illuminated sign erected in the snow-covered landscape facing the road.

"Yep, they got a nice view in the bar," Porter said, flicking his spent cigarette out the window.

"Uh, huh, blonde, brunette, or redhead?"

"You know me too well."

"Unfortunately."

Turning at the light, Porter went down the road and turned in at the Radisson hotel entrance, which shared the restaurant parking lot.

Parking, Porter and Mindy edged up in their seats. The double red front doors leading into the restaurant were decorated with airline stickers. Beyond them, the inside was dark.

"It looks closed," Mindy said.

"Well, yeah, what did you expect this late?"

"Dammit," Mindy sighed. She stared in the rearview mirror and squinted.

"What?"

"Hold on," Mindy left the cab and walked across the lot. There was a blue Charger parked near the hotel's entrance. Illuminating the car's interior with her phone, she nodded and returned to the truck. "She's here. That's her car."

Porter stepped out, "You sure?"

"Yep, I recognize the fuzzy dice she hangs off her rearview mirror. Plus, the passenger side is littered with trash. It's hers."

"Good enough for me."

Walking into the hotel lobby, a short brunette receptionist greeted them. "Good evening." Her voice was squeaky, and she looked young.

Mindy leaned into Porter and whispered, "So, how do you want to do this? How about you create a diversion, and I'll check the security cameras, or –"

"Or you can just ask if your sisters checked in."

"Well, yeah, I guess I can do that."

"Okay, all you."

"Where are you –" Mindy began to ask, but seeing Porter walk towards the bar, she nodded, "Oh, right."

"Can I help you?" the receptionist asked.

"Hi," Mindy said, "my sister checked in earlier and wanted me to meet her, but her phone died before she could give me her room number. Could you tell me what room she's in?"

"Sure," the receptionist said, "what's her name?"

"Jen Miller."

"Let me check." The receptionist clicked away at her computer. "No, I'm not seeing anyone by that name."

"Really?" Mindy pondered on this momentarily and shrugged, "Well, she does have a stage name, Esmeralda."

The receptionist smiled wide and nodded, "Yep, now I remember." She clicked away once more, "Pretty girl, wearing lots of jewelry, came in with some guy. He looks familiar, but I didn't get his name. Anyway, she's in room 107. Did you want me to call the room for you? I can let her know you're coming."

"No, that's alright, thanks."

Mindy crossed the deserted lobby to the black marble hightop at which Porter sat. He had his phone to his ear, sipping down a Coors Light.

Mindy declined a drink from the cute blonde with pigtails wearing a black shirt that said, 'All this and brains too.'

"Nope, we're still following the leads. Nothing on Frank Marion, yet. I'll let you know if we have an update." Porter flipped his phone closed and shook his head. "Bobbi says hi."

"What was that all about?"

"Just giving her an update. Any luck on your end?"

"Yep, room 107."

Porter slapped a five onto the counter and downed his beer, "Thanks, Terri."

Terri looked up from her phone, "See ya next time, Mr. Porter."

As they left the bar, they turned at the hall and, cutting past the corner for the swimming pool entrance, stopped at room 107.

Porter banged on the door.

No answer.

They waited a moment, and Porter banged away once more.

A man's voice pleaded inside, "C'mon, be a man, be a fucking man about it. Take it!"

"Well, someone's in there," Mindy said, with her ear pressed to the door

"Take it! No, don't, please, don't. Oh God!" the man inside squealed.

"Shit, someone's getting murdered in there," Mindy said.

Porter shook his head and lit a cigarette, "Rookie, trust me, no one's getting murdered in there."

"Help me please, let me go, let me go. Oh God, Timmy, take it. Noooo!"

"Do something!" Mindy shouted.

"I'm telling you –" Porter began to say.

"Porter!" she insisted.

"Fine, stand back!" With a heave, Porter kicked at the side of the doorknob, crashing the door in.

Mindy rushed inside and stopped at the bed. Porter slowly followed.

A naked, stout man wearing a black spiked collar and sporting short blond hair and a walrus mustache was on all fours atop the bed. Sweat dribbled down his flesh, and he was panting hard. A humiliated look streaked across his plump pink face.

A matching black leash was attached to the man's collar. Tugging on it was an alluring naked and familiar-looking thin woman. She had wide shoulders, long blonde hair that curled at the tips, and grey eyes. She wore elbow-length shiny black gloves and sported a strap-on buried inside the man's ass.

A cigarette was perched between her glossy pink lips, and she looked at Mindy and nodded, "Hey, sis."

Mindy returned the shrug, "Hey."

Porter pulled out his phone and snapped a picture.

18

Walrus mustache pulled away from Jen and rolled off the opposite side of the bed, hiding. "Oh my God, I don't have my pants on," he said.

"Yeah, I think that's the least of your worries," Porter said.

"Get out! Get out!" the man yelled in a panic.

Jen took out her cigarette and blew out a plume of smoke, "It might be best if you guys wait in the hallway. Someone has to collect himself."

Mindy was quick to exit the room.

Porter studied Jen for a moment longer. He liked what he saw.

"Before you leave, you want to hand me that bathrobe?" she said, nodding to the bathroom while unbuckling the strap-on fixed to her pelvis.

Porter pulled the thin white cotton robe from the hook on the back of the bathroom door and held it out for her.

Jen tossed the strap-on into a duffle bag and pulled off her gloves. She grabbed the robe from Porter, "Thanks." Covering herself, she fastened the straps across her torso and turned. "You mind?"

Porter smirked and tied her off.

Jen smiled and, blowing out a plume of smoke, eyed him. "Been a while, Boss. How you been?"

Before he could answer, the man who had rolled off the bed peeked over the top of the mattress and barked, "Get out! Get out!"

They both left the room, and Jen closed the door behind them.

Mindy was glued to the wall, eyes closed and shaking her head.

"What's your problem?" Jen said.

"I can never unsee that!" Mindy said.

"Don't be such a child. You've seen me at work before."

"But never...doing *that*. I mean, seriously?"

Jen shrugged, "Hey, some guys like a classic suck and fuck, some like getting their toes licked, others like getting pounded in the ass. Who am I to judge?" Taking a deep drag on her cigarette, she and her sister exchanged a silent argument with their eyes and facial expressions. She rolled her eyes and turned to Porter, "And this one likes blondes."

Mindy pointed a finger between them, "Oh, god, when you worked at the club, did you two? On second thought, nope, never mind, I don't want to know."

After a thorough inspection, Jen paced around Porter and smiled, "Boss, you haven't changed a bit. I never told you this back then, but I wouldn't charge you a penny."

Porter eyed her once more, "Likewise."

"Oh, thank god," Mindy said.

"So defensive," Jen said. "Or jealous?"

Mindy blushed, "Jen, don't be ridiculous –"

"I was sixteen once, too," Jen interrupted. "Didn't stop me from daydreaming about getting rammed by a much older Johnny Depp."

The door cracked open, and a clothed man inside hissed, "What do you want?"

Jen rolled her eyes, "Be nice."

Porter stepped past Jen and, forcing the door open with a kick, knocked the man onto his back. Porter got a good look at him. His '80s Action movie look alerted Porter to who he was. "Well, who do we have here?"

"You first! Who are you? Just who the hell are you? Her pimp?" the man said, getting to a vertical base. "You have no business here."

"Mr. Family Man, running for U.S. Senate, Tim Styles," Porter said.

"Oh yeah," Mindy said, "I thought I recognized him from somewhere."

Styles' cheeks went flush, and he pulled on his collar.

"What's wrong? You look nervous," Porter said.

Styles turned to Jen, "You know them, don't you? Did you set me up? You called that girl your sister. I'm not paying for this."

Jen sighed, "Timmy, it's just my sister and –"

"Just your sister?" Styles advanced towards her and reared back a fist, "You stupid whore!"

Porter caught the punch and sent out one of his own. Styles' face absorbed the impact, and he spun around before colliding into the window at the room's rear.

"Hurts, don't it?" Porter asked.

"Damn," Jen said approvingly.

Holding onto his swollen face, Styles turned to him, "You stupid fuck. You have no idea what you've done."

Porter stepped up to him and, grabbing a handful of his hair, slammed the back of his skull into the window, "Enlighten me."

Styles stared at him momentarily and then, summoning the courage, said, "You just hit a U.S. Senate candidate. Do you have any idea what connections I have? I have people all over this city. I say a name and point a finger, and they'll cut you into little pieces of dog shit. You're a dead man. You hear me?"

"Yeah, and what good does that do you right now?" Porter asked him before repeatedly smacking the back of his head into the window, cracking the glass.

Styles cried out.

"Damn," Jen said again.

"Uh, Boss," Mindy said.

"Okay, I'm sorry, I'm sorry," Styles whimpered.

Porter stopped and pulled him close, "What did you say? Speak up. Use your man voice."

"I'm sorry!" he yelled.

"Whaddya telling me for, Timmy? Tell her," Porter jerked his head towards Jen.

"I'm sorry, okay," he said to her. His eyes focused on Porter, "What do you want?"

"Pay the lady, leave a generous tip, and get the hell out of here." He released Styles, and the Senate candidate dropped to his knees. "Before I lose my temper."

Massaging his hair where Porter had grabbed it, Styles nodded and, using the bed for support, stood, "Wait, you're not here for me?"

"Figured that out all on your own?" Porter asked.

Styles fished out his wallet, "Uh, she was paid for in advance."

Porter turned to Jen, and she reluctantly nodded.

"Well, give her a tip."

Styles put twenty dollars on the nightstand.

"Really?" Jen said, blowing out a plume of smoke.

"Try again," Porter said.

Styles pulled out another twenty dollars and added it to the nightstand.

"Get," Porter said. "And just remember," he pulled out his phone, "if you don't forget about us real fast, I'm uploading a certain picture to the net."

Mindy sighed, "He means social media."

Jen turned to Mindy, "Who still says the net?"

Mindy shrugged.

Jen handed Styles his duffle bag, and Mindy held the door open. The three of them watched as he galloped awkwardly out of the room.

Mindy closed the door behind him and met Jen at the nightstand. "We need to talk."

Jen nodded as she sat on the bed and counted the money. "Damn, Porter, I need you to close out all my jobs." Jen opened the nightstand's top drawer and pulled out a red leather clutch purse with a gold clasp. Parting the top, she pulled out a wad of cash and added Styles' tip.

"Why are you still doing this?" Mindy asked, sitting next to Jen. "I thought you quit."

Jen took another drag and blew out a jet of smoke through her nostrils, "What can I say? Work at the restaurant has been slow. And, this pays the bills."

"Really, sis?"

Jen sighed, "What do you want me to say?"

"Were you getting my texts?"

"Yes."

"So, what? You just decided not to answer them?"

"That's right because you always start with 'what's up?' And I promised to never lie to you after Mom left. So, if I answered back, I don't think you would have liked my answer."

"Well," Mindy crossed her arms over her chest, "I was worried about you."

Jen put an arm over her shoulder and playfully hugged her.

Porter grunted.

"Right," Mindy said, "we wanted to find you and ask about American Iron?"

"What about them?"

Porter spoke up, "We saw security footage of you riding with their President, Scott, and going to the Peterson's house. You told the Petersons you worked for the U.S. Census Bureau?"

"Oh yeah, that was Scotty's idea. He's got the brawn but not the brains. What's your interest?"

"We're working a case," Mindy said.

"We? So you're taking this whole Detective stuff pretty seriously?"

"She's my partner," Porter clarified.

"C'mon, Sis, we need just a little help to connect the dots," Mindy said.

Jen puffed away on her cigarette, thinking, "Alright, I'm going to do you a solid since you guys got Timmy to give me that big tip." She gently bonked heads with Mindy, "Plus, I can't say no to my little sister."

"Go on," Porter said.

Jen winked at him, "You got it, Boss. Scott's the American Iron President and calls it a business partnership."

"Calls what a business relationship?" Porter asked.

"American Iron outsources its dirty work to several groups, including the Wolfpack. It's not the entire biker gang, just the ones Scotty recruited. Scotty's crew gets paid plenty for their home security stuff and discounted drug shipments."

"What type of dirty work?" Porter said.

Jen pushed her blonde hair back. "You know, the usual."

"I need specifics."

"Well, I was riding with Scotty and some Wolfpack members when they threw a Molotov cocktail into the front glass doors of that Circuit City up on Academy. I've heard them talking about stalking store managers at various businesses who refuse to buy into American Iron. They wait for them to get off shift and then either beat the crap out of them in a parking lot or force them off the road and do it there. They harass homeowners who don't buy into them, like the Peterson's."

"Check in the boxes," Mindy said.

"No shit," Porter agreed. "Jen, do you know where Scott is now? Word on the street is you're his girl."

Jen smiled, "I was his girl because he was paying me to be his girl."

"Was? Is that why you were with Tim Styles tonight?" Porter asked.

"Yep, Scott and one of his buddies met me for dinner, and when I asked for my week's pay for various services performed, he stormed out of the restaurant. Fucker and his friend didn't even pay for their meals. That's when I saw ole' Tim sitting alone at the bar. I recognized him from the TV ads and billboards. Figure I'd get to know him."

"We need to find Scott," Mindy said.

"I know he works at the American Iron Corporate office, but that place is a fortress."

"Does Scott live in the city?" Porter asked. "Did he ever take you to his house?"

"No, his aides would set up hotel rooms for me or escort me into the corporate building if I met him there."

"Was one of those aides, One-Eye?"

"No, one was a Russian guy with a knife tattoo on his neck. The other didn't talk much, but I think he was German," Jen said.

Porter and Mindy exchanged a confused glance.

"Tell me more about the German," Porter said.

"He Always wears a business suit and sunglasses, even inside a room, even at night. He's got this wicked scar that goes down the left side of his face. Scotty and his crew all call him Mr. Scarface."

Mindy exchanged another glance with Porter.

"You guys are doing that *thing* again," Jen said. "Wait, you know who I'm talking about, don't you?"

"Yeah," Porter said.

Mindy clarified, "Except they work for Bobbi Johnson."

Jen shook her head. "Okay, now I'm confused."

"That makes two of us," Mindy said.

"Three," Porter added. "Last question, does the name Frank Marion mean anything to you?"

Jen shook her head, "First I'm hearing of him."

❧

Walking across the lot to Porter's truck, they both got in and sat there momentarily. After some time, Porter turned the engine and lit a cigarette. He took a deep drag and massaged his temple. He pulled out his phone, flipped it open, and closed it again.

"You're not going to tell Bobbi about this?" Mindy said, turning up the heater. "Seems like her Russian and German friends are working against her."

"Or we're being played."

"What makes you so sure?"

"Frank Marion."

"Frank Marion?" Mindy asked.

"I don't think this guy exists. We're only following a lead on him because she pointed me in his direction but no one's heard of him. Something's not right."

"What do you think it all means? Why would she set us up?"

"I'm not sure."

Pulling out of the lot, they rolled onto the main road and turned onto Powers Northbound.

The roads were populated with a handful of cars. A closed-down Jiffy Lube was ahead of them on the right, just past the red light that had caught them.

At the light, Porter noticed the Jiffy Lube bay doors were open, and four bikes were idle.

"What?" Mindy asked.

Their front lights turned on in unison, and they pulled towards them.

"Shit," Porter said.

Porter gunned the red light and made a U-turn, barely dodging a Suburban crossing in the intersecting lane. Horns blared as he slid into the opposing lane.

Pressing hard on the accelerator, a rattle of gunfire sounded from behind.

Mindy looked back as the bikes weaved through the intersecting traffic. "They're shooting at us!"

"Yeah, that tends to happen when you fuck with their bikes," Porter said.

Breathing out a plume of smoke, Porter cut the wheel and turned hard onto Milton Proby. Glancing in the rear mirror, he shook his head and put the cigarette to his lips.

Mindy looked back again at the bikers.

"Relax," Porter said.

"You do have a plan, right?" Mindy said, her attention on the road as they snaked around cars.

"Sorta."

"Sorta?" She looked back again.

The Choppers were gaining on them.

"I'm telling you, relax."

"I am relaxed," she said impatiently.

"Really, that's your relaxed voice?"

"What if they catch up to us?"

"What do you think? Shoot them."

Porter pumped the brakes to avoid a collision with a Mercedes, then jerked the wheel, entered the shoulder lane, and accelerated.

He glanced in the rear mirror and, seeing the trailing bikers having difficulties in the traffic, sighed and turned on the radio.

"What are you doing?" Mindy said.

"You act like you've never been run down by bikers before."

"I haven't."

"They'd have a field day with you, Jailbait."

"Fine. Do you want to let me in on your master plan?" She did the math when Porter didn't answer and crossed onto Academy going southbound. "We're heading to I-25?"

Porter nodded. After a few minutes, they weaved through traffic and traveled down the length of Academy, taking the on-ramp to the interstate.

"Okay, the only places we could be going are Fountain, Fort Carson, or Pueblo."

As a Chopper pulled close behind them, Porter tapped the brakes. The bike veered to the left and collided with the side of a silver minivan with Girl Scout stickers plastered across the door.

As the motorcycle fell to its side, the rider flew off and rolled across the road.

A pileup ensued at the point of collision.

Looking back, Mindy saw the biker rolling into the shoulder and out of the way of an incoming truck.

"That guy dodged a bullet," Porter said, glancing in the rearview mirror.

Mindy pondered and then said, "The turn-off for Fountain has too many tight turns and narrow roads. It doesn't suit our situation if they pull alongside us and start blasting. We won't get too far on Fort Carson since I don't have a CAC. So, what's in Pueblo?"

"Jesus Christ, Nancy Drew, does being smart get annoying?" Before she could answer, he reached over and opened the glove box. "Do me a favor, will ya?"

"Okay?"

Reaching inside the glovebox, he rummaged around for a bit and then placed a green M67 hand grenade in her lap, "Pull the pin and toss this out the window towards our pals."

"Are you serious?"

"What's the answer you're looking for?"

"But I've never –"

"Just pull the pin and throw it out the window. It's not rocket science. Oh, and don't throw it in the back of my truck bed or something stupid."

"You throw it," Mindy said.

"I'm driving," Porter said.

"That's bullshit, you can easily throw it out your window."

"The air currents aren't right on my side. They're working better on your side."

"You're ridiculous," Mindy said. "So what do I do? Pull the pin and toss it?"

"You going to ask this much clarification the first time you have sex?"

"First, screw you," Mindy said, "second, am I aiming for someone in particular?"

"We're trying to get them off our tail, not annihilate all of them in one shot. I'm thinking the fear of the explosion will do the job."

"Does it explode immediately, or do I have 10 seconds?"

"Once you pull the pin, you hold down the lever. Once you let go of the lever, you have two to three seconds before it goes boom. Remember, don't hit my truck."

"Right, priorities," Mindy said. "Okay, here goes nothing." Lowering her window, she pulled the pin and lobbed the grenade out the window. "Okay, uh…short toss."

Porter sped up his truck.

They both looked back as the grenade exploded loudly, shooting up asphalt. The darkness was illuminated in a bright glow of orange and yellow.

The remaining trio of bikers stopped their pursuit, shouted curse words, and threw out their middle fingers. One man hurled a beer bottle, and it shattered atop the highway.

"Not bad, Jailbait," Porter told her.

"Thanks, it was my first grenade toss."

After a few more miles, Porter pulled off the road and, putting the truck in four-wheel drive, crossed a field and headed towards a cluster of buildings in the distance.

"Where are we going? And, don't say another biker bar."

"Why? We're they riding you too hard?"

"Piss off."

They jumped onto a road at the end of the field and pulled in front of a chain-link gate leading to a long one-story red-bricked building with blue trim and a sloped metal roof. A sizeable illuminated flagpole was out front with an American flag raised to the top and a POW flag beneath. Both flags were waving gently in the breeze. Above the brown double front doors, a large sign was affixed. The white letters on the black sign read '218, PUEBLO POST, and VFW.'

"The VFW, are you kidding me?" Mindy said.

"Nope," Porter said, lowering his window. Pulling alongside the silver intercom box erected in front of the gate. Porter read the affixed sign, 'Public Hours 8-4, After Hours by Exception Only.' Holding the red button on the intercom, he said, "Tell Big Chief the Rookie is here."

"Whose, Big Chief?" Mindy asked.

"You'll see."

"Okay, once again, not answering my question."

"How could you tell?"

"Wait one," a man barked through the intercom.

A man with a flashlight walked up to the gate a minute later. As he crossed the path of the headlights, Porter saw he wore a leather Wolfpack vest with a worn-out blue Denver Nuggets tee shirt. He yawned as he approached, removed his Army ball cap, scratched his scraggly head, and then put it back on.

"Porter, what the hell?" Mindy asked.

"Relax," he told her. Porter snaked his left arm out the window and smacked the exterior driver's door, "Evening, Jeff."

Jeff shielded his eyes from the headlights. Squinting, he said, "Porter, that you?"

"Why? Want an autograph or something?"

"Jesus, you haven't changed one bit. Hold on a sec." Jeff pulled a keychain from his pocket, fumbled as he looked for the right one, then put the key to the gate's lock.

As Jeff unlocked the gate and rolled it open, Porter pulled forward. There were only about twenty spaces. The few alongside the entrance were spoken for.

A late-model blue Chevy with an eggshell cab-over camper mounted in its bed was parked near the back.

Porter pulled alongside the Chevy and killed the engine.

"Why did they let us in?" Mindy asked.

"We're at the Wolfpack club headquarters. I told you, I know the biker club President, and that old bastard owes me some answers."

"But they've been trying to kill us all night."

"Don't be so dramatic. It was just a few of them. A few are not the majority."

"So, your plan is to go to their headquarters?"

"Yep."

Mindy face palmed as she stepped out of the truck.

Following her lead and stepping out, Porter noticed a faded rainbow bumper sticker on the back of the small camper he parked next to, which read 'SNAFU.'

Jeff walked up to them. He danced the beam of his flashlight across the Ram's frame, "Your trucks got a lot of bullet holes, bro."

"You noticed, huh?" Porter said.

One of the two entrance doors opened, and an overweight man walked out with a black cane support. He had thin white hair and donned large, thick, '80s-style glasses. His leather Wolfpack vest was worn open, and there was no chance of it being buttoned again. The title 'PRESIDENT' was embroidered across his left chest with a patch reading 'BIG CHIEF' underneath.

A snarky grin smeared across his face, "Well, would you look at that. Mindy and her sidekick, the Rookie, have come to grace my presence."

"Flick?" Mindy blurted, running out and hugging him. "What are you doing here?"

"I *was* avoiding Porter," he said.

"Clearly, and I'm not hugging you, Old Man," Porter said.

"Good, I don't want to catch whatever Millennial disease you're carrying."

"What? Hard work and good looks?"

Flick waved him off, "You're living in a dream, Rookie."

"Flick, I didn't know you were part of something like this," Mindy said.

"Yeah," Flick looked back at the building, "I run this club," he turned to her, "What? You think I sit at home growing old all day?" He turned to Porter, "Hell, that's his job."

Porter ignored the comment. He was focused on the woman who walked up behind Flick. She wore a denim patch jacket over a white shirt.

"Valentine," Porter said with a wide grin. "I thought I'd find you here."

"Detective," she said, exchanging a grin of her own.

"Dear God," Fick said to Porter, "How the hell do you know my niece?"

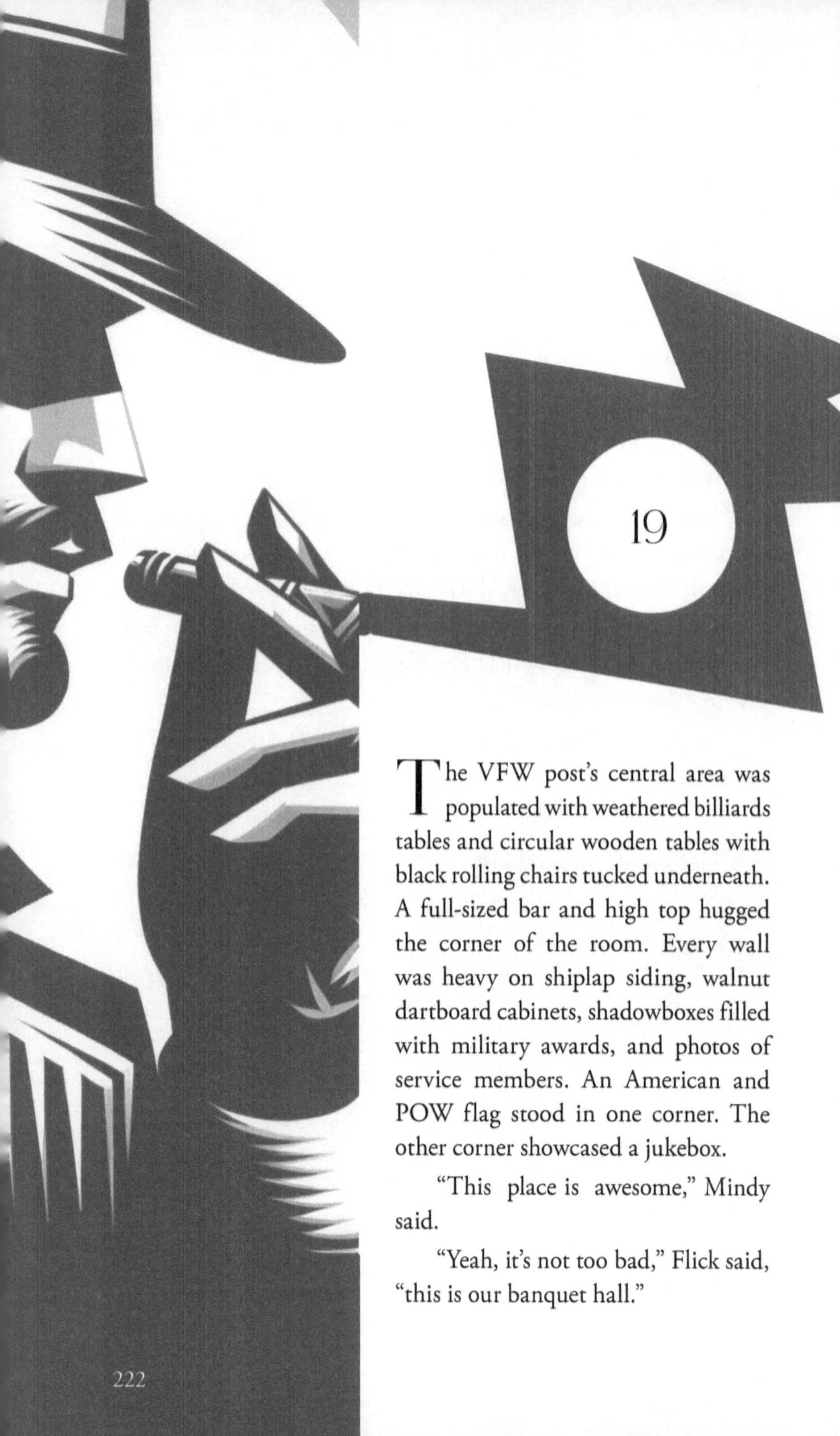

19

The VFW post's central area was populated with weathered billiards tables and circular wooden tables with black rolling chairs tucked underneath. A full-sized bar and high top hugged the corner of the room. Every wall was heavy on shiplap siding, walnut dartboard cabinets, shadowboxes filled with military awards, and photos of service members. An American and POW flag stood in one corner. The other corner showcased a jukebox.

"This place is awesome," Mindy said.

"Yeah, it's not too bad," Flick said, "this is our banquet hall."

"Wait, Porter, is this you?" Mindy said, inspecting a photo behind one of the billiard tables.

The photo showed six Marines standing side-by-side with arms around each other's shoulders and clear plastic cups of beer in their free hands. They all wore desert camouflage uniforms with sleeves up, had wicked tans, and were grinning ear-to-ear. The third Marine to the right was a much younger version of Porter with a clean shave and short hair.

Porter walked up to the photo, "Would you look at that?"

Valentine stood beside him, tilting her head, "Ah, how adorable."

"Out-processing at Camp Lejune, we had just returned from Afghanistan."

Flick grunted, "Hey, if you three are done goofing off, come back to my office."

Flick led the way down a narrow hall with recent, rather sloppy navy-colored walls across from the bathroom that reeked of a cinnamon floral-scented urinal cake.

Flick's office was nothing spectacular. There was just enough room for a mid-sized file cabinet against one wall, a tall locker against the opposite, and a heavy desk shoved into the back.

A pinup calendar was tacked to the wall. A short-haired brunette graced the centerfold. She was looking out to an orange and red horizon with pursed lips and donning patriotic lingerie.

"So, you're still alive, huh?" Porter said, taking a seat facing the heavy desk and putting his boots on it.

Flick maneuvered behind the desk and pushed Porter's boots off. "Knowing that I'm the bane of your existence keeps me alive." As he sat, the maroon leather chair under him groaned in pain.

"Dammit, you're going to live forever just to piss me off."

"Better believe it."

"I didn't know you were in charge of a biker club," Mindy said with a yawn. She sat in the chair next to Porter and slumped back.

Porter turned to Valentine, who leaned against the door frame. He offered his chair, but she waved him off.

"There's a lot about me you don't know," Flick said. "Let's keep it that way."

"Yeah, the Wolfpack share this club with the VFW and do all sorts of things here," Porter said, "VFW meetings, bingo night, football parties, book clubs, weddings, and for every single event, they overcharge for the beer."

"Damn right," Flick said. Grasping his oversized blue mug, he took a big sip and leaned back. The chair looked as if it would break. "So, we just finished helping with a Toys for Tots event with the Marine Corps Reserve Unit out at Buckley when I got a call telling me some shit for brains Marine Detective working a case was whacking some of my boys around at the bar. I expect there's a good story behind this?"

"I'll start the story with two questions and let you fill in the plot," Porter said. "First, was it Tattoo Tony who called you? Second, is there a reason you didn't return my call?"

Flick grinned, "Yes, it was Tony." He studied Porter and said, "He's turned on me, hasn't he? Well, it's about time that Seabee made his power play. So, what's the story?"

"Tony is in league with American Iron. They've recruited some Wolfpack military vets behind your back to do their dirty work."

"Whose they?"

"Scott Winters, heard of that asshole?"

"The American Iron President? Yeah, ex-Army. Scott and his buddies went into business for themselves after the war doing private security. It gets a little shady in between, but eventually, you get American Iron, and Scott was left at the top."

"You just happen to know all that?" Porter asked.

Flick waved him off, "You said they. Who's the other one?"

"Frank Marion, ring a bell?"

"Never heard of him."

"Neither has anyone else. Can you look into him?"

"You say you have two questions, and then you ask more. Your generation doesn't even know how to count, freaking Millennials," Flick said. He looked at Mindy, who had fallen asleep, "Damn, Porter, see what dealing with you all day does to poor Mindy?"

"Cute kid," Valentine said.

Porter turned to Valentine and stared at her tight denim pants that fit her ass like a glove, "Yeah, cute."

Flick noticed the gaze and said, "Porter, don't kid yourself. You don't have a snowball's chance in hell."

"Bite me," Porter said, getting up. He went to the Keurig and stacked Styrofoam cups on the file cabinet.

"No thanks, I don't eat junk food," Flick grunted.

"That gut of yours says differently."

"Porter, what your feeble mind fails to understand is that fat is a temporary caloric imbalance, but stupid is a permanent genetic malfunction."

"Be nice, you two," Valentine cautioned.

"It's alright, V," Flick said as Porter loaded a K-cup into the machine. "He's an ungrateful little Millennial twerp. You know, when he was a kid, his parents actually encouraged him to run away."

"Keep it up," Porter said as the Styrofoam cup under the brewer filled. The smell of Hazelnut filled the air. As the final drip of coffee spat into the cup, Porter took a sip and added Splenda. "Old Man, I swear I will call the retirement home and give them your location." He pointed to Valentine and motioned to the Keurig.

She waved him off again.

"Ha, they'll never catch me," Flick grinned. Interlacing his beefy hands on the table, he continued, "I missed your first phone call because my phone reception sucks at Buckley, and if you haven't noticed, it's not much better here. When I got reception, I had received a frantic call that you had hospitalized One-Eye, Sam-Wise, and Pup and messed up a few bikes at the bar."

"Someone's been busy," Valentine said.

"What can I say? I can go all night," Porter said, raising his brows to Valentine.

"And to think, people like you are allowed to breed," Flick said, rolling his eyes. "After the frantic phone call from Britney, I knew if you had roughed up my boys while working a case, it had to be for a good reason. So, it took a bit of coordination on my end, but I called off my club members from hunting you down. So excuse me, Mr. Self Entitled, if I didn't return your phone call immediately."

"Oh really?" Porter said, taking a seat, "Then why the hell was Mindy and I chased and shot at on the way down here? The bullet holes in my truck aren't for air conditioning."

Flick laughed, "Hell! That's not an admission of guilt. V, get this, the day I met Porter, I wanted to hit him with my car. He just has that type of personality."

"I'm beginning to see that," Valentine said.

"Thanks for the vote of confidence," Porter said. "Which brings us here."

Flick sat forward in his chair, "Listen, if Wolfpack members were still chasing you in the last hour, then they were acting independently," Flick said. "Besides, convincing guys not to want to kick your ass ain't easy, Porter. Hell, have you ever met you?"

"Yeah," Porter grinned, taking a sip of his coffee, "and I'm fucking awesome."

Valentine laughed.

"F'ing delusional," Flick said. "Alright, tell me about your case."

Porter took another sip. "We've been hired by Bobbi Johnson…"

"Time out," Flick said, "Bobbi Johnson?"

Porter nodded.

"What is she doing hanging around a bum like you?"

"Who's Bobbi Johnson?" Valentine asked.

"She's running for the Colorado U.S. Senate seat," Flick said, "Stick around long enough, and you're bound to see one of her terrible commercials."

Porter continued, "Bobbi's hired us to improve her public image before the election."

"And that's achieved how?" Flick asked.

"Bringing down American Iron."

"Wow, that's no small task."

Porter took another sip of his coffee, "She's convinced they're at the center of the crime wave surge hitting the Springs."

"American Iron," Valentine said, pointing to Porter, "from what you've said, they sound like a criminal organization." She pointed at Flick, "But from what you've said about their President, Scott, they sound like a home security company."

"Officially, they're a home security company," Porter said.

"And, unofficially?"

Porter finished his coffee and crumpled the cup. He lobbed it into the blue trash bin beside the wall locker. Lighting up a cigarette and taking a seat, he once again put his boots on the table. "Bobbi's friends with a family whose house got broken into a few nights back. The family is convinced it's American Iron's doing since they didn't buy into their home security system. We followed the breadcrumbs and confirmed their theory. The rogue Wolfpack members are acting as American Iron's QRF."

"Whose their supplier?" Flick asked. He swiped his meaty right paw at Porter's boots, knocking them off the table.

"The local Air Force supplies them with NVGs, gasmasks, grenades, pistols, and the works. One of your members, Pup, knows the armorer on base. Kids a piece of shit, by the way. The only things he's good at is pissing on himself and getting his nose broken."

"Pup, huh? The name doesn't ring a bell."

"Shouldn't the club President know everyone?"

"The Wolfpack has over 100 members. I don't swear in every person."

"But I bet you collect their membership fees."

"Damn right," Flick said. "Anything else?"

"Bobbi's bodyguards seem to be working with Scott and American Iron."

Flick stared at him for a long moment, "You're serious?"

Porter puffed on his cigarette, "As a heart attack. Which I'm hoping you have any moment now."

"Hardy, har, har." Flick massaged his jaw, "So what? You want a cake now that the plot has thickened."

"Old man, I'm only interested in a cake if she's popping out of it," Porter said, thumbing back to Valentine.

Valentine smirked devilishly, "Oh, you'd like that, wouldn't you?"

"Damn right."

Flick palmed his head, "God, youth is wasted on the young." Composing himself, Flick said, "Tell me about these bodyguards."

"One is a thick, bald Russian bastard with a beard and a dagger tattoo on his neck. The other has a thick German accent and has a scar on his face. He's a real chrome magnum-looking bastard. Here –" Porter fished out his phone and, opening the text picture Mindy had sent him, handed it over.

Flick pulled his glasses out of his vest pocket and put them on. He held the phone up to his nose and squinted.

"I figured you might recognize him with all your overseas work with the agency."

"What agency?" Valentine asked.

Flick handed the phone back, "What? No one said *agency*. You're hearing things." He delivered a stern look to Porter, who merely shrugged.

"Talk to me, Goose," Porter said.

"Bobbi keeps some nasty company. The Russian goes by Igor Volkov, the Butcher. Ex-KGB, and after the fall of the Soviet Union, he was part of an elite Chechen commando unit."

"A death squad," Valentine said.

"Call it what you will. We had reason to believe Volkov's unit took out several Ukrainian officials before Ukrainian forces got intelligence of one of their intended hits and intercepted them. He's supposed to be locked in a cell half a world away."

"And the German?" Porter asked.

"Krystofer Gunther goes by a few aliases; some call him Scarecrow, and others Teufelsmörder. The translation means Devil Killer."

"That's a hell of an alias."

"He was an Officer in the German Naval Special Forces Command, the Kampfschwimmer. Rumor has it he made quite a name for himself in the elite commando unit before being imprisoned for an unsanctioned hit."

"Unsanctioned?" Porter asked.

"So the files say. More likely, it was one of those ops where things go wrong, and you get disavowed."

"And things went wrong?" Valentine asked.

"That's the thought. Anyway, while incarcerated, Gunther brokered a deal with the Iranians to break him out. In exchange, he worked as an exclusive hitman for the Iranians to kill U.S.

Marines in Afghanistan. And as you know, since the battle at Belleau Wood, Marines are nicknamed Teufel Hunden."

"Devil Dogs," Porter said. "Why only target Marines, though?"

"An operation gone bad. Recon Marines called an artillery strike on what they thought was an insurgent family digging IEDs in the dirt road in front of their house. It was actually a family burying their dog. The family belonged to a high-ranking Iranian General. So, he waged a shadow ops war against Marines in Helmand Province."

"Well, fuck," Porter murmured.

"Needless to say, Gunther's exclusive rights to the Iranians were terminated when intel caught wind of this targeting, and allied forces took out the Iranian base of operations cell that was allied with insurgents as part of Operation DAN."

"Defeat Al Qaeda in the North," Valentine said.

"Gunther was thought to have died with the Iranians and insurgents during the joint airstrike with our British allies, but based on your recent encounter, it appears otherwise."

"Where do you even recruit people like that?" Porter asked.

"Politics obviously opens doors that would otherwise be closed," Valentine said.

"These are highly trained assassins," Flick said. "Porter, don't mess with Volkov, but really don't mess with Gunther. He was on our watch list, but we could never nail him. He is beyond bad news."

"C'mon, Old Man, I bet the only Marines he whacked were those pussies from Parris Island."

"Dammit, Rookie, if there is one time in your life you take me seriously, it is now. Be careful."

Porter didn't know how to respond. He wasn't used to Flick showing concern for him. This was uncharted territory.

"So, was that it?" Flick asked.

"I guess," Porter stood and stretched. "Well, we'll get out of here. Let me wake Mindy."

Flick checked his watch, "Rookie, it's late. Don't wake the kid up. Just bed down here for the night. Mindy can keep sleeping in here. I'll bring in a cot and get her a blanket."

"You don't have to do all that. It's not that long of a drive –"

Flick cut him off, "It'll give me some time to do more research on Volkov and Gunther. I told you to stay clear, so I know you won't because, well, you're an idiot. If I can find you an advantage over these guys, I will."

"Uh, thanks," Porter said. "I think?"

"Yeah, yeah, shut up," Flick told him. "As for you, I've got a sleeping bag. You can –"

"Porter, you can sleep in my camper," Valentine interrupted. "The corner bench converts to a spare bed. It's a little cramped but beats sleeping on the floor with a sleeping bag."

"He's a Marine. He doesn't need a bed," Flick said.

"Ignore him," Valentine said.

"I usually do," Porter said.

"C'mon, follow me," Valentine said, leading the way out.

"Wait, no, uh," Flick began to plead. As they left the office, Porter and Valentine heard him mutter, "Dammit."

"Drink?" Valentine asked, grabbing a clear bottle of Everclear 190 Proof from the camper's mini-fridge. She twisted off the gold cap and filled two lowball shot glasses from the overhead white cabinet to half. Her hand twitched as she poured, and the bottle's connection to the drink made a persistent clink.

She handed a glass to Porter and sat next to him on the corner bench.

The overhead ventilation fan whirred loud enough for Porter to notice and look. There was a cracked dome light affixed next to the fan.

Porter took a sip and placed his glass on the small table the bench encircled. A scratched purple laptop and a black and white composition notebook sat on the table. "Thanks for the drink and for letting me crash here."

Porter looked around the late model truck camper with its glaringly yellow interior walls. Across from the bench were a corner sink and a two-burner stovetop. The off-grey linoleum counter in between had just enough room for a coffee maker and a metal carrier filled with utensils and condiments.

White cabinets and heater vents were conveniently tucked here and there, leading to the green exit door.

A shelf filled with Goosebumps novels and various DVDs lined the right of the camper. The DVDs included all of Tarantino's work and classic '80s Action movies. A yellow bungee stretched across the outside of the shelf to keep the media from falling off.

An elevated bed adorned with a feather bed mattress, an assortment of loud-colored blankets, Build-a-Bear stuffed animals, and pillows filled the rear.

"I know, it's not much to look at," Valentine said, sipping her drink. "But, when you're single and travel as much as I do, something like this is ideal."

"You're talking to a guy who lives in a trailer home," Porter said.

"Okay, good point."

Downing more of his drink, Porter pointed out, "It would be nice if it had a head."

Valentine removed the brown cushion beside her and lifted a partition of the bench, revealing a portable toilet. "Behold, five gallons and up to thirty flushes of technological superiority."

They both had a good laugh.

Valentine put everything back in place. "I've even got a water tent in that cabinet above the stove."

"Well, when you need a place to crash, you can certainly do worse."

"True." As they both stared awkwardly at one another, Valentine got up and plugged her phone into her computer. "Care for some music?"

"Sure."

She thumbed away on her phone, then sat back down as a quick trio of piano strikes started the song.

"Nice," Porter said, immediately recognizing the tune as, '…Baby One More Time.'

Britney's voice, in all her lower-register sexiness, filled the air.

Valentine took another sip from her glass and nodded to the song, "Every time I listen to this, it brings back memories."

"Oh yeah? Like what?"

"A lot of bullshit Jr. High dances."

"Yep, I know that one."

"I would swear up and down to all my friends that I absolutely hated Britney and all her dumb, catchy songs. But secretly, I'd stay up late singing to her songs in my PJs in front of a mirror." Valentine mimicked, holding a microphone in her hand and swaying her shoulders.

"That's a good visual image," Porter laughed. "So, is Britney what got you into playing music?"

"God, no. That was Metallica."

"Makes sense."

"You know," Valentine said, "I never thought about this when I was a tween, the first time I listened to this? But what does this song mean? Does she literally want to be hit so she knows her boyfriend is paying attention to her?"

Porter finished his drink and shook his head, "No, she's saying hit me up on the phone." He mimicked, bringing a phone to his ear. "Remember your '90s vocabulary."

"How do you know that?"

"Know what?"

"Britney Spears song lyrics? Aren't you supposed to be some tough-as-nails, Marine?" Valentine finished her glass and poured herself and Porter another round.

"Well, naturally, but I also did have a first love in my life. Her name was Britney."

"How poetic."

Porter shrugged and took another hit of Everclear.

"At least you're honest," Valentine said.

"Brutally."

She took a big gulp from her glass, "Brutally honest guy, ass-kicking, former Marine, Detective, in love with Britney Spears. I bet you think you're just hot shit?"

"I don't think things. I know them."

"Aren't you just a cocky-son-of-a-bitch?"

"You say that like it's a bad thing."

She shook her head, "Not bad. It's refreshing, if anything. A lot of people change in life. A bully becomes a Bible-thumper. A Bible-thumper becomes a whore. A jock becomes a businessman. A businessman becomes a drug dealer. But I'm betting you were a cocky SOB in the Marines, and you're still one now. Good for you." She squeezed his left leg and poured them more shots.

Porter sipped more of his drink, "And what about you, Ms. Valentine?"

"What about me?" She brought the rim of the glass to her lips.

"Have you changed?"

She sat back and shrugged, "After my discharge from the Army, I had nothing. There was no place to go home to besides Flick, no family to speak of, and no real purpose. I had a few thousand in my bank account I saved up in Afghanistan and my old man's truck." She took another swig and stared at her hand, which held onto the glass and twitched uncontrollably.

"I honestly thought I'd be in the Army my whole life," she said. "I thought that by my age, I would have a husband, two kids, and maybe a dog. I was sure I'd have a nice house and be stationed somewhere on the East Coast where I could wake every morning to the scent of the ocean and a view to match." She waved a hand across the trailer, "But obviously, that's not the case."

"A married Army wife living on the coast just doesn't seem like you."

"Really, what do I seem like then?"

"A loner."

"A loner," she repeated. "Damn, you sure know how to talk to a dame."

"Hey, a loner's not a bad thing. A loner's a survivor, and there's no smarter thing to be in today's world."

"You know, I thought you were a loner, too," Valentine said. "And then I saw Mindy with you. You said she was your partner, but the way you look at her and talk to her, if I didn't know any better, I would say she was your daughter."

"I *am* her legal guardian."

"You don't seem the type to take on a stray."

"It's complicated."

"It must be. Can I make a recommendation, though?"

"Sure."

"Are you sure? You might not like it."

"That's life."

"Don't get too attached. If you're anything like me, which I think you are, you're constantly getting fucked over in life. Say she up and leaves tomorrow? Or gets hurt or killed working one of your cases. People our age can die from a broken heart."

Porter took in her words and nodded. The longer they knew one another, the more he trusted Mindy and enjoyed her company. He knew he wasn't her father, but he also knew she needed guidance, as Evans had told him. He liked it when he could give her some, though she rarely needed it.

"So," Valentine baited, using the collar of her shirt to wipe the alcohol off her lips, "you mind if I ask you a question, Detective?"

"Shoot."

"Are you stalking me?"

Porter downed his drink and wiped his mouth with his hand, "Now, why would you say that?"

"I've only been in town for a day, and you've conveniently run into me several times already." She smiled and swayed.

"What can I say? I'm drawn to you," he smiled back.

She rolled her eyes, "Jesus, when's the last time you," she stuck a finger into his chest, "got laid?"

"Not since last night, and I'll tell you what, it's been a long fucking day."

Valentine laughed. After a moment, her grin faded, and she said, "Anything serious?"

"They never are."

"Good…I think?"

"In all honesty, it saves on the bills. You get in serious relationships with women…" Porter gently brushed a strand of black hair behind her left ear.

Valentine bit down on her lower lip.

"They start wanting you to buy them shit," Porter said.

"Yep, jewelry sure does get expensive."

Porter pointed to the bed, "I was thinking more like Build-a-Bears."

"Oh, is that right?" She studied him, eyes boring into his like a lioness, ready to take down her prey. "You really think you're shit hot, don't you?"

Without answering, he pulled her in by the back of the head and locked his lips onto hers.

After the steamy kiss, she pushed off, finished her drink, and slammed her glass onto the table. She pressed on Porter's chest with force so his back was strewn across the bench.

With shaky fingers, she spread his legs and unzipped him. She dropped to her knees and buried her head in his lap.

Porter ran his fingers through her jet-black hair and held on as she bobbed up and down.

At the beginning of the next song, she resurfaced and straddled him.

He kissed her collarbone and neck, tasting her sweet-scented skin.

She guided his hands to her belt.

He unbuckled her and yanked her belt out of its loops.

She unbuttoned her pants, and he pulled them down with her panties. As she tossed them to the floor, she allowed space for Porter to do the same.

She hovered her slit over his groin and gently grinded against him. She tongued his ear and nibbled on his lobe, breathing hot breath onto him.

Porter snaked his hands under her bra and massaged her slender chest. Crawling his fingers around her back, he unclipped her bra.

Valentine slipped the bra off and added them to the growing pile. Porter did the same with his shirt.

They made their way to the bed and lay there for some time, caressing one another and fervently kissing.

Porter always thought something euphoric about running his fingers across every inch of a woman's body. Something about feeling all the perfections and imperfections. Only after this did Porter truly feel intimate with a woman.

Valentine had a thin frame, thinner than he expected but firm where it mattered. Despite her living conditions, it was clear that she led an active lifestyle. Her hair smelled of strawberries, and her flesh tasted sweet. His hands ran over a streak of scars etched across her back, and she quickly moved them elsewhere. Her body felt cold against his but was quickly warming up.

Porter began to pull her hips towards his and found his fingers running across a set of scars, entry, and exit wounds on her right side.

She pushed his fingers further down, so he now grasped her ass.

He pulled on her once more but felt resistance. Her gaze was fixated on his prosthetic leg.

She ran shaky fingers down the polypropylene socket and then felt the carbon fiber pylon leading to his foot.

"My eyes are up here, beautiful," Porter said.

Valentine nodded, "Sorry, it's just…I had almost forgotten."

"I hope this isn't a problem."

"No, of course not." She guided his hands up to her hips, "As I said before, we're both just a couple of broke dicks."

He massaged her hips, and she kissed him.

With a firm grip on his piece, she whispered in his ear, "Prove me wrong."

Porter did just that.

20

The glass doors parted as Hector removed his cowboy hat and entered the St. Barbara Hospital reception area. A heavy scent of disinfectant spray wafted through the air, emanating an aroma of crisp air coming through a window on a Spring day. There were brown signs with white arrows pointing one way or another and a list of associated areas. Beneath him, the gleaming white floors were situated with diamond-shaped sapphire tiles.

Rows of steel-framed chairs with blue leatherbacks and black foam cushions populated the reception area— about half were full. An assembly of children, teens, adults, and older people sat glued to their phones. A 32" TV was mounted above a water cooler on the sidewall. The cooler bubbled as a teenager dispensed water into a plastic cup.

The news was playing. A soft-faced girl with wavy brunette hair and ruby red lipstick, wearing a pink sweater, reported on a mass shooting at a Waffle House in Raton.

The rows of chairs parted down the center of the room, leaving an open path to the Check-In station. Hector made his way to the receptionist.

A teenage girl sat behind the counter, looking down at her phone. She had obnoxious neon green streaks in her short blonde hair, a stud in her left nostril, and a hoop in one of her brows. She wore a light blue one-pocket scrub top.

Hector rapped his knuckles across the counter to get her attention.

Still looking at her phone, she nodded toward the white self-check-in kiosk attached to the wall. "Just enter your information, and we'll call on you shortly."

"I'm not a patient. I'm here to see someone," Hector said.

She thumbed away for a few seconds before looking up with irritated hazel eyes. "Yes?" she said, forcing a smile.

"I'm here to see someone," Hector said once more.

The girl slowly chewed on her gum, "Okay."

"His name is –"

"It's like, after hours, you know?"

"After hours?"

"Yeah, visiting hours are from eight-to-eight. You can come back then."

"Come back?"

"Obvi."

"Obvi?"

"Obviously, yes, sir, you'll need to come back," she smiled again. This time, it was genuine.

She was as young and innocent as a girl her age could be. "What's your name?"

The girl hesitated before answering, "Liz."

"Liz, such a pretty name."

She nodded and shrugged, "Uh, thanks."

"I need you to tell me what room Joshua Guvera is in."

"Uh," she bit her lip, "I'm not allowed to do that. Really, you'll have to come back during visiting hours."

Hector stared at her for a long moment, "You will tell me."

Liz stared at him for a moment, confused at having been contradicted. "Uh, what? Sir, I just told you I can't do that."

"No, you said you weren't allowed to."

She shook her head, "Uh, what?"

Hector leaned into the counter and lowered his voice, "Listen to me and listen to me very closely, Liz. You are going to give me his room number. You will do this for me because if you don't, I will stop asking nicely."

"What does that mean?"

"Use your imagination," Hector told her with a cold stare.

The girl stared back, and after a few moments, her hand began to crawl under the desk toward the panic button.

"I wouldn't do that," Hector said.

Liz stopped, and her jaw went slack. Her hand retracted.

"You're a smart girl."

Liz nodded.

"Joshua Guvera, look it up."

With stiff fingers, Liz clicked away on her computer. She looked up at Hector when the room number appeared. She tried to tell him the room number, but the words were caught in her throat.

"Take a deep breath," Hector told her.

She hesitated at first but eventually said, "Room 432. That means f-f-fourth f-floor, room thirty-two. He's under p-police w-watch."

"Thank you," he said. He waited for Liz to respond, and when she didn't, he said, "You're welcome. That would be the polite thing to say."

"You're welcome," she squeaked, tears building.

A middle-aged man with long, unkempt brown hair and a goatee walked in through the rear swinging doors leading to the exam rooms' hallway. He was garbed in a white lab coat, a checkered green tie, and a stethoscope hanging off his neck. "Liz, did my wife call?" The man nodded to Hector, "Hey, how ya doin'?"

"Outstanding, and yourself?" Hector asked.

"Can't complain." He turned to Liz, "Hey, are you alright? Why are you crying?"

Liz looked at him, swallowed hard, and nodded, "I'm fine, Dr. Block. Really, girl stuff always hits me at the worst times, ya know?"

"Say no more," the man said, tossing his hands up and sitting at the computer behind Liz.

Hector nodded to her. Walking into the elevator, he pushed the button for the fourth floor.

"Hold it!" a man barked.

Hector reached back and ran his fingers up the holster clipped to the inside of his waistband.

Dr. Block rushed in just as the doors were about to close. "Whoo almost didn't make it."

"Lucky you," Hector said.

"Yeah, lucky me." He turned to Hector, "Believe it or not, this has been one killer night."

"Yes, it has."

The Doctor smirked, "You mind pushing three?"

Hector pushed the button, "Not at all."

⁂

Rounding the corner leading to Joshua's room, Hector stepped back as a pair of Registered Nurses walked past him. They looked at him, and he nodded and removed the top of the nearby garbage can. He pulled out the bag and tied the top.

As they passed, he returned the bag to the can and continued down the hall.

A blue-uniformed Officer sat at the end of the hall in front of room 432. He was plump with short hair and pink cheeks. A bottle of Coke stood next to his black shoes. He thumbed away frantically at his cell phone, deeply involved in the game he was playing.

Returning the way he had come, Hector looked at the drop panel grid ceiling. The panels were flat white and peppered with perforations. His eyes traced the length of the grid system tracks until he found a conduit and followed it to a fixed camera. One conduit led to another, branched to more cameras pointing down each hallway.

All conduits eventually led to one room. Hector knew the door had to be the security room for the floor. Pulling a trash bag from the nearest can, he stood by the door and gently knocked on it.

The door creaked open, revealing a dark room illuminated only by a computer screen glow. A wiry middle-aged uniformed guard with a comb-over stood behind the frame, "Yes?" The guard inspected Hector from cowboy hat to rattlesnake boots.

"Basura?" Hector said, holding up the trash bag.

The guard looked confused.

"Garbage," Hector clarified.

"Sure," the guard said, opening the door fully and stepping aside. The security guard wore a blue buttoned-up dress shirt and a black tie. A patch badge was embroidered on his chest, and a shield patch with the words 'AMERICAN IRON' stitched on his shoulder. "The can is under the desk," he said, pointing to it. "Hey, I don't see a hospital badge. Aren't all you workers supposed to –"

Hector stepped inside, opened the bag, and dropped it on the guard's black safety shoes. The garbage inside spilled.

"Hey man," the guard protested, looking down. "I just had my pants pressed, and now they're covered with, I don't know what."

When the guard looked up, Hector was behind him. The steel chord from the wrist of Hector's glove slipped around his neck.

The guard struggled against the pull, but Hector was stronger, pulling the guard away from the door. Bracing himself against the back wall, Hector bent down, adding pressure to the pull, and ignored the frantic clawing and punches from the guard. The guard stopped resisting within seconds, and Hector dropped him to the floor.

Hector retracted the chord into the wrist of his glove.

Closing the door, he sat behind the desk. Hector looked up at the computer video wall of three monitors stacked atop three monitors. Each showed a different hallway on the fourth floor.

Hector watched the video feed of himself from when he entered the fourth floor until now. His hat covered his face. Navigating the feed from the current floor to the reception area, he rolled the timeline when talking to Liz. With a few clicks of the buttons, Hector erased the video timeline of himself.

Looking at the current feeds. Few people were walking the halls, and only one had an Officer sitting outside the door. Hector stared at the slouching Officer for a few minutes, staring away at his phone. He was such an easy target, but Hector knew he couldn't make a move. A guard was one thing. A badge was another.

On the side wall was a fire alarm pull switch. Getting up, Hector pushed in the plastic and pulled down on the switch.

The alarm rang out.

The Officer dropped his phone in surprise and picked it up. Talked into his walkie and then ran from the door to investigate the alarm.

Hector disabled the fourth-floor cameras and made his way out.

Walking into room 432, Hector closed the door behind him. The room was white-themed with walls, ceiling, blinds, and floor. A mixture of revolting aromas wafted in the space, stemming from the patient's unhygienic condition.

Hector squirted hand sanitizer from the dispenser above the corner sink into his palm. He swabbed the isopropyl alcohol inside his nostrils.

At the gurney where Joshua lay, Hector noticed his right wrist was cuffed to the matching side rail.

Bandages secured Joshua's forehead, long hooked nose, and narrow jaw. Blood and puss seeped through the cloths, making them discolored in hues of brown and yellow. A brace was affixed to his neck.

Joshua's hazel eyes fixated on him, and his thick brows furrowed. "Hector," he whispered.

It was the same look Joshua had given him in their youth. A look of both disappointment and concern. On countless occasions, Hector would come home from school with bruises, black eyes, and cuts courtesy of his classmates.

Being the older brother, Joshua would shake his head and get the ice pack from the freezer. Hector would plead with his brother to beat those kids up, to deal with them, but Joshua never would. He would always tell Hector that to be a man meant fighting your own fights.

"Is that really you?" Joshua asked.

Taking a knee, Hector held his brother's arm, "Yes, it's me."

Joshua studied him, "What has it been ten years since you left the country?"

"Yes, that sounds right."

"I missed the memorial service, didn't I?" Joshua asked.

"Yes," Hector told him.

"How was it?"

"The service was small. I said a few words for Mom and Dad, mostly Mom. Once you get past the military service, there's nothing positive to say about Dad."

"Agreed," Joshua said with a cough. He tried to sit up and struggled.

Hector grabbed a paper cup beside the sink and filled it with water. Bringing it to Joshua's lips, his brother sipped on it slowly.

"Is that better?" Hector asked.

Joshua nodded.

Hector looked him over, "Who did this to you?"

Joshua shook his head, "I shouldn't have taken this assignment. I knew it was bad from the outset. I knew it –" he coughed again, and this time it didn't seem like it would ever end.

Hector struggled to see his brother like this.

"Who did this?" Hector said once more.

"Does it matter?" Joshua asked. He turned on the gurney, "I'm tired."

"What can I do?"

"Leave. Please leave. You shouldn't see me like this."

"I can get you out of here, take you with me, disappear."

"After the things I've done. What I did to keep my cover. This is my penance." Joshua sighed, "I'm in God's hands now. He has chosen my fate. I don't have much time left."

"Who did this?"

Joshua stayed silent.

Hector squeezed Joshua's hand and realized this would be the last time he would see him, "Goodbye, brother."

"Porter," Joshua muttered.

"What?" Out of all the names Hector was prepared to hear, Porter wasn't one of them.

"His name was Porter."

"Are you sure?"

"Yes, he called himself Porter," Joshua said before turning away.

Walking out, Hector closed the door and contemplated his brother's words in the hallway.

21

Streaks of mud and patches of black ice were etched into the blacktop. Fat, heavy flakes kissed the Bronco's windshield before melting into the night.

Hector adjusted his heater and, drinking the warm milk in his thermos, nodded to the Cash song, 'Folsom Prison Blues.'

Driving past the three-bay fire department on the corner of Bradley and Horizon View, Hector read a sign as he turned into the neighborhood, 'AFFORDABLE HOUSING STARTING IN THE MID $300s.'

Hector remembered a decade ago when that billboard read 'IN THE LOW $150s.'

The two-story houses were all a decent size. The matching dog-eared fenced-in backyards were nothing to brag about but nothing to complain about. Every home had a long driveway sloping from the two-car garage to an American Iron home security sign planted just short of the road.

The neighborhood was quiet, and all the streetlamps were in good working condition. The snow-frosted roads had minimal potholes that had become an indicator of a neighborhood's quality in Colorado.

Hector slowed his Bronco to a crawl at the corner of Cheyenne and Bramble Lane. The house was illuminated from within. Smoke hissed from the chimney on the roof.

Hector parked across from the house alongside the sidewalk.

Walking across the road to the house, Hector was flooded with memories. He had been to this house so many times. Between dinners, beers out on the front deck, and Sunday BBQs after Church, he knew this place like the back of his hand.

Ascending the sloped driveway and making his way around the garage, Hector walked up the deck's stairs, a deck he had helped build. He knocked on the purple front door.

Maggie always liked purple.

A pitiful yappy dog barked.

On the second knock, a woman inside shouted to the dog, "Vete, vete tu pequeña mierda." The door creaked open, and a young woman with a warm face, long brown hair, and painted black brows nursing a baby peered out. "¿Si?"

Hector didn't recognize her.

"¿Si?" she said again.

"Does Ryan Porter still live here?"

"No ingles."

"Ryan Porter," Hector said, "or Maggie Porter?"

"No ingles," she repeated. Her small, fluffy Pekingese dog began yapping again, and the woman pushed it back with her foot. "Silencio!"

"¿Eres el dueño de esta casa?" Hector asked, inquiring about the ownership of the house. "¿Sabes dónde vive el dueño anterior?" He continued, seeing if she knew where Porter now lived.

"No lo sé," she said, slamming the door.

Hector stared at the closed door for a moment. He contemplated breaking it in and interrogating her for answers. At the sound of the baby screaming, he decided against it.

"They moved!" a woman yelled from the neighboring house.

The well-aged woman wore a thick grey coat, a beat-up trapper hat, and knitted grey and black gloves. She had a thin face and a great smile. Something about her reminded him of his mother.

The woman dragged a heavy blue and white ice melt pail out her front door.

"Let me help you with that," Hector said.

"Oh, that would be nice," she said. Her voice had an Upper Midwest twang to it.

Walking down the drive, he rounded the house's fence and approached the woman.

"Frances," she said, extending a hand. "But you call me Frankie. Everyone does."

"Hector," he said, shaking her hand. Hector popped open the top of the pail and began scooping out pellets and scattering them across her driveway. "Porter moved, you said?"

"Oh ya, a few years back, I reckon. It was after his wife left. Poor thing."

Hector nodded as he continued spreading the pellets over the driveway. "Do you know where he moved?"

"Where, hmm, that is a good question. Couldn't say," Frankie said with a shrug.

Hector continued working and was done in no time. He put the pail next to her door.

Frankie balled a knitted fist under her jaw and squinted her eyes, "Ya know, come to think of it, I think I overheard he moved into one of the trailer parks in the city."

"Do you know which one?"

"Now that I couldn't tell ya. But you could always look up. I wouldn't think it'd be that hard to find. Given his profession and all."

"Profession?"

"Ya, he's one of those Private Detectives or Private Investigators or whatever they call themselves nowadays."

"Really?"

"You betcha. I'm sure you could just google his name and find his address quickly."

"Thanks, I'll do that."

"No problem." Frankie looked up at the falling snow. "Do me a favor, Mr. Hector. You drive safe out there. It seems like a front might be on its way."

Hector nodded, "Oh, it certainly is."

Returning to his Bronco, Hector turned over the engine and pulled out his phone. He thumbed Porter's name into the search engine and within seconds had the address for 'Leathernecks Detective Agency.'

Hector selected the 'guide me there' option on his phone and kicked the Bronco into gear.

He turned up his deck finishing the Johnny Cash song.

❧

Twenty minutes later, Hector drove up to Porter's trailer. For a while, he just stared at the home.

Tire marks were etched in the snow where a vehicle had backed out of the attached carport some time ago. Remnants of footprints led to and away from the rotted front screen door.

The trailer wasn't much to look at. It wasn't much at all.

Walking up the steps, Hector opened the screen and banged on the door.

He waited for a response.

There was none.

He put his ear to the door.

Nothing.

Next to the doorknob, he sent a kick into the door.

The door didn't budge, for it was reinforced.

Staring into the ring doorbell cam, he crouched and put a finger to his lips.

Making his way to his Bronco, he opened the back and pulled out his Mossberg 590 shotgun with the Salvo 12 suppressor.

Putting the barrel on the doorknob, he squeezed the trigger.

The cylinder lock blew back, and the remains of the deadbolt crumbled.

An alarm whined as Hector entered. He swept the corners of the living room with his barrel, and then, behind the door and over it, a shotgun was suspended on hooks over the doorway.

Taking a knee and training his weapon on the open living space, he steadied his barrel, looking for any movement, a wayward sound, anything.

There was nothing.

He let the alarm whine for several more seconds before locating it on the side wall and smashing it with the butt of the shotgun.

The kitchen on the opposite side was lined with dirty coffee mugs and ashtrays.

Porter's wedding picture hung on the hallway wall. Porter was in his dress blues, two rows of medals hanging off his chest. Maggie wore a trumpet ivory dress.

A closet was next to the open bathroom door. An old washer and dryer combo was in the utility closet, and a box of detergent pods filled the space.

In the bathroom, Hector was surprised to find an assortment of nail polish lining the vanity, various boxes of makeup, and a collection of hairbrushes. His surprise didn't stem from the products themselves but rather the teenager-themed style of each.

Avril Lavigne and Evanescence rock posters adorned the walls in the first bedroom. A long mirror cluttered with stickers and sticky notes hung on the back wall. A computer desk with a chrome book, school books, and various notepads hugged the main wall. A colorful twin-sized bed took up the middle of the room.

In the opposite room was a vintage '90s poster of Britney Spears clutching onto a faded white post. The Princess of Pop wore a pink sweater revealing her mid-drift and sported cut-off Levi's.

There was an unkempt bed with tangled white sheets and a single heavy mink-red blanket. Spent cigarettes hung off the sides of an ashtray on the end table. Crumbled condom wrappers decorated the dresser. An empty bottle of Coors Light in the mix and a taped-together free-standing punching bag in the corner tied the room together.

Something on the bed caught Hector's eye.

Digging with the shotgun barrel, he lifted and examined the red lace panties that hung off. He let the panties fall off the barrel.

Hector slung the shotgun onto his back and walked to the kitchen. Opening the fridge, he pulled out the milk carton, found the cabinet of mugs, and poured himself a drink. He nuked the mug and, taking it out, went to the hallway.

Sipping on the drink, he stared at the picture of Porter and Maggie and could only speculate about what happened between them.

Motorcycles rumbled outside, and the sound intensified as they neared the trailer.

Hector took another sip of milk before placing it on the office table. He plucked a 12 gauge from the front pocket of his jacket and loaded the shotgun.

"Detective!" a voice yelled from outside.

Their bike revved menacingly.

Hector thumbed additional slugs into the shotgun.

"We know you're in there!" Another yelled.

"Get your ass out here!" A third called out.

Hector peeled back the front window curtain and counted four riders illuminated by a Molotov cocktail one of the bikers held. All wore bandannas over their mouths, donned matching Wolfpack vests, and were heavily armed.

Hector walked out the door as the others lit their Molotov cocktails. There was a look of surprise on their faces.

The biker with the lit Molotov hurled his bottle.

Taking aim, Hector blasted the bottle out of the sky, and a rain of fire showered the air.

A few heads popped out of their trailers to see what was causing all the noise.

Hector paid them no attention.

Hector blasted the man's hand before the next biker could throw his Molotov. Consequently, the bottle ignited, exploding into the man's face and knocking over the biker beside him.

As Hector walked down the stairs, a biker sporting large GI glasses with a bandage across his nose turned his bike in the opposite direction to retreat. "Fuck this!"

"Jason, where the hell do you think you're going!" the lead biker with a face covered in tattoos yelled.

Jason got ten feet before Hector sent buckshot into his back.

The man slumped forward, and the bike veered lazily off the icy road, over a curb, and fell into a ditch.

The tattooed-faced leader began to pull his pistol from his side holster. Hector nailed him in the chest, sending him flying off his bike.

The toppled-over biker took aim with his SIG Sauer M17 and fired two shots.

The first 9mm Luger missed.

The second hit.

Feeling a sharp pain in his arm, Hector swapped the shotgun from his right to his left. He returned fire at the man's head, which disappeared in an explosion of red.

Blood dripped off Hector's fingertips as he shakily fished a 12-gauge from his flannel pocket. He slowly thumbed the round into the shotgun as he approached the man Hector had shot in the back.

At the bike wreckage, Hector descended the ditch and circled around the crawling biker, leaving a crimson trail etched through the snow.

"Help me, man, help me," the biker pleaded. He reached and tugged on Hector's pants leg with fingers more blood than skin.

The biker was young, thin, and sporting a high and tight military cut. The name patch on his Wolfpack vest read, 'Pup.'

"Why are you after Porter?"

Jason spat out blood, "I need to get to a hospital, man, a hospital."

"Yes, you're bleeding to death."

"Help me," Jason pleaded. He tugged again on Hector, "Please."

"Answer my question. Why are you after Porter?"

"Fuck that guy. He broke my nose twice."

"Seems a little overkill for a guy who broke your nose."

"Twice."

"Even if I were to call right now, an ambulance would not arrive in time. I am the only one who can get you to a hospital in time. Tell me more."

Jason spat more blood and said, "You promise you'll help me?"

Hector nodded, "If you tell me what I need to know."

"Tattoo-Tony told us to go after Porter."

"Where can I find Tattoo-Tony?"

In pain, Jason looked back at the dead bikers in front of Porter's trailer, "You blew a six-inch hole into his chest,"

"Who did Tony get his orders from?"

"Fuck, I don't know. We were all recruited by Scott."

"Scott?"

"The American Iron President."

"If Porter wasn't here, where would you look next?"

"A whore from his club he sleeps with."

"Who?"

Shakily reaching into his pocket, Jason pulled out his phone, unlocked it, and slid it across the snow towards Hector. "The information is in a text. It's all there."

With the gun still trained on him, Hector picked up the phone and thumbed on the text.

Sirens sounded in the distance, and Hector looked towards them.

"Please, man, I'm dying, I'm dying," Jason whimpered.

Hector pumped the shotgun and leveled it at Jason's face, "I know."

"No, what the fuck?" Jason quivered in surprise and anger. "No!" He cried, "You promised you'd help me."

Hector pulled the trigger. "I just did."

22

Evans' cell phone rang. She awoke in bed and stared at the phone, vibrating and playing the theme song to Cops, 'Bad Boys' by Inner Circle, on the end table beside her. The time read 2:20 a.m., and the number said, 'Private.' In her line of work, there were many numbers this could represent, but she hoped it was only one or two. She unplugged the phone and stared at the screen.

Her black cat jumped on her chest.

Evans rubbed behind his ears, "It's okay. Down, Bauer." She shut her heavy eyes, debating whether or not to answer the call. Despite her better judgment, she answered, "Finley, I told you not to call me anymore tonight with your apologies. I don't want to hear any more of your excuses."

"Sarah, sorry to wake you."

"Harry?" Evans asked, sitting up.

"Yeah, sounds like you're already having a rough night," Amberson said concerningly. "Listen, we've got a situation here, and I'm going to need you at a crime scene."

It was odd for a senior Detective to request another Detective at a crime scene. Even for a guy like Amberson, who had a good relationship with Evans, Detectives usually liked to work and solve cases alone.

"You need me now?" Evans asked.

"Yeah," Amberson answered. "Trust me, I know it's late."

"Is everything alright?"

There was a long pause.

"Harry?" Evans asked.

"Listen, your buddy, Porter –"

"What did he do this time?" Evans snapped.

"I'm at his place right now. There's a lot of bodies."

"Is he okay?"

"Interesting that this is your first question after I tell you that."

"Harry?"

"I don't know. He's not at the scene, and we have no idea where he's at. We tried calling him and his partner, Mindy, but no one answered. I put out an APB a few minutes ago. You wouldn't happen to know where they're at, would you?"

Evans ran fingers through her hair and, shrugging, shook her head, "Who's to say? His club, a bar, a random blonde's bed." Bauer inched closer up her chest, and she rubbed behind his ears again. Even in the dark, she perceived a look of sincerity from the cat.

"Okay…" Amberson sighed. "Listen, Sarah, we trust each other, right?"

"What are you getting at?"

"You would tell me if he was with you, right?"

Evans rolled her eyes and, instead of saying something she would regret, instead said, "I'll be there in forty minutes." Ending the call, she looked at her unkempt bed. Years ago, the plan had been for Porter to be next to her every night. That was before the Marine Corps, before Maggie. She exchanged another look with Bauer, "Looks like I just got you."

Unplucking Bauer from her chest and walking to her kitchen with Bauer's claws clicking across the wooden floorboards behind her, she flicked on the lights, reached into the cabinet, and pulled out a can of cat food. Peeling open the can, she put it on the counter and watched as Bauer gobbled it up. Bauer never waited for her to put the food in his dish.

On her cell, she selected Porter's number from her favorites and listened for his answer, but it never came. When prompted, she left a message, "Porter, it's me, listen, Harry put out an all-points bulletin on you. I'm heading to your place now. Where are you? Call me back." About to end the call, she said, "I hope you're alright."

Returning to her room, she rummaged through her dresser for undergarments, then went into her closet for a black turtleneck and matching dress pants. Grabbing the fold of clothes, she lingered on a framed picture atop her end table.

Finley wore a classic black suit, Evans, a red dress with a black shawl draped over her shoulders. They were in Quantico, standing in front of an empty stage filled with various flags and a podium stamped with the blue FBI seal. Finley held up his brand-new identification badge and wore a wide grin.

Evans turned the picture face down. Starting the shower, she unclothed and stepped in.

Turning into the trailer park, a gaggle of police tape, news vans, and reporters lined the neighborhood awash with alternating blue and red police lights.

Evans slowed the Jeep to a crawl as she took in the scene, "What the hell happened?"

A tow truck was loading a wrecked bike into its back. The flatbed was already packed with a mangle of steel and tires.

Various mounds of snow had oil and dried blood soaked into them.

Residents stood outside their homes, inspecting bullet holes that had peppered their exteriors. Some people were talking to news crews, and some were trying to get on-scene Officers' attention. One older man just stood outside with his shirt off, drinking a beer and cursing at everyone within earshot.

An Officer controlling traffic into the neighborhood recognized Evans' vehicle and rushed over. He was tall, with a lazy eye and big ears.

Evans lowered her window, "Hey, Mock."

"Detective Evans, I was supposed to go on my lunch break half an hour ago, and I really gotta pee, but Ellingson –"

Evans raised a finger, "Stop, that's way too much information. Where is Detective Amberson?"

"There was some sort of shootout, like the O.K. Corral or something. From what we can tell, a few Wolfpack bikers got mixed up, and some guy took them all out. I've never seen anything like it."

"I bet," Evans said.

Navigating through the controlled chaos, Evans parked alongside Porter's bullet-riddled trailer, blocked from the public with orange barricades and police tape stretched over the entrance.

Stepping out, she looked down at the dirt and snow driveway splattered in blood and shell casings.

Evans hoped to God the blood wasn't Porter's.

A tripod work light illuminated the property in 4000 lumens, and a forensics crew collected prints off abandoned pistols in the front and took pictures. Another team placed yellow placards across the property, marking and categorizing the evidence. There were multiple body bags lined one next to the other.

"Sarah! Over here," Amberson said, peaking his head out from Porter's trailer with a cup of coffee.

Allowed entry by the controlling Police Officer, Evans tiptoed around the placards and forensics crew.

Stepping into Porter's trailer, Amberson handed the Starbucks cup to Evans, "Here you go, got you a Café Latte." Amberson was wearing the same clothes he had on last night. Grey and wrinkled never went out of style with him.

Evans took a sip and cringed.

"Not a winner?"

"You want it?" Evans asked, handing it back.

"Sure."

"Appreciate the gesture."

Walking to Porter's kitchen, Evans grabbed a clean cup from the dishwasher, a bottle of creamer from the fridge, the big bag of Splenda from the top cabinet, and a spoon from the leftmost drawer.

"Uh, should I even bother to tell you that going through a suspect's personal belongings…" Amberson began to say.

Tossing a coffee pod into the Keurig, Evans placed the mug under the dispenser and began the brew. She looked at him and stared indifferently.

"Never mind." Amberson sipped his coffee. "I take it you've been here once or twice?"

Evans leaned back across the kitchen counter and looked up at the hooks above the front door where a shotgun was usually nestled. "Yeah, you could say that."

Combining the Splenda into the coffee, she stirred in the creamer and sipped.

"How is it?" Amberson asked.

"Frothy," Evans said. "Say what you want about Porter. He has the good coffee fixings."

"So yeah, let's talk about Porter."

"Give me the details."

"It ain't pretty, to say the least. I mean, I'm sure you saw enough on the way in. It's a slaughterhouse out there. We are still gathering the details, but the residents were awoken by explosions, gunfire, and screaming. When the units arrived, everyone was already dead, and Porter was nowhere to be found."

"The rounds in the vics, you confirmed they're from a .38?"

"A .38?" Amberson tapped away on his tablet. "Nope, forensics say the casings in the Wolfpack bikers are from a shotgun."

Evans looked at the hooks over the door again, "A shotgun, huh?"

"Yeah, but not that one."

"What do you mean not that one?"

"We have Porter's shotgun categorized already, a Mossberg Silver Reserve II double barrel shotgun taking 20 gauge. The vics were hit with .22 caliber from a suppressor-fitted shotgun."

"A suppressor-fitted shotgun?"

"Is that a type of weapon Porter carries? Maybe in his truck?"

"Not that I'm aware of."

"Sarah, these bikers came looking for Porter, and whether or not they found him, he's on their radar. The Wolfpack is looking for him, and after the carnage here, they will not stop until he's dead. We need to find him before they do. What did he get himself into?"

"He's working a case for Bobbi Johnson right now."

"Seriously?"

"Yeah."

"Wow, nothing against Porter. I know he's your friend and all, but Johnson is not the clientele I would associate with him."

Evans shrugged and drank more of her coffee, "Preaching to the choir."

"Okay, I'll have someone give her office a call. What is he hired for?"

"It concerns Johnson's Zero Tolerance Crime Crack Down."

"But she hasn't even been elected to the U.S. Senate."

"She wants Porter to shut American Iron down, which happens by going after their muscle. That muscle seems to be the Wolfpack or at least elements of the biker club."

"Elements of the biker club, you don't buy it's the entire club?"

"I know the Wolfpack President. He wouldn't go into partnership with American Iron, let alone condone a hit on Porter."

"I'm not going to even ask how you know a biker club President. What's the name?" Amberson asked.

"Flick," Evans told him.

Amberson punched it into his tablet, "Is that a first or last name?"

"I don't know. We just all call him Flick."

"You gotta give me more than that."

"He lives in this trailer park, pretty close to Porter," Evans said.

"Alright, I'll run it to ground." Setting down the tablet, Harry crossed his arms. "You said Flick wouldn't condone a hit on Porter? Why is that?"

"Flick trained Porter to be a Detective."

"Ahh, I see. If Wolfpack bikers are after Porter, they must be unsanctioned without Flick's knowledge."

"My thoughts, too."

Scratching his beard, Amberson said, "Well, from what I hear, a few bikers wouldn't push a guy like Porter around."

Evans shook her head, "Nope, not Porter."

"If Porter can prove the rogue bikers are connected to Amerian Iron and shut them down, it's a good talking point for Bobbi Johnson heading into the election. Pretty much guaranteeing a win for the U.S. Senate seat," Amberson said.

"Exactly."

"Still, quite the task for one guy and his teenage partner."

"Porter's not just a guy, and Mindy's not just a teenage partner."

Amberson nodded, "Fair."

Evans finished her coffee and placed it in the sink, "Okay, Harry, what do you need from me?"

"Take point on finding Porter. I've sent a few badges to his club and – "

"A few?" Evans asked. "How many cops does it take to check out one club?"

"You really think it's possible to only pick one badge to check out a strip club? I was about to have a full-blown riot on my hands. So, yes, I had to pick five badges. And guess what? In two hours, five different badges will rotate to replace those. These boys are treating this assignment like the lottery."

"How shocking," Evans said sarcastically.

"I was just about to start going through Porter's known associates and sending more badges out before you rolled up. Sarah, you know him better than any of us. If anyone knows which blonde, redhead, or brunette he's sleeping under, it's you."

"I'll be in touch," Evans said, making her way for the door.

"Where are you starting?"

"Not too sure, yet. Figure I'd start driving and go from there."

Harry stepped in front of her, "Here's the thing, Sarah, the Captain wants you to bring a badge with you."

"Seriously?"

"Yep."

"She doesn't trust me?"

Amberson sighed, "She knows your relationship with Porter."

"Harry, do you trust me?"

"Sarah, this isn't an issue of trust. This is an order from the Captain."

"Do you trust me?"

Harry sighed once more and rolled his eyes. He stepped aside and held the door and screen open for her, "Pretty girls like you are so damn persuasive at talking me into bad ideas."

"I'll find him."

"You better, or it'll be both our asses."

"One last question, Harry."

"Shoot."

"I'm guessing you also have a rotation at the strip club?"

"Well, of course, someone has to supervise, right?"

❧

As Evans Jeep rolled down Academy, few cars were on the road. Many people were still asleep, and even fewer establishments were open. A McDonald's she now passed being one of the few places available at this hour.

A memory crossed her mind of Senior Skip Day, or at least the day she, Porter, and their trio of friends determined it was Senior Skip Day. Porter was living with his mom, and she was off on a business trip. All his siblings had moved away. He had the house to himself.

They all met up in the gym before the first bell. They ran past the school security Officer and made their getaway, all five crammed in Porter's white '96 Thunderbird. Their first stop was McDonald's.

Rebellion never tasted so damn good.

It was no *Ferris Bueller's Days Off,* but the day of video games, laughing, loud music, movies, and pizza at Porter's house was great. At the day's conclusion, Porter rolled back into the school's parking lot just as the last bell rang. Their friends bailed out, and Evans stayed behind in the T-Bird with Porter, making out. Things were starting to progress when there was a knock on the window, and Evans' dad stood on the other side.

Since Evans first met Porter in Junior High School, trouble has followed him wherever he went, and today was no exception.

Glancing at the McDonald's again, Evans realized how hungry she was. Having rushed out when Harry called, she hadn't bothered to grab food and regretted it. Coffee only made so much for a morning breakfast. She made a mental note to grab a bite the first chance she got.

Nearing her turn, Evans said, "Hey, Siri, call Porter."

On the third ring, he picked up.

"Sarah?" Porter asked in a groggy voice.

A sense of relief washed over Evans, and she let go of built-up tension she didn't even know she held. Anger filled the stress, "It's about time you picked up. You know how many times I've tried to call you?"

There was a long pause before Porter responded, "It's…4:30."

"You noticed, huh?" she snapped.

"You wanna get laid that bad?"

"Where are you?" Evans asked, slowing to a stop at a red light. A sign was affixed to the light pole: NO TURN ON RED.

"You been thinking about me all night, huh? That's cute."

The light winked green, and she turned, "Dammit, I'm not in the mood."

"You sure about that? This call seems to contradict that statement."

"Where are you?"

"Where am I? More importantly, where are you?"

"On my way to Alice's place, where I assume you're staying. Listen, I'm nearly there and –"

That's when the SUV slammed into her.

23

Porter awoke in a cold sweat as his phone rang. Sitting upright, he banged his head into the top of the truck camper. He cursed and looked around in the darkness for his phone. Of course, his phone wasn't on him; *that would be too convenient.* His phone was in his pants, and his pants were on the camper's floor.

Reaching out, he scooped up his pants and dug out his phone. Only so many people could reach him during his set *Do Not Disturb* hours, and those that could were worth answering. He read the screen, saw he had one signal bar, and flipped open the phone, "Sarah?"

Anger filled the line, "It's about time you picked up. You know how many times I've tried to call you?"

Porter looked at Valentine's LED clock, "It's…4:30."

"You noticed, huh?" she snapped.

Porter smirked, "You wanna get laid that bad?"

"Where are you?" Evans asked.

Porter could tell she was driving from the distorted voice and low, rumbling background sound. With a yawn, Porter laid back in the bed. He turned to his bedmate and brushed a finger across her flesh, wondering if it was even worth telling Evans about Valentine. "You been thinking about me all night, huh? That's cute."

"Dammit, I'm not in the mood."

"You sure about that? This call seems to contradict that statement."

"Where are you?"

"Where am I? More importantly, where are you?"

"On my way to Alice's place, where I assume you're staying."

Porter rolled his eyes.

Evans continued, "Listen, I'm nearly there and –"

A loud crash sounded.

Porter's eyes went wide, "Sarah?"

She didn't answer.

Sitting up, Porter once again smacked his head into the camper. Cursing, he rolled out of the bed and sat on the corner bench at her table. He held the phone close to his ear, listening for any sounds that might clue him into her whereabouts.

There was hissing and panting.

"Sarah? Talk to me. Sarah!" Porter yelled.

There was a sound of metal crunching.

"Get her out," a man barked in the background.

"Get back," Evans groggily said.

"Take her gun!"

"Sarah, what's happening?!" Porter yelled.

"Porter!" Sarah yelled before being carried away.

Someone picked up the phone, and with it came a man's breathing.

"Who is this?" Porter asked.

"I heard you've been looking for me," the voice said smugly.

Porter deciphered the voice and said, "Scott, this is between you and me. Leave Sarah out of this."

"You've been hurting my operations, and now I'm going to do something to hurt you. It's a shame, really. I was looking forward to seeing her work a pole."

"You want to talk about hurt, fine," Porter said. "Mess with someone I care about, and I will hurt you in ways you've never dreamed. No amount of Army Special Ops training will keep me from drinking your blood from your skull."

There was silence.

"Did you hear me? Say something, you fuck."

Scott chuckled, "It's been a while since someone threatened me like that."

"Yeah, you get high enough in the food chain that you get complacent," Porter said. "You start to think you're immune to getting your teeth kicked into the back of your throat."

"God damn, Porter, you're like a professional asshole, aren't you?"

"Tell me where you're at so I can show you the laminated lifetime membership."

"We'll be at the cemetery, you know, the one by Alice's apartment. Alice has a cute kid, too. What is she in, second grade?"

"Really? You piece of shit."

"Such a shame the kids recently paroled daddy picked her up from school to see Grandma and Grandpa. We weren't expecting that, but we'll catch them when they return to the city."

"I can't wait to snap your neck, Scott."

"And you think we only know about Alice? We've got addresses for all your whores. Erica, Molly, Jen, to hell with that two-timing whore, by the way, you want me to keep going?"

Porter couldn't contain his fury and seethed with anger, "Make your peace with God."

"Come alone, or your partner, Mindy, or should I say your legally adopted daughter? She'll be the first to eat a bullet," Scott said before ending the call.

Porter stared at the phone, wanting to crush the piece of aluminum and metal in his hand as it would somehow bring him pleasure, but he knew it wouldn't.

Putting two fingers to his neck pulse, he felt his blood was still racing. His head was pounding from a sudden migraine or bashing his crown into the camper, most likely both. Finding his jacket among the pile of clothes, he took his bottle of Excedrin out of the inside pocket and, careening his mouth under the faucet, downed two capsules.

Sitting on the corner bench, he fished his contact lens case from his jacket and popped the contacts in his eyes. As his eyes adjusted, he pulled back the side window curtain and watched the snowfall. He usually found peace in watching the snowfall in the night.

There would be no peace tonight.

He knew this would be a trap and hoped to clear his mind, but it wasn't happening. He felt so much anger, and he knew it was clouding his judgment. He felt this way only one another time. The day Maggie had left him, but this was different.

Sarah was worth saving.

Porter finished getting dressed and lit a cigarette before heading for the door.

Still lying on the bed, Valentine propped up onto her side. "What are you planning?"

Porter stopped and turned to her, "Oh, you know, something heroic."

"Jesus, you going to get yourself killed?" Valentine asked in all seriousness.

"Trust me, if I go down, I'm taking all those mother fuckers with me."

"Porter –" Valentine began to protest.

"Make sure Mindy doesn't follow me," he told her.

Valentine got out of bed with a blanket wrapped around her flesh, "Porter, I can help."

"They're going to come after, Mindy. I'm sure of it. If I don't make it back, keep her safe. That's how you can help, but be careful with her. She's too smart for her own good," he took a deep drag on his cigarette, and the ember cast an orange glow inside the camper. "You know, there's not a lot of good I've done in this world, but taking her in, I feel like that's one of them."

Stepping up to him, Valentine grabbed the back of his neck and pressed her lips to his. After a lingering moment, they parted lips, and gazing into his eyes, she said, "This is the last time we can be together, you know that, right?"

"Why do you say that?"

"That woman who Scott took, Sarah, you love her, don't you?"

Porter didn't answer.

"You're willing to die for her."

"I am."

"Then that's a yes. Go get her."

❧

Unlocking his 8 x 10-foot storage container, Porter rolled up the door and stepped inside the freezing brown corrugated steel.

Reaching up, he flicked on his six ft LED work light, which was velcroed to the ceiling, illuminating the free-standing three-tier shelves filled with armor and weaponry.

Pulling a black flak jacket off one shelf, he plucked AR500 Steel Body Armor Plates from another shelf and inserted them into the flak's front and back openings.

Taking off his jacket, he tossed it onto the green cot, taking up the floor space between the two shelves, and pulled on the flak. He made the flak extra snug as he often did before a firefight.

Propping a foot on the cot's frame, he clipped a side holster to his thigh. He secured his revolver to his side as he nodded to 'Kryptonite' by 3 Doors Down, playing from his truck parked outside the container.

A cloud of condensation formed from his breath as he muttered along to the song lyrics.

Porter added six-shot speed loaders to his utility belt and dropped full metal jackets into the pouches on his flak.

Rummaging through a bin, he pulled out a M18 smoke grenade and a pair of M67 grenades. Placing them into the pouches on his flak, he walked to another bin, pulled out a Ka-Bar adapter, and secured it onto the flak. About to insert the Ka-Bar into the sheath, he decided to sharpen the seven-inch blade.

Finding the sharpener, he sat at the cot and ran the blade directly through the center. On the 10th pass of grinding the edge against the sharpener, the image of his drill instructor ran through his mind.

Porter recalled three weeks into Boot Camp, hearing the loud clicking heels of Corfram dress shoes walking up and down the freshly mopped squad bay as lights went out. Drill Instructor Staff Sergeant Lopez, a short, grizzled veteran wearing a crisp campaign cover, pressed Charlies with three stacks of ribbons, speaking to them in a frog voice, "It was a frozen day in hell during the

Chosin Reservoir campaign in Korea in November 1950. On this day, Ole, Chesty, one of the most stubborn Devil Dogs to ever wear the Eagle, Globe, and Anchor, said, we've been looking for the enemy for several days now. We've finally found them. We're surrounded. That simplifies our problem of getting to these people and killing them."

With the knife finally sharpened to his satisfaction, Porter scooped brass knuckles out of another bin, slipped them into his pockets, grabbed the M204 rifle from the bottom shelf, and slung it over his body. Securing the container, he returned to his truck.

Pulling out his phone, Porter shook his head, "I hate doing this shit." Thumbing away, he sent a mass cautionary text message to his contacts, warning them of the impending danger lurking behind the name of American Iron.

Parked in the McDonald's lot across the road from the cemetery, Porter pulled out his pocket scope and put the monocular to his right eye, adjusting the focus to compensate for the distance. A single car was visible past the tall iron-rusted arches leading into the parking lot.

Evans' smashed yellow Jeep was sitting sideways, taking up a trio of spots and surrounded by a minefield of glass, aluminum, and metal debris. The length of the driver's side was smashed in. The driver's side door had been forcibly removed, and smoke hissed from the engine.

Porter glassed the empty, fenced property with his scope. Colorado Blue Spruces scattered across the snow-covered landscape past the lot and the small funeral home, towering 75-100 feet tall. An assortment of black granite headstones comprising various crosses and angelic symbols took up much of the space. Cedar gazebos, 12 feet tall, with metal roofs flanked on either side of the property. A 15 x 30-foot memorial wall was adorned with first responder flags and plaques running along the center space. Behind the first responder memorial stood a stone mausoleum with flanking pearl angels.

Porter watched the property for a few moments longer. All seemed relatively quiet. He wondered where Scott and his team would attack from. Better yet, Porter wondered the best place he could shoot from.

Pulling into the lot, Porter stepped out, walked past the Jeep, and scanned inside. The cloth seats were sprinkled with glass and blood. The airbag was a crumbled heap hanging limply out from the steering wheel.

Porter yanked on the door handle to the funeral home. It was locked, and the only disturbed snow was from where his hands had touched the pull handle. Peering inside the etched window, all was dark and empty.

Porter made his way up the cemetery in a tactical crouch, taking what cover he could. At the memorial wall, he found a square urn enclosure with a cross and plaque that read, "Mike Porter, Sgt. 1st Class, US Army, Nov 10, 1960 – Dec 18, 2003, Bronze Star, Purple Heart, Operation Iraqi Freedom, Father, Husband, Soldier."

Staring at the etched letters, Porter remembered the day they cremated him and placed the urn in the wall. The day he didn't say a word, his brother and sister said little. That day, they saw their mother cry and not stop crying for the whole day. It was just a constant flow of tears and sniffling to the point mom's eyes were bloodshot, and her nose was cherry red by day's end.

Porter knelt and readjusted the green wreath that had fallen over at the base of the memorial wall. A nickel was sitting atop the marble base. He picked it up.

"I came by earlier and put that there."

Porter leveled his rifle at the voice and saw a man he hadn't seen in years, "Gunny?"

The years had been unkind to Hector Guvera, who was thinner than Porter remembered. Hector was still tall and broad-shouldered, but there was now a slight hunch to his stance. His eyes drooped and sagged, making them look heavy. The hazel in his eyes had dulled. His once-dark skin looked stretched and faded, like an old leather jacket.

Hector wore a black felt cowboy hat, red suede jacket, deerskin gloves, blue jeans, and snowy black and white rattlesnake boots. A discolored bandage was wrapped around his right arm. A Sig Sauer P226 sat on his side. A Mossberg 590 shotgun fitted with a Salvo 12 suppressor was slung around his chest.

Hector gestured to the memorial wall, "Coins on a military gravestone signify someone visited to pay their respects. A penny means they visited. A nickel means they were in boot camp with them."

"A dime means they served with them," Porter said, weapon still trained on him.

"I see you're ready to go to war again. But your fight isn't with me."

Porter lowered his weapon.

Hector stared down at the coin, "OIF 2003. I was just a young buck then, a Corporal serving under your dad. I was there when it happened." He reflected on the memory and said, "He was a good man."

"So, I'm told," Porter said.

"To think you would serve under me just a few years after your dad passed."

"Small world," Porter said. Seeing his old Gunnery Sergeant any other day would have warranted war stories and rounds of beer, but today wasn't that day. Porter scanned the scenery and, taking in the emptiness, turned his attention back to Hector. "What are you doing here?"

"I've been tracking you for some time, Sergeant. Or should I call you Detective?" Hector asked. "You've been going after some dangerous people lately."

"Well, that's what pays the bills."

"I read about the Sandman case you solved earlier this year. And seeing you now, you know there's no room left in this world for heroes. You're a dying breed."

Porter looked back at the memorial wall, "Hero? That's them there, not the guy in front of you."

Hector nodded, "I went by your trailer and didn't find you or your daughter there."

"Is that right?" Porter noticed there were splatters of blood on Hector's face and neck. Things were beginning to add up. Hector must have been why Sarah told him an APB was put on him. Porter could only imagine all the Wolfpack members Hector had killed en route to his location, "Why are you tracking me down?"

"We do anything to protect family," Hector said, looking up at the sky. "Family is what brought me here. You see, my parents died. Their funeral was just the other day, and someone put my brother in the hospital."

Porter stared at him, "Someone?"

"They broke both his arms and legs, then marked his face with cigarette burns," Hector turned to him, and his eyes burned into Porter's.

Porter returned the stare. "The only person I've done that to recently was a spaghetti-eating fuck. A greasy bastard who liked to chain up, drug, and screw little girls."

Hector didn't blink as he said, "I always find it interesting how families come to be, a blend of cultures, traditions, heritage. Take my family for example. My father came from Mexico, gained citizenship, and joined the Army. One day, he gets stationed at

Longare U.S. Army Base in Vicenza, Italy, where he meets my mother. My parents have two boys, myself and –"

"Joshua," Porter finished his sentence. "You do realize what that greasy brother of yours was about to do to my partner, my daughter, don't you? What he did to all those other girls? I couldn't allow that."

"Whatever Joshua has become, he's still my brother and mine to deal with when this is all over."

"When what's all over?" Porter asked.

"My intentions were to find you and do to you what you did to Joshua, but there's something more at play. Someone has set you up, so circumstances would bring us together today. Given our history, it's no coincidence. There's a mark on both of us. We've been brought here together for a reason."

"A mark?"

"A group has been trying to kill me ever since I reentered the country."

"Why? What did you do?"

"We have a common enemy," Hector said, not answering the question. Instead, he continued, "That should be enough for now."

"Listen, what I did to your brother –"

"What if I told you that my brother was working for the Rizzo family, those Italians you ran into the other day. The Rizzos were in partnership with American Iron," Hector said. "But Joshua was working for them undercover. Truth be told, I think he got in too deep; the lines were blurred, and he couldn't get out. He got lost in the monster he had to become to maintain his cover."

"Undercover for who?"

"A shadow organization based out of Europe with operatives strategically placed in crime organizations across the globe. This organization is well-connected and funded by the elites of the world. They have heavy influence in political world affairs."

"Do they now?"

"They call themselves The Pride." Hector studied Porter, "But you already know of them, don't you?"

"I know of them."

"Few do."

"I'm sure."

At these words, SUVs rolled up to the cemetery.

"To the mausoleum," Hector said, leading the way.

The tall white mausoleum with granite exterior stood 150 feet away. Steps and railings preceded bronze doors, and fluted pillars flanked either side. Angels were sculpted inside the gable leading to the triangular roof.

The sun was to their backs, and being at the top of the hill, they had a line of sight to the below lots, providing a tactical advantage.

They made it to the exterior wall of the mausoleum as a silver SUV with black tinted windows pulled into the side lot with a screeching halt. The vehicle positioned itself parallel to the curb. Moments later, a matching SUV pulled into the main lot where Porter was parked.

Instinctively, Porter and Hector took cover behind pillars, and each man pointed their weapons at a separate vehicle.

In tandem, the doors of each SUV opened, and out stepped seven armed men and one woman. The men were tall, muscular, hairy, with thick eyebrows and chiseled jaws. Each sported slick back hair and rocked gold chains. They wore a mix of black and red tactical gear, including flak jackets and bandoliers of ammo. Their arms were layered with various tattoos. Their fingers were adorned with rings. They rested their Beretta ARX160 assault rifles above the car doors they took cover behind.

Porter searched for Scott but didn't see him. Who he did see surprised him. Amongst the crowd was a thick, bald Russian with a beard and a dagger tattoo on his neck, Volkov.

"You order take-out?" Porter asked. "Pizza Hut with a side of Mother Russia?"

Hector shook his head, "More of your friends?"

A Britney Spears song sounded as Porter's phone went off.

Hector turned to him, "Seriously?"

Porter held up a finger and dug in his jacket. He looked at the screen, which read, Sarah. Flipping open his phone, he said, "Too chicken shit to show up yourself, Scott?"

"Porter," Scott said, "when the Italians contacted me asking to set up a reunion with you for what you did to them earlier this week, who was I to say no?"

"And the Russian?" Porter asked, looking down at Volkov. "Bobbi Johnson in on this too?"

"In on this?" Scott asked with a laugh. "For being a Detective, you sure are a dumbass."

"A dumbass, really, Scott? C'mon, don't bullshit yourself, no one can take that title from you."

"Shut your mouth," Scott said, "Put Hector Guvera on."

"Not until I talk to Sarah, I want to know she's there," Porter said.

Scott sighed and then said, "Talk to him."

Sarah's voice came over the line, "I'm at the American Iron Corporate –"

A whipping sound came over the phone, and Evans groaned in pain.

"Sarah!" Porter yelled.

"Talk again, and I put a bullet in you," Scott said to Evans. He then barked at Porter, "Put Hector on the phone now!"

"I can't wait to break your fucking neck." Porter turned to Hector and put the phone on speaker, "It's for you."

"Talk," Hector said.

"My investors, let's call them that," Scott continued, "would like to know your funereal preferences? Six feet under, cremation, or should we settle for a burial at sea? Surely the latter has symbolic meaning to you."

"I don't make threats," Hector said. "So, when I tell you that you will die painfully, know it's guaranteed."

"And you, Detective," Scott said, "I'm actually impressed with your skills. You've caused a lot of damage to my operation, and let's face it, you handled yourself well as of late."

"I already told you, we ain't swapping spit in the shower," Porter said.

"Kill Hector Guvera now, and not only will you be given the job as my top security advisor here at American Iron, but you will also be paid $1 million."

Hector turned to Porter and studied him.

Porter let him study him for a moment longer before slowly moving his free hand into his jacket and slowly taking out his pack of Lucky Strike cigarettes. With a flick of the wrist, a cigarette extruded, and Porter bit down on it. Exchanging the box for his lucky lady zippo lighter, he lit up and turned his attention to the phone.

"$1 million? For a man of my skills? That's fucking insulting. I want at least $10 million," Porter said. "All in crisp dollar bills. I got a lot of girls I need to put through college and not just the Community College."

Hector smirked for the first time in a long time.

"You see, these club girls want to go to these fancy State Universities," Porter said. "And you may not know this, being the ASVAB waiver you are, but the tuition rates rise yearly. So, as you can see, $1 million just isn't going to cut it."

"Well, that's bad news for Sarah," Scott said. "Such a shame, too. She's played such a good damsel in distress."

There was a sound of what sounded like struggling over the phone, then shattering glass and a man's screaming voice.

Evans's distant voice said, "I'm no one's damsel in distress."

The phone went dead.

"Seems Sarah's doing alright," Porter said to Hector.

Hector shook his head, "Were not."

"Aprire il fooco!" one of the Italians yelled before they opened fire.

Porter and Hector exchanged gunfire. The pillars they took cover behind began to quickly disintegrate.

"Contact right! Adjust to sixty meters!" Hector yelled.

Porter adjusted the range knob on the M203 mounted to his M4, took aim, and let loose a 40 mm grenade round. A pop sounded as the round shot off into the air and struck the SUV parked in the side lot. The SUV jumped in the air, and the fire and car parts explosion tossed the Italians and Volkov to the asphalt.

"Contact left! Adjust to ninety meters!" Hector said, continuing to exchange gunfire with the main lot.

Porter adjusted the range knob, plucked a 40 mm from his flak, opened the barrel, inserted the round, and slammed it shut. Taking aim, he let fly the grenade.

"Mettersi al riparo!" The Italians yelled at the sound of the pop. They scrambled away from the SUV moments before it leaped into the air, leaving a trail of fire, metal, and aluminum.

"How many more rounds you have?" Hector asked.

"Not enough. Just hold them off for a second!" Porter yelled. Focusing on the mausoleum door, he exposed the barrel and slammed in his last 40 mm round. Taking a step back, he took aim at the locked bronze door and blew it open.

Reaching on his flak, he pulled out a smoke bomb and, pulling the pin, lobbed it in the space between them and the Italians. "Take cover inside."

Hector gave the front doors a kick, widening the opening.

The white marble mausoleum was narrow and deep. The tall walls on either side were lined with crypts, five stacks high and fifteen across, each adorned with an inscription accompanied by a flower in a mounted vase. Benches lined the center, leading to stained-glass windows in the back. Despite the best attempts at proper ventilation, there was an underlying smell of dustiness and various other disagreeable odors.

"You take immediate right," Hector said, pointing with his Sig Sauer barrel to the location next to the door. "I'll take a staggered position to the left. We'll shoot them as they come in."

"Fine with me, as long as they all die."

Trained on the entrance, the sound of one of the back windows shattering caught them off guard. They looked down as a green M84 grenade rolled towards them.

"Flashbang!" Hector yelled.

A blinding light illuminated the room as the grenade exploded, and a deafening boom sounded. The velocity sent Porter onto his back, and Hector slammed into the nearest wall. A portion of the ceiling came apart and showered onto them.

Grey smoke filled the room.

"Entra adesso!" an Italian shouted from outside the building.

Porter's head pounded and swirled. His eyes burned, and his throat was dry. Blood swelled in his deafened ears. His vision was blurred. He tasted blood.

Reaching for his leg, Porter unbuckled his gas mask carrier. Pulling out and strapping the mask to his face, he took short sips of air.

Porter pulled an M67 grenade from his pouch and pulled the pin on pure instinct. "Frag out," he weakly said as he tossed it out the door. Within seconds, the grenade exploded, and screams sounded.

Porter looked around the smoke-filled room for Hector but couldn't see him.

At the door's entrance, a man-shaped shadow pierced the smoke. The shadow was wide and tall. The laser sight on its ARX160 danced across the room as it advanced through the doorway.

It wore NVGs, making the eyes look glowing, and donned a gas mask. This was the same gear the Wolfpack had worn when they broke into the Petersons. Porter could see how the Petersons would mistake anyone wearing this gear for something supernatural.

Porter shakily raised his M4 to meet the Italian and fired a round. He missed wide. His balance was off, and he suffered from an afterimage in his vision. Everything seemed a fraction of a second off.

The Italian focused on him, "Ciao, Amico."

"Yeah, fuck you, too, Amico," Porter said.

Porter was ready to take rounds to the chest when he saw Hector adorned with a makeshift gas mask. Hector snuck behind the man and stabbed every inch of his Strider SMF knife with a downward thrust into the man's jugular.

As another man entered, Porter flicked his M4 rate of fire from Semi-to-Burst and sprayed the doorway with bullets. The man dropped with a handful of rounds to the chest and face.

Hector said something, but Porter had trouble hearing. He could only assume it was along the lines of "Get up, Marine."

Grabbing Porter by the flak, Hector was helping him up when he suddenly dropped to his knees.

Blood exploded from his left shoulder. An exasperated look reflected in his eyes. Hector pulled Porter's revolver from his side holster and, turning to meet his foe, emptied all six rounds into the Italian before falling over.

"Gunny," Porter said. He checked Hector's faint neck pulse.

Pain exploded in Porter's back as his sappy plate ate a trio of 5.56x45mm NATO rounds. He fell chest-first into the marble floor.

At that moment, Porter's mind returned to Iraq. He remembered the searing heat licking his face a moment before the explosion as his platoon was ambushed from all around. As gunfire came at them from rooftops and buildings, a sharp pain ripped through his leg. Screams and gunfire were all around as he fell.

Falling over, Porter landed on his chest. His face was lying in the sand. He had just enough strength to turn over and see Lance Corporal Wilson lying across from him on his side in a pool of red sand. Blood drooled down his face, and his bottom lip shook. His emerald eyes were wide with shock. The bottom half of his body was missing. Parts of him were strewn out all over. He reached out to Porter before dying, "Ser-geant."

"Trasferirsi!" one Italian shouted to another.

Cautious, soft footsteps sounded as an Italian made their way to Porter. Porter could tell it was a woman from the woody, spice, vanilla perfume. With a grab on Porter's flak, the woman turned him over. Porter met her gaze by sliding his Ka-Bar into her throat.

"Sorry, beautiful," Porter whispered.

"Beh, è morto?" the second Italian asked, checking on her, who was still hunched over Porter. His voice was gruff, his steps heavy, and his Italian seemed a second language.

Porter pulled his knife from the neck of the woman and, shoving her aside, buried the blade into the man's chest.

Looking up at the man, Porter saw it was Volkov. His beard was sticking out the bottom of his gas mask.

The blade pierced through the Russian's body armor but didn't penetrate, and he lurched backward. Porter fired off his M4 and tagged the man's ARX160. The Russian tossed it to the ground before leaping and rolling out the door.

"What? Had enough!" Porter yelled.

Backing up into the nearest wall, Porter used it to brace himself as he got to a vertical base. Panting, he looked down momentarily at his M4 and ejected his magazine. He was in the middle of reloading when Volkov came running full speed into the mausoleum.

In a bull rush, Volkov shoved Porter into the back wall. Before Porter could react, he ripped off Porter's mask and punched him in the gut. With the punch, Porter was forced to exhale a lungful of the tear gas lingering in the air.

Porter couldn't even curse as Volkov held Porter by the throat with one hand, ripped the sling of Porter's M4 from his chest with the other, and flung the weapon across the room.

In desperation, Porter cracked the top of his head into Volkov's big, crooked nose, creating distance. He then sent a front kick into the Ka-Bar's handle, still lodged into Volkov's beefy chest, which sent the blade deeper.

Volkov staggered into the adjacent wall, grabbed the knife's handle, and screamed as he attempted to pull it out, "Kozyol!"

Reaching out, Porter grabbed Volkov's gasmask and yanked it off. He then kicked the Russian in the balls, "How's it feel?"

Bending over and coughing, Volkov sent a haymaker into Porter's face, followed by a body shot. The combined blows dropped Porter to the floor. Volkov grabbed Porter by the throat with both hands and, pinning him against the wall, lifted him off his feet.

Porter first tried chopping Volkov's elbow pit of his right arm, but it wouldn't give. He delivered his best open-palmed punch into the man's chin, but it didn't budge. Porter gripped the man's sweaty hands, trying to break the hold, though nothing worked. By the time he thought to gouge Volkov's beady blue eyes, he was already starting to black out.

Porter's strength had nearly dwindled, and he felt inside his jacket pocket for anything useful. He felt brass knuckles, a pack of cigarettes, and his lighter.

Volkov began growling in anticipation of the kill.

Pulling out his yellow Lucky Lady Motor Oils lighter, Porter thumbed it open and flicked it alive. He had just enough strength to touch the flame to Volkov's beard.

Volkov screamed, and his grip immediately released. The Russian frantically patted his face to extinguish the fire that consumed his beard.

Porter dropped and coughed out saliva and blood. Color began to override the black and white stars swirling in his vision. He looked up as Volkov danced backward.

With an opening, Porter lunged forward, plucked the Ka-Bar out of Volkov's chest, and, yelling, buried the blade into the top of the man's bald head.

Porter stepped back, dropped to a knee, and, sipping air, watched Volkov freeze in place before crumpling to the ground. Volkov's body lay on the floor, beard kindling in green and white smoke.

Putting back on his gas mask, making his way back to Hector, and rechecking his pulse, Porter found his revolver buried in the smoke. Thumbing open the cylinder and letting the empty brass shells fall from the chambers and onto the ground, he took out a speed loader and reloaded.

Porter looked around at the corpses littering the mausoleum and shook his head, "Today sucks.'

❧

With both doors closed and the locking bars secured, Hector Guvera lay unconscious on the cot inside the brown corrugated steel shipping container Porter had prepped inside just hours earlier. Doc was knelt beside him, hard at work on the wound. "So, Porter, I still can't get over that you texted everyone."

Porter stood shirtless and shrugged, chugging down a Coors Light.

"Yeah, Porter texting, that's a new one," Molly said.

"Laugh it up," Porter told them.

"Arms up," Molly said.

Porter did as told, and sitting in her wheelchair, Molly reached around him, securing a surgical bandage around his torso.

"G – S – W," Doc said, pulling the bullet out of Hector's back with a pair of long needle-nose pliers and dropping the round into the glass of disinfectant sitting on the TV tray beside him. "Been a while since I pulled one of these out." Adjusting the light on his headlamp, Doc examined the wound and, after a thorough search, held out an open palm, "Wet wipes."

Porter pointed Molly to its location. She rolled to another shelf and, grabbing the pack, handed them over.

Doc pulled out a few pieces and began dabbing around the wound.

"Is that hygienic?" Molly asked.

"Don't worry, they're alcohol-free wipes, right Porter?" Doc asked, still wiping away.

"Uh, I guess," Porter told him, still sipping his beer. "What's the package say?"

Molly examined the pack, "I don't know, everything is faded. How old is this?"

"Don't worry about it. It should be fine. Or, you know, it's not. Either way, our friend here won't mind," Doc said, wiping away more blood. After a few more swipes, he tossed the used wipes and his blue latex gloves in the trash can. Getting out of the way, he said, "Molly, you're up."

Molly wheeled over, unzipping her blue travel sewing kit, and threaded a needle.

"Let me ask you something, Molly," Doc said, "is that thread of yours hygienic?"

"Absolutely not, but it's what I have." She turned to him, "You've made your point."

Doc nodded, "Carry on."

"You said, G – S – W," Molly said, beginning to work on Hector. "What does that mean?"

"Gunshot wound." Doc turned off his headlamp and looked at Porter, "It's the type of thing you usually have to report to the cops."

"Usually," Porter said.

"So, why didn't you just bring him to the hospital? This whole thing," Doc gestured to the container space, "seems very Spy vs. Spy."

Porter finished off his beer, "Ignorance is bliss." Reaching for a box of Icy Hot patches on the top of one of his shelves, he groaned in pain.

Doc grabbed the box for him and handed it over, "You should really let me patch you up. Your body looks like a colored page where a kid ran out of the right colored markers, so they just used any available color. And your back, man, the size of that bruise. Did you get shot or something?"

"Yeah, a few times," Porter said.

"Damn, hope you gave the other guy hell."

"Well, I sent him there if that's any consolation."

Doc nodded, "Remind me never to shoot you in the back."

Porter applied an Icy Hot pad to the back of his neck and another to his shoulder.

Looking around the container, Doc walked to a shelf and pulled out an MRE. "Porter, what the hell is this, an end-of-the-world bunker?" He walked to another shelf and picked up Hector's shotgun, "You got enough weaponry here to invade a small country." Doc leveled the weapon and pretended to blow someone away, "Boom."

"Oops," Molly said.

Porter and Doc looked over and saw her shake her head.

"Oops, isn't good," Doc said.

"No, it's okay. I just poked him a little too deep."

"He won't mind," Porter said. He then turned to Doc, yanked Hector's shotgun from him, and put it back on the shelf.

Doc looked around, "Porter, you got any real food in here? Something that doesn't say," he held up the MRE, "Meals Rejected by Enemy?"

Walking to a shelf, Porter opened a black footlocker and tossed him a bag of jerky. "All you and beers are in there, too."

Doc ripped open the bag and stuffed his face. "Thanks, so…" he nodded to Hector, "you gotta explain this. You guys get in a firefight, or did you shoot him?"

Porter cocked a brow.

"Hey, man, just asking. Cool if you did."

Doc cracked open a Coors Light and, drinking it, winced, "Tastes old. How often do you restock your food supplies?"

"Yearly, if I remember."

Doc shrugged, "Better than nothing."

Porter plucked a fresh shirt from another shelf and strained to put it on. Upon doing so, he pulled his flak back on and started to reach into various bins on shelves, gearing up. Yelling over his shoulder, he asked Molly, "How's it coming?"

"Almost done," she said, continuing to seal the wound. "This is my first time doing something like this on a person, so I'm a little nervous, ya know?"

"You're doing great," Porter said, leaning over and kissing her on the top of her pink hair.

Molly grinned at him, sweetly saying, "Your face is still covered in blood." She handed him the wet wipes.

"Right," he pulled a wipe out and began working his face.

A ringtone sounded, and Doc pointed to him, "I think that's you."

Porter pulled out his phone and stepped outside the container due to the bad reception. As the phone rang again, he looked at the screen, saw Flick's name, and flipped it open, "Old Man, have you not died from a heart attack?"

"You know, it's a damn shame you got too old to die young," Flick said in an oddly cheerful voice, "though not for a lack of trying."

"Yeah, figured I'd live another day just to piss you off."

"Well, mission accomplished."

"What do you got for me?"

"Rookie," there was a pause as Flick thought for the right words. "For what's it worth, eh, I'm sure there are some ill-minded people, not me, obviously, but others, like Mindy, who knows no better, who would be happy to know you're alive."

Porter lingered on the statement, lit a cigarette, and surveyed the gated shipping container yard. The yard was small, with two dozen containers in single stacks across the snow-dusted yellow grass.

Looking past the row of containers, his truck, and Doc and Molly's cars, fifty yards of ice-covered dirt was between them and the main road. Sometimes, the most concealed hiding positions were in plain sight.

"That almost sounded sentimental," Porter said.

Flick grunted, "Almost."

"What do you have?"

"I contacted one of my old friends in Langley."

"Flick, all your friends are old."

"Shut up and listen. First, Volkov –"

"Flick, the Russian is no longer a problem."

Flick grunted, "Took you long enough to wipe one of them off the table."

Porter shook his head. "That's it? Took you long enough?"

"What do you want, a fruit basket? Okay, I take it Gunther's still in play."

"Yep, I'll get to the Sauerkraut eventually."

"Gunther has a daughter in Frankfurt, Germany, named Heidi. She's a medical student living at the Adickesallee campus. Our records indicate that after her mom died, she was raised by various foster families and is now alone."

There was a pause as Flick went through his notes. "Uh, it says here that last year, Heidi was approached by what she thought was German officials and thinks she's inherited a college grant for her dad dying in the war, only releasable when she turned eighteen, but really Gunther fabricated the grant and is paying her bills. She doesn't know he's alive."

"And Frank Marion?"

"You called it. Marion is a phony but an interesting one."

"How so?"

"I was able to pull up the fake credentials from the NSA, which alone raises a lot of red flags if you're asking me. Frank Marion is a former Marine with advanced combat training, multiple deployments, and was a POW in Iraq. After his medical discharge, his wife left him, he became disgruntled, suffers PTSD, and is a gun for hire…you know, they made him sound like your typical run of the mil bum. Sound familiar?"

"Well, better rap sheet than some bums who run biker clubs. Anyway, figured they were setting me up to be their fall guy," Porter said.

"Yep," Flick agreed.

"What do you know about Hector Guvera, my old Gunny I served with?"

There was a long pause on the line.

"Flick? You still there? A clogged artery didn't take you out, did it?"

"I'm still here. You're not that lucky. Why are you asking about Hector Guvera?"

"Because he's bleeding out on the cot in my storage container."

Flick sighed, "Anytime you can't sink any deeper, Marine, you find a way."

"Listen, I didn't go looking for him. He was looking for me. The same people gunning for me are after him."

"Your old Gunnery Sergeant, Hector Guvera, is bad company, even for you."

"Bad company, huh? My folks said the same thing about all my Junior High and High School friends."

"Guvera was a Seal," Flick said.

"Yeah, I know. Gunny was part of the team that rescued me in Iraq."

"Did you also know that he was part of DEVGRU?"

"What the hell is DEVGRU?"

"Naval Special Warfare Development Group. In '87, Seal Team Six was dissolved and became DEVGRU. But everyone still considers them Seal Team Six, got it?"

"I didn't know that." Seal Team Six was the most popular Seal Team of all time. Porter remembered the countless movies and video games that portrayed them. Sometimes Hollywood got it right, but often, they didn't.

"On May 2, 2011, Guvera was in Pakistan," Flick said.

"So what?"

"You do remember what happened that day, don't you?"

Porter thought back and blew a stream of smoke out of his nostrils, "That's the day Bin Laden got whacked, right?"

"Yeah."

"So, you're saying he was with the team that killed him?"

"Porter…" There was a long pause. Flick continued, "My reports say Guvera may have been the one who killed him."

Porter plucked his cigarette from his lips and looked at the barren blue sky. "Well, fuck."

"My thoughts exactly."

Porter dove deep into his memory banks and shook his head, "No, that can't be right. I remember the reports that a helicopter got shot down a few months after the Bin Laden thing, and everyone in the raid died."

"August 6, 2011, a Chinook helicopter was shot down in Afghanistan during an operation to kill a Taliban leader involved with plotting the 9/11 attacks. There were fifteen Seals in the chopper, one being Guvera. Reports said everyone in the chopper died."

"Apparently not."

"Apparently," Flick agreed. "Hector's been laying low for almost a decade, probably living in Europe or someplace. For some reason, he came back to the States, and what's left of Bin Laden loyalists either thinks or knows he was the trigger man and put a bounty on his head in the amount of $50 million. It's been all over interagency flash reports for months now."

"I must have missed that memo."

Flick sighed, "Porter, I don't care how much this guy means to you. You have to distance yourself from him. It doesn't stop with American Iron. Heavy hitters won't stop coming for him, you know that, right?"

"Noted," Flipping his phone closed, Porter lit another cigarette.

Stepping back into the container, he watched Molly finish and zip up her sewing case. "You did great, thanks."

"What the hell? I didn't get a thanks," Doc said, stuffing his face with the last of the jerky.

"Your medals in the mail."

Doc waved him off and motioned to Hector, "So, what's this guy's deal?"

"You do know what ignorance is bliss means, right?" Porter said.

"C'mon man, that's bullshit! You just called us completely out of the blue and asked for our help. Molly and I walked off our job to help you. Hell, we might get fired for that."

"Actually, I just called in sick for my shift," Molly said.

"Hmm, why didn't I think of that?" Doc asked. "I just decided not to come back from my lunch break. Anyway, the least you can do is tell us what the hell is going on."

Porter looked at each of them, "Fine, but you keep this information to yourself, understand? I'm trusting the two of you, and that's saying something. Don't make me regret this."

Molly held up three fingers, "Scout's honor, I won't tell anyone." She exchanged a look with Doc and Porter, "Girl Scout for 11 years."

Doc said, "I buy Girl Scout cookies every year. Does that count?"

"They let you near Girl Scouts?" Porter asked.

"Hey, they come to my house. I don't go to theirs. Speaking of which, do you have any Thin Mints? I'm craving them?"

Porter shook his head. "Erica's running late and bringing doughnuts."

"Not the same," Doc said.

"Fine, then don't eat them."

"Well, I'm not saying I won't. Fine, I'll keep the information on Hector to myself under penalty of doughnut death, happy?"

"Fine, Hector here," Porter said, pointing to him with his cigarette, "is the man who might have killed Bin Laden."

They stared at him in disbelief.

"Well, you wanted to know."

"Holy shit," Doc said.

"Okay, I wasn't expecting that," Molly said.

Grabbing his M4 off the shelf, Porter headed for the door, "Be back in an hour, hopefully. When Erica gets here, feel free to fill her in."

"What?" Molly asked. "Where are you going?"

"I'm going to pay the American Iron Corporate office a visit. Scott has Sarah there, and I'm getting her back." He pointed to Hector, "You guys got this, right?"

"Got this?" Doc said, "You're leaving us with him? After what you just told us? Screw that!"

"Umm, I'm uncomfortable with this," Molly said.

"Yeah," Doc added, "what happens when he wakes up and has no idea who we are?"

"I'm sure you'll think of something," Porter said, walking out.

"You suck, Porter!" Doc yelled.

As Porter walked to his truck, Erica pulled up in her banged-up, faded purple 2000 Dodge Dakota. She stepped out in a green CSU Pueblo jacket and matching beanie. In one hand was a coffee mug, the other a box of donuts. "Hey, Boss, I got your text and got outta class as fast as I could. But it's a long drive from Pueblo."

Opening the box, Porter pulled out a white sprinkled donut and took a bite. "It's okay, I appreciate you coming."

"You look like a semi ran you over," Erica said. "What's going on?"

Porter took one more donut, "Doc and Molly will fill you in."

"So, should I expect you to be texting me all the time now? Early mornings, late nights, daytime? Kinda sexy."

Getting into his truck, Porter mumbled, "One little text, and everyone loses their minds."

25

Years ago, on a dreary day in mid-January, when a cold front brought biting rain and a stiff breeze, Evans parked her yellow Jeep Wrangler in front of Porter's trailer. Walking up the creaky, discolored, wooden steps. The lyrical vocals of Garth Brooks within sounded. Evans knocked and then opened the screen door of Porter's trailer.

There was an intense aroma of wood and fruit mixed with sweet caramel and grass, Jack Daniels. Evans knew the drink well as it was the poison of choice her dad abused on many hard nights when he was in the Force.

The house was in disarray, with kitchen cabinets flung open, dishes shattered in multiple rooms, clothes piled everywhere, the trashcan knocked over, holes in the wall, torn down family pictures, a bottle of Jack sticking through a flickering 40-inch TV on a stand, and a Ka-Bar stabbed into the hallway wall. A pair of dog tags hung from the knife's edge, and with it, a pair of wedding rings.

Walking to the console table in the hallway, she paused the iPod in the docking station.

"I was listening to that," a slurred voice said.

Evans followed the voice to the bathroom, where Porter lay on the white and black marble linoleum floor. He was shirtless, wearing only a pair of grey sweats, no prosthetic. In one hand was a bottle of Jack and a lit cigarette in the other. His sleep-depraved emerald eyes behind his glasses were staring up at the ceiling. He had not shaved or bathed in several days and looked thinner than Evans had ever remembered.

Evans walked around him, flushing the toilet and sitting atop the lid. "You haven't returned my texts or calls in a week."

Porter took a deep breath and, coughing, puffed on his cigarette, "You know me, I'm bad at returning calls, and I don't text."

Evans stared at him for a long moment, "Maggie's not here anymore, is she?"

Porter took another puff on his cigarette and shook his head.

"What happened?"

Porter opened his mouth to answer, thought better of it, and straining, sat up against the black wood cabinet vanity and took a swig of his Jack. "Shouldn't you be out catching bad guys right now?"

"Catching bad guys?"

"Yeah," Porter pointed up and down her body with his cigarette. "You're wearing your flat foot uniform, pressed shirt, pants, shoes, and shiny badge. Shouldn't you be out catching bad guys right now? If you ever want to be a Police Detective one day, you won't do it hanging around a worthless person like me."

"You're a lot of things, Porter," Evans said, gently tugging Porter's bottle of Jack away from him. "But you're not worthless."

"I woke up, and Maggie was in the middle of packing. She said I had another night terror."

"Another?"

"Sarah, I can't stop thinking about that day in Iraq. That day, everything went to hell." He looked at his leg, "I at least came back, but I can't stop asking myself, why me? Why did I come back and not them? It doesn't make any sense."

"God has a plan for us all," Evans told him.

Porter banged his head back on the vanity, "Shit, not this again. You know I don't believe in that stuff."

"Just hear me out," Evans told him.

"You're welcome here, but your God isn't." He looked down at his leg, "Not after what happened."

"Fine, let me rephrase then," Evans said. "It is *my* belief that you just need to find a new purpose. You have all these skills, all this training, all this –"

"Anger," Porter added.

"Okay, anger," Evans said, "That you can still put to good use. You need to find a good outlet." Evans reached into her front pocket and pulled out her field notebook and pen. She scribbled on the pad, "There's a guy named Flick who worked with the Force earlier this year as a hired Private Investigator, a Detective. I think he has a similar background to yours. I think he can show you how to apply your skills to the private sector."

"The private sector, huh?"

Evans ripped off the sheet and set it on Porter's bathroom sink. She sat on the toilet again. Conflicted feelings flooded her thoughts, and a clump formed in her throat. "You're a horrible person, you know that, right?"

Porter puffed on his cigarette, "I've been called worse."

"You got married."

Porter shook his head, "What?"

"Why did you get married to Maggie?"

There was a long moment of self-reflection. "Doesn't seem to really fucking matter now, does it?"

"Actually, to me, it does." She stared him down, "I'm not going anywhere, so you might as well stop your self-pity crap and answer."

"I don't feel like talking about it, okay?"

"Too bad."

"Suit yourself. I got nothing better to do today, but I would think you would."

"Fine," Evans pulled out her phone and dialed a number.

"What are you doing?"

Evans put the phone to her ear, "Yes, I'll hold." She looked at Porter, "I'm ordering you a pizza, and then I'm going to start cleaning your place."

Porter growled in frustration, "You are ridiculous. You know that?"

Evans smiled, "Yep."

Porter took a deep breath and muttered, "You're like a drill bit to the temple." Reaching over, he grabbed her phone and ended the call. "Fine, you made your point. I'll stop my self-pity crap, happy?"

"Here's the thing," Evans said. "We've known each other since 7th grade. You know more about me than anyone. And I know more about you than probably anyone else in your life. But the things I don't know about you keep me up at night. So, tell me."

"Fine." Porter conceded, returning her phone, "Okay, after High School, you and I broke up. Remember, you told me that–"

"I told you that if you took one step into that Marine Corps recruiting station, I'd break up with you," Evans said.

"And I did," Porter said.

"And we did," Evans added.

"My first duty station was Camp Pendleton, and that's where I met Maggie while on weekend liberty," Porter paused, deep in thought.

"Go on," Evans nudged.

"You've gotta understand, at the time, after going through boot camp and SOI, everything back in High School seemed like it had been a million years ago." Porter put his head in his hands, "I guess I assumed that everyone, including you, had moved on with their lives."

"Quite the assumption," Evans said.

"What can I say? Maggie and I hit it off. She supported me, and everything was great for a while. Everything was fun. Then, she told me she was pregnant," Porter trailed off and shrugged, "I had to do the right thing, I had to marry her, I wasn't ready. Hell, I was scared, but I wasn't going to run." He looked at her, "That's not who I am."

"I know," Evans whispered.

"Five months into the marriage, she had a miscarriage. It just went downhill from there. Then, after what happened in Iraq, and when I got out and came home earlier this year…it was just too much for her. My problems were too much for her."

Porter and Evans exchanged a long stare, and she finally said, "Did you love her?"

Porter shrugged, "At the time, I thought I did, but I'm not so sure."

Evans voice wavered, "You once told me you loved me." She wiped away a tear, "The night of our Senior Prom, you told me you loved me."

"Prom sucked."

"So, you do remember?"

"Yeah, I remember."

"Be honest with me, and I don't even care what the answer is, but please, Ryan, be honest with me. Did you mean it? Because I'll be honest with you, it broke my heart when I learned you had gotten married." Tears began to form in Evans' eyes, "You said you loved me."

Porter shook his head, "Sarah, I can't, not right now."

"Okay, when?"

"Hell, I don't know." Snuffing his cigarette onto the floor, Porter shook his head, "When the day comes that I can face the hell inside me. When I can make peace with myself. It's not today. I'm sorry."

Evans kissed his cheek, "Whether that day comes tomorrow or years later, I will always be there for you. Remember that."

Porter looked at her, "Why won't you give up on me? Everyone else has?"

"I won't let you off that easy."

⁂

Evans awoke, looking down at her swaying gold cross hanging off her neck. Sitting in a black office chair, she immediately felt her hands were restrained behind her back by zip ties. Her hair had fallen over her face, and she tasted blood in her mouth. She felt dehydrated, hungry, sore, and exhausted.

Blowing hair out of her eyes, Evans saw she was in an enclosed 12x12 office, sitting behind an executive desk. A computer monitor on the desk had a 3D Pipes screensaver. Next to the computer was a jar of Clif Bars, a mug full of pins that said, 'WARNING May Start Talking about ARMY Shit,' and a four-row Challenge Coin Display stand with an assortment of military coins. She focused on a poster next to the closed door that stated, 'ARMY, Because No One Played Navy as a Kid.' A spacious window covered the main wall that overlooked a call center below.

The clock on the wall above the mini-fridge reflected that it had been roughly an hour since the car wreck.

Getting her wits about her, Evans stood from the chair, bent at the knees, leaned forward, raised her arms back, slapped them down against her hips, and pulled her hands apart as hard as she could. On her second attempt, the zip ties broke.

She rubbed her bloody and bruised wrists and walked to the window overlooking the sizeable open-floor call center. A trio of elongated mahogany tables was on each side of the room. Atop those tables sat forty computer workstations.

Each seated worker wore various colored polos, lanyards, and khakis. Most were at their desks, looking down at their phones and slowly thumbing away. Others were talking by the bars at either side of the room, which were made up of a water cooler, a Keurig coffee dispenser, and a microwave. Even fewer had headsets and were typing on the keyboards at their workstations.

Standing in open view of those below, and no one paying attention, Evans assumed she was looking through a two-way mirror.

At the sound of digits entering the keypad on the other side of the door, Evans returned to the office seat and placed her hands behind her back.

A muscular man with a high and tight military cut, glassy blue eyes, chiseled jaw sporting a skintight grey polo and tan khakis walked in. A skull donning a green beret with a bayonet pierced through it was inked into his right bicep. The badge attached to his American Iron lanyard read, 'Scott.' Evans could smell his thick cologne, which reeked of douche and testosterone.

Scott closed the door behind him, leaning on the frame, and crossed his arms on his burly chest, "Ahh, Sleeping Beauty has awoken. About time."

"You owe me a new Jeep," Evans said dryly. "I only had six months of payments left."

Scott grinned, "Hot damn, that raspy voice of yours. I can tell why Porter has such a hard-on for you."

"So, let me get this right: you came after me to draw Porter out? Going after a badge? That's a dangerous game you're playing."

"What are you, his girlfriend, fuck buddy, wife? I still can't figure it out. Doesn't matter. You can't tell me you are seriously buying into the badass Porter myths that run rampant in this city. Marine solves one high profile case, roughs up some thugs, and magically, he's the Chuck Norris of the Rockies."

"You got it all wrong," Evans told him.

"Oh yeah, which part?" Scott asked.

"You shouldn't be worrying about what Porter will do to you. Your focus should be on what I will do to you."

"Wow, you got bigger balls than some of the guys I served with. They don't make women like you anymore." Scott opened the mini-fridge and pulled out a Vitamin Water. He offered one to Evans, and she shook her head. Opening the cap, he took a swig and pointed out the window, "So, what do you think of my operation?"

Evans met his gaze, "Sloppy."

"That's because you don't see what I see," Scott wheeled her chair next to the window ledge. "You know, this company was originally formed by me and my buddies as we were about to leave Afghanistan. Smoking victory cigars, waiting for our C-17. We decided to leave the military and go into business for ourselves for a change. We formed a security detail and started taking on cannabis retail clients all over Colorado after it passed Amendment 64."

"For a time, the money was good, but when I grew out this company, it was because I realized what my buddies didn't. I realized the money wasn't in physical security but the illusion of security. If people think they are safe, they pay just as much as someone standing outside their door with a rifle. So, you realize the things you can cut back on, physical security, proper training, state-of-the-art electronics."

Evans shook her head, "The illusion of security built on lies."

"Of course, that's American capitalism for you. So, when you see sloppy, I see profit."

"And when people won't buy into your American capitalism and your vision of profit, you force it onto them with fear tactics? You outsource the physical security you cut back on? You form partnerships with the Italians and the Wolfpack? And by association, those partnerships bring in even more money with drug trafficking?"

"See, you get it, when American Iron wins, they win. It's a lucrative partnership. Everyone wins."

"In this story of lucrative partnerships, someone in political power has to be backing you," Evans said. "You might be running American Iron, but you aren't running the show, right?"

Scott turned to her and raised a brow.

"Someone has to be high enough on the political food chain to not only get the other home security businesses out of town but to make the cops look the other way when your outsourced physical security enacts fear tactics in the name of American capitalism. Tell me I'm wrong?"

"You're not," Scott said.

"With Styles and Johnson running for Senate, both need to raise millions, and partnering with someone like American Iron is, as you say, lucrative, financially."

"So, I guess you're asking yourself, which one is pulling the strings?"

"Well," Evans shrugged. "One hired Porter to shut you down, and one didn't."

"It's interesting how you can be both right and so wrong at the same time."

It was now Evans who raised a brow.

Scott's phone rang, and he nodded as he listened to the voice on the other end, "Good, patch me through." He momentarily turned to Evans, "Looks like your knight in shining armor came for you just like we knew he would."

"Porter, get out of there," Evans whispered.

After a moment, Scott said, "Porter, when the Italians contacted me asking to set up a reunion with you for what you did to them earlier this week, who was I to say no?"

Evans leaned forward in her chair, trying to hear the opposite end of the conversation, but could not decipher anything.

Scott rolled his eyes, "In on this?" Laughing, he continued, "For being a Detective, you sure are a dumbass." Scott stopped and raised his voice, saying, "Shut your mouth. Put Hector Guvera on." Scott sighed and then walked to Evans, holding the phone out, "Talk to him."

As the phone screen touched her ear, Evans took comfort knowing Porter was on the other end. She also knew the few words that came out were vital. Evans blurted, "I'm at the American Iron Corporate –"

Scott yanked away the phone and, reaching to his side, pulled his tan P320 Sig Sauer out of his holster. With a backstroke, he whipped the gun across her face.

Evans yelled out in pain and spat blood.

Taking a few calculated steps back, Scott leveled the weapon at her chest, "Talk again, and I put a bullet in you." He then brought the phone to his ear and barked at Porter, "Put Hector on the phone now!"

The phone conversation continued for some time, with Scott keeping his distance. The plan was for both her and Porter to get all the information out of him that they could.

"Well, that's bad news for Sarah," Scott said as he took a few steps forward to get a better aim at her head. "Such a shame, too. She's played such a good damsel in distress."

Evans felt the conversation was nearing its end.

In one quick motion, Evans reached up and pulled Scott's gun towards her. The act caught him off guard, as reflected in the flash of surprise in his eyes. She then exploded out of her chair and turned her body into his. Pulling his gun arm down and crouching, she turned her hips, followed through, and tossed him through the window.

Peering over the window ledge, Evans saw Scott writhing on the landing below, surrounded by shattered glass and blood. She yelled, "I'm no one's damsel in distress!"

After the screaming in the room had ceased, some call center workers rushed to his aide. A few looked up at her in disbelief before cheering and clapping. Others made way as Security guards wearing blue buttoned-up dress shirts and black ties stormed into the room and yelled, "Lockdown!" One middle-aged man with a comb-over dropped to his knees and, praying to Evans, exclaimed, "Thank you. I've wanted to do that every single day for six months!"

Evans exited the office, checking that a round was chambered in Scott's P320 Sig Sauer she had lifted from him.

26

Reaching into his tackle box, Dustin pulled out a hook. He used the P-38 on his key chain to cut the old line on his pole and tied off a new one. He attached a weight and bobber and cast his line.

He sat next to Mindy on the wooden pier overlooking the lake. The water reflected the stars twinkling above. A thin layer of mist hovered above part of the water, and there was a buildup of foam on the water's edge where it touched the stone enclosure.

Mindy breathed in the early morning dew, unscrewed the top of a dented steel thermos, and poured coffee into the cap, handing it over.

Dustin sipped his drink, breathing in the steam, "Thanks, my little Fortuna."

"Fortuna is the Roman Goddess of fortune and personification of luck," Mindy told him, drinking from the thermos. She let the coffee warm her throat and chest, reached into her coat pocket, and took out a bag of gummy worms.

"Precisely, that's why I call you that, and hopefully, we will have plenty of both," Dustin said, stealing a worm. He wrapped an arm around her shoulders and smiled that smile of his. "When I spend time with you, I'm always lucky."

Mindy yawned, "It's just because mom and Jen don't want to wake up at four in the morning."

Dustin shrugged, "Their loss." He took another sip of his coffee and pointed at the open water. "You hear that?"

Mindy looked around. They were the only ones on the pier, not a soul in sight, "No."

"Exactly," he said. "No phone calls, sirens, cars, it's perfect." He sipped more coffee, "You're gonna find the older you get, the harder it is to find a little peace in your life, a little quiet. But when you finally do, it's so worth it, even more so when you're with the people you care about most."

They both looked up at the stars above. Bright and sparkling.

There was a bob on his line.

"You got something," Mindy said, edging forward on the pier.

Dustin's legs stiffened, and he sat up, "See, that's why I bring you." He stood and began to reel it in. "Looks like a big one."

Sitting there watching him, Mindy smiled. As he continued reeling, she heard a faint sound of guitar strings being plucked. "What is that?"

"Almost got it," Dustin said.

Whispers filled the air. A woman singing a song from Metallica's '…And Justice For All,' album. The lyrics and guitar strings got louder. Mindy recognized them as the opening to the song, 'One.'

She looked around. There was no source of the song. It was just there, playing from a distance.

She once again looked at her father, still reeling away.

He should have reeled in whatever was in the water by now.

This wasn't real.

"This guy's really fighting me," Dustin said. He looked at Mindy, "Give me a hand, Fortuna."

Mindy hugged his side, "Don't go."

He let the pole slip from his hands and into the lake. Putting an arm around Mindy, he said, "I have to."

"But, I miss you," she cried, "so much."

"I know you do. But we can't change things which have already happened."

"But –"

"You're tough, and you are smart. Remember, luck is always on your side when anything bad happens because you're my Fortuna."

"Don't go." When Mindy looked up, her father was gone.

❧

Mindy awoke and stared at the blank ceiling of Flick's office. Hot tears rolled down her cheeks. She turned in her cot and, pulling her phone from her pocket, scrolled through her pictures and found an old photo of her and her dad. She was about to text her sister about her dream but saw she had no cell service.

She heard the guitar playing somewhere close in the distance. There was also the smell of coffee and bacon. Mindy got out of bed and stepped out of her room.

A scraggily-headed man wearing a faded Denver Broncos shirt sat in a metal folding chair beside her door. The man was eating bacon and scrolling on his phone, giggling.

"Uh, hi, Jeff, right?" Mindy asked.

"That's right, good morning," Jeff said. "Valentine asked to talk to you when you woke up."

"Okay?"

"You know, Flick's niece, she's in the camper playing her guitar."

"Right, what's this about?"

Jeff shrugged.

"Is Porter with her?"

Jeff shrugged.

"Good talk." Passing the table of coffee and trays of breakfast food on heating elements, Mindy grabbed a strip of bacon. Opening the door next to the closed garage doors, she wrapped her arms around her torso as snow flurries hit her body.

Mindy saw tire tracks in the parking lot leading away from the VFW post where Porter's truck would have been. Reaching Valentine's camper, she stepped up and thumbed the silver latch of the rear door.

The smell of cigarette smoke and coffee filled the camper. There was a scent of something else, too, something familiar that Mindy couldn't quite place. Running water could be heard from the camper bathroom. Valentine was sitting on her corner bench. A black guitar hung off her neck, the instrument's body resting on her lap. She plucked at the vinyl strings. An American flag blanket was draped over her shoulders, and she wore only red panties.

As she sang the lyrics to Metallica's 'One,' and picked away at her guitar strings, she noticed Mindy.

"Jeff said you asked for me," Mindy said.

Valentine plucked the cigarette from her lips and tapped it across the ashtray atop the table. "Close the door."

Mindy stepped inside the camper and, staring at her lack of attire, said, "Hey if this is a bad time, I can come back."

"Nope, don't mind me, I was just about to hop in the shower," Valentine told her. "It takes a few minutes for the water to get warm."

"Sure, whatever," Mindy said, closing the door. "So, uh that song, I recognize it. That's a famous Metallica song, right?"

Valentine picked at her guitar more and nodded, "The song 'One' is about a World War I soldier. A landmine takes away everything. His arms, legs, eyes, and jaw. He's just wishing for God to end him."

"Well…that, sucks."

"Yup."

"Okay, uh, while I'm here. Do you know where Porter is? His truck is gone."

"Yeah, he had to run out. He asked you to stick around until he got back."

"Stick around?"

"The VFW post. He said it's not safe with the recent friends you made. But he should be back soon. He wanted me to let you know that since the cell service out here sucks." Resting the cigarette on the ashtray, Valentine raised her mug and took a sip. "You didn't sleep well."

"Excuse me?"

"You've got that look in your eyes."

"What look?"

"That walking dead look." Valentine smiled. She pointed to the Keurig coffee maker secured by a bungee atop her kitchenette. "I made a fresh pot. Go ahead and pour yourself a cup. Mugs are in the cabinet above with the sugar. Creamers in the mini-fridge."

"Uh, okay, thanks," Mindy said, getting a mug and pouring herself a cup. As she added sugar and creamer, she looked around the camper. Valentine's current living situation wasn't much to look at, and suddenly, Mindy's trailer life didn't seem so bad.

Mindy looked at the elevated bed full of Build-A-Bears and messy sheets and then focused on the bottle of Excedrin sitting on the table. "I take it Porter stayed with you last night?"

Valentine nodded, "Umm hmm."

Mindy shook her head, "Jesus, you have any idea how many women he's been with?"

Valentine sipped her coffee, "Probably a lot."

"And that doesn't bother you?"

"Why would it?"

"Wow," Mindy shook her head. "Whatever."

Valentine cocked her head, "You don't think I'm good enough for him?"

Mindy was caught off guard, "Uh, I didn't say that."

"You sure about that?" Valentine puffed on her cigarette, then stood, took off her guitar, placed it on the bed, and reached a hand into the shower, then retracted it. "Damn thing takes forever to heat up." Leaning on the doorframe leading into the bathroom, Valentine crossed her arms over her chest, "So, what's the problem?"

"With what?"

"With me. Clearly, something about me is not up to your standard."

"Lady, I don't even know you. So, why should I care?" Mindy said.

"Yeah, I can see that."

Mindy shook her head and mimicked Valentine, putting her arms across her chest, "Listen, you don't know a thing about me, so don't act like you're all high and mighty, got it?"

Valentine didn't answer. She stared and smirked.

"And stop looking at me like that."

"Like what?" Valentine asked.

Mindy tried to match Valentine's stare, but she couldn't. Her stare was too cold, too calculated, too predator-like. It was like she was about to go in for the kill.

"Do I scare you?" Valentine said.

"No, I just. –"

"I do, don't I?"

"No, you don't…I just don't like how you look at me."

"Why?"

"Because I don't, alright?"

"Alright," Valentine told her slyly. She broke her gaze and picked the guitar up again, draining her coffee. She began plucking at the nylon strings once more.

"Those hands," Mindy whispered.

"What about them?"

"Well, when you were drinking coffee, your hand shook. But now that you're playing your guitar, it's fine."

Valentine nodded and continued playing, "Ever since my accident, my hands have never been the same. I'm fine when I play the guitar, not so much when I try to do anything else."

"The accident?"

"Suicide bomber," Valentine told her.

"You were in the military?"

"An MP in the Army. I was on a patrol in Afghanistan, and a bunch of kids came up to us like they always would."

"Kids would come up to you guys?" Mindy said, still looking at Valentine's hands, which were severely scarred.

"Yeah, we'd give them candy or toys, kick soccer balls their way, stuff like that. We were instructed to win the hearts and minds of the people of Afghanistan," Valentine said. "There was one boy, his name was Amad. Good kid, about your age. Always gave me high fives. He wanted to be a village doctor like his brother."

"What happened?" Mindy asked.

"Amad came up to me like he had for the last four months and…" she shook her head, "he didn't give me a high five." She raised her shaky cigarette to her lips.

"That's horrible." Mindy noticed that Valentine's cigarettes were the same brand Porter smoked, Lucky Strike.

Taking a puff, Valentine let the cigarette hang off her lips, "Like I said, good kid. I learned later that he did it in exchange for the Taliban paying off his parent's house mortgage."

"Their house mortgage?" Mindy said as she finally figured out the scent she smelled when she entered was perfume. The rose-scented aroma was the same that Porter's ex-wife used to wear.

Something wasn't right.

The cigarettes and the perfume were all things Porter liked. Either she was trying too hard, or something else was at play. A terrible thought went through Mindy's mind. An idea that Valentine purposely baited Porter to her, but for what reason? Was it simply for sexual reasons or something else?

"Yeah, ironically, the house was hit a week later," Valentine said, cutting Mindy's concentration, "artillery strike. Blown to smithereens – what are the odds?" Valentine continued plucking at the strings, "I find, whenever I play, my hands don't shake. Can't explain it. It's just one of those things. I think it's God's messed up way of telling me to make love and music, not war like all those hippie bumper stickers say." She continued to pluck away on her guitar.

"Well, you play pretty good at the music part," Mindy said as she slowly backed out of the camper.

Valentine looked up from her guitar, "You going somewhere?"

With one foot out the door, Mindy froze. "Uh, yeah," she thumbed behind her, "gonna head back inside and get some of that breakfast they had out. I'm starving. Then, hang out until Porter gets back. See if I can get a cell signal somewhere."

Valentine's eyes narrowed on Mindy's grey eyes for what seemed like an eternity but instead were only several long seconds. "Alright, good idea, you go do that."

Internally, Mindy breathed a sigh of relief.

Valentine headed towards the shower.

"Right," Mindy said, stepping outside the camper.

"Wait!" Valentine hollered from the shower.

Mindy stopped, "Yeah?"

"You mind leaving the coffee mug? I only have a few of them."

Mindy looked at the drink in her hand, "Oh, right, sorry, my bad."

"Thanks, and uh, close the door on your way out, will ya?"

"Sure."

Mindy dumped her coffee in the sink and then washed out the mug.

She looked back at the bathroom.

A thick fog of steam emanated from the shower.

She opened the camper door and, about to step out, turned to the table where Valentine's computer sat. She loudly shut the door and instead sat on the corner bench. She peered cautiously at the steamy bathroom, made a mental note that she maybe had five minutes, and opened the laptop lid.

A blue screen with a semi-translucent overlay map of the world's continents showed. In the middle of the screen was a seal of an eagle head above a white shield and a sixteen-point compass star. The words 'CENTRAL INTELLIGENCE AGENCY' surrounded the seal. The 'Agent ID' field below was prepopulated with asterisks. The 'Password' field needed to be filled in.

"Damn, I knew there was something off about you, Ms. Valentine," Mindy whispered.

On the keyboard, a few letters were faded, 'a-e-d-c-t-h-g-n-m- i.' Mindy also noticed certain letters were faded more than others, the thought being they were entered more than once on login, 'a-e-t.' Pulling out her phone, Mindy opened her anagram app and typed in the letters, generating a series of phrases.

Attic henge mad

Candie math teg

Dam eating tech

The last one made her smirk; the list went on, but nothing seemed right. Mindy looked around the trailer, focused on the guitar, and remembered Valentine had been playing a Metallica song when she walked in. She looked at the anagram generator once more. The word 'Death' could be spelled out in one way or another in each instance.

Googling Metallica albums, only one had the word 'Death' in the title, 'Death Magnetic.' She entered the album name into the 'Password' field, and the computer unlocked.

A sudden rush of fear and adrenaline pumped through Mindy's veins. Out of all the things she had done, breaking into a CIA computer was at the top of the list. Her eyes darted to the steamy bathroom and then back to the computer.

The desktop was cluttered with various files and folders. Mindy skimmed through memos about security policy changes. TPS reports cover page changes and updates in the most wanted interagency listings. A folder caught her eye, "Operation Hermes II."

Mindy clicked open the folder, and there was a listing of POWs from Iraq, one of which was Porter. There were multiple files on him. The death of his father, his time in the Marines, his cases as a Private Detective, and his known associates, which were many. The list of names included Sarah, Erica, Molly, Doc, a blacked-out file of someone named Agent F, and the list went on.

Mindy read a short blurb about herself. There was nothing much that wasn't already public knowledge. The death of her stepfather Dustin in the Black Forest fire. Information on her biological serial killer father, Joe, whom Porter had killed earlier in the year after he had abducted her. Documentation of when Porter adopted her several months back. Worst of all, they had her Freshman picture on file, which made her cringe. She had worn her hair in pigtails that day and still wore braces.

Navigating to the root folder on the Iraq POW files, Mindy opened a folder revealing a group of Navy SEALs. It occurred to Mindy that these were the SEALs who were part of Porter's rescue in Iraq. Each SEAL had their own file. And all but one file ended with a headshot that said KIA.

The lone SEAL without the KIA stamp instead said MIA.

His name was Hector Guvera.

Mindy read about Hector's father's service in Vietnam, his upbringing in El Paso, and time served in both the Army and the Marines, leading up to him joining the SEALs. A folder in Hector's file was dedicated to 'Operation Neptune Star.' Mindy watched a short video of Hector and other SEALs raiding Bin Laden's compound.

"Holy shit," Mindy murmured.

There were other video files in his folder. One was labeled 'NSA Decrypt' and was outside a bullet-riddled Waffle House. The restaurant was filled with smoke. Screaming and erratic gunfire could be heard from within. A man wearing a makeshift gasmask blurred across the frame, killing a man. The video ended with the cameraman being shot and the gunman crushing the camera.

Another was of a hospital lobby. A man who matched that of the previous video wore a cowboy hat and red suede jacket. He looked up at the camera.

The final video was from a traffic camera. The footage showed a white Bronco leaving Porter and Mindy's trailer park. The man in the cowboy hat sat bloody-faced in the car as he passed by a light, and Police vehicles passed by him in the opposite direction.

The time stamps on the last three videos were from yesterday.

"Porter was right. You really are too smart for your own good," Valentine said.

Before Mindy could react, Valentine slid her wet right arm under Mindy's chin and gripped her left bicep with her right hand. She then secured her left hand around the back of Mindy's head and began applying pressure.

Mindy kicked out and yanked down on Valentine's arm, but it wouldn't give. She struggled for air, but none came. Mindy's eyes began to flutter.

Within seconds, everything faded to black.

27

Speeding into the spacious Corporate lot filled with employee vehicles, blue and white American Iron service vans, and motorcycles, Porter could hear an alarm from inside the elbow-shaped two-story building made of large grey and white exterior panels. Slamming on his brakes alongside the fenced-in manicured front landscape, Porter began surveying his surroundings when his phone rang. The number said, 'Private.' He hoped Evans had found a phone, and he answered, "Sarah?"

"It's Detective Amberson," the voice on the other end said. "What's your location?"

Porter let the disappointment wash over him and said, "I just pulled into their lot."

"Okay, I've got the calvary with me, and we're almost there."

Porter focused on the sound of gunfire exchange sounding within the building. He searched the windows for a source of muzzle flash but didn't see anything.

"Kid, listen to me," Amberson said, "I know what Detective Evans means to you, but do not go charging in. Wait for us to get there. Let the police do their job. Do you understand me?"

At the sound of additional gunfire, Porter revved his truck and focused on the front door of the building, "Too late."

"Dammit, Porter!" Amberson yelled before Porter flipped his phone closed.

Pushing down on the gas pedal, Porter's Ram sped through the parking lot and leaped over the sidewalk. Cutting his wheel of the truck, Porter navigated under the front awning, and the steel front bumper collided first with the outer, then into the inner commercial-grade security double doors. Glass and metal exploded behind him as he crashed into the American Iron Corporate building.

Shots peppered his driver's side door as the truck entered the lobby. Porter pointed his revolver out the window and, spotting the Wolfpack member inside, returned fire.

Nailing his target on the second shot, Porter cut his wheel and looked out the front window just in time to see a man leap from the customer service desk. The Ram ran through and annihilated the desk before coming to a complete stop.

As Porter shifted the truck into park, the passenger side window exploded. Porter ducked and was about to return fire when shots impacted his dash. Keeping his head low, Porter shifted the Ram into drive, turned the wheel to the gunfire, and pushed on the gas.

As a round impacted the truck's hood, Porter peeked over the dash to ensure he was on target, adjusted the wheel, and sped up as he smashed into the Wolfpack member and pinned him between the truck's grill and the side wall.

Sitting up and putting the truck in park, Porter saw the member's body sprawled lifelessly over the hood, blood oozing from his mouth. Grabbing his M4 from the backseat, Porter slung it over his chest and attempted to open his driver's side door but could not because of the stampede of screaming workers in polos and khakis pushing up against it in a rush to exit the building.

Making his way to the back seat, Porter slid open the rear window, pulling himself through and onto the truck bed. He kneeled, readjusted his three-point sling, nestled the butt of the M4 into his shoulder, and took aim down the iron sights.

As screaming people ran past the truck, Porter yelled, "Sarah? Does anyone know where Detective Sarah Evans is? Anyone!" No matter how loud Porter yelled, his voice couldn't overtake the yelling frenzy.

But something else did.

A deep rumbling sounded from outside the building. Porter focused his iron sights on the rumbling. It was coming from the opening his truck had made.

Everyone inside the building had exited, and it was just Porter and the rumbling.

Tires screeched on the marble floor as three Harleys sped into the lobby. The Wolfpack members aimed at Porter with their pistols and erratically fired off their weapons as they advanced.

With a controlled short burst, Porter took out the first biker with a series of rounds to the chest. The second, he nailed in the face with a single shot as he was nearly on top of him. Biker three leaned back on his bike and forced their Harley into a wheelie, using their bike's undercarriage to absorb Porter's gunfire. With the back tire on the floor and the front spinning over the bed, the Harley frame impacted the truck bed and sent Porter to his back.

Revving up his Chopper, the biker leaned forward and slammed down while jerking his handlebars to crush Porter under the spinning front wheel.

Porter rolled side-to-side and fired off rounds from his M4 but couldn't hit the rider maneuvering his bike and body with each shot. The front Harley's front wheel was nearing Porter's crotch. After Porter fired and missed again, the Wolfpack member yelled, "Is that the best you got!"

Reaching in a pouch on his flak, Porter pulled out a grenade, pulled the pin, let go of the latch, held onto it for a second, and then tossed it at the biker's chest, "Catch."

Jumping over the side of the truck, Porter rolled under the bed simultaneously as an explosion roared. Metal shook above Porter, and oil from the undercarriage of the bed spat into his face.

The Chopper flew through the air in a blast of flame and screams. From Porter's limited view, he saw the bike and corpse crash in the distance.

Once the ringing in his ears subsided, Porter crawled out from under the truck bed. Using the truck frame as an assist, he stood and surveyed the lobby carnage consisting of shell casings, buckets of blood, dead bikers sprawled across the floor, flaming Choppers, destroyed furniture, and the gaping hole where Porter had smashed his truck through the front. Amid the screeching building alarm that continuously sounded, the fire sprinklers above the pipes activated, distributing water cones across the lobby.

Porter turned his attention to his truck. The bed was scorched and bent inwards where the grenade had gone off and had many more dents and tears than this morning. The tailgate was only attached on one side and hung lazily on the other. Bullet holes peppered each side of the truck, and nearly every window was cracked, shattered, or bullet-ridden. The front grill was smashed inwards, and the engine was starting to hiss smoke. Ironically, the rear window was still intact.

At the sound of approaching rumbling outside from several more bikes, Porter reached on his flak, pulled out a smoke bomb, and, pulling the pin, lobbed it across the lobby. White smoke enveloped the space between his truck and the wall opening.

Turning tail, Porter exited the lobby and quickly crossed a hallway with award plaques and mission statements painted in cursive black ink across the walls. The end of the hall gave way to a spacious call center filled with tables, chairs, and computer workstations, all in disarray from the mass exodus of workers. On the back wall, overlooking the call center, was a large, shattered bay window.

Heading up the stairs at the rear of the call center, Porter made his way into the overlooking offices. The first room's door was wide open. The Army-themed office was empty, but he could smell the remnants of Sarah's Rainforest Fresh Suave shampoo. He fixated through his iron sights on the broken zip ties on the carpet.

Exiting the office, Porter followed a trail of blood that led down the hallway, the walls of which were wallpapered with bullet holes and blood. A trio of Wolfpack corpses riddled with bullets lined the once white linoleum floors now awash in red.

Porter swept each identical office he passed with the barrel of his M4. They were empty. Reaching a door at the end of the hall marked 'Armory,' Porter tugged on the silver lever, and it didn't give.

Taking a step back, with a squeeze of the trigger, he sent a controlled burst to the lever, and with a front kick, the door gave.

He dropped to a knee and pointed out with his M4 into the darkness.

A tan barrel of a P320 Sig Sauer pointed back at him, the silencer glinting.

Porter was about to shoot first and ask later when a husky voice called out, "Ryan, pull that trigger, and you'll never get laid again." Sarah crept out of the darkness and limped towards him.

Porter lowered his weapon and saw that her face was drained of color. Her eyes looked heavy, and she was breathing hard. Her turtleneck and cross were splattered in blood. He then saw that she was holding her piece in her left hand because her right arm was wrapped with a blood-soaked bandage.

"I'm fine," she told him, out of breath with shaking lips. "Bullet went clean through." She stumbled into his chest and embraced him in a hug. "My morning has sucked."

Porter returned the embrace and ran his fingers through the back of her hair, "Been a while since I've seen you covered in this much blood. Not since you beat the shit out of Gabby Stone in High School when she called you a slut in Math Class Junior Year."

"Yep, I remember," she groaned.

"It's a hot look for you."

Evans sighed, "You would say that."

"You know me too well."

"Unfortunately," she said, exhausted.

A High School memory came to mind as Porter ran his fingers through her hair again. After getting off work on the 4th of July between Junior and Senior year, Porter picked up Evans in his T-Bird. They were on their way to the annual city fireworks display, but the traffic was backed up too deep. Instead, they pulled into a Taco Bell parking lot. With Evans' head on his shoulder, they watched fireworks through his cracked front windshield, and Porter ran his fingers through her hair all night.

The crackle of gunfire sounded from the lobby below. A parade of footsteps and yelling could be heard.

"Sweep every office!" A familiar voice shouted from the hallway. "Find her!"

Porter and Evans exchanged a look.

"Amberson! We're in here!" Evans yelled.

A few seconds later, Detective Harry Amberson, flanked by two Police SWAT team members, entered the room.

"Identify yourselves!" a SWAT member yelled. The flashlight attached to his M4 illuminated Porter and Evans.

"Drop your weapons! Hands in the air, do it now!" the other SWAT member yelled.

Harry turned on the light to the room, illuminating the armory. Multiple gun racks filled with serialized military-issued M18 pistols, M16A2 rifles, M240 machine guns, and a M82 sniper rifle. A variety of green ammo boxes were stacked against one wall. A long white table lined another wall filled with weapon cleaning kits. A red weapons-clearing barrel was propped at forty-five degrees in the corner of the room.

"Stand down," Amberson said to the gun-happy SWAT members. "These two are with me. Now, you two, stand guard outside the door."

"Yes sir," they both said, exiting.

"Sarah, you look like hell," Amberson said.

"Good to see you too," Evans told him.

"Glad you're okay. And Porter," he said with an accusatory finger, "what part of wait for us to get here did you not understand?"

Porter shrugged, "Oh, is that what you said? Funny how similar that sounds to I don't give a fuck."

Amberson shook his head, "Okay, I should have seen that one coming."

"Yep," Porter agreed.

"Yep," Evans concurred.

"Alright, if you two are ready, let's get outta here. Porter, why don't you lead the way. You seem more heavily armed than my SWAT guys."

Stacking behind one another with weapons drawn, they were about to exit when Amberson's phone went off.

"Hold up, it's probably the Captain," Amberson said, clicking his earpiece. "Go for Amberson." He looked at Evans and Porter, "Yep, I'm here with them. It went about how you thought it would." Amberson nodded as he listened to the voice on the other end of the call. "Want to tell them yourselves? No? Okay, I'll take care of it."

"What was that about?" Evans asked.

Amberson holstered his sidearm and, reaching in his jacket, pulled out a pair of blue latex gloves. Putting each glove on, he shook his head, "Sarah, work in this business long enough, and you'll soon find out everything always comes down to what's best for business."

"Best for business?" she asked.

Lunging forward, Amberson yanked Porter's revolver from his thigh holster. He then bent down and exploded with an uppercut, smashing the revolver's chrome under Porter's chin and sending him to the floor. Spinning to face Evans, he pointed the Smith & Wesson at her stomach and fired a round.

As the two SWAT members rushed back into the room, Amberson killed each with a .38 round to the face. Smoke trails gaped out of the blood oozing holes in their heads as they fell dead beside where Porter had dropped.

Evans' cries of pain stirred Porter awake. Upon doing so, he did his best to ignore the searing pain under his jaw and saw Evans writhing in distress across the room in a puddle of her own blood. He attempted to reach a vertical base when he felt steel nudge the back of his skull.

Amberson's calm, gruff voice said, "Remove your M4 and kick it back towards me."

Porter paused, thinking of his options.

"I know what you're thinking. Can you send an elbow to my face fast enough, or maybe spin around and disarm me with one of your slick, killer Marine Corps moves? Either way, will it be quick enough? You know, once upon a time, I was Army Special Forces. Did Sarah ever tell you that? I already snuck up on you, so don't try me, kid."

Porter knew he was outmatched at the immediate moment. He unclipped the three-point sling across his chest and, placing the attached M4 on the floor, nudged it backward with his boot.

"Now interlock your hands behind your head and stay on your knees."

Porter did as told. "You just going to let Sarah die?"

Amberson took a few calculated steps around Porter and stepped past Sarah, with Porter's revolver trained on his face. "Don't you worry about her. I'll be done in a few minutes, and that's all the time needed to frame you. Getting shot in the gut isn't like Hollywood movies. You don't actually die immediately. There are a lot of variables. The caliber of the bullet. Vital organs. All that stuff. The ambulance will get to her in time."

"Yeah, but I guarantee they won't get to you in time when I'm through with you."

Amberson ignored him, reached inside the hole at the weapons-clearing barrel, and pulled out a clear bag filled with pills. "Must be $250 grand worth of stuff here." He tossed the bag to Porter, and it bounced off his chest, "You were supposed to catch that."

"And get my fingerprints all over it?"

"See, now you're getting it. Go on, pick it up. Open the bag, too. I don't care."

"I got a better idea. How about you shove this bag up your ass?"

"Kid, don't take it so personally."

"You just killed two cops with my gun and shot Sarah. You now want to get my fingerprints all over a bag of drugs. Betting there really wasn't a Frank Marion, was there? Or better yet, since I just took out half of the Wolfpack, I'm essentially Frank Marion, doing an aggressive takeover, a coupe?"

"Everyone says you Marines are dumb as rocks, but you know what, I don't care what they say, you're okay. Kid, I can see why Sarah likes you."

"What's her role in this?"

"Role? Her only role, sadly, is being associated with you. It's a shame, really. She was just promoted and everything."

"So what? You just woke up and randomly decided to be a traitor to your nation?"

"Wow, so dramatic. It's actually pretty simple. I'm in debt up to my eyelids. It's just business. I needed the money, you understand, right?"

"Yeah, I understand you've got two options, asshole."

Amberson's eyes tightened, "Given your position, you're going to threaten me? Oh, this should be good."

"Option one, you fire the weapon, my weapon, but it's not a killing blow because you still need me alive. Once you fire the shot, you realize no more rounds are left. That's when I cut the distance between us and kill you. I'm thinking snapping your neck will do just fine."

Amberson forced himself not to examine the revolver and provide Porter an opening, "You really think I can't draw my primary weapon fast enough if needed. Kid, you really are full of yourself. Okay, out of curiosity, option two?"

Porter unsheathed his Ka-bar attached to his flak, "This goes in your heart."

Amberson knelt by Sarah, pushing the revolver barrel to her head, "I need you alive. I don't need her, and like I told you earlier, you're not fast enough. Kid, trust me, you don't scare me."

Porter nodded, "I believe you."

Evans reached up to Amberson's key chain and yanked off his key ring Pepper Gel. Thumbing the latch, she pushed down on the button and, taking aim, shot the gel into his eyes.

As Amberson cursed out and stumbled back, grasping his eyes in pain, Porter hurled his Ka-bar into Amberson's chest.

Amberson dropped the revolver and held himself upright on a gun rack. His face sagged as he looked down at the knife in his chest. After a moment, he dropped to a knee and grabbed the knife's hilt before falling to his back.

Porter picked up his M4 and dashed to Amberson. Standing over him, he leveled the barrel at his face, now gurgling blood. About to pull the trigger, Evans tugged on his pant leg. Porter looked at her, and she shook her head.

"Okay, that was a good throw," Amberson said, spitting blood. "You're good."

"Talk," Porter said.

"Fine, you win. I've always wanted a boat."

"What?"

"After this job went down, I was going to finally retire and get a boat."

"I don't care about your fishing plans."

"No, I hate fishing. Just a boat. Nothing special, just something structurally sound, with a good motor and big enough to lay in and sleep my life away on the waters. I was going to name it Lauren, after my first wife. I cheated on her, but damn, I loved her more than any of my other wives. I wish I could have had a second chance with her."

"Who are you working for?" Porter asked. "Is it Bobbi Johnson?"

Amberson smiled as blood continued to roll out of his mouth, "Can I just pretend I'm in my boat and lay here?"

"Give me something," Porter urged.

"We all work for Bobbi Johnson," Amberson said before closing his eyes and lying motionless.

"Porter," Sarah whispered.

Porter knelt by her and held her in his arms. "Sarah, you're going to be okay."

"I know, but Porter, this fucking hurts."

"Wow, you cursed."

"Yeah, I cursed."

Porter felt immediate dread and fear. It was a feeling that foreshadowed anything he had previously felt. Even more so than anything he experienced in Iraq or in his marriage to Maggie. It was one thing for him to get hurt and another for Sarah to get hurt.

Porter cut the bottom of his shirt using his Ka-bar and wrapped it into a ball. He lifted Sarah's hand and pressed it against her wound. "Here, put pressure on this." He tried to stand her up, "C'mon, get up. Let's get you out of here."

Evans cried out in pain, "I can't move. I can't."

"Sure you can, c'mon, I'll carry you."

Police sirens began wailing in the distance.

"An EMT will be with the backup. It'll be okay," Evans said. "I'll signal them when they get here."

Porter held onto her and stared into her face as she shook with pain. "Fine, I'll stay with you."

"No, you have to go. This is all a setup, you know that. Bobbi Johnson is out to get you."

"I don't care. I'm not leaving you." Porter held her even tighter.

Evans stared into his eyes, "Why won't you give up on me?"

"You don't get off that easy."

"C'mon, everyone else has. My parents, the Captain…Finley."

"Fuck that Fobbit," Porter said. "Sarah, you're stuck with me whether you like it or not."

Evans shook her head, "Ryan, we just don't work. No matter how hard we try, we just aren't meant to be and –"

"Sarah, you're all that matters to me."

"How can you say that, considering you're with different women every other night?"

"Dammit, Sarah," Porter said. He stared into her blue eyes, "If you don't think I'd give that all up for you in an instant, then you're a fucking idiot."

Evans smiled and studied him briefly before saying, "That's an interesting way to say I love you."

Porter smiled back, "Yeah, I thought so too."

They exchanged a soft kiss.

"Porter," Evans whispered, "Stop Bobbi Johnson and go."

Making his way to one of the downed SWAT members, Porter put on the man's helmet and vest. Exiting the room, Porter made his way down the hall, and nearing the stairs, he heard a gaggle of footsteps.

He stood off to the side and waved the SWAT members and EMT to the armory at the end of the hall. "We have an Officer down, go, go," he said.

Moving downstairs and quickly through the call center into the smoky lobby filled with police and EMTs, Porter noted that everyone's attention was elsewhere and opened the door to his truck.

Getting inside, Porter removed the SWAT helmet and turned over the engine. It took more than one crank to get the truck going, and when it finally did, the check engine light flashed.

"Figures," Porter sighed. Shifting the truck into reverse, he nearly made his way out of the lobby but stopped as someone walked into the view of his backup camera.

Holding onto the back leather headrest of the passenger seat, Porter turned to see Captain Easley standing behind him.

She wore dark glasses and a blazer to match. Her Beretta was drawn and leveled at the rear window.

The two exchanged a long stare.

Easley grinned that self-righteous grin of hers.

She had a clear shot, and Porter was surprised she didn't capitalize on the opportunity. Porter surmised she, too, was working for Bobbi Johnson.

"Out of the truck!" Easley barked.

Porter watched as a squad car outside the lobby approached and cut the wheel, positioning itself across the width of the building opening, blocking him in.

"Out of the truck," Easley repeated.

Nearby Officers ran to the truck and pulled their guns on Porter.

Porter kept eye contact with her and pushed down on the accelerator.

As the truck reversed, Easley leaped out of the way as Officers opened fire.

The truck screamed in reverse as it sped out of the lobby, and the truck bed slammed into the side of the squad car with such velocity that it caused the latter to spin across the asphalt. Porter created an opening, turned the wheel, flicked off Easley through his open window, and shifted the truck into drive.

As another pair of squad cars pulled up, Easley stood and pulled out her radio. She yelled into it so loud Porter could hear, "Suspect fleeing the American Iron Corporate building in a red Ram 2500. Give me ground and air support, now!"

The Hemi of Porter's truck roared as he drove past the squad cars and EMT. Speeding up, he turned and skidded onto the main road and cut off an oncoming car in the process.

With an angry horn behind him, Porter glanced in his rear-view mirror as three squad cars and an unmarked silver SUV pursued him.

Porter lit a cigarette, feeling it was as good a time as any.

In the distance, Porter saw that traffic was building up. He had to get off the road.

Swerving around a minivan and forcing himself into the far-right lane, Porter took the on-ramp for the highway.

At the top of the hill, there was a ramp meter. The light alternated red and green to ease traffic congestion. A metal sign next to it read, 'One vehicle per green.'

There were several vehicles in either lane, each waiting for their turn. A cement barricade lined the right shoulder of the ramp.

Glancing in the rear-view mirror, Porter could see the alternating red and blue police lights bouncing off the paint jobs of the surrounding cars far behind him.

He was ahead of them, but they would catch up if he stalled long enough at the light.

Swerving off the road, Porter exhaled a plume of smoke and, reaching out the driver's side window, patted the cigarette against the truck's outer frame to let the ashes fly. Porter's truck began ascending the left side of the ramp on the snow-dusted hill. He had to mow down a merge sign on the way but eventually made it past the line of cars and cut the wheel to get back onto the ramp.

Upon getting onto the ramp, he exchanged paint with a heavily hail-damaged Cadillac. The Cadillac blared its horn, and Porter cared little, for he kept cutting the wheel and forced the car into the cement barricade, hugging the right shoulder.

Porter sped ahead and merged onto the highway.

There were six lanes, half Northbound and half Southbound. Between them was a road lane divider. The highway stretched above and over the Cheyenne Reservoir.

Porter quickly got up to speed and cruised with traffic until he heard a siren wailing behind him and the rumble of a deep-throated hog.

In his rear-view mirror, he saw multiple vehicles slowing and pulling off to the side. He also noticed the black and white paint job of a 1700 cc police Harley rolling towards him.

Porter raced ahead and took a puff on his cigarette.

The Harley gained on him, its siren blaring and its lights flashing. The cars in front peeled off to either side, allowing passage of both the pursuer and Porter's truck.

After another quarter-mile, the Harley caught up and sped alongside Porter's driver's side window. The police Officer looked at Porter through the black visor of his helmet. He aggressively pointed and yelled, "Pull over!"

Porter took a final puff on his cigarette and flicked it at the Officer.

The cigarette landed in the Officer's lap, and the Officer feverishly patted himself down. In doing so, he lost control of his bike and crashed hard into the road.

The road coughed up metal and plastic, and the Officer rolled across the highway.

Porter looked back to see the Officer stumble to a vertical base, remove his helmet, and angrily spike it into the road. An expletive left the Officer's mouth as Porter lost view of him.

Ready to light another cigarette, Porter stopped mid-motion as he saw a roadblock ahead. Five squad cars lined the road end-to-end, and orange pop-up barricades stood before them. Additionally, Officers were in the middle of rolling out a tire spike strip across the width of the road.

Porter slammed on his brakes, and his truck groaned to a stop.

The heavily fortified blockade was less than a quarter of a mile before him.

"Well, shit," Porter said. He felt his racing neck pulse and took a deep breath. For a moment, he sat there, smelling the burnt rubber on the pavement he had just created. His white-knuckled grip on the steering wheel loosened.

Reaching in his jacket, Porter took out his pack of cigarettes, shook one free, and lit up.

As he took a deep drag, the whir of chopper blades sounded. Porter careened his neck out the window and saw the blue and white police helicopter hovering above him in the cloudless grey sky.

The side door was open, and tethered inside was a police Officer armed with an M24 SWS. The twenty-four-inch barrel of the sniper rifle was pointed at him.

A sniper rifle…just like Iraq.

The wind whipping all around, courtesy of the helicopter, made Porter squeeze his eyes shut. In doing so, he saw himself fall at the crack of the sniper rifle from the shooter above the rooftop.

He smelled sand in his nostrils and felt heat lick his face.

"Step out of the vehicle!" A voice blared from a megaphone inside the Chopper.

He could hear police sirens from the opposite end of the road. He looked back and saw that the original five had added three more squad cars and were nearly on him.

"We will take you down!" The man behind the megaphone yelled.

Porter reached into the backseat and pulled out his megaphone. Turning the volume to max, he leaned out his window and yelled at the helicopter, "Go fuck yourself!"

Cutting the wheel hard, Porter accelerated against the traffic flow, heading toward the approaching squad cars.

The cars that had pulled off to the side remained in place. Many stood outside their vehicles with their phones out. They were either taking selfies with the police blockade behind them or filming Porter and the approaching squad cars like a documentary.

Porter figured if he could return to the off-ramp, he had passed by earlier than he had an out. All he had to do was beat the approaching police vehicles.

As he neared the exit, Porter figured that the only way to make the turn was to drift into it. It had been a while since he drifted, not since drag racing against Finley Junior Year of High School. Drifts weren't complicated, but it had been a while, and Porter was confident he could still pull it off.

Nearly at the exit, the approaching squad cars were so close Porter could see each driver clearly behind the wheel. Half were angry, and the other half was scared as hell. There was one person whose facial expression differed from the rest. In the unmarked silver SUV sat a passenger with a sadistic grin, and it was Captain Easley.

As Porter reached the highway off-ramp, he engaged the emergency brake and spun the wheel for the drift, but he couldn't help but stare back at Easley.

"What the fuck are you smiling about?" Porter murmured.

Porter heard tires squealing first and saw the black unmarked Ford Crown Victoria second. Third, he saw the driver, Gunther. His vehicle, modified with a steel push bumper, broke from the group of pulled-over cars and, accelerating, smashed into the passenger side of Porter's truck.

The force sent Porter's truck spinning uncontrollably across the road. Within moments, the Ram crashed through the shoulder barrier and toppled over the highway's edge.

Plunging towards the reservoir, Porter gripped the steering wheel and held his breath, bracing for the inevitable impact. The drastic change in scenery from road to water to the free-fall floating sensation to the sudden hood first impact shook Porter to the bones.

The truck immediately sank and took on water from the open driver's side window. Porter tried for the door, but it wouldn't budge due to the water's pressure against it.

As the vehicle continued to plunge and the water reached his chin, Porter took a final deep breath just as water completely engulfed the cabin.

He was ready to unbuckle and swim out the window when the truck rolled and landed at the bottom of the reservoir on the driver's side.

The impact once again rattled him, and pain shot through his body. In an instant, Porter remembered his Marine Corps HMMWV Egress Assistance Trainer, more commonly known as HEAT, he went through in Camp Lejune. The HEAT exercises have various scenarios, but the one most prevalent in the current situation placed four Marines in an armored suspended Humvee and tumbled multiple times. The Marines inside then had to safely exit the Humvee while it was upside down. Communication, teamwork, speed, and presence of mind were vital.

Porter unbuckled and used the steering wheel to pull himself upright. Reaching up to the passenger door, he tried to open it. Still, he could not due to the collision with the Crown Victoria warping the metal.

The passenger window had been shot at in the lobby, but it wasn't a clean opening. Porter punched out the remaining glass with his fist. He grabbed the jagged window frame glass and propelled himself out of the cabin.

With a few strokes, he quickly rose to the surface.

Breaking the plain, he coughed violently and breathed a lungful of air.

His eyes stung, and his contacts had fallen out, rendering his eyesight minimal.

Looking up, he saw what he believed to be blurs of people looking over the edge of the highway at him.

He turned in the water and, finding land, swam to it.

Crawling through icy reeds, snow, and sharp rocks, Porter exhausted his energy and laid on his back, just happy to be alive.

Porter was so overcome with pain and tiredness, and his ears clogged with water and muck, he failed to notice the squad cars pulling into the snow-dusted grass fifty yards away.

When the police finally got to him, they pulled him to his feet. As they were cuffing him, Porter could only break one guy's nose and kick another in the balls before they beat him to his knees and tasered him unconscious.

28

With a bump, Mindy awoke. She sat in the passenger seat of a '74 blue Ford F100 Explorer and looked at a long, sloping, open grey road with no other cars in sight. The purple and brown Rocky Mountains stood dominantly against the cloudy sapphire sky. To either side were fields of yellow grass – their pungent scent reaching her nostrils through the open passenger window. A warm breeze blew through her hair.

"Morning, Fortuna."

Mindy turned to her dad, who was driving. Clothed in a flannel-red long-sleeved shirt and a tan cargo vest, Dustin kept his eyes on the road and brought a silver dented thermos to his lips.

"How long was I out?" Mindy asked. She smelled the coffee. It was Hazelnut, her dad's favorite.

"Almost a day," he said.

"Really, that long?"

"Yeah, she did quite a number on you."

"She?"

"You don't remember?"

"Nope," Mindy opened the glove box and, finding a bag of gummy worms, took them out and began eating.

Dustin reached over and stole one. Popping a gummy in his mouth, he winced.

"What?"

"I swear the yellow ones are sourer than the others."

"They all taste the same to me," Mindy said, popping another into her mouth.

"If you say so."

As they continued to drive, the road just got longer, with no curves or turn-offs in sight. Mindy knew something wasn't right. Looking at her dad, she knew everything about this wasn't right. She knew this wasn't real.

"How come you never taught me how to fight?" Mindy asked. "Or how to get out of a headlock or fire a gun? You know, real skills?"

"Real skills, huh?" Dustin took another sip of coffee. "Well, not every father sees the world the same way."

"Porter is not my father."

"He's trying his best."

With her hand out the window, Mindy surfed the passing breeze. "He sucks at it."

"Okay, here's the thing, I never went to war. I don't know what Porter saw or what he went through. After experiencing something like war, I'm sure you come out differently. I'm sure you see the world differently. You see a threat around every corner. The world seems like a scary place."

"But you are –" Mindy stopped herself and rephrased, "were a firefighter. How did that shape you?"

"Well, it's not an easy life. Marines and firefighters are willing to make the ultimate sacrifice daily. We both see the horrors of the world. But there is a significant difference. As a firefighter, you do everything you can to lie to the world."

"Lie to the world?"

"Yes, you use all your powers to shield the world from true horrors. To make them think that heroes exist and every story has a happy ending."

Mindy shook her head, "What do you mean?"

"When someone is hurt, we tend to their wounds. When someone is trapped in their car, we cut them out. When a house catches fire, we rescue those inside. When someone dies, we cover them so the public can't see the truth."

"What truth?"

"Every day, people succumb to wounds, die in car wrecks, burn to death in fires," Dustin paused and stared at the road.

Mindy nodded through tears as she thought of how Dustin died in the Black Forest fire all those years ago. She regained her composure long enough to mumble, "I know."

"A firefighter doesn't get the luxury of seeing a blanketed corpse. We get exposed to everything. Without us, a lot more people would be exposed to everything."

Mindy wiped away hot tears, "So, that's how you raised me? To shield me from the horrors of the world?"

Dustin took a sip of his drink, "That's right." Setting down his mug, he turned to Mindy, "Look at me." He waited for her to do so, then continued, "There are dads like me who do everything they can to shield their children. Then there are those like Porter who know the horrors and do everything they can to prepare their children to confront them, head on."

"Dad –"

"Brace yourself."

"What?"

In the middle of the road was a speed bump.

⁂

Mindy awoke in a sweat and, taking a deep breath, gripped the sides of the cot she lay on. She stared at a 65-watt canopy LED affixed to the ceiling of a brown corrugated steel shipping container. Hearing the hum from the nearby 1500-watt space heater, she felt electric heat lick her skin.

She immediately knew she was inside one of Porter's bug-out shelters, what he called 'Bugs.'

Sitting up, Mindy pulled off the military tricolor Woodland poncho liner that blanketed her and looked around the 20 x 8 foot enclosure. In the corner of the container sat a blue bucket with a garbage bag liner and a toilet seat affixed to the top. A three-tier free-standing shelf lined one wall. The shelves had foot lockers, guns, body armor, toiletries, and canned goods. Set up next to her cot was a TV tray. A deck of nudie 'Freedom Cards,' a black compact shortwave radio, and a sticky note were atop the tray.

She pulled up the sticky note and read the cursive writing:

"Sorry, it's for your own good. You'll be safe here. I'll make sure someone comes by in a few days." Signed, "V."

"A few days?" Mindy repeated. "That, bitch."

After what Mindy had found on Valentine's computer, she knew her predicament must have something to do with Porter, which meant Mindy had to get free and help him. Waiting a few days was not an option.

Mindy stuck the note back to the TV tray and stood. As she stretched, she realized her neck and jaw were sore from Valentine's chokehold. She made a mental note to return the favor one day.

Checking her pockets, Mindy was relieved she still had her cell phone. When she tried to turn it on, the relief passed, realizing it was dead.

Walking to the roll-up door, she felt cold being out of range of the heater. She knelt and tugged up on the inner handle, which refused to budge. The internal lock was unhinged, so Mindy figured it must be locked from the outside. "Shit," she said to herself.

She banged on the rolling door for several minutes, hollering for help.

No one came.

Wrapping the poncho liner around her shoulders, Mindy found a thin red flashlight. She began rummaging through the footlockers and shelves for a cell phone charger cable. Not seeing a cable, Mindy moved the bins on the shelves and searched high and low in the container for an AC outlet. After not finding a power outlet, she fixated on the LED light bar on the ceiling but realized it was battery-powered.

Mindy grabbed a water bottle from the case on the ground and sat on the cot. Breaking the seal on the bottle, she took a swig and lay down.

"Well, this sucks," Mindy muttered to herself.

Reaching over, she turned the knob on the radio and listened to the National Public Radio station broadcast.

A segment was playing about tooth decay and dental diseases.

Mindy listened for a minute, scanned for other frequencies, listened to them, and, in dissatisfaction, turned off the radio.

Repositioning herself on the cot, she interlaced her hands and drummed on her stomach. Mindy stared up at the light, contemplating her options.

She didn't have a phone cord to charge her phone, and even if she did, there were no outlets. Her eyes bounced to the flashlight, shortwave radio, and LED light. "All of you have a power source," she mumbled.

Sitting up, she popped open the back of her phone and removed the battery. She examined the required voltage, which read 3.7-volt cells.

Mindy turned her attention to the shortwave radio. Unhinging the battery cover on the back, she exposed the AA battery and popped it out. The battery read 1.5 volts.

Mindy twisted the flashlight apart and shook out the pair of AA batteries.

A black duffle bag was on the top shelf of the nearest three-tier rack. Unzipping the bag, Mindy pulled out a red and white first aid kit. She opened the kit and unpackaged the tape and scissors.

Using the white first aid tape, Mindy fastened the three AAs side-by-side. She flipped the middle AA battery upside down.

Needing copper wires, Mindy smashed the radio into the floor.

With the plastic and aluminum outer casing shattered across the floor, Mindy plucked out the inner copper wiring she needed and got to work.

She cut the wires and tape to size using the TV tray as a workbench. She used multiple short wires and strips of thin tape to connect the AA batteries in series, positive end to negative end.

For the final step, she secured a longer wire to both negative and positive terminals separately. Those two wires went to the charging contacts on her phone battery.

Securing the final pieces with tape, Mindy double-checked each contact and then carefully set it on the TV tray.

Mindy knew this would take some time. She found a bag of beef jerky in a bin and devoured it. Finishing off her water bottle and chugging another, Mindy lay down on the cot and closed her eyes. Her thoughts were on Valentine, her connection to the CIA, and, more importantly, the link to Porter.

After an hour, Mindy returned the battery to her phone, and it turned on. She only had 20% battery, but it was more than enough. The date displayed indicated Mindy had been out of reach from mainstream society for almost a full day. She had multiple notifications from her home security app indicating their trailer had been broken into. She viewed the video feed and watched Hector pull up in a Bronco to their trailer. With a blast of a shotgun, he forced himself inside. He entered the trailer, and the video timed out at the sound of approaching motorcycles.

Mindy's first call was to Porter, but there was no answer.

Opening her GPS app, she realized she was in a 'U-Store It' lot in Sidney, Nebraska.

Mindy scribbled down the address and called a local locksmith to her location.

In the hour and a half it took the locksmith to arrive, Mindy inspected the bug-out bag on the top shelf. Inside was a change of clothes, a beanie, a dark brown bomber jacket, gloves, Leatherman, Ka-Bar, e-tool shovel, and $300 in cash. Putting on the jacket, something about the leather reminded her of Porter and gave Mindy an immediate sense of calm.

Mindy placed the tape and scissors she had removed from the first aid bag into the bug-out bag. She added two water bottles.

She took her pick from the various guns on the middle shelf and decided on a Beretta 92 FS. Porter had trained her on it, and it was the weapon she was most comfortable with.

Mindy loaded a clip with 9mm rounds and then packed another clip for reserve. One of the footlockers had a tangle of holsters in it, and Mindy found a suitable one and freed it from the knot. She secured the weapon to her belt.

Mindy was playing her fifth round of solitaire with the deck of Freedom cards when she heard a car pull into the lot, and a man stepped out yelling, "Hello? I'm the locksmith you called!"

Mindy banged on the rolling door, and the locksmith quickly found her storage unit and unlocked it. A cold breeze swept in as the door began to roll up, and dying sunlight stretched across the corrugated steel floor.

The mid-thirty-something man behind the door was fluffy with a smug grin and chaotic black hair. He wore a black apron with red pockets full of various tools over a white polo shirt. The collar was stained with sweat marks.

"And there we go," he said, watching the roll-up door ascend into the aluminum box top.

"Thanks," Mindy told him, walking outside the unit.

"Nothing to it," he said, placing his screwdriver into his apron. "Name's Hank," he said, holding out a hand.

"Mindy," she said, shaking his hand.

Hank placed his hands on his sides as he looked into the container, "I gotta admit, not every day you get a call from someone trapped in one of these."

"Well, I wasn't trapped, not really. It was a stupid school prank, that's all."

"Right," Hank nodded. "Which school do you go to?"

"It's the one here in town. I'm from outta state, and it's my first week. I think the High School kids do this prank with all the new kids."

"Right," Hank said, unconvinced.

"Uh, yeah," Mindy changed the subject, "Do you take cash?"

"Cash?" Hank scratched the back of his head, "We don't really do cash anymore. I can type your card into my phone."

"Can you just mail me a bill?" Mindy said.

Hank shrugged.

"You have a PayPal account? I can pay you that way."

"Is cash no longer good in America?" Mindy asked.

"I'm not sure. Let me call my manager," Hank said, pulling out his phone and walking to his white van in the lot. Vinyl decals of overblown doorknobs and keys crowded the lousy paint job. A minute later, he returned to Mindy, "Alright, Donny says he'll take cash, forty dollars."

Hank watched with interest as Mindy pulled out an envelope from the bug-out bag and plucked a pair of twenty-dollar bills.

About to hand over the money, she asked, "Any chance you can lock the unit up?"

"Uh, yeah, sure," Hank fished the master lock out of his apron. "Didn't even break it." Walking to the unit entrance, he reached up to the outer handle and stared at the contents inside. "Wow, you got a lot of interesting stuff in here. All this stuff yours?"

"Uh, it's my dad's. He goes hunting a lot."

"Yeah, I can see that."

"Can you close the unit?"

"Sure," Hank pulled on the outer handle of the rolling door until it was down. He then attached the lock and checked that the door was secured.

"Thanks," Mindy told him.

Hank nodded, tossed his screwdriver, let it flip, and caught it. "Of course." Leaning his back on the rolling door and crossing his arms, he grinned, "Anything else I can do for you?"

"Yeah, actually," Mindy told him. "Can you give me a ride somewhere? I'll pay."

❧

An hour into the drive, they had just entered the city limits of Raton. For $200, Hank had agreed to drive Mindy as far as Denver. It had been primarily a one-sided conversation. Hank had told Mindy about his life, from being a Varsity Linebacker on the High School football team to almost joining the Marines to becoming a locksmith on a dare.

Using Hank's phone charger that only worked if you held it at a certain angle, then only for short periods, Mindy nodded along to the stories and stayed busy texting away on her phone. Occasionally she dropped in an "Oh really?" a, "no way," and the always important, "Yeah, those bitches."

Finishing his story about the first time he got high, Hank turned down the country music blaring over the radio. "You know something? I feel like I've been talking about me this whole time. I want to hear more about you."

Mindy shrugged and continued sending her text.

"Uh, who are you talking to?" Hank said, leaning over to look at her phone. "You telling them about me? Telling them how cool of a guy I am?"

Mindy stuffed her phone in her pocket, "Obvi."

Hank laughed, and Mindy did, too.

Mindy looked out the window. Speeding across the highway, they passed a billboard saying, 'Vote for Bobbi Johnson' and a billboard saying 'Vote for Tim Styles.' They then passed an exit ramp for a hotel and restaurant. The illuminated Motel 5 and the Waffle House were the only signs of life off the road.

The restaurant looked like it was under construction.

"So, you said you were in High School?" Hank asked.

"That's right," Mindy said.

"You're one of those High School girls who looks like she's in college, huh?" Before Mindy could answer, Hank continued, "Yeah, buddy, I bet all the boys like you."

"I guess," Mindy said. She knew Hank's type, and it made her cautious.

"You have a boyfriend?"

Mindy sighed.

"C'mon, it's a simple question. You have a boyfriend?"

"Can we change the subject?"

"Girlfriend?"

"I really don't want to discuss this."

"Sure," Hank said, turning the radio music up. After a minute, he turned the radio down. "I gotta know. You're a hooker, right?"

Mindy rolled her eyes and, massaging her forehead, said, "Pull over."

"C'mon, don't be like that."

"Pull over," Mindy said again.

"That's why you were in that container, right? Did your pimp put you in there or something? You were escaping. Somebody oughta give me a Ph.D."

"Just let me out. You can keep the money."

"I'm not a bad person. Why are you talking to me like I'm a bad person? I rescued you. Someone like you should reward me," he ran a finger up her thigh, "with something other than money."

Mindy pulled the Beretta from her holster and stuck it in his side. "Pull over, now!"

Hank looked down at the gun and said nothing for a moment.

The moment passed, and he grinned, "C'mon, you wouldn't."

Mindy pulled back the hammer, "Try me."

❋

With the bug-out duffle bag strapped across her body, Mindy walked the shoulder of the highway against traffic. After ten minutes of smelling car fumes, getting a few car honks, and nearly freezing her fingers off, she reached the exit ramp she had seen earlier.

Following the descending curve of the ramp and crossing a street, Mindy stopped in front of the Waffle House parking lot. The restaurant looked like it was a candidate for a rehab show on the Discovery Channel. The Waffle House sign had missing letters. Half the windows were replaced with plywood. A corner of the store was caved in, and a blue tarp covered the gapping damage.

A sign on the door read, "Yes, we are still open."

Looking into the lobby, Mindy saw one employee sweeping the floor and another eating at a table.

Mindy walked across the nearly empty parking lot. The only car was a late-model purple VW adorned with peace symbols and ladybug stickers. A bicycle was parked next to the green dumpster in the enclave on the side of the building.

Walking through the boarded-up doors, Mindy was immediately hit with warmth and the smell of coffee and hashbrowns.

Half the restaurant was roped off with a sign saying, "Sorry for the construction. Limited capacity seating." Aside from the high seats at the counter, only four booths were available.

"Hello, sit wherever you'd like," the sweeping woman with freckles and short brunette hair told her. A flower was pinned to her visor, and a gold cross hung down her long neck. Mindy recognized her from the memorial earlier in the year following the Sandman case.

Mindy looked at the woman's yellow nametag, which read Emily.

"Work, work, work," the employee with the cleft lip eating at the table said as he shoveled his remaining hashbrowns into his mouth and maneuvered his way back to the kitchen.

Mindy placed her bug-out bag in the closest booth and sat on the opposite-facing bench.

Emily put up her broom and came to her table. "Okay, before you ask," she said, "we are legally obligated to say that a car hit the restaurant."

"Is that what really happened?" Mindy said, looking at the construction.

Emily smiled and shrugged, "How about a coffee to start with?"

"Sure."

"Just scan the QR code on the table to pull up the menu." As she began to walk away, she stopped and asked, "Have we met before?"

"At the funeral. You hired Detective Porter to find your brother, Gary."

"That's right, you're his partner, Mindy?"

"That's right."

To Mindy's surprise, Emily came around and, sitting next to her on the bench, hugged her. "Wow, small world, what brings you out here? Working a case?"

Miny shrugged, "Yeah, guess you could say that."

"Wow, you guys certainly keep busy."

"Sure do. How is your brother doing?"

"Gary's good. He works across the street at the hotel. He's the night receptionist. He's about to get his GED. I'm really proud of him."

"Wow, that's awesome."

"Okay, well, as a thank you from me and Gary, your meal is on the house."

"Oh, you don't have to do that."

"Mindy, I don't know you that well. But I know your look."

"My look."

"You look exhausted, stressed, and a little rattled, too. This case you're working on must be a tough one. You and Porter do good work. The least I can do is treat you to a meal."

"Okay, well, when you put it like that…" she lingered on the cross Emily wore, "no arguments."

"Are you a person of faith?" Emily asked.

"No, I don't go to church. But someone I know wears a cross, too. She's a good person. You remind me of her."

Emily nodded, "Cream and sugar with your coffee?"

Mindy nodded, "Yes, please."

"Alright, you figure out what food you're having. I'll be right back.'

Mindy began to scan the code when her phone died. "That's just perfect."

A minute later, Emily brought Mindy's coffee. "What are you eating?"

"Uh," Mindy nodded to the cook, "whatever he was eating. It smelled great."

"Johnny, what were you eating?" Emily asked the cook.

"Drop one scattered, covered, chunked, and topped with a splash of tabasco," Johnny said, holding up his spatula proudly.

"Sure, whatever all that means, sounds good," Mindy said. "Minus the tabasco."

"Hashbrowns with ham, cheese, and chili, coming up," Emily said, writing down the order.

Mindy closed her eyes and buried her head in her arms. She was tired, and the case did have her stressed. Mindy found it odd that sometimes it took stating the obvious for you to realize the reality of the situation.

"Well, hi there," a familiar voice said.

Mindy smelled the scent of roses and looked up to see Valentine sitting on the opposite-facing bench. She wore a denim jacket full of patches and a Metallica tee. Her guitar case sat underneath the table.

Valentine gestured to Emily, "I'll take a coffee, black."

"So, that's why you left me with my phone," Mindy said. "I didn't notice the tracker in it."

"You'd have to take it completely apart to find it. Well, I will give you credit. I put you out in the literal middle of nowhere. I thought I'd bought myself some more time locking you in there. Should have known you'd find a way to charge your phone and call for help. It appears I underestimated you, Ms. Miller."

"Apparently."

"Apparently," Valentine repeated. "It's interesting. You remind me so much of me when I was younger."

Mindy stared at her with malice.

"Ahh, that look, yes, I know that look, too," Valentine told her.

Emily returned with the coffee, "Here you go, and your meal will be right up, Mindy. What can I get you to eat, honey?" she asked Valentine.

"I'll take a bowl of tomato soup with some crackers," Valentine said.

"You got it," Emily told her, returning to the kitchen.

"Why are you here?" Mindy asked.

"Same reason as you."

"Porter?"

"Porter," Valentine confirmed.

"What is your interest in him?"

"Oh, c'mon now, you spent enough time on my computer to figure it out."

"Nearly, until someone put me in a headlock and choked me out."

Emily returned with their food, "Here you go." She set the hashbrowns in front of Mindy and the soup in front of Valentine, "Let me know if you need anything else."

Neither touched their food. Valentine and Mindy continued to stare at one another. The tension was thick.

Emily took her cue and returned to the kitchen, "Okay."

"He knew people would be after you. That's why Porter asked that I keep you safe," Valentine said.

"Bullshit, that was your idea of safe?"

"Oh, if you only knew the things I've done in the last twenty-four hours to keep you off the grid."

"Tell me, what exactly have you done?"

Valentine smirked, "That's classified."

Mindy face-palmed herself, "How did I know you'd say that?" Mindy watched as Valentine swigged her coffee and added sugar. "What type of trouble has Porter got himself into with this case?"

"The worse type of trouble," Valentine said. With shaky hands, she crumbled her crackers into her soup.

"Because of whoever this Hector Guvera guy is?"

"That's right."

"So what now?" Mindy asked.

"Listen, I know you don't know me, I know you don't trust me, and I know you sure as hell don't like me –"

"You're not wrong," Mindy interrupted.

"Let me finish," Valentine continued, "I told Porter I'd make sure you are safe until he gets back, and I always keep my word."

"You try and lock me up again –"

"Oh, I'm well aware of what you're packing in your holster," Valentine told her. "Nope, you'll be coming with me from now on. And it's time I show you what else is in my case besides my guitar."

"Coming with you?"

"Yeah, but first, we need to let Porter sink himself in the hole just a little deeper."

"Why?"

"If you want to solve this case, you need to trust me," Valentine told her. She then pointed to Mindy's food, "Eat up before it gets cold. Oh, and recommend you add some Tabasco, it'll taste better."

From the kitchen, Johnny yelled, "Right?"

Mindy shook her head and stared at Valentine, "What exactly do you have hiding in your guitar case?"

Valentine smirked, "Ever see the movie, Desperado?"

29

There was a potent smell of bleach cleaner, cotton sheets, something metallic-like, and flowers.

Stirring awake, Porter's temples throbbed.

On cue, he heard old piano tunes from a nearby television. It sounded like something from an early 1900s cinema.

Everything was a blur as Porter opened his eyes. Searching for his glasses, he found them on a white end table beside the bed.

He began reaching for them but stopped short.

Then, he realized his left wrist was cuffed to the gurney.

He yanked on the restraint, but it refused to give.

"Well, look who's up," a man said in a slow, gruff voice.

Porter looked at the voice and saw a blurry uniformed Officer sitting at the foot of his bed. The badge grabbed the handset clipped to his uniform, "Tell the Captain that our resident Detective is awake."

"Where am I?" Porter asked.

"St. Barbara's hospital," the Officer told him as he stood and stretched.

"What's with the cuffs?"

"Ahh, you don't recognize me, do you?" the Officer shook his head and walked closer. Taking a knee beside Porter's bed, he leaned in, "Well, I was wearing a helmet, and we were both going pretty fast on the highway."

Porter shrugged. He took in the man's hazel eyes, dark features, and bushy mustache. The Officer looked close to retirement, if not a year or two past it. Multiple bruises and band-aids lined his aging face.

"You were in your truck. I was on my bike. The bike was brand new. Just issued to me this week."

Porter sighed, "Yeah, I remember."

The Officer sent a punch to Porter's gut.

Porter coughed out.

"That's for my bike." He punched him again, "And that's for my face."

When his coughing subsided, Porter gasped in pain and asked, "Alright, you feel better now?"

"Well, it's a start."

"Good, now uncuff me, Gramps, and let's find out how tough you really are."

"No one cares how tough I am, but we're gonna find out how tough you are." The Officer said, walking out the door, "Yes sir, we will find out."

"What the hell does that mean? Hey, get back here! Where's Sarah! Get Officer Evans!" Porter pulled again at the cuff to no avail. He rolled painfully onto his bandaged side and, reaching across his body with his opposite arm, grabbed his glasses.

At the foot of the bed, beside the chair, stood a small table with a white ceramic vase with flowers. A pea-colored love sofa hugged the sidewall. Next to the door, a wheelchair was parked. On the front wall, a mounted TV was playing the black and white 1920s version of Dr. Jekyll and Mr. Hyde.

Text came on the screen, "Sir George Carew [to Jekyll]: A man cannot destroy the savage in him by denying its impulses. The only way to get rid of a temptation is to yield to it."

Examining the cuff more closely, Porter turned his wrist to expose the keyhole.

He removed his glasses and began pulling apart one of the temple pieces to get at the screw that secured the hinge to the endpiece when the door opened.

Porter threw his glasses on as Captain Easley entered. Her lips were painted with a loud layer of red, giving her a Joker-like grin.

"Where's Sarah?" Porter said. Yanking hard on his wrist, he rattled his cuff against the bed, "And, you wanna explain this?"

"Seriously, you know how much property damage you caused on the highway?" Easley asked.

"Who gives a shit about property damage? Where's Sarah?"

"Did you know that most of the states in this country have the Death Penalty right now? If you live in California, Florida, or Texas and shoot a cop, you most likely get the Death Penalty. Beautiful, isn't it?"

"Answer me, dammit! Where's Sarah?"

Easley ignored Porter and continued, "Unfortunately, we have a Governor-imposed Moratorium here in Colorado. A suspension of law, the death penalty specifically. And right now, it seems no incoming Governor will ever change that because it's a neutral stance, and they don't want to lose potential voters. It's pretty fucking cowardice if you ask me."

"What's Sarah's condition."

"Critical. You shot her in the abdomen, after all."

"It was Amberson."

"Ballistics says differently."

"He had my gun."

Easley grinned, "Yeah, good luck proving that in the courtroom, Detective Porter. Or should I say, Frank Marion, your alias?"

Porter shook his head, "Ahh, now it makes sense."

"We have multiple sources pointing you as the man behind brokering the deal between American Iron and certain violent members of the Wolfpack biker club. Also, multiple reports and surveillance photos of you meeting with known Wolfpack members in the last twenty-four hours. Not to mention, numerous payments have been made to you that led to your offshore accounts."

"My offshore accounts? Can I have access to those? There's a new truck I need to buy and some upgrades to my club I want to make. Also, can I meet some of these sources? I'd like to knock out some of their lying teeth."

"You killed them all during your coupe of the American Iron Corporate Office."

"My coupe? That's what we're calling it? How about Scott Winters? Where's that asshole? I bet he'd have something to say about all this."

"Mr. Winters is willing to testify in a courtroom that you violently coerced him into a partnership against his will."

Porter studied her, "That's if I get to a courtroom, right?"

"What happens between now and your sentencing is out of my hands. But I hear inmates love it when they learn a Detective resides with them, even if you are only a Private Detective. They treat them real kindly."

"Is that right?" Porter said, sharing a grin of his own.

"Did I say something amusing?"

"I was just thinking, if you're so sure they're going to treat me kindly, I can only imagine how they'll treat the Captain of the police force. When they're done with you, your pussy will look like a box of cow tongues."

Easley laughed, "I knew you were a cocky loose cannon, but now I know you're delusional."

"Am I? I know all about you, your connections with American Iron, and your slumber parties with Bobbi Johnson."

Easley's grin faded, and the color drained from her face.

"Kickbacks, kickbacks, kickbacks, I guess a Captain's salary ain't what it used to be. If you need the extra cash, go work a corner. It would be simpler, but I doubt even my competitors would hire you. People in my business do have standards."

Easley stepped to his bed and smacked him across the face.

Porter massaged his cheek, "Was it something I said?"

At these words, a scraggily-looking doctor in scrubs wearing a face mask walked in. He closed the door and began cleaning his hands at the washing station.

Easley barked over her shoulder, "Not now, come back later!" With a crooked finger, she pointed at Porter and grinned through flared nostrils, "You're finished, you hear me? I cannot wait to —"

There was a slapping as the doctor pulled latex gloves loudly onto each hand and wrist.

"Did you hear me? I said, not now," Easley said.

The doctor nodded and removed a washcloth from the overhead cabinet. "Sorry, this will only take a moment."

"Make it quick," Easley returned her attention to Porter, "Don't get too comfortable because –"

"Quick question," the doctor said, tapping Easley on the shoulder. She turned to him as he sprayed a solution on the rag, "Does this smell like chloroform to you?"

"What?"

The doctor wrapped an arm around Easley and pushed the cloth across the Captain's nose and mouth.

Easley fought for a few seconds before going limp.

"Ooh, someone's a kicker," the doctor said as he gently lowered her to the floor.

Making his way to Porter's gurney, the man pulled down his mask, "It's okay, really, I am a doctor."

Porter breathed a sigh of relief, "Doc? I have never been so happy to see your ugly mug."

"Thanks, I think." Doc surveyed him, "I gotta say, Porter, you look like shit."

"Um, hmm. Lucky I'm cuffed."

"Well, yeah, that's why I chose to say those words here and now."

The door opened once more, and in limped a female Officer with shoulder-length red hair, thick glasses, and a face full of freckles. A bug-out bag was slung over her shoulder. She closed the door and looked at Easley.

"This is awkward," Porter said.

"Well, how do I look?" the Officer asked.

Porter recognized the voice, if not the face, "Erica?"

"It's kind of sad when your own boss doesn't recognize you in daylight hours."

"Erica, what are you doing here?" Porter asked.

"Oh, but it's okay that I'm involved?" Doc said, "Okay, I see how it is." He turned to Erica, "You must put out."

"Depends who's asking," she said.

"Me, I'm asking," Doc told her.

"Then that's a hard no."

Porter exchanged a look between them, "Have either of you heard from Mindy?"

"No," Erica said, "Do you want me to call her?"

"I'd rather she stay out of this."

"Your call, Boss."

Porter made his cuff link rattle, "Either of you got a key?"

"I got ya, Boss," Erica pulled a lockpick set from the bug-out bag and handed it over. "Here you go." She placed the bag on his gurney, "You got a change of clothes and a revolver in there."

"Damn, someone's getting a bonus when I get back to the office," Porter told her.

As Porter worked the cuffs, Erica and Doc dragged Easley to the back of the room.

Porter pointed to the Captain, "How long does that stuff last?"

"Don't worry, we'll be long gone before she wakes up," Doc said. "The chloroform usually knocks them out for a solid two hours."

Erica turned to him with a look of shock.

"I mean, I hear it's two hours. I don't know for sure."

"Right," she said.

"Is Sarah going to pull through?" Porter asked.

"I don't know. She was sleeping or in a coma or something when I went by the room," Erica said.

"Which one? Sleeping or a coma?"

"I don't know."

"I looked at her charts. She'll be fine," Doc reassured.

Freeing himself of the cuffs, Porter pulled off his hospital gown, exposing himself completely. Grabbing clothes from the bag, he pulled out his prosthetic and began attaching it to his nub.

Doc shielded his eyes and turned, "Damn, Porter, at least a warning next time."

"Grow up," Erica said.

Doc waved her off.

"Besides, some guys are comfortable with being nude."

"Just like Michelangelo's statue," Porter said, tightening the prosthetic.

"Let me know when you have pants on," Doc said.

Throwing on his pants and fastening his belt, Porter nodded to Erica, "Enjoying the view?"

Erica smirked, "C'mon, like I've never seen your bare ass before."

"True," Porter said.

Doc wagged a finger, "I'm sure there's an NC-17-rated story behind this."

"Wouldn't you like to know?" Erica asked.

"Actually, yes, I would," Doc said.

"There's something seriously wrong with you," Erica told him.

"You sound like my ex-wives."

Porter stepped off the gurney and, securing the gun and holster to his thigh, looked at both of them, "So, if you two are here, don't tell me you left Molly alone with Hector?"

"So, about that," Erica said.

"What?"

"Molly is working the receptionist desk. She'll discharge you from the hospital."

"So if you two are here and Molly is the receptionist, who is with Hector?"

"He bolted," Doc said.

"What do you mean, bolted?"

"He woke, grabbed me by the throat, and was about to kill me when Molly and Erica talked him down."

"To be honest," Erica said, "it was more Molly than me. I don't know what it was, but I think she reminded him of someone. We told him you had charged us with caring for him, and then he ran out of the container."

"And I sure as hell wasn't going to stop him. Especially not after all that killer stuff you told us about him. That dude is scary when he's awake and has one hell of a grip," Doc said, rubbing his neck. "Couldn't tell you where he went after he left. He just kinda disappeared."

"Yeah, he does that," Porter said.

Erica handed him the hospital gown, matching surgical cap, and a cloth facemask, "Put these on and park it in the wheelchair."

"Right," Porter said, putting the garbs on and securing the facemask straps behind his ears. "So, what's the game plan?"

"Doc will push, and I'll escort. Once we go down the elevator to the lobby, Molly will buzz you out. Alice will be our ride out of here."

"You found Alice?" Porter asked.

"What do you mean found her?"

"I thought Scott, that American Iron douche had gone after her," Porter said.

"She called me," Erica told him, "she saw you on the news, and after I told her our plan, she insisted on helping."

"I was on the news?" Porter asked.

"Yeah, check it out," Doc said. He pulled out his phone and, thumbing away, opened TikTok. They all watched a video of Porter's Ram stopped on the highway with a helicopter hovering above. From the chopper, a man with a sniper rifle pointed at

Porter's truck; another had a megaphone and yelled, "We will take you down!"

Porter pulled out his megaphone, leaned out the open window, and said to the helicopter, "Go fuck yourself!"

Cutting the wheel, Porter accelerated, and the video ended.

"That was hot, Porter," Erica said.

"Hey, I got a megaphone in my shop," Doc said.

Erica shrugged, "Good for you. Okay, moving on, we head to the club once Alice picks us up. I already talked to Ursula."

"Ursula, who is she?"

"My club manager. She runs the daily operations," Porter said.

"Manager, huh?" Doc asked. "A woman in power, is she hot? Think you can hook me up with her?"

Porter and Erica exchanged a glance and smiled at one another.

"You got it," Porter told him.

"Okay, that was too easy. Ursula is hideous, isn't she?" Doc asked. He shook his head, "Of course she is, hence the name. Damn, I knew something was wrong when you agreed so quickly."

"Once we get to the club," Erica continued, "we lay low until this clears up."

"Lay low?" Porter asked. "Maybe you guys."

"Okay, we're taking bets. Who are you going after, Styles or Johnson?" Doc asked.

"Johnson," Porter said.

"I knew it!" Erica said. She held out her hand to Doc, "Pay up."

"C'mon, now, I don't have the money on me," Doc told her. "How about this? After everything blows over, we go back to my place and discuss repayment over a nice microwavable TV dinner. I got a new Vegas Naked Wrestling Girls DVD we can watch."

"DVD? What is this 1999?" Porter asked.

"Seriously, a DVD is your concern?" Erica asked. She shook her head, "No, thank you. Just pay me when you can, with cash."

"Details, details, details," Doc murmured.

"What about the Officer sitting in front of this door?" Porter asked.

"I wouldn't worry about him," Erica said. "I slipped something in his drink, and someone's taking his place."

"Slipped something in his drink?" Doc asked. "You do that type of thing a lot at the club?"

"Oh yeah, all the time. Porter didn't only hire me for my good looks. When needed, if a customer is being a jackass or getting a bunch of drinks and not tipping well, I slip something in his drink to make him leave."

Doc turned to Porter, "Seriously? You condone that?"

"Doc, it's not like we chloroform people," Porter said. "Erica, you mentioned someone is taking the Officer's place?"

"Yeah, someone."

"Wait for the signal," Erica said.

"Signal?" Porter said.

A trio of quick knocks sounded on the opposite side of the door, followed by a pause and two more knocks.

"Here we go," Doc said.

Erica held open the door as Doc wheeled out Porter. Exiting the hallway, they watched an Officer making long, awkward strides down the hallway. He was holding his rear and knocked over an orderly on his way to the bathroom.

"Laxatives?" Porter asked.

"A special cocktail for sure," Erica confirmed.

"This is undignified," an annoyed man grunted in a low voice.

They turned to Flick, sitting next to the door, playing with one of the buttons, screaming for release on his tight Police uniform. "These things were made for toddlers, I swear."

"Flick," Porter greeted.

"Don't Flick me. You know, Rookie, even when you're admitted to a hospital, you still somehow manage to be a pain in my ass."

"I owe you one, Old Man."

"Damn right, you do." Flick gestured him forward, "Go on, get moving."

Rolling down the length of the hall, they almost made it to the elevator when Porter heard a beeping sound from an EKG. He looked to the sound and watched a doctor walk out the door, and as he closed it behind him, Porter glimpsed Evans with eyes shut and lying on a bed with tubes hooked to her.

Porter gripped the wheels and stopped them from turning.

"Porter, c'mon, man," Doc said.

"Boss, we got to get a move on," Erica added.

Porter shot them both a sharp look.

Doc rolled his eyes and wheeled him in.

Porter sat at Evans' bed momentarily, staring at her sleeping face. Even with an IV running to her arm and bruises on her face, she looked beautiful.

Porter held Evans hand and ran his other through her blonde hair. He leaned forward and planted a kiss on her lips. He focused on the cross hanging around her neck, "Do your job."

On the first floor, Doc wheeled Porter down the hall, thick with the scent of freshly brewed coffee and glazed doughnuts. A large gathering of Officers huddled by the main desk in the lobby, sitting in the surrounding chairs and watching reruns of Jerry Springer on the mounted television. They were loudly conversing over last night's lottery numbers. Everyone was joking that, yet again, their badge numbers screwed them. There was a spacing of chairs between the Officers and the regular hospital patients waiting to be seen.

"You said a few cops. This is a freaking doughnut convention," Doc whispered.

"Just play it cool," Erica whispered to Doc.

"Both of you, shut up," Porter whispered.

Doc wheeled Porter towards the desk, "Excuse me, Officers, coming through."

Still deep in conversation, the Officers hesitantly made a hole for them.

"Excuse us," Doc said, parking the wheelchair at the receptionist's desk.

"Good morning," a woman in a wheelchair with pink hair in a bob wearing a light blue one-pocket scrub top said. The lenses in her pink sparkle-framed glasses shimmered as she glanced at Porter and held back a smile.

"We're here to check out a patient," Doc said.

"Name?" Molly asked.

"Wait a minute!" an Officer said, pointing at Porter. He was the motorcyclist Porter had encountered on the highway. "I know that son-of-a-bitch!"

Another Officer with a bandage across his nose put his doughnut down and nodded, "Yeah, that's the bastard who broke my nose! Porter!"

"Boys," Erica said, "there's been a mistake. Mr. Bauer here –"

"Remove your face mask!" Another Officer yelled, pointing his weapon at Porter.

"Shit, someone do something," Doc whispered out of the side of his mouth to both Erica and Porter.

"Lower it now," another commanded.

"Everyone just calm down," Erica said.

"Guys, c'mon, this is just a misunderstanding," Doc pleaded.

"Step away from him," an Officer said, yanking Doc back.

"Relax," Erica said, stepping between the Officers and Porter, "this is not Porter."

As another Officer began reaching for his shoulder radio, Flick burst into the hallway. He pulled out his gun and fired a single shot into the ceiling.

As everyone ducked in fear, the lobby patients screamed, and guns began to point in all directions. Flick clutched his chest and screamed out in pain. "My heart!" he gasped, reaching out for the nearest Officer.

He fell to the ground with a large thud, taking down the closest Officer.

In all the confusion, Molly swatted the release button for the exit door. "Go!" she hissed.

Porter winked at her before he, Erica, and Doc rushed out of the lobby and entered the parking lot. After only wheeling and taking a few steps, an older tan Honda Civic screeched to a halt in front of them with Alice at the wheel.

With the side window rolled down, Alice yelled, "Porter, get in!" Reaching over, she opened the front passenger door.

Getting up from the wheelchair, Porter rushed into the passenger side.

As Doc and Erica ran to the rear passenger door, Alice floored it. Her car tires squealed across the blacktop, leaving Erica and Doc behind.

"Hey, wait!" Doc yelled, jumping and waving his arms.

Erica looked on in disbelief.

"What the hell's going on?" Porter asked.

The Civic was out of the parking lot and onto the main road before the Officers made it outside. He watched as they drew their weapons on Doc and Erica, forcing them to drop to their knees and interlace their fingers behind their heads.

"Porter, I'm sorry," Alice said.

Porter took a deep breath and exhaled before looking in the back seat. Scott lay on his side, a gun trained on the back of Alice's head. "Detective Porter, if you value her life, hand me your weapon and do exactly as I say, understand?"

Porter turned to Alice, and her face was full of dread and fear as she drove. She was breathing hard and sweating. Porter nodded to her and squeezed her leg like she liked, "It's going to be alright."

Alice nodded, "I trust you."

Porter turned to Scott and handed him his revolver, "What do you want, shithead?"

"Drive," he said.

"Where?" Alice asked.

"We're going to the Lady Luck."

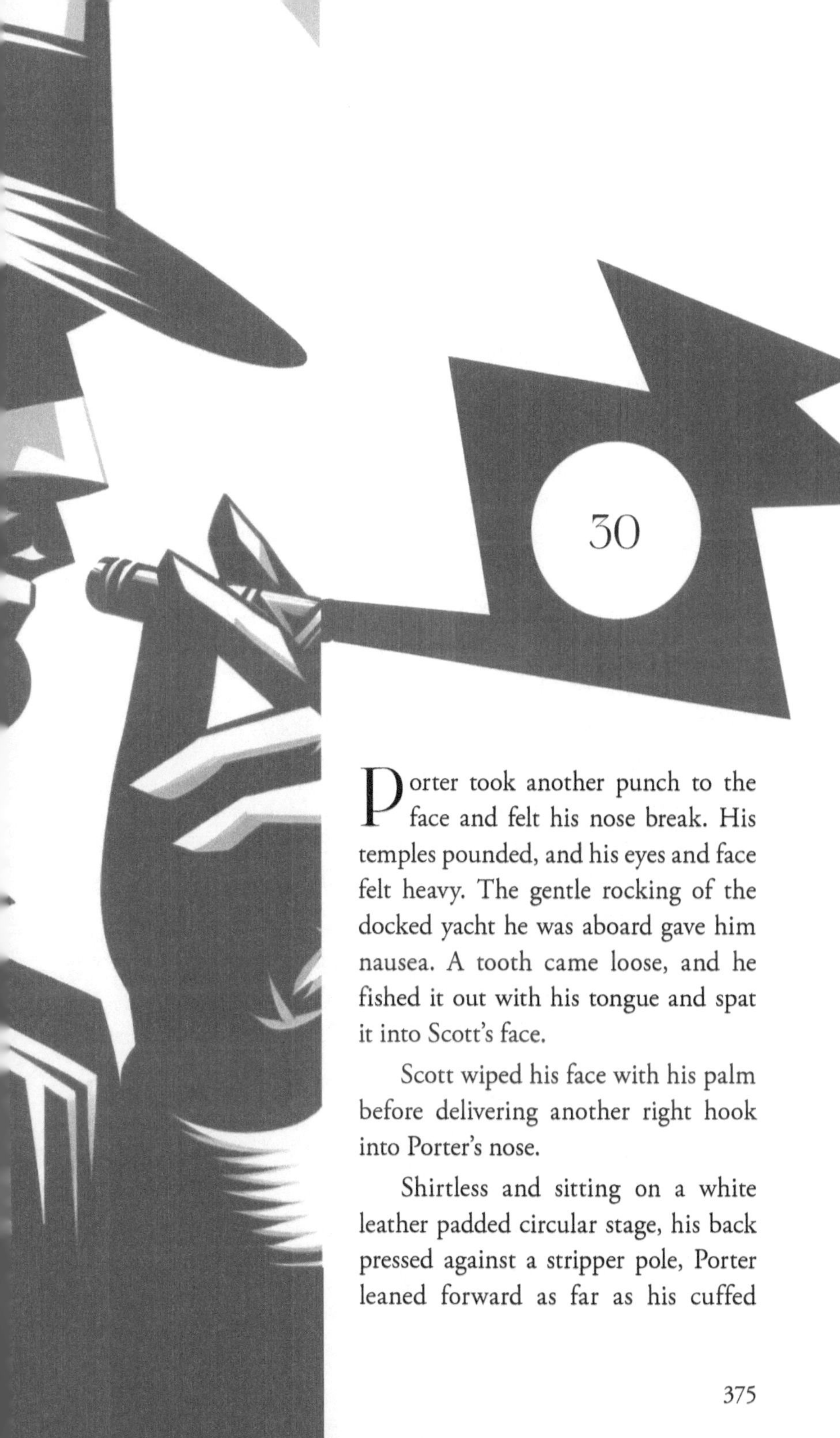

30

Porter took another punch to the face and felt his nose break. His temples pounded, and his eyes and face felt heavy. The gentle rocking of the docked yacht he was aboard gave him nausea. A tooth came loose, and he fished it out with his tongue and spat it into Scott's face.

Scott wiped his face with his palm before delivering another right hook into Porter's nose.

Shirtless and sitting on a white leather padded circular stage, his back pressed against a stripper pole, Porter leaned forward as far as his cuffed wrists secured behind the pole would allow him and let the blood drool out of his mouth.

Gunther walked down the stairs and crossed the deck to them. Pulling up a chair, he took a seat, inching forward, putting his elbows on his knees. His fingers interlocked to form a steeple under his chin. "Where is Guvera?" He looked up towards the upper deck at the sounds of hoots and hollers. "The boys are trying to get your woman to warm up for them. She's being difficult."

"Good," Porter said.

Porter watched Scott make his way to the dark cherry bar table. Stepping around the counter, Scott turned on the sink and washed the blood off his knuckles. Taking a shot glass from the lower cabinet, Scott grabbed a bottle of Crown Royal from the curio cabinet behind the table and poured himself a drink.

He offered a glass to Porter, "Something to wash away your bullshit excuse for a life?"

"Yeah, I'll take a tall go fuck yourself," Porter said.

Scott looked at Gunther and shrugged.

Gunther eyed Porter cautiously for a long moment before grinning. "I heard you were a tough bastard." He stared at Porter's bare chest, weathered with years of scars and bullet holes. "You're on a whole different level, aren't you?"

"He's just shit for brains," Scott said, pouring himself another shot. "Just like all jarheads."

"Hooah, I'm going to kill you first," Porter groaned. He then swiveled his head to Gunther, "I'm going to break his fucking neck. You want to watch?"

"Oh, you'll break my neck?" Scott pounded down his drink and decked Porter in the face.

"Get some fresh air," Gunther told him.

"What?" Scott asked.

"Now."

"Right," Scott said before heading up the stairs.

Gunther listened for the upper deck door to close before getting up, folding his arms behind his back, and pacing around Porter, "Every man has a breaking point. Even Marines. I will find yours. It is only a matter of time."

Porter spat blood, "Yeah, I've heard that about you."

"Heard what?"

"Heard you hunt down Marines and kill them."

"Oh, you Marines take such pride in being elite. You tout your thirteen-week boot camp, your crucible, your legacy from the Halls of Montezuma to the shores of Tripoli, the tip of America's spear. But Marines fall easily once you break them from the pack and ingest a little fear into their system. They lose their confidence, their battlefield dominance, their brutality."

"Take a hard look in my eyes, Sauerkraut, you see any of that fear in me?" Porter asked.

"Let's find out," Gunther said. Walking to the bar, tearing a strip off a roll of duct tape, and reaching into the underside of the curio cabinet roof, Gunther unscrewed the 5.5-watt medium base LED light bulb. "Do you know what happens when you ingest glass?"

"I'm going to fucking kill you!" Porter growled at him.

With a punch to the gut, Porter gasped in pain. Pulling Porter's jaw open, Gunther held back his head and forced the bulb inside. He then applied the strip of tape over Porter's mouth.

Porter growled in anger once more, and Gunther sent a haymaker into the side of his face.

A crack sounded inside Porter's mouth.

"Another two punches will break the glass," Gunther said. Grabbing Porter by the hair, he forced his head back and asked, "Where is Guvera?"

Porter refused to answer.

Gunther's next punch cracked the glass even more, "Tell me where Guvera is, and I'll kill you quick." Gunther held his fist back, waiting to send a third punch into Porter's face. "The pain will be excruciating."

Gunther studied him for a long moment. "Even now, you give me that look. Even now, you look at me like you're superior. Few times have I been on the receiving end of such a look. You really are something else, Detective."

The upper deck door opened, and Scott said, "Welcome to the Lady Luck. Follow me, Ms. Johnson."

"I thought Tim Styles would have a bigger yacht," Bobbi said. "What's with the girl cuffed to the pole? Why is her mouth taped."

"It's necessary," Scott said.

Porter watched Bobbi in a three-piece cherry business suit and high heels hold the steel railing as she walked down the mahogany steps leading to the lower deck. Reaching the bottom, she held onto the railing as the yacht swayed.

"Careful, ma'am, we have rough seas tonight," Scott told her.

Bobbi grimaced as she looked around the hull at framed prints of scantily clad Bond girls, from Ursula Andress coming out of the water in her swimsuit in "Dr. No" to a golden nude Shirley Eaton in "Gold Finger" to the backside of Eva Green smoking a cigarette in "Casino Royale" and everything in between. "So, this is Tim Styles' infamous Lady Luck. Quite the family man."

Upon seeing Porter's current state of health, Bobbi awkwardly pulled at the white collar of the beige fashion-notched lapel she wore under her vest. Looking away from Porter, she crossed her arms and loudly cleared her throat, "Scott, Gunther, a word, please."

As the two walked to Bobbi, Porter could hear Gunther whisper, "Not yet."

"You assured me you could break him," Bobbi hissed.

"It's only a matter of time."

"We don't have time," Bobbi whispered. She looked back at Porter momentarily and then continued, "The ambassador will be here in the next few hours. If Guvera is not here, then all this is for nothing." Motioning to Porter, Bobbi said, "Clean him up. I want a word with him."

Scott filled a shot glass with water and, walking to Porter, pulled the tape off and the bulb from his mouth. As Porter coughed, Scott splashed the water into his face. "There you go, all cleaned up."

"Leave us," Bobbi said. She turned to Scott and Gunther, "Wait for me topside with my other guards."

"Ms. Johnson," Gunther protested.

"I can handle myself."

Bobbi watched as they went upstairs and exited. Turning her attention to Porter, she squeezed her temples and shook her head, "Tell us where Guvera is, and this can all stop."

Porter spat blood on her shiny red high heels.

Bobbi looked at her heels in disgust and sighed.

"Don't tell me you have the balls to pull all this off but not to look at blood," Porter said. "C'mon, take a good fucking look at what all your money has bought."

Bobbi shook her head, "What my money has bought? Do you have any idea how much it costs to run for Senator? How much money I need to raise to win at the polls? To bribe the right people?"

"I'm sure you have deep pockets."

"Direct solicitations, website contributions, fundraisers, rallies, and party endorsements bring in money," Bobbi said. "But at the end of the day, if you're a woman and black, you still fall short, and you need other means."

As she spoke, Porter searched the room for anything to help him, anything at all. The pole he was secured to was a little shaky, but not much. There wasn't anything he could reach out to with his feet. Porter kept thinking he could slip out of the cuffs, but they were on tight, and the blood and sweat on his wrists weren't enough lubrication.

"You see," Bobbi continued, "I was only recently made aware of the significant bounty on Guvera from a certain Middle Eastern family. A bounty that would solve all my financial problems and ensure I won at the polls. Unfortunately, Guvera's whereabouts have been unknown for the last ten years, so I had to lure him in. I had to give him a reason to show his face."

"So, you had his parents killed?"

"Sometimes there has to be collateral damage," Bobbi said. "It should have ended there, but the team I sent after him failed."

"The team? Do you mean your hit squad? You say that so politically correct, figures," Porter said.

"Detective, you ensured he stayed in the States when you went after his brother, Joshua."

"I have you to thank for the lead?"

"That's right. Then, all you had to do was work the case I assigned you to"

"And be the bait, your Frank Marion. Your fall guy."

"That's right. It was so simple, and you found a way to fuck that up, didn't you?"

"The cemetery?"

"The cemetery, but you joined forces and helped Guvera escape. So, I'll tell you what my money has bought. Nothing but frustration."

"Sounds like you made some piss poor investment decisions," Porter said. "I'm glad to have been part of that."

"Tell me what I want to know."

Porter grinned, "Fine, you want to know how I'm going to kill you? Is that it? I'll give you two options, A or B. Your choice."

"Where is Guvera?"

"Option A, I rip out your lying tongue first, then your eyes."

Bobbi raised her voice, "We know you're hiding him somewhere. Where is he?"

"Option B, I rip out your fucking throat."

"Dammit, Porter!" Bobbi yelled, "You owe me."

Porter's grin faded, and he stared at her for a long moment, "What?"

"Did you ever stop to wonder why, you?"

"Me?"

"I could have had the pick of anyone I wanted to draw Guvera to me. The police, private military companies, hell, even Homeland Security, but I picked you for this case. Someone barely qualified, someone who overcharges for his services, someone who lives in a trailer park."

"Must have been my dashing good looks," Porter said as blood continued to dribble down his face and nose.

"You haven't figured it out, have you?" Bobbi walked to the bar and opened the curio cabinet. "Where is it?"

"What are you talking about?"

"You haven't figured out just how long fate has connected us."

"Fate?"

"Here it is," Bobbi said, finding a blue bottle with the words Hypnotic on it. "This was his favorite." She poured herself a shot and took a sip. She squinted and shook her head, "Nope, not for me."

"Government, I'm talking to you!" Porter barked, "What do you mean about fate?"

Bobbi walked to him and crossed her arms. "I want you to look into my eyes and tell me you haven't figured it out! Figured out why I chose you."

Porter stared into her emerald eyes. There was something familiar about them, but he couldn't recall. He tried to think of every woman he had slept with over the years, but the list was too long, and his memories blurred.

Where have I seen those eyes?

"Look at my mouth. Look at my skin. Do I look familiar?" Bobbi asked.

Porter searched the features but still couldn't pin it down.

"Think hard, Ser-geant."

It was the inclusion of his rank that caught his attention. And not just the rank Bobbi had said but how she had said it. There was a Southern slur to the 'r' and the 'g' in the rank, a familiar slang.

A voice echoed in his head, "Ser-geant, I'm scared. I'm scared."

He saw Lance Corporal Wilson lying across from him on his side in a pool of red on the sands of Iraq. Blood drooled down his face, and his bottom lip shook. His emerald eyes were wide with shock. The bottom half of his body was missing. Parts of him were strewn out all over. He reached out to Porter before dying, "Ser-geant."

"Wilson," Porter said.

"That's right," Bobbi said, "Fitzgerald Davidson Wilson, my little brother. He was a beautiful human being, and you sent him to his death out there in Iraq. You didn't even come to his funeral."

"I didn't –"

Bobbi smacked him, "Don't lie to me! Don't you dare, don't! I've heard it all. I heard how he sacrificed himself for our country and died a hero! I've heard it all from people who script out those damn letters to families where they just insert the names into the blank spaces on the form."

Tears began running down her cheeks, and she shook with anger. "Out of everyone, why did God spare you! You, a man who has no regard for human life, who uses women like tools, and who is an absolute monster." She smacked him again, "Why you! Tell me!" She slapped him again and took a step back. "Talk! Say something!"

Porter shook his head, "Bobbi –"

"God! I'm talking about God. Why would he spare someone like you? What makes you so special? Tell me. I've waited years to learn why you were spared, and my brother wasn't."

Porter stared at the blood pooled beneath himself. "I've asked myself that question every single day since it happened. Every single day since I left Iraq. I've had nightmares and woken up each night thinking about it. Why me? And you know something?" He looked at her, "Your God doesn't have the answer, and neither do I. I have made peace with the things that have happened in my life and the person I have become. You're right. I am a monster, and I have my demons, but I use them to fight people like you."

Bobbi shook her head, "No, I don't accept that answer. I cannot!"

"Too bad, it's the only one I got."

Bobbi pulled back her blazer, revealing the Glock holstered to her side. She pressed the tip of the barrel to his forehead and cocked the hammer. "You will tell me where Guvera is!"

Porter looked past the barrel and up at Bobbi. "Pretty close, afraid you're going to miss?"

"You have no idea how much I want to."

"Then what are you waiting for?"

Bobbi held the gun there for several seconds before lowering it, "No, I have to think of the bigger picture." Putting the barrel to his right thigh, she said, "But still."

She pulled the trigger.

Porter screamed out in pain.

Walking up the stairs, she opened the upper deck door. "Scott, get in here."

"Yes, ma'am," Scott said, walking inside.

Bobbi pointed down the stairs, "If you don't make him talk in the next hour, you can kiss your next option year contract with the state of Colorado goodbye. Do you understand me?"

"I'll make him talk," Scott said.

"For your sake, you better!" Bobbi snapped before slamming the door behind her.

Scott walked down the stairs to Porter. He removed his jacket and washed his hands under the sink, "Now, where were we?" Seeing the lightbulb on the counter, he picked it up and went to Porter.

An explosion sounded from topside, and the entire yacht trembled. Moments later, the fire alarm activated, and a whine blared obnoxiously. The overhead sprinkler activated, and water began to rain into the deck.

"What in the hell?" Scott said, standing on shaky knees after being knocked over.

Gunfire and screams sounded from topside.

Pulling out his Sig Sauer, Scott took a knee and aimed down the sights of his gun, pointing the barrel up the stairs.

Porter quietly stood from the leather stage, maneuvered himself behind Scott, placed his back against the pole, and painfully extended his arms and wrists as far back as possible, creating a small pocket of space. He looked back, slowly lowered, and quickly slipped his cufflinks around Scott's beefy head and over his neck.

Dropping to his knees, Porter pulled back on his wrists as hard as he could.

Scott gasped and struggled against his pull. He ferociously beat at Porter's hands and arms and fired off several wayward shots into the hull. Scott tried to stand, but Porter's pull kept him from doing so.

Porter clenched his teeth so hard he felt as if they would shatter and strained his muscles so hard he thought they would burst. The cuffs cut into his wrists so deep he felt as if they would cut right through his bones.

As the struggle ensued, Scott's body fought less and less, and Porter's pull on him became more vigorous.

Scott eventually stopped struggling altogether, and the only sounds coming from him were short whines and desperate gasps for air. When those finally stopped, Porter yanked back one final time.

Feeling and hearing no resistance, he loosened his hold. Porter stood on shaky knees and caught his breath. "Told you I'd break your fucking neck."

Scott's body dropped with a splash.

Porter looked down at the water filling the lower deck and followed the source to the holes in the hull where Scott had shot. Water was gushing through the holes, slowly flooding the yacht.

Pulling at the cuffs, Porter still couldn't break free. Staring at the water now rising to his ankles, he sighed, "Well, fuck."

At the sound of footsteps, Porter looked up to the steps where boots descended.

She was short and thin, wearing black and yellow leather and a matching web belt. Her eyes were viper green, and her long black hair parted down the middle and fell to either side of her face. She donned a black skull lower-half face mask. A three-point sling hung off her yellow military spec body armor splattered with blood, and an M4 fitted with a silencer was leveled.

In a tactical crouch, she quickly moved to Porter. "Well, hi there. Don't you make a cute damsel in distress?"

"Valentine?" Porter asked. "A soldier saving a Marine? I'm never going to hear the end of this one, am I?"

"As a thank you, you can give me head in the parking lot after this," Valentine said. Pulling out a curved karambit knife from her belt, she moved around him. "In the meantime, let's get you out of these cuffs."

A large splash sounded as Valentine began working the blade into the cuffs.

"What the hell?" Porter asked.

Valentine walked in front of him, the silencer of her M4 pointed at the ripples of water that had now risen to her waist. Aiming at blurs, she fired off bursts from her weapon. After expending fifteen rounds, she took aim once more when an arm reached out of the water and buried a seven-inch stainless steel Maserin knife into the ejection port of her rifle.

Looking down at the knife, Valentine was pulled into the water.

"Valentine!" Porter yelled.

As the water rose to his naval, Porter struggled against the restraints that still didn't give. He watched moving blurs under the water where Valentine had been pulled under. There was occasional splashing from the blurs, and a few moments later, Valentine came up for air, and as she did, an arm was wrapped around her throat.

Gunther surfaced behind her, and with gritted teeth, he pulled his arm tighter against her throat and asked, "Haben Sie schon einmal im blassen Mondlicht mit dem Teufel getanzt?"

Valentine sent two punches over her shoulder into Gunther's face, followed by swinging her wet head back, breaking the grip. Turning, she sent an uppercut under his chin. As Gunther reeled, she planted a front kick into his chest and sent him flying back first into the water with a dramatic splash.

Pulling her karambit knife out, she stabbed at a ripple of water but hit nothing. Crouched, she backed up to Porter, ready for his follow-up.

As the water was now at her chest, she turned to Porter, her lip bloodied. "Okay, I think –"

She could not finish these words as an arm wrapped around her throat, and Gunther held back Valentine's knife-hand. Leaning forward, he dunked her head into the water and didn't let her up. Valentine kicked as hard as she could but could not break his hold. After some time, Valentine stopped resisting.

Gunther's chrome eyes fixated on Porter. Pulling the knife from Valentine's hand, he was ready to plunge it into her chest.

"Stop," Porter said. "What would Heidi think?"

Gunther hesitated. He wasn't expecting Porter to say his daughter's name.

Gunfire snapped, and Gunther's hand blew apart courtesy of a 7.62x55mm NATO round.

They looked up at the stairs where Hector lay at the base of the upper deck in the prone position armed with an M24 steadied on a bipod. Hector aimed down his Leupold Mk 4 fixed-power scope at Gunther's head.

Gunther dove into the water, avoiding the subsequent shot.

Valentine's body sank into the water.

"No, Valentine!" Porter yelled.

There was a splash at the base of the stairs as Gunther flew out of the water and made his way up. Hector fired off a round but missed. In an instant, Gunther had ascended to the upper deck and was exchanging gunfire with Hector.

From Porter's position, Gunther and Hector advanced out of sight, and all he could hear was gunfire.

The water had now risen below Porter's chin, and he frantically looked out at Valentine's last position and called out her name.

With the sound of rushing water and his own yelling, he almost didn't hear the yelling of, "Boss! Boss!" Porter turned to the stairs where Mindy stood. She wore a faded black Evanescence tee and blue jeans. "Hang on, I'm coming!"

She dove into the water.

A few seconds later, she resurfaced in front of Porter.

"Mindy, get Valentine. She's a couple feet away from me. Get her to the steps," Porter told her. "She needs CPR."

Mindy nodded and dived under.

The water had now reached his face, and Porter leaned his head back, doing his best to keep the water out of his nostrils.

After what seemed like forever, Mindy appeared above him and said something, while holding up his spare glasses. It was difficult for Porter to hear, but he nodded anyway, hoping whatever she was saying was good news regarding Valentine. Reaching into her blue hair, Mindy pulled out a hairpin and dove under once more.

The water reached his nostrils, and Porter did his best to control his breathing. He hated this feeling. This feeling of helplessness. The sense of creeping death. A feeling of drowning.

He felt Mindy's hands on his wrists as she frantically worked her hairpin into the key post of the cuffs.

As seconds dragged on and blackness faded into his brain, the things he thought about were odd. Porter didn't think much about whether Mindy could free him in time, for it was entirely out of his hands. He thought about his life and those in it.

Porter recalled looking past his brother Chris and sister Olivia, staring at his mother's tears streaming down her cheeks at their father's funeral. He remembered his Senior year of High School, losing to Finley at the NJROTC military ball and watching Sarah dance with him on the dance floor. Images surfaced in his mind of being at Camp Pendleton during Marine Combat Training, calling Maggie from a payphone. She told him she was pregnant, and they were getting married. His mind went to the dark red pool of blood that surrounded him in Iraq as the RPG took out his squad. Thought of the day he woke up to find Maggie gone and the bottle of whisky in one hand, the revolver in the other, and the contemplation of death.

Porter then remembered Evans coming to his house and telling him he could use his monster for good. He remembered being at the club, laughing with Alice, sitting on his lap, and the music playing loud. Porter recalled teaching Mindy to throw a punch and laughing when she broke her thumb. He remembered staying up late with Mindy, watching Marvel movies, and eating popcorn. The thought of kissing Evans went through his mind, and he could taste her lips and recall the smell of her hair.

The blackness turned to light, and rushing water entered his eardrums, "Stay with me, Dad!" Mindy yelled.

Porter looked around and realized that, with an arm across his chest, Mindy was buddy-dragging him across the water-filled lower deck towards the steps. Porter shrugged her free and swam the rest of the way by himself.

At the steps, Porter saw that Valentine was lying across the middle steps, accompanied by Alice. With a bloody lower lip and a ripped Halestorm tee, Alice had pulled off Valentine's body armor.

Alice pinched Valentine's nose and gave her two short breaths. She then placed her hands atop one another and, positioning them atop Valentine's chest, proceeded with fifteen quick compressions. Alice listened for breath, and when she heard none, she repeated the process.

"Is she?" Mindy asked, reaching the steps out of breath.

"I don't know," Alice said.

At the sound of gunfire, Porter looked to the upper deck where Gunther and Hector were still fighting. "I can't let Gunther get away." He turned to Alice, "Do everything you can–"

"I know, I'll keep on her," Alice said, continuing the CPR.

"What about me?" Mindy asked.

Porter plucked Scott's pistol out of the water. "You have to protect Alice and Valentine."

"But I can help you," she said.

"You are. I trust you, kid," Porter told her.

Mindy nodded and, handing Porter his glasses, pointed her gun up the stairs, "Kick his ass."

Holding onto the guard rail, Porter put his glasses on and limped up the stairs, hugged the door frame leading to the upper deck, and peered inside. The crystal chandelier reflected light off warm hardwood floors, covered with a large black bear rug. Facing blue couches with white stitching, a glass table with a stripper pole going through the middle, a kitchenette on the starboard side, a grand piano on the port side, and a navigation terminal with a large wooden helm at the bow made up the space.

Hector took cover behind the closest blue couch, firing off rounds from his Sig Sauer P226 at Gunther, who hid in the navigation enclosure.

"Get down," Hector said, gesturing for Porter to take cover.

Upon doing so, 9x19mm rounds from a Glock 19 peppered Porter's previous position.

"He's running out of ammo," Hector said, handing him a Beretta.

Porter nodded, chambered a round, and aiming down his sights on the navigation enclosure Gunther hid inside, waited for movement.

"How did you find me?" Porter asked.

"I've been following your CIA friend for some time, and when she used you as bait to lure in Gunther, I followed her trail," Hector turned to him. "What, not the answer you were looking for?"

"Shut up and fight," Porter said.

Hector smirked.

Gunther popped up and fired and was met by rounds from Porter and Hector.

"He only has one more shot," Hector said.

"You think he's going to use it on himself?" Porter asked.

"We can't let him," Hector said, "Take him on three?"

"On three," Porter agreed.

Hector said, "One."

Porter said, "Two."

They nodded to one another, and that's when they heard the whir of chopper blades, and the yacht began to rock.

"No," Hector said.

Gunfire sounded as Gunther used his final round to shoot the navigation window, cracking it.

Porter and Hector fired at Gunther as he ran and leaped shoulder first through and out the window onto the sundeck.

Following him, Porter and Hector were nearly at the window leading outside when 7.62x39mm gunfire reigned down onto them from fully clothed tactical men sitting inside a blue and white Bell 205 helicopter.

In between bursts of gunfire, Porter took aim and fired away. He took out a single man in tactical gear who fell lifelessly out of the chopper and onto the sundeck before another two took his place, opening fire.

Within the chopper, Porter could make out a well-dressed elderly man of Middle Eastern descent.

The surrounding windows in the upper deck exploded, and sparks exploded all around them as the electronics of the navigation terminals they hid behind absorbed the gunfire.

As Porter and Hector took cover, a rope ladder dropped from the helicopter's deck onto the sundeck. Gunther picked up the AKMSU assault rifle from the downed tactical man on the sundeck. Then, wrapping one arm around a tier of the ladder and a leg around another, he signaled for the helicopter to go and sprayed bullets at Porter and Hector's location.

"He cannot get away!" Hector yelled as the chopper began to ascend.

"No shit!" Porter said.

Porter and Hector made one final attempt to gun down Gunther with no success. They fired until their guns were empty.

As both reloaded, Gunther was nearly out of reach.

"They're going to circle us for a better assault position," Hector said.

"Hell, that simplifies our problem of getting to the enemy and killing them."

"In the words of Chesty," Hector said.

"Damn right," Porter answered.

A roar sounded.

Looking up, they saw a white AIM-120 AMRAAM missile streak across the sky for only a second before it collided with the Bell 205. The helicopter exploded instantly, illuminating the sky in a brilliant flash of orange, gold, and azure. The rope ladder detached, and Gunther was sent falling thirty feet to the yacht's deck.

As fire and metal debris showered the lake, Porter could feel the heat of the flames on the water beyond the yacht.

Stepping out of the upper deck onto the sundeck, they watched a silver F-35 Lightning II fighter jet scream by. Five seconds later, another F-35 followed the first. The two jets streaked past them towards the distant purple snowcapped mountains.

Porter wondered if one of the pilots was his sister, Olive.

Walking across the sundeck, Hector and Porter stood over Gunther, writhing on the cracked hardwood. On his back, and blood spooling at his lips, Gunther was reaching for an assault rifle that was just out of reach.

Hector kicked the rifle away and put a rattlesnake boot on Gunther's chest, "You killed a lot of people."

Gunther spat out blood, "You're one to talk. You, me, the Detective, none of us are any different. Hector Guvera, you are a walking plague of death. And you, Porter, bring Hell with you wherever you go. Each night we relive our nightmares and each day we create new ones. We all have blood on our hands."

Hector exchanged a look with Porter. "That may be true," Hector told him. "But you killed my parents."

"And how many parents have you killed?"

Hector looked at Porter, "This man killed my parents to lure me back to the States. There's nothing you can say to stop me from killing him."

Porter shook his head, "Whoever said I was here to stop you?"

"And Bobbi Johnson?" Hector asked.

"And Bobbi Johnson," Porter said.

"Heidi," Gunther said, spurting blood as he did so. Looking at Porter, he said, "Keep her away from our world, do you hear me? Don't tell her about me or about the things I've done."

Porter nodded.

"Give me your word as a father."

"You have my word."

Gunther turned to Hector, "Do what you must."

Porter nodded to Hector. While returning to Mindy, Alice, and Valentine, Porter had nearly made it through the upper deck when a single shot sounded. He paused at the doorframe leading downstairs for a brief moment.

At the stairs, the water had nearly risen to the top steps where the girls were. Valentine was breathing, and Alice and Mindy struggled to get her to a vertical base.

"Here, let me help," Porter said, wrapping Valentine's arm around his neck and assisting her up. "Take the lead, Mindy," Porter said as she led the way up the final step and through the upper deck.

Making their way to the sundeck, they looked down at Gunther's corpse. There was a single bullet hole between his eyes, still smoking.

"Is it over?" Mindy asked.

Porter looked for Hector, but he was gone.

"It's over," Porter said.

They stepped off the sinking yacht onto the wooden pier, and as they began to walk, police and EMTs swarmed their location. Leading the convoy was a black SUV with a CIA logo, and stepping out of the vehicle were Tim Styles and Flick.

Upon seeing the damage, Tim Styles removed his sunglasses and shouted, "Porter, what the hell did you do to my yacht?"

"I'll take that," Mindy said, taking a break from her Algebra homework. Sitting at the Fantasies bar, she downed the frozen pink drink in the shot glass.

Britney Spears was blaring over the speakers, and 'Oops!…I Did It Again' was currently playing.

With nearly a foot and a half of snow outside, only a few girls made it in tonight, and the club was almost empty. The roads had been paved, but the snow was still falling, and roads were iced over, keeping customers home.

The only occupied table sat Ursula. She wore a brown mink fur coat and was surrounded by empty shots of vodka and a French version of the novel, 'The Three Musketeers.' She buried her head in her arms and was snoring.

"So, what do you think?" Erica asked from behind the counter with a grin. She wore a red CSU Pueblo hoodie and denim pants.

"Good, but where's the alcohol?" Mindy asked.

"I told you, it's a frozen Shirley Temple."

"Don't Shirley Temple's have alcohol?"

"You can make it with or without alcohol," Molly said, her wheelchair pulled up to the bar. Wearing a burgundy puffer jacket and fingerless gloves, she knitted a sock.

"You're a teenager, Mindy. I'm not putting alcohol in it," Erica said. "I didn't even put any in Molly's."

"I'll be twenty-one next month," Molly said, setting down her double-pointed needles on the bartop. She sipped her green and clear Virgin Mojito. "Still, she wouldn't budge."

"You suck, Erica," Mindy said.

"What a sweet kid," Erica said.

Leaning over Mindy, Doc pointed at Mindy's tablet, "That answer's wrong. It should be thirty-six."

Mindy growled in frustration, adjusting her answer.

"Wow, someone's bitchy tonight," Alice said, sitting next to her, smoking a cigarette. She wore a blue sweater and matching sweats she could quickly shed if customers came in, but until then, it kept her comfy and warm. "Here, have some of mine," she slid over her drink.

Mindy picked up the glass, "What is this?"

"Vodka Martini."

Erica shook her head at Alice, "Seriously?"

Alice dismissively waved her off.

Taking a sip, Mindy cringed, slid the glass back, and coughed. "No thanks, disgusting."

"Want to talk about disgusting," Doc said, sitting on the stool beside her. Over a long-sleeved flannel, he wore a green tiki shirt with repeating prints of a naked girl playing the ukulele, wearing a red lei covering her chest. "Ever heard of the Prairie Oyster?"

Mindy shook her head.

Erica shrugged while cleaning a glass. "Heard of a lot of drinks but never a Prairie Oyster. Okay, what's in it?"

Doc smiley smugly, "Tomato juice, vinegar, pepper, Worcestershire sauce and raw egg."

"That sounds disgusting," Mindy said.

"Agreed," Alice said.

"Sounds like a hangover drink," Erica said.

"Yep, you're supposed to drink it in one gulp." Doc smiled, "You girls are good at swallowing, right?"

Reaching over, Alice smacked him, "Mindy's a teenager, cut it out."

"Oh, you can give her an alcoholic drink, but I make one little joke about swallowing and –"

Erica smacked him again, "Seriously?"

Doc smiled, "Actually, keep smacking me. I'm starting to like it. Alice," he turned to her, "can we roll this into some sort of package deal?"

As everyone laughed, the news coverage playing on the TV caught their eye.

Erica turned up the TV.

On the news, Audrey Peterson dolled up in heavy makeup, wearing a thick blue jacket stood before a T-Mobile. With a mic in hand, she said, "…and this store is just one of the dozens we've heard from today who have reported that security company American Iron has, without notice, removed security equipment from their stores."

The camera focused on a man in a polo and khakis unscrewing an American Iron sign affixed to the front of the store. Audrey motioned for the cameraman to follow her and jogged across the parking lot to the man. "Excuse me, sir, is it true American Iron is getting ready to file for bankruptcy, and you're pulling all of your equipment so you can begin the liquidation process?" She shoved her microphone towards the man.

The khaki man waved her off and continued unscrewing the sign.

"Sir, we have unconfirmed reports that illegal money racketeering funded the company. Is this true?"

"No comment," the man said.

Audrey shrugged, then, taking a few steps away from the man, turned to the camera, "Well, no one's talking much as is often the case with a situation like this. For Action News 8, this is Audrey Peterson. Back to you, Tom."

The segment ended, and the news transitioned to a young man sitting behind a desk wearing a blue suit and a bright orange tie. "Thanks, Audrey. And now, back to our ongoing story," the news reporter continued. "For days now, we've been covering this bizarre story about former police Captain Denise Easley. As we reported earlier, she had just recently been assigned as the Captain of the Colorado Springs Police Department when, seemingly out of nowhere, she had a mental breakdown and confessed to various crimes."

The news segued to a video of Easley in handcuffs being escorted by police Officers. Her hair was a mess of tangles, her eyes bloodshot, and her body language mirrored that of a junkie looking for a fix.

Those sitting at the bar cheered at her new look.

As the news showed Easley being escorted out of the police station and guided towards an unmarked police car, Easley struggled against the Officer's pull so she could address the news crews.

"Yeah, it was me! Bobbi Johnson ordered me to do it, and yeah, I framed a few people for it. Is that what you want to know! It was me! Me! What else do you want to know? C'mon, ask me, ask me!!!"

An Officer held off the news reporters as they advanced on her. "We will give an official statement later. Thank you."

The news transitioned once more to the news desk. "With the disappearance of front-runner Bobbi Johnson, Tim Styles is the leading candidate on the ballot for the Colorado U.S. senate seat. By law, if Bobbi Johnson isn't found in the next seventy-two hours, Tim Styles will win by default. We'll continue to follow this story as it develops," the news anchor said.

"Yeah," Doc said, "whatever happened to Bobbi?"

"I'm curious about that, too," Erica said. "Did the Boss Man say anything?"

"According to Porter, she's being taken care of," Mindy said.

"To hell with her," Alice said. "That lying bitch, Bobbi, is going to get exactly what she deserves."

"I'll drink to that," Erica said, pouring herself a margarita. About to drink, she gestured her glass to Evans, who had walked in through the beaded archway. She wore a grey top and a brown leather flight jacket. Her multiple layers of torso bandages were still visible under her clothes. The clubs' alternating red and green lights reflected off the gold cross that hung off her neck. "Officer Evans, care to join us for a round?"

"It's just Sarah here," she told Erica. "I'll take a Bud."

"You got it."

"Nice sock," Evans said to Molly.

"Oh, thanks," Molly said, "it's for the Sock Madness competition."

As Erica grabbed the beer from the cooler, Evans stepped beside Mindy. "First off, thanks for watching Bauer while I was on the mend. Second, Porter wants to talk to you. He's at his truck."

"Uh, okay," Mindy said. She shrugged to Alice, "Be right back, I guess." Putting on her Bagheria black leather jacket with an inner grey hood, she zipped up and walked out of the beaded archway and through the doors into the cold, dark parking lot.

Only a handful of cars were in the lot, and Porter's new red Ram truck looked the best. Mindy opened the passenger door and stepped inside. The heat was blasting, and music was blaring inside the cab.

Mindy recognized the song playing as Five Finger Death Punch, 'I Apologize.'

Looking out the front window, Porter puffed his cigarette and petted Bauer, who lay on the center console, "Hey you."

"Sarah's cat has really attached itself to you." She looked out to where Porter did. Stars peppered the night sky. The surrounding shopping areas and homes were caked with thick snow. The various street lights illuminated flakes as they fell through the air. "So, what's up?"

"Sarah's quitting the force," Porter told her.

"Really?"

"Yeah, she was thinking about getting her Private Investigator license and wondering if she could join us."

"And what did you say?" Mindy asked.

Porter turned to her, "I told her I'd have to discuss it with my partner first."

Mindy shrugged, "I like Sarah, and she can definitely handle herself."

Porter smirked, "No shit."

"But will it work between you two? You guys are, how do I put this, complicated?"

Porter shrugged and sipped from the thermos of coffee beside him, "Things get complicated as you get older. Relationships aren't really black and white."

"Relationship? So, you guys are like dating, right?"

"You and your 7th grade talk. So cute."

"Screw you, you know what I mean."

Porter brought the cigarette to his lips and took a deep drag, "You had asked me a while back if I loved her, and for whatever the hell it's worth, I do."

"Yeah, I know you do."

"Yeah."

"So, that means you're finally done with all your bullshit?"

Porter turned to her, "My bullshit?"

"All the girls you sleep with. You know that crap has to stop, right?"

"Wow," Porter said.

"No, I'm serious. I don't want Sarah killing you in your sleep because you decided to do the nasty with Alice."

"Christ," Porter said.

"Or Valentine," she continued.

"You don't have to worry about Valentine," Porter said. "She's already off on another assignment. The agency keeps her busy."

"Or Erica."

"I never said me and Erica —"

"But you never denied it either," Mindy interrupted.

"Shut up, I get it."

"So, you promise?"

"Promise? What are you going to do next? Make me pinky swear?"

"Say you promise, and I'll agree to Sarah joining us."

Porter turned to her, "Why do you care so much?"

"Because Sarah's good for you, and you need someone like her in your life to make you a better person. I don't want to see you fuck that up, understand?"

Porter stared at her long hard before saying, "I promise."

"Then it's settled."

"Yeah, I guess so." He puffed on his cigarette again and then chugged a mouthful of coffee.

Mindy saw that Porter was once again staring up at the stars. "What do those mean to you?"

"Quid pro quo."

"What?"

"Quid pro quo, you answer first, then I'll answer, deal?"

Mindy shrugged, scratching Bauer under the chin, "I guess."

"What do you think of when you look at the stars?"

Mindy looked across the night sky. "I think of fishing with my stepdad, Dustin, early in the morning before the sun would come out. We'd set up our pole and stare at the stars. He always said I was his Fortuna. Your turn."

"My turn," Porter said. After a moment, he said, "Each star reminds me of someone I lost."

"In Iraq?"

"Marriage, life, friendship," he took a long drag on the cigarette, morphing the ember tip into a short stub, "Iraq." He lowered the window and flicked the spent cigarette to the snow. The smoke that escaped from his lips was evident in the dark night. "I think of all those things, but mostly, I think of the Marines I lost. I question why I'm here, and they aren't."

"At some point, you have to forgive yourself."

Porter shook his head, "I don't think I ever can."

Mindy put an arm over his shoulder, and although it surprised him, he didn't resist. "I may be young, but it seems things happen for a reason. My stepdad once told me that the struggles in our lives define who we are. If my parents hadn't left us, Jen and me, I wouldn't be who I am today. I wouldn't have met you. Some people can look at loss and drown in it. Others can adapt to it and learn from it. You're a fighter, Porter, a survivor. That's who you are. That's who you've taught me to be. I'm better because of you, and I know you're better because of me."

"That's pretty presumptions of you."

"Am I wrong?"

Porter smirked, "No, you're not wrong."

"Exactly."

"You're too good for me, kid. I'm supposed to be the one trying to be a good role model, but I suck at this parental shit."

"As someone named Porter would say, I have low standards."

"Don't ever change, jailbait."

"I'll try not to, old man," Mindy told him.

Squeezing her shoulder, Porter said, "I owe you. You saved Valentine, hell, you saved me, thanks."

"You saved me first, remember?"

"We're not keeping score."

"Besides, looking out for each other. Isn't that what family is all about?"

"You're damn right," Porter said. "I'm proud of you."

Mindy nodded and wiped away a tear, "Okay, listen, I'm going to head back inside and try to convince Erica to make me an alcoholic drink. She's stingy."

"Yeah, I guess she's worried about us losing our liquor license by serving to minors, man, she sucks," Porter said.

"Okay, I get it." Opening the door, she turned to him, "You coming? Erica is doing some sort of Britney Spears concert in the bar in your honor."

"I'll be there in a minute," Porter said. "There's something I need to do first."

"Okay, don't take too long," Mindy told him. Exiting the truck, she made her way back inside.

Porter watched Mindy leave and then, pulling out his phone, scrolled to Maggie's number. He stared at the listing for a long time before deleting the contact.

With relief, he grabbed Bauer and opened his car door when his phone rang. The caller ID displayed a number he hadn't seen in years. Answering the call, he said, "What do you want?"

"Hello, little brother," the voice on the other end said.

Porter paused for a moment. It had been years since he had heard this voice.

"You seem surprised," the voice said.

"It's been a while, Chris," Porter said.

"I heard you solved another high-profile case. Congratulations."

"What's this about?"

"The Pride has become interested in you," Chris said. "With Gunther's death, you helped eliminate an NSA operative we've been after for some time. But you must be aware of the consequences of your actions." There was a pause before he said, "*They* will be coming after you. Our organization can offer the necessary assets to assist you. Take some time to think about –"

Porter hung up his phone before Chris could finish and lit another cigarette. Staring at the stars once more, he shook his head and said, "Fuck."

⚜

In a Motel 5 on the New Mexico – Colorado Raton Pass, Gary Suthers popped the tab on his Pepsi and reclined in his seat. With his boots propped on the desk, he took a swig and belched as he watched 'The Late Show.'

They were doing a skit on Bobbi Johnson's political agenda.

An actress wore a red and white striped long-sleeve top and matching beanie. She then walked on stage and was mobbed by identically dressed cast members. A banner rolled across the skit, "Where's Bobbi?"

A familiar low guttural growl sounded from the parking lot, and headlights flooded the lobby.

Gary watched as a white Ford Bronco pulled into a vacant space.

A thin man wearing a suede jacket and holding a coffee travel mug walked across the lot and into the motel lobby.

Gary sat up, "Hello, sir, sir, sir. W-Welcome b-back."

The man nodded to him, walked to the side counter with a Keurig coffee maker, rummaged through the creamers, and shook his head. "I forgot you guys don't have milk?"

"C-correct," Gary told him.

Hector nodded, "I'm going to need a room."

"Yeah," Gary said.

After paying and being assigned a room, Hector returned to his Bronco. Getting inside, he turned over the engine to pull the vehicle to the rear of the motel. About to put the vehicle in drive, he heard a banging.

Leaving the Bronco in park, he circled to the back of the Bronco and opened the back window.

Something wiggled fiercely under a military tri-color poncho liner.

Hector pulled back the liner and looked down at a woman gagged and restrained by the wrists and ankles with duct tape. She wore a beige dress shirt and pressed cherry pants. Her emerald eyes were filled with hate and fury.

Pulling out his knife, Hector held it to her throat, and the woman stopped wiggling.

"Bobbi Johnson, I will pull your tape off and allow you a drink of water. But if you scream, if you make a scene, well –" Hector gently nicked her neck with the blade, causing a drop of blood to run down her flesh.

Bobbi nodded, and Hector pulled off the tape.

He plucked a bottle of water from the plastic twelve-pack case in the back. Unscrewing the blue cap, he held it to Bobbi's lips and let her take a few swigs.

She coughed after a few sips, and he pulled the water back.

"I want more," Bobbi said.

"Soon," Hector told her.

"Where are we going?"

"Somewhere you can repent for your sins. Somewhere hot, I think you'll fit right in."

"Somewhere I can repent for my sins? You won't get away with this," she hissed. "People will come looking for me."

"They will never find you. Not where we're going."

Bobbi shook her head, "God will judge you for this."

"God?" Hector asked. Grabbing the roll of duct tape, he stretched out a long piece. "Bobbi Johnson, did you ever think that maybe your God sent me?"

"God sent you?"

"Yes, in the words of Johnny Cash, to cut you down."

As she began to scream for help, Hector secured the tape over her mouth.

Peter Edward Boroch is the author of the 'Gothic Opera' military-fiction/fantasy series and 'The Man in the Leather Jacket' fiction/action series. His work is available on many digital platforms, including CreateSpace, Amazon, Barnes & Noble, iTunes, and Books-A-Million. Pete is a former Marine with multiple combat deployments. He studied writing at American Military University. In his spare time, Pete can frequently be found writing, drawing, reading comic books, and enjoying life with his family. Pete loves to interact with readers and other like-minded authors. He is currently working on the next great American novel.

Read more of Pete Boroch's books! Available at Amazon.com, and anywhere else great books are sold

- Gothic Opera Nightmares Labyrinth (2012)
- Gothic Opera Hunting Season (2015)
- Daughters of War (2015)
- The Man in the Leather Jacket: Predator Games (2017)

www.ingramcontent.com/pod-product-compliance
Lightning Source LLC
Chambersburg PA
CBHW032110310726

48972CB00001B/167